DYING IS EASY

K. J. HERITAGE

*For Jill Edwards,
stand-up comedy guru
extraordinaire*

DYING IS EASY

I've died many times. Far too many to remember. But that's what happens when you're starting out as a stand-up comic. Even the established acts are not immune.

The sudden realisation that you're going down. No matter what you say, no matter how you try to turn it around, no matter how much it hurts.

I suppose we all die sooner or later. On stage and off. The hard part?

Not knowing when it's going to happen.

***

STRONG HANDS sit me down while someone else manacles my wrists and ankles before roughly pulling the hood off my head. After a few moments, my eyes adjust, and I find myself strapped to a chair surrounded by bright lights.

To my right is a man in stained leather overalls standing in front of a bench of tools. I see power-saws, screwdrivers, drills, knives and hammers. It's then that I notice his overalls are stained with old blood. And, as if in sympathy to this information, my own blood runs suddenly cold.

I spit out my gag and start screaming for help.

The men laugh at me. I look at them properly for the first time.

They are big guys. Bald-headed, muscular and covered in tattoos. Their black clothing stretched over powerful muscles like a second skin.

"Strip him!"

My clothes are cut off me with one of those military knives—all gleaming curves and wickedly serrated edges. A blade is a blade in my world. You can kill someone with a fruit knife if you have the inclination. No, this knife has another purpose. To instil terror and fear. As I look at the eight-inch, horrific shank, I realise that it's doing its job pretty much as intended.

While I'm being 'prepared', the guy in the apron puts on a terrifying, smiling pig-mask and runs his fingers lovingly over his set of macabre tools. He selects a large rough-looking metal file, throws it up in the air and expertly catches it, before slowly coming towards me.

"No! Don't!" I shriek. What the hell have I gotten myself into?

Before I realise what's happening, he expertly scrapes the metal file over my left hand, stripping the nail from my forefinger.

I throw myself back in the chair, screaming in agony as the nail rips free...

TEN DAYS AGO

TUESDAY NIGHT

I CLING to the greasy bricks, still wet from the recent thunderstorm, my grip loosening, my feet scrabbling to find a ledge to take my weight. Three floors up, a nasty fall onto concrete below. It's way past midnight and silent—the quiet that descends after a torrential downpour. A silence only punctuated by the drip, drip, drip of rainwater falling from the eaves and the frantic thud of my heart.

"Fuck!"

I've done this more times than I'd like to mention—climbing up to the balcony of my top floor flat in Hove—simply because I can't manage to remember my keys like any normal person. And I'm still quite drunk, not that that has stopped me in the past.

Tonight, my focus is elsewhere. Distracted and filled with a terrible sense of foreboding. Thinking about my stupid argument with Jozee, the love of my life. She'd wanted to talk to me. About something important, I guess. But I'd caused a stupid scene— and she'd driven home alone, leaving me to make my own way back in the pouring rain. Jozee was either sitting upstairs in the dark, punishing me, or she hadn't come home. Without my keys, I had no choice but to make this ill-advised climb. Now, half-sober and halfway up this stupid wall, I've somehow forgotten how I do this—climbing like a spider quickly into its hole. My normally reliable autopilot has switched itself off to leave me hanging a hundred feet from the ground, wondering what the hell I am doing.

What the hell *am I doing?*

I change my grip, aware that I can only carry my weight for a minute or two longer.

"Fuck!" I repeat, as if the English language's most simple, yet most powerful, word has some as yet undisclosed magical power to save me.

Fear, like most of my over-dramatic emotions, is an all-or-nothing affair. No in between. My mind slips from the calm confidence of a seasoned climber into the realms of cruel terror as easily as I can slip off this greasy wall and fall to a sudden and hopefully quick death.

"Fuck!" I say for the third time, really getting the hang of it. "Fuck, fuck, fuck!"

I see flashes of myself falling—like in a thousand movies and TV shows. A frozen look of horror upon my face telling the audience that this *really is it.* Followed by a long, drawn out moment as I dangle there, almost trapped in time, accompanied by jarring, incidental music. And then… the gut-wrenching horror of the drop filmed from multiple angles. The director extending the fall to eke out every morsel of terror until—

I'm wrenched from the fervent imaginings of my own Hitchcock-esque death by the slide of a window above and a well-controlled, posh and familiar-sounding voice.

"What on earth do you think you're playing at, Adam? It's past one in the morning."

"Oh, hi, Clive," I respond to my next-door neighbour, my feet still scrabbling. "I um forgot my keys so I was forced to—"

"I honestly don't know what's gotten into you since that girl moved in. It's like I've been living in one of those awful soaps. Screaming and shouting at all hours, god-knows-what in the afternoons and now this. What do you have to say for yourself, young man?"

"Sorry, but I'm actually in a little bit of troub—"

"Couldn't *she* let you in? That girlfriend of yours? Jozee?" Clive spat out Jozee's name like poison sucked from a snakebite.

"We had an argument and she's probably gone to bed or—"

"When aren't you arguing?"

"I'm sorry, but—"

"Oh piffle!" Clive slams the window shut and angrily closes his curtains.

"Clive!" I shout, annoyed by his irrational dislike of my wonderful girlfriend. The woman who over the last six or so months has come to mean more to me than even Willow from Buffy or that striking girl at work with the cheeky tattoo who I'd totally failed to ask out. But it's just the distraction I need. My autopilot switches back on, my foot finds a ledge and I quickly ascend the wall to pull myself over the rail of my balcony. I slide back the balcony-door, that never seems to shut properly, and stagger, shaking, into the living room of my flat.

"Jozee!" I shout. "Jozee! You here? I nearly fell to a quite horrific death. *Nearly...* Jozee!"

No reply. The flat we've shared for the last six months feels peculiarly empty. Barren almost. Like all the life has been sucked out of it—like it was before Jozee moved in with me. I experience her absence like a physical thing. An expanding ball of black nothingness, consuming me. I forget about nearly falling to an artistically-filmed, Oscar-winning death and check the bathroom, kitchen, and bedroom. Opening closets and even looking under the bed.

She's not here.

I somehow knew she wouldn't be at home, waiting for me. Knew it when she got into her ancient Mini Cooper and drove away after that dumb argument. Knew it before I arrived home and rang the doorbell. Knew it when I phoned her mobile and it went straight to voicemail.

But more than that, I can't shake the dreadful feeling that Jozee is never, ever coming back.

2
EIGHT
MONTHS
AGO

THE COMEDY GODS!
Every Thurs at the Cathedral Bar, Hove

Come up on high and join us for some divine comedy!

This week's fantastic headliner:

JOZEE JACKSON!
"A rising comedy star worthy of your attention"
Comedy Sauce

"A comedy masterclass"
Cackle

"Beyond f**king hilarious"
Hrumph Magazine

Joining Jozee in the pulpit are our special guests:

Jim Laker "This guy KNOWS he's funny!"
Nat Naylor "Sweet, thoughtful and dark"
Shirley Sands "Caution: Man-eater! Will swallow you whole!"
Pari Chabra "A dirty old lady you can't help but love"

And in the newbie spot:
Songs from brand new talent: **Scott Wong**

**Compered by the high-priest of comedy:
Donnie 'The Doozy' Coogan**

£8 Advance / £10 on the door
STUDENTS 2-4-1 with valid ID
OAPs £5

Box Office/Book Tickets:
https://www.tickets-into-comedy.co.uk/251224

A CRACKING line up and the very first comedy gig I watched as an aspiring comic. The first time I saw those—as I then thought—brave, hilarious souls on stage knowing that, one day soon, I would be up there with them. Telling jokes. Making people laugh. Living the life I dreamed of. It was also the first time I saw Jozee.

Beautiful, funny, Jozee Jackson.

Everyone was brilliant that night. Especially newbie, Scott Wong and Northern Irish compere, Donnie Coogan, who kept the laughs coming and the night flowing.

But I only had eyes for Jozee.

A storm had been threatening and, when Jozee stepped on stage, the heavens heralded her appearance with a fanfare of thunder, quickly followed by a torrential downpour, pounding the roof of the building like thousands of marching, iron-clad ants.

Unlike the other comedians, she walked slowly onto the stage. A petite, blonde haired girl in her early 30s. Not a typical blonde   she possessed a look that was all her own. Short and curvy, with a cheeky grin and big, green, welcoming eyes.

The moment when an unknown comedian comes on stage is like no other. The audience waits in anticipation.

Who is this? What will they be like? And, more importantly... *will they be funny?*

Jozee seemed vulnerable, nervous. Her face down-turned, like she was scared of the growing storm. A flash of lightning dimmed the lights followed by an instantaneous bang of thunder, jumping everyone out of their seats, myself included.

"I knew an atheist playing the Comedy Gods was gonna be one major fuck up," she said. And the audience erupted into a howl of relieved laughter.

Jozee's wide eyes looked into mine. Just another punter in a comedy club, I suppose. And yet, in that moment, I did the thing that I always said was impossible, that was make-believe and just for the movies… I fell in love with a golden-haired, green-eyed storm-queen, heralded by the very elements themselves… I, Adam John Hanson fell in love with Jozee fucking Jackson.

Stand-ups come from a wide-range of backgrounds. From the shy to the egotistical, from the privileged to the poor, and from every race, gender, and sexual orientation—all suffering from a personality disorder or two and saving on expensive psychiatric bills by getting their therapy free on stage. For the first time in my life, I felt I belonged to this group of eccentric characters and fruitcakes. Hell, I was made for them.

I'm socially awkward and always have been. A misfit. The odd man out. A fish out of water. The list of clichés goes on. Unfortunately, for myself and society in general, this disability was never going to stop my pursuit of social success. Sure, I was a decahedral peg in a nonagonal hole, but I also suffered from an over-developed enthusiasm for life. I wanted to be out there, in the social world, meeting people, finding friends, having fun.

Just like everyone else…

But, from the start, things didn't really work out that way. I was an anxious kid, scared of bridges, water, electricity, next-door's hoover that 'looked like a Dalek'… and just about everything else you can think of. Even sunlight terrified me. I was convinced it would make me blind and was such a fear that I always wore a pair of outsized sunglasses whenever I left the house, strapped to my head with a grubby elastic band.

My best friend as a kid, *my only friend,* was a perpetually snotty-faced, freckle-covered boy called Jeremy Dexter. He lived a few houses away and we'd play for hours throughout the long, never-ending summer months of the school holidays. I'd imagine a whole host of wonderful, fantastical worlds and he would enter them with me. We spent days on the sandbanks behind the house where I grew up—an old, overgrown quarry—pretending we were astronauts, explorers, spies, snipers or anything else that my over-active mind could conjure. We always got on brilliantly well. But as soon as any other kids joined us, everything changed. I became side-lined. Made a fool of. Laughed at. And Jeremy would join in with them.

Why? I would ask myself. It was a question that would haunt me for the rest of my life.

School was a trial and adulthood no easier. Jobs filled me with trepidation—interviews, commuting, the dreaded small talk. All magnified by my non-stop, Olympic-standard, A1 anxiety. I found it hard to cope with the constant worry, the social failures, and the gaping hole where all my friends should have been.

I struggled along until my early 30s. Managed to get a full-time job in a quiet office where my creativity could be exploited—mainly for designing websites and databases. I found a place to live, consorted with the odd girlfriend—and most of them were very odd indeed—and settled into a safe, but mostly anxious life living in Hove, the posh part of Brighton by the sea.

It was only when my anxiety was threatening to overwhelm me that I finally went to the doctor. She questioned me about things that seemed irrelevant at the time and sent me off to the local brain doctors for a two-day assessment. Questionnaires, tests and a day-long interview.

I was diagnosed with Asperger's Syndrome, although the term is not officially used anymore—possibly due to the fact that Hans Asperger turned out to be the worst kind of child-murdering Nazi bastard. But I digress. I have full blown, high-scoring, top-of-the-range autism with advanced social and verbal skills. I laughed when I heard that. My social skills are a joke. Always have been.

I should've been relieved that I now had a valid reason for being such a total dickhead around people, that I said and did things that they didn't understand, that I used incorrect body language, stressed the wrong words and found eye contact so disagreeable. But instead, it made me angry.

Very angry.

I didn't want a damn excuse—to be seen as some social freak with a medical exemption certificate. No way! Despite all this Asperger's nonsense, I was actually a nice guy—deep down. People realised that once they penetrated through my crap. This knowledge should've been enough for me, but it wasn't… I needed more, I needed everyone to realise I was a cool guy—I wanted them to all think I was 'great' like Jeremy Dexter did all that time ago when we played together as kids. And so, feeling affronted, miserable and more than a little angry and peeved, I chose the nuclear option… *I chose stand-up.*

And that's what I was doing in the Comedy Gods the night I fell in love with Jozee Jackson—learning to become a comedian.

I'd been on a comedy course with a few other hopefuls. A way to bridge the immense gap between the bedroom and the stage. We did mini-gigs in an actual venue with the other comedy students as an audience, culminating in a 'Newbie Night' where friends, family and anyone else who cared to buy a ticket were in attendance. One of the best nights of my life.

People laughed at my jokes. *Result.*

And even though I knew that night was artificial, that making a room of strangers laugh would be an entirely different prospect, I was hooked.

I was cool at last.

3
WEDNESDAY MORNING

I WAKE up dull-headed and hungover at 5.48am after a few troubled hours of sweaty, dream-laden sleep, if you can call it that. More like a series of insomniac fits and starts, although I'm used to it.

I've had many nights like this before. Unable to sleep because of the horrors that 'tomorrow' will bring. In my life, these horrors are usually everyday things like a work meeting, a trip to the supermarket or even using the bus during rush-hour. Thankfully, these petty, self-involved night terrors are now usually reserved for my new life as a novice comedian, spent sweaty and half-awake fretting about a five-minute gig in the back end of nowhere. It makes no difference that I can rationalise how a single five-minute segment of my day is unimportant. My Asperger's—Aspie—brain just doesn't care. It dives on the minutest atom of worry like a flock of Brighton seagulls on a dropped bag of chips.

Last night was different—Jozee hadn't come home. And for the first time in a long time, I was kept awake worrying about someone other than myself.

I grab my phone and get up. No message from her. No messages from anyone. There's no way she could've arrived without waking me, but I check the flat anyway. Even the damn closets and under my bed again.

Why?

The answer is simple. If I don't check, I can't relax. It will play on my mind all day, driving me mad.

Obsessive Behaviour 101.

I go back to bed and look at my phone again, worried that it's somehow broken, switching it off and on to no avail. Afterwards, I close my eyes, but I can't get to sleep. I lie under my duvet, listening for the high-pitched spluttering whine of Jozee's 1970s white Mini Cooper. I yearn for it amongst the steadily growing purr of early morning traffic.

Is Jozee trying to teach me a lesson?

I don't think so. She knows about my condition—how easy it is for me to fret over the smallest thing. If she's really pissed off with me, this is the perfect revenge. But I can't stop myself worrying.

Has she crashed her car?
Is she in a ditch somewhere?
Is she lying dead in a morgue?
Is she in hospital, terribly injured?
Has she been abducted?
Is she tied up in some dreadful basement at the mercy of some weirdo?
Is she at another guy's house? Waking up with him for the early morning sex she so loved to share with me?
Or at a girlfriend's? Or…?

My mind races with the possibilities. Hundreds of them. Driving me mad.

A long time ago, I discovered meditation, a form of self-hypnosis used to calm my excessive nerves, mostly for everyday work meetings or those awful outings where I'm forced to chat to work colleagues socially. No one sees the turmoil bubbling under the surface of my professional demeanour. I'm excellent at hiding in plain sight. At the pretence of confidence. Even my comedy mates mention how confident I am on stage… if they only knew the real story.

Meditation works wonders for me—how else did I manage to attend that first stand-up comedy lesson without a week of meditating every morning and every evening? How else can I calm myself before going on stage? But there's no way I can meditate today. I'm too anxious. Too messed up.

I make a bowl of cereal, grabbing milk from the fridge, noticing the carton of goat's milk that nestles next to mine. Jozee is lactose intolerant and swears by the stuff. I love seeing her milk and, as daft as it may seem, it usually makes me feel connected to her. Today, the sight fills me with dread.

I take a mouthful of bran flakes and stare at the road outside. My flat is on the third floor of a newish Hove development built about fifty years ago, when aesthetics were not as important as they are these days. A featureless, brick-built oblong lacking any character going by the unfortunate name of *Eaton Palace Gardens*. The place is no palace that's for sure, and the gardens are nothing more than concrete and a few overgrown shrubs. And yet it does have a certain appeal. From my vantage point, sitting in the kitchen, I can see the road outside, the Georgian period houses opposite, and a clear view of the sea beyond. Serene and bluey-green, squatting just below the horizon.

Despite this quite beautiful, early morning vista, my eyes keep darting back to the road, still expecting Jozee's beat up Mini Cooper to pull up at any moment. *Will it ever be there again?* Parking is a nightmare in Hove. She may be forced to park roads away…

"Shit!" I splutter, spitting out cereal and milk like some crazed, bran-spouting human volcano. Jozee could've slept in her car! She'd done that tons of times in the past when she was unable to get digs in Edinburgh, or sometimes when she was late coming back from a gig. Or when she was too tired to walk. We laughed about it before. Many times.

The more I think about it, the more it makes sense. She's asleep in some Hove backstreet. Sure, Jozee is annoyed with me, but how better to teach me a lesson than by sleeping in her car overnight? And it was chucking it down last night. She could've been waiting until the rain stopped and just nodded off. Jozee could sleep anywhere.

Why didn't I think of this before? I'll go and check the streets now. Find her and take her out for breakfast. My treat. I can apologise and… I take a long breath… whatever she wants to tell me, she can tell me. How bad can it be?

A massive bang breaks into my thoughts, spiking my heart— something has slammed into my window. I gingerly walk towards it and see a small sparrow dead outside on my balcony, its neck broken, its brown wings twitching. The sun is so bright this morning that it didn't see the glass—which is odd as I've never cleaned it in the two years since I moved in. And this has never happened before. Poor little bast—

Another bang, and then another. Two more birds smash into the glass.

"What the…?"

I quickly grab a stack of Post-It notes from my desk and go out onto the balcony, sticking them over the glass door and windows. Hopefully this will prevent other suicidal wildlife from bashing their brains out in my general direction. To be honest, I'm a little spooked. I pick up the dead birds using double-wrapped kitchen towel and throw them in the trash. They're almost weightless, and I'm suddenly struck by the fragility of existence. One moment, these birds were full of life, flitting excitedly here and there on a beautiful summer's morning, the next, they are lying dead in my kitchen bin. I never react well when I see death up close like this. It gives me an empty, sick feeling… an overwhelming emotion that brings tears to my eyes and, like the sparrows crashing into my window, I'm hit by stabs of sudden panic about Jozee.

I have to find her, I just have to!

I race out of the flat and into the darkened stairwell—automatic lighting flicking on to reveal sterile steps reeking of lemon and bleach—and jog down them two at a time, arriving seconds later in the communal entrance area. I push through the front door, running through the small forecourt garden and into the road, dodging traffic and jogging past parked cars. Modern vehicles are huge compared to Jozee's tiny Mini Cooper, her car could easily be hidden behind any one of them.

I race down the road, phone jammed into my ear, ringing her number once, twice… multiple times. Going straight to voice mail. I leave breathless message after breathless message, cut off each time by the mailbox time limit. I don't care if I'm making a fool of myself. I just want Jozee to call or text back, telling me she's safe. So I can stop this cycle of worry.

I check my phone almost continually, but no reply. Nothing.

I'm now running manically, grunting and babbling incoherently to myself, fully in the grip of panic. My head buzzes like a nest of irritated hornets, blood swirls through my ears, and my veins burn. I see a flash of white paint and run towards it, crossing the road with no regard for my safety, a car hooting at me. I don't care. I arrive on the opposite side and trip over the pavement, landing heavily on the concrete.

People at a nearby bus stop stare at me. I know what they're thinking… *just another Brighton nutter.*

I push myself back to my feet, only to find an old Ford that's seen better days, its white paint rusting and covered in seagull shit. The fall is enough to quell my raging panic. I sit up and take slow breaths, aware of a cold, clammy sweat crawling over my skin and sticking to my clothes. My heart slows, the buzzing in my head reduces to a background hum and the panic thankfully recedes.

Running around Hove like a madman isn't going to get me anywhere.

After a few minutes to catch my breath, I navigate the internet on my phone and bring up the Brighton and Hove City Council website. I live in Parking Zone R. A map of the area pops up. If Jozee is parked somewhere nearby, it's likely she will be on one of these streets. My panic is now replaced by a logic problem—finding the most efficient way to check all the roads in our parking zone—and soon, I'm methodically zig-zagging through the leafy streets of Western Hove, although I can't help but feel a little silly. I overreacted, like I've done hundreds of times before when things have got on top of me. Jozee is still missing, but that dreadful knot of worry has been swapped for something more rational. Part of me wonders if I should stop this search and go back home, and I almost do that, but a vision of Jozee lying in her car after suffering a stroke or some other illness enters my mind, and I know I will have to make sure.

Hove is eerily quiet this Wednesday morning, especially along the leafy backstreets. Last night's storm has lent the day a special feeling of newness. The air is cleaner than usual, absent of the stiff sea breeze, the sky a perfect, mesmerising blue, dotted with a few early morning clouds. Even the damn seagulls are silent, taking a day off from their petty domestic squabbles.

Half an hour later, after finishing my search with no sign of Jozee or her mini, I'm back outside Eaton Palace Gardens. It's still early, not even 7am. I'm hoping that Jozee might've turned up while I've been out. The flat is as I left it. Cold and empty without Jozee's presence.

I tell myself she'll get in contact when she's ready, although I can't stop looking at my phone, fiddling with it, checking the volume and reception, and for missed calls. On a whim, I open my favourites menu and stab my finger at Stevo's number.

Stevo, my best and only mate.

He's one of the few people who I can truly be myself with. Mainly because he's just like me, an Aspie, or I guess he is. We were mates long before I was diagnosed. Now I know why—although I've not told him my suspicions about his possible autistic tendencies. Once my condition was spotted, I saw it everywhere, in everybody, although I'm pretty much on the nose about Stevo.

A couple of rings and he answers.

"What the shit?" he blurts, his deep voice pushing the lower-bass limits of my phone's earpiece. "It's not even 8am. Someone better've died Adam… No one has died, have they? Fuck!"

Stevo always speaks like this. A stream of unfettered consciousness littered with more than the occasional expletive.

"Can you send me a text? I need to check my phone."

"What do you want a text for? You're already talkin' to me."

"I need to check they're getting through."

"Oh right. Why didn't you bleedin' well say? Jeez."

"Just shut up and send it."

I off the phone and wait.

A beep and Stevo's text comes through.

> Loser!

I stare at the message and sigh. My phone appears to be working perfectly. Which means… Jozee hasn't texted me. I shake my head and reply.

> *Thanks mate, you're a star.*

Another beep.

Whatevs. Beers soon?

I don't reply. I take a shower and get ready for work. Jeans, shirt and an old jacket I bought from a charity shop a couple of years ago. Smart casual is the Brighton way. I'm purposely taking my time, but the clock moves inexorably towards 7.30am. Time for me to go to work. I pen a note and place it on the floor in the hallway. A note Jozee won't be able to miss. A note with two simple words.

Call me x

4

ON THE way to the bus stop, I make a quick decision—I'm gonna walk into work. I hate the bus, and even though the usual drunks, tramps and schoolkids will be absent—they make this form of transport a full-on sensory hell—I decide I still can't face it. It's a lovely post-storm morning and I fancy more fresh air. Walking only takes fifteen or so minutes longer anyway and it will help me to clear my head.

I leave the wide, leafy streets of Western Hove to walk along Church Road and the hustle and bustle of this seaside city slowly returns with an increase of traffic. I walk fast—I always have done—head down, legs pounding, shoulders hunched.

Loping like Bigfoot, Jozee described it.

She told me to stand up straight, or I might get a back problem. I joked that she wanted my back in the best possible condition for her morning demands, but from then on, I've always walked tall. It makes me feel arrogant and, strangely, more in control. And why shouldn't I be those things when walking with the most beautiful girl in the world? With Jozee, my sexy and talented girlfriend?

I try to do the same today, but the weight of worry is too much, and I fall easily into my old habit. I feel safer with my head down, cut off and stomping along. The *new me* is nothing more than a veneer, I realise. It will take a lot more than telling a few gags and walking upright like proper homo-sapiens to sort myself out.

Determined not to fall into the same cycle of self-deprecation that has dogged me all my life, I try instead to think positive thoughts. Starting with where Jozee might be. Not lost and dead in a ditch but at a friend's place. She has no family. Or no family she talks about. As far as I know, both her parents are deceased, and she has no siblings.

As far as I know.

Jozee is secretive about her life, but I'd managed to get information in dribs and drabs. I swallow. If she has no family, then…

Jozee has no one looking out for her except me.

I'm filled with a sudden urge to text everyone in my phonebook asking if they've seen her. I take out my phone and begin to quickly write a message. I get halfway through and think better of it. I may be worried sick, but I understand myself. Jozee hasn't exactly disappeared… not yet. I over-think things, worry too much and always imagine the worst. I save the message in my drafts folder, telling myself that if I don't hear from her in the next few hours, maybe by lunchtime, I'll send it. I may have pissed her off, but there's no need for me to play the obsessed boyfriend just yet. Well, not to anyone but Jozee.

Church Road turns into Western Road. Tree-lined pavements giving way to a more urban vibe—but only just. I leave Hove and enter Brighton. The number of pedestrians increases. A mixture of those going to work, those going home and those other people who never seem to belong to any time of day. But that is Brighton all over. A fantastic mix of all types of people and lifestyles crammed into its Georgian houses now converted into flats. It's like no other city in England. Welcoming, diverse, damn exciting and a little scary.

The heat at this early hour is becoming oppressive and I loosen my shirt. I remember something vague about a heatwave. Perhaps it was starting today? The wispy morning clouds have rapidly burned away, leaving a blue, empty sky.

I walk through the town centre past a bustling Churchill Square, shop-fronts covered by yet another development, people crowding around bus stops and sitting outside coffee shops. I head down the hill toward the Old Steine, feeling sorry for the many beggars and drunks sleeping rough in doorways, their sad-eyed dogs staring hopefully at me. I find the innocuous red door of my office, nestling in a backstreet, and buzz myself in using my ID card and pin.

First in as usual. A quiet time that I've grown to love. Today, the quiet is oppressive. I power up my PC and pop into the kitchen, making myself milky tea in my favourite mug and sit down.

I've a ton of emails waiting, yet I'm in no mood to face them.

Instead, I log onto Facebook—the comedian's essential ally—even if they are selling all my data to third-parties, sending me adverts for things I have no interest in and constantly asking me to keep in touch with my dead dad. That was comforting in an odd way, my dad somehow staying alive within Facebook's complex algorithms, haunting cyberspace. He died a couple of years ago. A silver surfer who was on Facebook long before I was. I skip straight to Jozee's page.

No updates.

Same for her Twitter, Instagram and blog. She wasn't that prolific on social media, but I always enjoyed reading her posts. I'm a stickler for grammar, and Jozee's missives are the antithesis of good writing practice. All conjoined words, bad-spelling and a total lack of punctuation, unless it was the ubiquitous exclamation mark. Same for her texts. It took me quite a while to understand her particular Sanskrit. But I love her messages. I've saved them all.

I post direct/personal messages on all her platforms…

Please contact me ASAP. I'm getting worried! x

…and check her website *www.jozeeisnotfunny.co.uk* for her list of upcoming gigs.

Jozee puts everything into her comedy career. When she's not working her part-time job at the local superstore, she's at a late-night café writing new material, rehearsing or gigging. Some weeks, she gigs almost every night.

I wince when I see the date for last night's gig at the Dog and Duck in Burgess Hill. I'd been so looking forward to it—even if it was run and compered by Jim Laker, a comedian I've come to despise. I'd hoped doing this gig again would've reminded Jozee where it all started—the first place where I shared a stage with her. Afterwards, we had our first kiss, followed by a drunken grope that got my heart racing all the way home back to her seedy Kemp Town bedsit—where she was living before she met me.

Our first night together.

A clumsy coupling to get it out of the way, before we learned to understand each other's bodies. And I'm not unashamed to say that

I drank in every inch of her. The sensory overload of having sex can sometimes be overwhelming for me. Not with Jozee. She told me we had 'a good fit' and despite trying to find a more descriptive way of putting it, I realised that this summed up our relationship perfectly. We were a good fit. In all ways. *Or we had been.*

I turn my attention back to her webpage. Jozee is scheduled to headline a gig in London tonight. A new act night at a pub called *The Horatio* in Seven Sisters. The kind of gig where she'd try out new material or get other promoters to come see her. A bread and butter gig—cash in hand. Not that these gigs paid that much. Jozee never misses a gig, especially a paying one. She's very professional in that respect.

I put the address in my phone. If push comes to shove, as my nanna used to say, and Jozee doesn't turn up, I can visit her there tonight. Hopefully Jozee will get in contact long before then. And if she doesn't…?

I clamp down my thoughts and attack that stack of emails.

A short while later, my workmate, Ollie, arrives. A tall, skinny guy in his early twenties carrying an egg and bacon roll, a cup of coffee and a blueberry muffin. I like Ollie, but it took a while for him to like me. He even said the line that I have come to despise the most in life…

'When I first met you, I thought you were a real twat, but now…'

I've often wondered if I should get that phrase printed on a t-shirt.

"Morning!" he says, sitting down opposite me.

Like me, he's an early morning person—another reason why we get on well.

Ollie raises his eyebrows. "You look rough, mate. Heavy night?"

"You could say that."

"Drinking on a school night, that's not like you." He opens his bacon and egg roll and takes a large bite, yolk running down his chin that he wipes away with the back of his hand.

I've always envied his twenty-something metabolism, but today, watching him eat makes me queasy. He's right. I overdid it. I get a flash of me shouting at Jozee, of her getting into her mini and angrily driving away. The rain pounding down around us.

Two more bites and the bacon roll disappears. He takes a swig of coffee and starts in on his muffin.

"So how did the gig go last night? You were looking forward to it, yeah?"

"What?" I reply, almost forgetting I'm having a conversation.

"The gig? That's all you could talk about yesterday. Some important place where you met… what was the name of that girl again?"

He's being playful. Since Jozee came into my life, she's all I talk about. Her and comedy. Today, I don't want to chat about either subject. As ever, my mouth has a different take on things.

"It was a cluster-fuck," I rasp in reply. "I'm not funny. I don't think I ever will be."

"Didn't you tell me, you have to die on your arse hundreds of times as a rite of passage?"

"I don't know what I said," I snap back, aware that I'm sounding somewhat sullen.

Ollie pauses half-way through his muffin. "Hey, man, I was only asking."

"Sorry. I'm not in my right head today."

"It must've been a bad gig. How was Jozee? Everything still okay with her?"

I nod, but the truth of the matter is somewhat different. Recently, things have become strained between us. Jozee has been… *odd*. It's difficult for me to read people, but I'm more in tune with Jozee than anybody else. And yet I can't ignore one simple fact.

We haven't made love for nearly two weeks.

Unprecedented in our relationship so far, although I've not pushed the issue. Relationships always start out with an intense marathon of sweaty, non-stop, 'can't get enough of one another' fornication before the ardour dies down into predictable routine—which I admit to preferring. But Jozee had been coming home late and was still asleep when I woke up to go to work. We didn't seem to find the time anymore, and I couldn't help worrying that there was more to it. And worry is what I do.

Jozee said she needed to talk to me. That's what she was going to do last night, before our argument. I wince again at last night's memory. I was a class-one dick and now I'm paying the price.

5
LAST
NIGHT

*"**I HAVE** a very healthy, varied diet..."* I say, hitting the audience with my next set-up, the back of my neck prickling with terror. I'm performing my new five minutes set and so far, not one single laugh.

"...I eat all the different pizza toppings."

A titter, just enough to keep me going.

"Apparently you can lose a lot of weight by thinking very hard...

"...So, I thought about a kebab and put on three pounds."

Another titter. Oh hell.

"I went to an Egyptian restaurant last night...

"...I ordered from the Set menu."

Silence.

Thoughts race through my brain, consuming me in a tidal wave of negativity. What was I thinking? I'm rubbish. Everybody knows it. The other comics know it. Even Jozee knows it. I'm such a loser!

I try to calm myself, remembering to keep my delivery slow. Everyone dies. It's part and parcel of the profession. I need to go back to my tried and tested material and get off-stage as soon as I get a laugh.

"I was walking past my local church the other night...

"I say my local church. I don't go in...

"I'm an atheist... thank God!"

Someone on the front row likes that and laughs out loud, the rest of the crowd? Not so much.

"There was a sign outside that read, 'You don't need a mobile phone to read God's text messages'...

"And I thought, that's absolutely true. Cos what you do need...

"...Is quite a serious mental illness."

The woman abruptly stops laughing and there is a general intake of breath. Maybe Burgess Hill is full of Christians? There has to be some hiding somewhere, I suppose. And that was one of my best lines...

I'm what you call an edgy comedian. My comedy is dark and can sometimes split an audience. Not this one. They're absolutely convinced I'm not funny.

I take a breath to continue and Jim Laker, tonight's compere, a tall, confident, striking looking man in his early thirties—who I hate—comes on stage. He strides up to me offering his hand. Comedian speak for 'get off now'. I grab the hand of shame, shake, and make my way back into the audience, feeling their eyes burning into me.

"A big hand for Adam Hanson!" Laker says to muted applause.

I recall what my comedy coach always used to say: 'Record your gigs. And remember... dying is the best teacher of all.'

That all sounded great in the comedy class, but so far, I've not listened to any of my gigs. I'm almost physically unable to hear my own voice played back to me. It's just too horrible to contemplate. And I've also died more times than I'd like to mention.

"Actually," Laker continues. *"Egyptians find me quite irresistible..."*

The crowd, who are loving his over-confident compere act, wait with bated breath.

"Yeah... it's my pharomones."

A deafening howl of laughter and groans, and I can't help but feel annoyed. Laker is arrogant. Someone who took against me as soon as he met me, although Jozee adores him. Meaning I have to pretend to like the annoying, cocky git. I bet he's loving the fact I fell on my arse again.

"Sorry about that... I get all my compere gags from a pyramid scheme," Laker continues.

More groans.

"I could go on like this all night... but my mummy won't let me."

While Laker gets the crowd going again after I almost killed them with my terrible set, I go to the bar and order my free pint—payment for tonight's gig—shutting my ears to Laker's annoying voice, his annoying puns and all his annoying laughs.

I glance over to the green room area where the next comedians pace white-faced, or manically scribble into their gag-books. Jozee sits there, a smile on her face, looking distractedly into the distance. She never gets nervous. Like she's permanently on beta-blockers.

Did she notice me dying? That my new five minutes hardly got laugh-one? Very probably. But she's been distant of late. I'm feeling angry at her and I'm not sure why. Maybe my subconscious has picked on something my useless conscious brain can't process. Whatever it is, it's worrying me. She hardly spoke on the drive here from Hove. Instead, I babbled on about my new gags and this, that and the other. I really should just shut up sometimes.

The free pint arrives a few minutes later and I down it in one, ordering another that isn't free. Jozee is driving me home so why shouldn't I have a drink or two?

Laker comes over to the bar after introducing the next act. His brown, collar-length hair frames thick sideburns, like some cheesy 70s porn star. His nose is thick and wide, his eyebrow ridges pronounced—a modern day Neanderthal hiding amongst humans. I thought him an attractive, fascinating-looking man until I got to know him better.

"Sorry about dragging you off stage like that," Laker says, his sneering voice unable to confer a single hint of apology.

The next act hits the room with his first gag, getting a bigger laugh than all my set put together.

"But you were stinking the place out," he continues. "You know the drill? You die, you leave the stage pronto. The landlord is getting itchy feet about the night as it is without you killing it dead. *The bloody Set menu?* Man, you couldn't raise a laugh out of a demented hyena with that gag. At least it gave me something to get the crowd going again."

The petite form of Nat Naylor pushes in between us. Her purposely designed and expertly judged sickly sweet set normally had the audience, including myself, in stitches. She lived in a world of love and boyfriends, of girlie nights out and baby showers. I used to guffaw at her perfect world that hinted at horrors lurking just below the surface. Recently, she'd gone off the boil, although she didn't seem to notice. Her gig tonight was a lacklustre affair.

"Leave Adam alone," she says, poking her finger into Laker's chest and pursing her thick, lipstick-covered lips in my direction. "Some nights are bleurgh, yeah? I loved your new set. The crowd didn't get you, is all. Don't give up on it just yet. And that pizza gag was great."

Jim Laker smirks and orders a Jack Daniels.

"Thanks," I say to Nat, staring down into her big, flirty eyes, framed by a short black bob that emphasises her childlike features. Nat has always had a thing for me… or so Jozee believes. I never noticed, of course. I suppose she's quite pretty, but I only have eyes for Jozee.

I glance over to Jozee again, but she's looking away from the bar.

"Your girlfriend is gonna smash it tonight," Laker says, following my gaze. "The punters will at least get value for money. She *can* be relied upon."

"Oh, stop it, Jim," Nat says, giving him a playful tap.

I grab my next pint and leave them to it. The last thing I want to do is chat to that smug bastard. I see a few other comedians, and lower my eyes, I don't want to talk to them either.

"Ouch!" says a familiar voice behind me.

I turn to face Billy Belter. I'm sure his second name isn't 'Belter', but comedians do seem to favour alliteration and Billy is on the old-fashioned side.

"That was quite some set," he says in his trademark jovial tones.

Billy is in his late fifties but young-looking with a full head of bright-white hair, slim build and muscled arms. He wears a t-shirt bearing the legend 'Ooh, Matron!' and a shocked-looking photo of Kenneth Williams. It's a balmy summer night and I'm envious of his shorts and open-toed sandals.

"Yeah? What about it?" I reply, noticing a belligerent tone to my voice.

"Calm down! Don't shoot the messenger. I'm your friendly-neighbourhood Billy Belter, remember?"

"Sorry Billy. It's not you that's put me in a bad mood."

"It's not? Well that certainly makes a difference!" he jokes, seemingly relieved.

I wonder if he's like me, saying the wrong things and annoying people all the time. He can sometimes be a jerk.

"I actually liked your new gags, Adam, but as I said, *ouch!*"

"It wasn't one of my best gigs, that's for sure."

"You can say that again… but I won't force you." He laughs at his own bad joke, another one of his annoying habits. "Did Jozee help you with your new stuff?"

I shake my head.

"Maybe she should!" He fist-pumps the air. "That's another of Billy's belters, right there!"

I finish my pint, realising that I'm going to need another one. Two pints is usually my limit, but… why not?

"How is Jozee?" Billy asks, following me to the bar. I wish he'd leave me alone. I try to get along with him, but he's tiresome company. Always trying to make jokes and mostly failing.

I shrug. "Dunno. Preoccupied."

"Something on her mind?"

"Wish I knew. She says she wants to have a talk," I admit begrudgingly, wondering why I'm telling Billy any of this.

He grimaces. "I'd go get your tin hat, mate."

WEDNESDAY MORNING

"IS THE Gannet in?" Ollie asks me.

"Not yet."

'The Gannet' is the nickname we secretly call our boss, a rather sweaty, stressed-out, wine-smelling woman whose real name is Stephanie Bird. An overbearing micro-manager who makes our work-life an utter misery. Curiously thin, and unfortunately birdlike in demeanour with a sharp pointed nose and eyes a little too close together, the Gannet regularly sits at her desk compulsively munching crisps, biscuits and chocolate like there is no tomorrow—hence her nickname. She is very possibly the worst manager I've ever worked for, and that's against some pretty stiff opposition. I've never wanted to be a manager, but even I could do a better job than Stephanie. She does however possess one quality in over-flowing abundance. A quality that I have lacked all my life.

Confidence.

She mostly comes in late, sits at her computer, sighs, moans, disappears for regular cigarette breaks and goes home early. Unless she has a meeting, which she attends under duress and on the implicit understanding that when she returns, we'll have to drop everything to listen to her blow-by-blow account of corporate mismanagement.

Despite all of this, the Gannet is easy to deal with, except on those days when she arrives in the office with a bee in her bonnet about something or other, forcing us to attend an 'emergency meeting' about it. Whatever that 'it' might be. Usually something irrelevant and pointless.

Recently, the Gannet has been working from home a lot. I hope today will be one of those days. Not that it'll make much difference to my workload. Stephanie passes most of her work onto me and Ollie and nakedly takes credit for it.

Soon Ollie quietens down and starts tapping at his keyboard, and I throw myself back into my emails. A whole raft of changes to the website database. Boring stuff, granted, but the morning is going slowly. The work is dumb and repetitive, leaving me to worry and fret, to constantly check my mobile, Facebook, Twitter and Instagram for a message from Jozee, and to sigh loudly every other minute or two, according to Ollie that is.

The Gannet arrives at 11am on the dot—a bad sign. She normally ambles in at around ten, curses at her emails, takes an early lunch and goes home.

"Meeting in fifteen minutes," she announces with no preamble, throwing her things onto her desk and searching her pockets for her ever-present packet of cigarettes. "So, get your combined acts together."

She sticks a cigarette in her mouth and heads to the fire door, outside of which, the smokers congregate to perpetuate their foul habit.

I lift my head and stare over my monitor at Ollie, but he beats me to it.

"Aw shit!"

7
LAST
NIGHT

JOZEE'S SET goes down a storm, the crowd clamouring for more. Laker strides onto the stage and bows theatrically at her, before giving her a long, lingering hug that makes my blood boil.

Jealousy isn't a normal emotion for me. I don't feel it with anybody else Jozee hugs. And believe me, she hugs a helluva lot of everybody.

By now I'm on my fourth or fifth pint and more than a little bolshy. Drink is my friend only in small doses, although this doesn't seem to stop the occasional binge.

Laker finally lets Jozee go and he winds the night down. She comes off-stage and over to the bar. I see the punters looking at her, giving her *that look*. She's the girl who made them laugh their socks off for the last twenty minutes. A star in their midst. A special human being. And they probably believe she's going out with Laker. Especially after the way he publicly groped her.

Jozee is annoyed when she sees the pint in my hand and what is no doubt a drunken expression on my face.

Jozee's parents are both dead, a fact that she took a long time to reveal. Her dad, who she adored, was an alcoholic. As a result, she lived in a weird world where she hated drunks, unless she was drunk herself, which she was on far too many occasions—an odd dichotomy.

She once told me, in a rare moment of self-revelation, that she couldn't stand seeing me drunk because it reminded her of her father. He was a kind man who could turn nasty when he was on the booze. She'd had a sober meal with him after one of his many hospital dry-outs. The last time she'd ever seen her dad... *as he used to be*. He died three years later, although she says he'd died the moment he took his first drink at that same meal.

"Didn't you listen to me earlier?" she says, disappointedly. "We need to talk, Adam. And now you're drunk as a bloody skunk."

"So what? I'm having a drink! Not everyone can smash it night after night. Or didn't you notice I died a godawful death?"

A few heads turn to look at us.

"Oh, piss off!" I shout back at them.

"C'mon, Adam," Jozee says, grabbing my arm. "You're no good to anyone when you're like this."

"Like what?" I reply, genuinely feeling that I've done nothing wrong. Other than have a few drinks. I'm fine, if not a little hard done to. Why doesn't Jozee understand that?

"Let's get you home."

I pull myself free. "Why now? I've still got half a pint left," I say belligerently, holding up my glass and accidentally sloshing lager onto the floor. "Or aren't I allowed to stop out every night like you do? What about Adam? Doesn't he get a chance to let his hair down?"

Behind Jozee I see a concerned looking Nat Naylor. Billy Belter stands next to her, he jokingly mimes shooting himself in the head and pulls a horrified face. Maybe I am being unreasonable, I think through my drunken haze. Aware that perhaps I've had a few too many. I'm about to go with Jozee when Laker appears behind her back.

"Just what do you see in this jerk?" he says.

I notice some of the audience watching this exchange. They obviously agree with him.

"C'mon, I'll take you home," Jozee says.

Laker puts his big spatula-like hand on Jozee's shoulder and gives it a squeeze. "Yeah, get him out of here pronto."

Doesn't Jozee see what he's doing? Trying to purposely wind me up. I hate all that ownership crap, but I can't stop the way I feel. Jozee is mine. She shouldn't let Laker touch her all the bloody time. "Why don't you take *him* home?" I shout, sloshing my glass again, the remaining lager splashing onto Jozee. "He's all over you like a rash anyway! You can take him back to that shitty little bedsit you used to live in before you came to sponge off me."

Jozee tenses and I know I've gone too far. She is fiercely independent and hates the fact I'm the main breadwinner, doing all she can to earn a little money working menial jobs here and there. Instead of erupting, her jaw sets, and she walks towards the door.

"Jozee! I'm sorry!" I shout after her.

"Leave it," Laker says, blocking my way. He's a big guy, thick-set and heavy.

"He's right, mate," Billy says. "Let Jozee cool down. Give yourself a few minutes to try and sober up, you've had too many."

I ignore them both.

By the time I get outside and into the car park, Jozee is standing by her mini, the driver door open.

A crunch of thunder above and the cloud-heavy sky cracks open, rain bouncing off parked cars and slapping into trees and bushes. An insistent, growing torrent.

"Get in and let's go home," Jozee says, the rain quickly dampening her yellow hair. "We need to talk. Once you've sobered up."

"Talk about what? How much you love Laker?"

She stands there for a few seconds, the rain pummelling the off-white paint of her mini, seconds that I will play over and over again for the rest of my life.

"Sod you, Adam," she says, dropping into the driving seat, slamming the door and roaring away.

8

WEDNESDAY MORNING

THE MEETING with the Gannet is another waste of time. Nothing that hasn't happened before, and yet, as I watch her sitting there, stinking of cigarettes and banging on about God knows what in the tiny back room that is as far away from a corporate meeting area as physically possible—a sink, exposed pipes running across one wall, cobwebs drifting from a roof too high to clean and a filthy, stained carpet—I realise I'm unable to deal with her nonsense any longer.

Normally, me and Ollie would sit back, 'listening with rapt attention to our most glorious leader'. Making notes and contributing considered nods of our heads. Today, I am in no mood for her particular brand of bollocks. And we've been here almost an hour already. It's getting close to lunch-time and still no word from Jozee.

I need to get out of here, to go home to see if she's finally turned up. Even if she's not there, I just need to go. To escape. Instead, I'm stuck in this oppressive little room with this idiot.

The Gannet has an annoying habit of saying a questioning 'right?' at the end of every sentence, as if she desperately craves validation. Ollie is giving her an echoing *Right* in a variety of ways to relieve the boredom and, I guess, to entertain me, but I don't join in. Not today. Plus, I can't stop checking my phone. The Gannet hates phones in meetings and I am flouting one of her golden rules... god forbid.

"Something wrong, Adam?" the Gannet finally asks. "You seem, I dunno, distracted. And put that phone away."

I entertain the possibility of coming up with some answer to placate her, but I'm in no mood to play her games this morning.

"Actually, there is something wrong," I say a little too belligerently, aware that I'm flying very close to the edge of my professional disguise. "This new pointless initiative that's got you so hot under the collar, is just the latest in a long line of similarly pointless initiatives."

The Gannet's over-plucked eyebrows manage to somehow rise and furrow at the same time—it's quite a sight.

"You regularly call these meetings," I continue, "to drone on and on about something that isn't remotely important to anything we're working on. And yet, we're expected to come up with a plan of action, with spreadsheets and objectives and God knows what else. We nod. But we've learnt to do nothing. And you know why? Because these meetings are only for your ego. As soon as we leave, you'll forget all about them. So we don't even bother."

A strange noise comes from the Gannet's throat.

"And nowhere in my job description does it say that I'm to do your work. Quite frankly, I'm sick of your laziness and the way you expect us to take the strain while you swan about doing nothing, other than stuff your face with rubbish, moan and smoke cigarettes. Does that answer your question?"

The Gannet turns a peculiar shade of red. I've never spoken to her like this before. In fact, I've never spoken out of turn in such a rational way at any time during my work life. I've ranted in the past in other jobs, but I soon learned that was a no-no in the office. Stephanie lives under the delusion that I think her an efficient and effective manager. This new, alternative information has come as a real shock to the fragile world she's created for herself.

The Gannet says nothing, packs up her files and walks out of the meeting room, slamming the door behind her.

"Bloody hell, Adam!" Ollie splutters, and even I can see that he is shocked—wide eyes, eyebrows raised, mouth open—just like the 'astonished' emoji, one of the few emojis I can actually understand.

"You really gave it to her that time," he continues. "And to her face. What were you thinking? You know what a mad bastard she is. I thought her head was gonna explode. And why the hell did you involve me?"

"It had to be said. We're both carrying her. And on top of everything else, she wants us to stop what we're doing just so she can grandiosely mouth off at us—while we're missing our lunchbreak. I've had enough of that buffoon. Enough."

"I suppose you're right, but Stephanie is gonna come down on you like a ton of bricks."

"I don't care. I'm having a bad day," I reply, feeling the oppressive weight of my irrational boss leaving my shoulders. "Aren't you sick to death of her riding us?"

"Well yeah, and you certainly told her. What didn't you tell her?"

I shrug and check my phone again. "I have to go back home just in case…"

"Just in case of what?"

"I need to be home."

I leave the meeting room and enter the main office, hoping the Gannet has gone outside for an angry cigarette in the nicotine corner of shame. Instead, she is waiting by my desk. The last thing I want is to continue the confrontation. I've said all that needs to be said. I quickly walk past her towards the exit.

"Where do you think you're going?"

"Home."

"You can't just leave after talking to me like—"

"It's my lunchtime," I reply.

"No way!"

Never has my office life seemed so utterly inconsequential and stifling. "I'm sorry," I say calmly, more calmly than I feel, "we can talk about this another time."

"Come back. Now!"

WEDNESDAY AFTERNOON

THE OPPRESSIVE heat of a stiflingly hot sunny afternoon hits me as I emerge from the office. The day has warmed up and then some. Brighton is shimmering, even in these backstreets. I think about walking home, but it will take forever. So will the bus, which, in this weather, is gonna be an oven. Instead, I stride to a nearby taxi rank and go straight back to my flat.

The Gannet WhatsApps me while I'm in the taxi, using the work group she set up to harass me and Ollie at the weekend. Her tone is unexpectedly conciliatory.

> *Not like you to behave like that, Adam. Ollie says you have something on your mind. I wish you'd talked to me privately about it. Always willing to help. Take the rest of the day off if you like. I have taken your concerns seriously and scheduled a meeting for tomorrow with HR. I don't want to make this any more formal than it has to be, but the things you mentioned must be properly discussed and—*

I give up reading. Talking to the Gannet like that was something I thought I'd never do. Like one of my rants, but more satisfying. It felt good to get it off my chest… *for now.* And yet there's an inevitable downside. I've created a world of pain for myself. Work is going to be hell for a while, but I don't care as long as I can find Jozee.

The taxi arrives at Eaton Palace Gardens, and I get out, checking up the road for Jozee's mini. It's not there. And the first thing I see when I push open my flat door is the note I left on the floor. Jozee hasn't been back yet.

I'm hit by a wave of sickness, not helped by the fact I haven't eaten all day. But my stomach is in too much of a knot to eat.

"Why can't she just come home, or phone me or leave me a bloody message!" I shout impotently into my flat.

"Adam, are you okay?"

I turn to face Clive standing in his doorway. A prissy man in his middle sixties. Thin and immaculately dressed in slacks, shirt and tie, over which is buttoned an expensive looking beige cardigan.

"Oh Adam, you look terrible. Is everything okay with you? That girl, locking you out of your own flat. It's disgraceful."

"Have you seen her, have you seen Jozee?" I almost shout at him.

He doesn't move a muscle. Instead he stands and shakes his head at me, a pity-filled expression upon his face, milky green eyes staring at me from behind effete, golden-rimmed glasses.

I've known Clive ever since I moved in a couple of years ago. We were good friends until Jozee appeared. He'd invite me around for meals once a week and we'd watch a movie, while he plied me and himself with copious amounts of gin poured, ready mixed, from an ornate glass jug. After which, he'd try to drunkenly chat me up—which I always politely ignored. He was harmless, or so I thought, but recently, I've noticed a nasty side to him.

"No, I haven't seen the little bottle-blond," he says, his smile disappearing to be replaced with a sneer. "Please tell me she's left you for good this time."

"What do you mean *this time?*"

"I mean that you're forever arguing. Night and day. It was only a matter of time. Surely you can see that?"

"They're not arguments… they're…" I'm at a loss for words. Jozee understands how I need to have a rant from time to time. She even joins in with me. Telling me she finds it cathartic. We'd often let it all out. Screaming and shouting like a pair of mad banshees. It doesn't surprise me that Clive has purposely seen this as negative.

"If she's finally gone, that can only be a good thing," Clive says with a sympathetic nod of his head.

"She's not left me! Jozee just hasn't… come home."

"Oh, I see. It's like *that* is it? Well I for one am not surprised. She has 'stop-out' written all over her. You want to hope she doesn't come back. You'll be well rid, young man. Well rid."

I'm filled with an intense desire to tell Clive to shut his mouth, to step inside my flat and slam the door. Instead, I take a deep breath. "Have you talked to her recently?"

Clive seems taken aback and a little guilty.

"Have you said anything to upset her?"

"We have had the odd altercation. Of course, we have," he says too quickly. "You don't know what it's like when you're away at work. She's noisy. Very noisy. And the things she's says to me when I'm just trying to go about my business? Scandalous!"

Jozee has often mentioned how Clive terrorises her after I go to work, waiting for her whenever she left or entered the flat. Door-stepping her with his unwanted comments and complaints. She always laughed it off.

"She's told me how you've been harassing her," I say.

Clive blinks, his body quivering. "She's… she's a liar. Plain and simple. You know me, Adam. You've known me a lot longer than her. I wouldn't do such a thing. Why would I? She turned you against me as soon as she realised I could see through her *little girl lost* act. I don't fool that easily."

I don't believe him. But I do know he's a nosey so and so. The type to twitch his curtains at every coming and going. "Last night, before you caught me climbing up to my balcony. Did you see Jozee?"

"See her? What do you mean?"

"I need to find out if she came home before me and left again, or never got home in the first place. It's important."

Clive pauses, and I get the impression he's hiding something.

"How would I know? he finally answers. "I had an early night until you woke me up swearing and banging below my window like that. I didn't see or hear anything of her."

"An early night? That's unusual isn't it? You usually wait till I'm in bed and then start playing that damn awful classical music at full blast until 2am in the morning."

Clive's jaw drops, quietly flexing as if he can't manage to vocalise his response to my insult.

"How dare you," he croaks. "No one else complains about my nightly Schubert. No one. How dare you! And after everything I've done for you since you moved in." He stomps back into his flat and slams the door.

If Jozee came home last night, I'm sure Clive would've told me. Which means she never came home, unless he is lying. But for what reason?

I enter my flat. Despite today's heat, it feels cold and unlived in. Jozee's absence is oppressive, but I still check all the rooms again. The closets and under the bed. Within moments I'm sitting on the sofa in my living room wondering what to do. Thanks to my belligerence with the Gannet, I now have the afternoon to myself. A whole eight hours to fill before Jozee's gig in London.

Eight hours!

The time seems immeasurably distant and I feel the beginnings of the panic that overwhelmed me this morning. I can't let that happen again. I make myself a mug of tea and a slice of toast that I force down and go sit at my makeshift desk. I open my iPad and create a list of 'To Dos'. I'm always happier with a list… who isn't?

It sounds silly, but I've used lists all my life to help with my condition. Even before I was diagnosed with Asperger's, my list-making habit was well entrenched. A way to order the manic whirlwind of my errant mind.

Firstly, I phone the hospitals. Talking to admissions. Asking for Jozee by her full name, Josephine Margaret Jackson—a name she despised—or for any Jane Doe who matched her description. It takes me over an hour. The result? *Nothing*.

I pop onto the local newspaper website, the Argus, and go through the last twenty-four-hour news looking for possible road accidents and other incidents, but if anything, it's been an exceptionally quiet time in the world of local happenings, other than multiple stories about today's unprecedented heatwave. The hottest day in Brighton since 1922, apparently.

I go onto Twitter: @FunnyAdamHanson. My go-to platform. Twitter is usually well ahead of the news, but find nothing, apart from reports of police activity on a beach near Eastbourne. I focus the search and find a tweet that mentions it directly, my heart suddenly lurching into my mouth.

> **Beach Wanderer**
> *@flotsamjenny*
> Loads of police down on the beach close to Normans Bay. I asked what was going on. A body was washed up. That's the second in a year. The police won't tell me any more than that.
> *4 hours ago*

I search for Normans Bay on Google. It's located on the far side of Eastbourne. About twenty or so miles away. There's no other mention of washed-up bodies anywhere. Just that single tweet.

Worried, I ring up the Argus news desk and talk to the editor. The woman is disappointed that I'm asking about the news, rather than phoning up with a story. When I ask about the body found on Normans Bay beach, she goes quiet.

"You will need to talk to the police about that," she says guardedly.

"So there was a body!" I take a deep breath and tell her about Jozee being missing and the woman takes pity on me.

"It was a woman's body," she confides, "dismembered, but it'd been in the sea for a long time. It can't be your girlfriend."

I breathe a sigh of relief. "Thanks."

"There's been a spate of these bodies washing up recently. All hush, hush. Illegal immigrants, from what I've been told. The police have asked the media to stay quiet. And so our hands are tied… If your girlfriend doesn't turn up in a few days, give me another ring. We may make a story out of it once the police take it seriously. You know the kind of thing, a plea for information."

"Thanks," I say. "But why wait? Surely if someone close to a missing person is convinced something is not quite right the authorities should take that seriously, shouldn't they?"

"I understand, but we usually hang off until these things are official. Have you contacted the police yet?"

"No, but it's on my list. Thanks for your time." Sighing, I finish the call. Another dead end.

I go through my phone contacts hoping a name might jog a memory or two. There's hundreds of comics on there. Half of them I have forgotten, but a lot of names stick out. Jim Laker is one of them. I often wonder if Jozee'd had a fling with him in the past. I'm not normally jealous or care one jot about who previous girlfriends have slept with. None of my business. But, like I said, it's different with Jim Laker. I can't stand Jozee to be near him. He knows how much it annoys me. He often winks at me over Jozee's shoulder when she gives him a greeting hug. And what he'd said last night… my blood begins to boil. As one of Jozee's best friends, it makes sense to phone him to see if he's heard from her… but I just can't do it. Not yet. Instead I call Shirley Sands.

Shirley is the closest Jozee has to a best mate in female form. My girlfriend doesn't get on well with other women, or so she tells me. She likes hanging out with men. Prefers their company. Except for Shirley Sands that is, who apparently made a bee-line for Jozee as soon as she arrived on the scene a few months before I started. Shirley doesn't seem to have any other friends to speak of, she's very much a keep-herself-to-herself kind of person. But she's always phoning Jozee up and arranging gigs together. And they're a great match on stage. Jozee, her set silly, funny and delving into her own twisted, hilarious off-beat world, and the tough-as-nails Shirley Sands, with her barbed tongue and devastating one-liners and put-downs.

She has a statuesque profile, hidden behind thick makeup and shoulder-length, raven hair, rocking a sixties look—mini-skirt, high-heeled boots and fantastically long legs. I've never seen her in normal life, but what she wears on stage is like a costume.

A form of protection, Jozee says.

She's cold to the blokes who are always pestering her, cutting them dead with her famous 'Fuck off!' line she uses on stage. Jozee tells me it's because she's such a stunner, that she's had to fight off guys perving on to her all her life. Shirley is polite to me though, even if she acts like I don't exist, which I've taken as quite a compliment. I never feel the urge to chat to her, or to make stupid small talk when she's around. Refreshing company. I wish more people were like her.

I bring up her contact details and her face appears on my phone.

The girl would be quite beautiful if she didn't cake herself with all that dark eyeliner and makeup. The call goes straight to voicemail.

"Hi Shirley, Adam Hanson here. Just wondering if you'd heard from Jozee. She's not come home and I'm a little worried. Please… can you call me when you get this."

I off the phone and try to think of who else to contact. And then I realise… that's it. That's everyone Jozee is close to. Jim Laker, Shirley Sands… *and me.*

It's difficult to believe that she has so few close people in her life. Everyone else… they're just acquaintances.

Then again, what about my life? *Who do I have?* I shake my head and whistle. It's just Stevo and Jozee and no bugger else. Unless I count Ollie, but he's only a work buddy…

A thought pops into my mind. Jozee works part-time at the marina superstore on the other side of town. A shelf-stacker. How did I forget about that? I'm always moaning at her to leave.

'Shit work but it pays', is the way Jozee put it. And she likes to pay her way.

I earn enough money for Jozee to not work at all, but she's fiercely independent. Something that I love about her. But which also means… *she might be at work now!*

It takes an age to get across Brighton. I ordered a taxi that took over twenty minutes to arrive and we hit traffic on the seafront. The sudden heatwave has brought everyone out. Hove Lawns is covered with illegal but traditional BBQs, couples making out, families and people playing football, cricket and drunkenly throwing frisbees at one another. I'd go and join them, if this was any other day.

Finally, I'm dropped off at the marina. It sounds a beautiful place. In reality, the concrete, characterless monstrosity is a Brighton embarrassment. Sure, there's a marina, and some restaurants, if you fancy taking out a loan to buy your gastro fish and chips and single coke, but the rest is designed with the same flare as the multi-storey car park that is its centrepiece.

The sun washes out all the colour, a harsh white glare, reflected by the swathes of hot concrete. I jog into the ASDA superstore, an enormous barn of a building, the aircon refreshing after the heat of outside.

I normally try to avoid places like this due to the people, the stupid non-stop beeps, other irritating sounds, and the overpowering smells, but not today. I grab a basket as cover and charge up and down the multitudinous aisles searching for Jozee, feeling an urge to kick at all those people blocking my way. I go up and down the immense store twice. No sign of her. She could be in the back or on a break.

I'm considering walking through the employee's door when it opens, and I spot a familiar face, a young kid who came to one of Jozee's gigs recently. He's short and wiry, appearing somewhat younger than I remember. His black hair is greased down, the same grease seemingly coating his blotched and spotty face. I'm nearly six foot and tower over him.

"Hey!" I say a little too loudly. "It's um… who are you again? You saw Jozee a few weeks ago. At a comedy night. Not sure which one. I'm Adam, her boyfriend, remember? Is Jozee in today. Is she back there?"

"It's Vinnie," the kid answers, sullenly, like I should know the name of every spotty kid who turned up to one of Jozee's gigs.

"That's it. Yeah, Vinnie. Great to see you. Is Jozee in?"

He gives me a quick once over and sneers. "Yeah, I remember you. You were on that night as well… ouch. Man, you died a death."

I'm getting a little frustrated. "About Jozee?"

"She ain't in. Not today. As far as I know," he says lazily. He narrows his eyes. "Why you askin'?"

I consider coming up with a lie, but why? Vinnie is no one important. "She didn't come home last night. I'm worried about her."

"Sounds like she don't want to see you, if you ask me."

"That's not important," I reply, wondering why he would say that, feeling suddenly irritated with this cocky teenager. "Can you find out when she's next in for me."

"Not sure that's… um… ethical, is it, man? Freedom of information and all that shit."

"What?"

"I'm just saying I might lose my job, you know what I mean?"

"Huh?"

"Jozee told me you were slow on the uptake… I'm talking money."

"Money?"

"Call it twenty quid."

"You want me to pay you twenty quid to go check the bloody roster?" I say, not quite believing my ears.

"That's the size of it. No skin off my nose, is it?"

I'm torn between punching Vinnie in the face or calling his supervisor, but neither option will get me the information I'm after. "Okay, you weaselly little twat. Twenty quid it is. But this is extortion."

Vinnie smirks. "Ain't it just! And I ain't no twat, so watch your lip, unless you want it split."

His confidence far outweighs his physical presence and I quell an intense desire to grab this little prick by the neck and shake him.

"Meet me outside in ten," he says. "And drop the attitude."

I go back outside, locate a cash-machine, and pull out fifty quid, squinting at the screen that's almost impossible to read in the harsh sunlight. Afterwards, I find a shadow to wait in. The heat is dizzying. I stand there for what seems a lot longer than ten minutes until Vinnie finally makes an appearance. Sauntering over like he doesn't have a concern in the world, now wearing a cheap pair of mirrored sunglasses too large for his face. At least it covers up some of his spots.

"You got the cashola?" he asks.

I pull out the twenty and offer it to him.

"Not in front of the CCTV!"

He pushes me aside and snatches the money off me when he's satisfied we're not being seen or videoed.

"Ta, mate. That will do very nicely. Jozee is in at 10am tomorrow." He takes out a packet of cigarettes, flicking it open in a way that I'm guessing is supposed to impress me.

"Tomorrow? Shit!"

"Hey, don't shoot the messenger," Vinnie says, taking out a cigarette and inexpertly lighting it. "You want me to give her a message or sumfin?" Vinnie digs out his phone from a back pocket. "Give me your phone number."

"What for?"

"Just in case I hear from Jozee. If she calls or messages me, I'll let you know. For an extra few quid that is."

"She calls you?"

Vinnie takes a long drag of his cigarette and stifles a cough. "Don't be surprised, she's a very friendly girl."

I don't like his tone. The kid is a complete creep, but I give him my phone number anyway. And he phones me back to check it's correct. What have I got to lose?

It's 5pm. Time to get to Brighton station to head up to London and Jozee's gig at Seven Sisters. There's a bus that goes straight there, which I catch. I'm not made of money and I must now pay for a ticket to London as well. Plus, I'm in no rush. The gig doesn't start till 8pm.

It's another slow journey on the bus and I can't help wondering why Jozee would give a creep like Vinnie her phone number, never mind text him. Then again, she was always very trusting. Too trusting.

I console myself with the fact that I'll be seeing Jozee soon. She can then explain what is going on.

10
WEDNESDAY
EVENING

BRIGHTON TRAIN station is packed with eager commuters with a long queue for the one working ticket machine. I'm impatient, cursing the people in front of me who are taking forever to get their tickets—even though I'm not in a rush. My eye roving around for Jozee.

She'd normally catch the London train rather than driving, although that option is cheaper. But her Mini Cooper is in a perpetual state of disrepair—indeed, some vandal kicked off one of her wing mirrors only a few days ago. Jozee is always afraid of it breaking down on the M25, the dreadful London circular.

I wonder if that's what Jozee did last night—drive to London?

The more I think of it, the more it makes sense. She has friends in North London, or so she told me. She grew up in Wood Green.

The queue lurches forward, but I don't move. I realise what I'm saying to myself. If Jozee went to London, she must be purposely ignoring me. She wanted to talk last night. And, even though I didn't think much of it at the time, I can't help worrying that it was something important. The curse of my condition, of my Aspie nature, is that I'm unable to pick up on all the little hints and social cues. And no matter how much I may tell myself that I know Jozee better than anyone else, it's possible I have misread her. Sure, we hadn't made love for a couple of weeks, but at night, when she was asleep, she'd still snuggle up to me, wrapping her arms around me in that childlike way I love so much. That spoke volumes... didn't it?

But something has been bothering Jozee. Something that I'm sure happened before she met me. Could that be what all this was about?

Was she finally willing to reveal some personal inner pain and I'd not taken her seriously enough, gotten drunk and accused her of fancying Jim Laker? Without knowing what she wanted to tell me, all I can do is speculate. I messed up though, that much is sure. The question is, *how big was that mess up?*

A guy taps me on the shoulder, irritated that I've not moved forward. I tell him to "Get lost!" followed by a conciliatory, "I'm sorry. Bad day."

He shrugs, giving me a knowing look. "You don't need to apologise. The trains suck. Everybody is irate. I've already missed one train due to this ticket machine screw-up."

Half an hour later, I'm crammed into the train on my way to London, wishing I'd brought headphones to drown out the cacophony of human noises. Mainly sneezing, sniffles and raspy breathing. Does everybody suffer from hay fever? It sure sounds like it.

Victoria Train Station is similarly rammed with people, but it's a relief to get off the train, heading for the Underground. The Tube is one of the few forms of public transport that doesn't bother me. It's so loud down there that every other sound is drowned out. And then there's the almost magical way you can travel around London. I love it.

I emerge from Seven Sisters station a short while later, and find my way to the Lord Horatio pub.

The time is 7.25pm and the little pub is already packed. A burly bouncer, an Asian guy with a skinhead, black uniform and an immaculately trimmed beard stands threateningly by the door. Bouncers on a Wednesday night? That doesn't bode well. Then again, Seven Sisters is a little on the rough side.

I push through the single door and walk inside, my eyes searching for the blonde head of Jozee. Instead, I see Billy Belter standing at the bar. I clap him on the shoulder.

"You seen Jozee?" I say to him with no preamble.

Billy almost chokes on his pint.

"Is she here?" I continue.

"Here?" he replies, looking shaken. "No, no. I've not seen her, mate, you mad bastard. What were you trying to do, coming up behind me like that? Do you want to give me a bloody heart attack?" He takes a quick chug of lager and licks his lips. "Luckily for you the alcohol will probably take me first. I've only just arrived myself. You on the bill as well?"

I shake my head, unable to hide my disappointment.

"I drove up from Brighton in Cheryl's new car," Billy continues. "Thought I'd start early—you know the traffic—but zero problems along the way. Since Cheryl put me on the insurance, I've been driving every opportunity I get. A lovely motor, an Audi TT Sportback— modded by its previous owner, blue paintjob, wheel rims and a nifty little spoiler, a real fanny magnet—but don't tell Cheryl I said that."

"Your girlfriend's car?"

"Yep, I'm very much a kept man these days."

"You didn't ask Jozee if she wanted a lift?"

"I wasn't aware she was on, and Cheryl is a complete green-eyed monster where other ladies are concerned. I can't help it if I'm god's gift to women, can I? If she heard I was driving alone with a hot pocket-rocket like Jozee, she'd first remove my car privileges and then my bollocks."

A young Asian guy comes over, his hair artificially dyed white-blond above dark skin and darker eyebrows. "Hey, you wouldn't happen to be performing tonight, would you?"

"Indeed, we are," Billy says, putting out his hand. "Billy Belter at your service. I take it you're the promotor?"

"I thought you guys looked funny! I'm Maz, Maz Tanik. Promotor and compere." He shakes Billy's hand before offering it to me. We also shake.

"And you are?"

"Adam Hanson. I'm a comic, but not on tonight. I'm here to see Jozee Jackson. Has she arrived yet?"

"Tonight's headliner? Nope. Not heard from her. As long as she turns up before it's time to go on, I don't mind. I've already had one act drop out though. You're welcome to the spot if you want it?"

I'm taken aback. Gigging is the last thing I'm thinking about. "No thanks."

"Never say never!" Billy says. "It's all experience, even in a dive like this."

Maz frowns.

"Only joking! I'm a comic. That's what we do."

"The place is a bit of a dump," Maz says, "but we get a lively crowd in. We're nearly full already."

He points to the other end of the small pub and I spot a microphone stand surrounded by fanned seating and quite a few punters.

Billy raises his hands. "Like I said, just a joke. I'm a comedian. Geddit?"

Maz forces a smile.

"Do you have a running order?" Billy asks.

"Sure, you're on first."

"First? I drove all the way from Brighton. At least stick me on in the second half."

"No can do. But I tell you what, I'll let you close the first half. Okay?"

"That'd be brilliant. Ta mate, I owe you one."

"Just make sure you're fucking funny." Maz winks and disappears into the crowd.

"Prick," Billy says. "Putting me on first? What was he thinking?"

"First is a great spot," I say, knowing that for a comic like Billy, first on was a poison chalice.

"In a shit hole like this? No way. Maz is the compere, it's his job to get the punters warmed up, not mine." He takes another swallow of lager and finishes his pint. "Dutch courage," he says in explanation. "You ever seen Maz before? Is he funny?"

I shake my head. Billy is his own worst enemy. The golden rule is to never annoy the promotor. No matter how big a dick they are. It is so easy to get a bad name in this business… and promotors talk to one another. "Maz seems a decent enough guy though," I venture.

"Looks like a wanker to me. You want a pint?"

He points a finger at an array of lager pumps and I'm nodding before I have time to think. I down the pint in two long gulps.

"Bugger me!" Billy says. "And I thought I was the only one with his booze-foot in an early grave. Another?"

"Why not, I need it."

"After last night? You were steaming mate. That was quite a barney with Jozee, yeah?"

I'd forgotten that Billy Belter was there and blush.

"You were shouting in her face. Then chucked booze all over her. Pretty nasty. I once got into the same state with Cheryl. Never again. I was proper in the shithouse. I suppose the make-up sex was damn good though, huh?"

I shake my head. "She drove off and I made my own way home. I've not seen her since."

After my second pint arrives we sit on the seats reserved for the comics at the back of the room. I take a long slurp of lager, my stress and tension ebbing away.

"I'm worried sick. Jozee's not been answering her phone all day."

"That sounds ominous."

"I don't know where she is. She's gigging here tonight, so I came down to chat it out with her."

"I thought it might be something like that," he says, knowingly. "Jim Laker vowed to never put you on again, you know?"

"That's not fair!" I blurt.

"Don't you remember? You told some of the punters to piss off. And you're always getting angry, mate."

"No, I'm bloody not!" I shout, making heads turn even above the bar's loud music.

"I think you just proved my point."

Billy is wrong. Last night was the first time in ages that I'd ever done anything like that. And never in front of the comedian crowd.

"I really screwed up."

"Yeah, you did. Big time. My advice—serve your porridge, let it blow over and buy her some flowers. The chicks love that kind of shit."

Billy Belter was always dishing out sage advice, like some aged sexist shaman.

"Flowers aren't Jozee's style. I'm hoping she'll turn up soon and we can sort it out."

Billy claps me on the shoulder. "She'll come around. I'm sure of it."

"Thanks Billy," I say, meaning it.

"Good man. Now, if you'll excuse me, I need to go and rehearse."

I nod, and watch Billy leave the pub to join two other comics who are wandering up and down the street outside practising their sets. I've done the same myself. A lunatic muttering to himself while passers-by stare.

THE NIGHT kicks off with Maz chatting to the crowd. Despite Billy's disdain, the guy is funny and very personable. *All the things Billy lacks,* I think to myself before remembering I'm trying to now like him. Maz thanks everyone for coming, tells them what will be happening and starts to warm them up.

Compering is a thankless, sometimes soul-destroying, job most of the time, but Maz has a lot of personable energy. The guy is good… *very good.*

"So now to the contractual obligation part of my duties," Maz says. *"Where I pick on some very attractive young ladies and shamelessly flirt with them in the hope of a leg-over later…"*

Maz does his thing with aplomb, flirting with everyone, even some of the guys. After he introduces the first act to thunderous applause, I go over to him and ask if he's heard from Jozee.

"No," he says. "Nada. I was told she's reliable, but now I'm getting nervous. Why you so interested?"

"I'm her boyfriend."

"Lucky you. Have you phoned her? Her number goes straight to voicemail when I call. She might answer you."

I shake my head. "I get the same."

"Shit. If she can't make it, it means I'm down two acts on the night. You've got to cover for her. These punters have paid for six comedians. I can't give them just four. Yeah? Is that okay? There's a free pint in it for you."

Even though gigging is the last thing I fancy doing right now, I like Maz and find myself nodding. He's also a promotor. I don't want to get a bad name, especially with Jim Laker no doubt bad-mouthing me. Besides, the sudden jolt of comedy fear takes my mind off Jozee.

"That mate of yours, Billy Belter, is he good enough to headline in

Jozee's place if she does a no show?" Maz asks me. "He seems pretty confident."

I hate to be put on the spot like this. Billy isn't funny. I've seen him occasionally smash it. But he's not up to headlining, and probably never will be. "He wouldn't be my first choice."

Maz shrugs. "Beggars can't be choosers I suppose. And he has come all the way from Brighton. The comedy scene is strong down there. I'll go and tell him the good news."

Billy returns and sits next to me. Gone is his relaxed demeanour and I see the same mixture of terror and excitement I've witnessed hundreds of times in the eyes of new comics.

"My first headline," he whispers. "Bloody hell."

"Jozee may still turn up."

He turns to look at me with a face creased with theatrical fear. "Let's hope so, yeah?" And we both laugh.

I get another beer in the interval. I know I shouldn't, but I can't help myself, and go and stand outside, hoping to see Jozee on her way from the direction of the station.

Where is she?

Punishing me with the silent treatment I can understand, but missing a gig? Jozee is too professional to do that. Plus, there's thirty quid in it for her. I know Jozee, even after the expenses of getting here, that's a payday she wouldn't miss. But I have more pressing concerns. I'm on any minute now. I calm myself with a few long breaths, aware of my heart chugging in my ears—as it always does before a gig—and even though my pulse doesn't slow, performing my pre-gig breathing exercises takes the edge off my panic.

I make my way back inside just in time for Maz to introduce me. I walk purposely to the stage. A raised area, six inches off the floor. Maz offers me his hand and I shake and step up to the mic. I'm not as nervous as I normally am. Maybe because of worrying about Jozee. Or it could be the beers. Billy is right. This place is a dive. Who cares if I die again? I've died enough times in the past.

Sod it!

12

I SAY nothing for a few seconds, letting the tension build. A trick I learned from Jozee. I've practised this before, but on stage, time speeds up so much that a second can seem like thirty, and I've always jumped the gun. Not this time.

As I'm waiting to speak, a police car roars past the pub, sirens blazing.

"He won't sell many ice creams going that fast," I say, blatantly stealing the famous Eric Morecambe gag, while also adding a half-okay impersonation. And whether the audience understand my little homage or not, they roar with laughter.

"My name's Adam Hanson," I continue, after the laughter has died down. *"But don't let that put you off."*

More laughter. They get me. That's the tester line. Not funny in itself, but if they laugh, things are gonna go well. I hit them with the next gag and settle in.

"I'm the kind of guy who likes to urinate on my happy-go-lucky neighbour's front lawn, just to prove the point...

"...His grass isn't always fucking greener."

Another howl of laughter. I'm surprised, that joke has never done that well before. An attractive red-haired woman wearing a fetching green dress in the first row, sitting with a well-to-do guy in a sharp suit, can't stop laughing. An infectious, weird cackle. It gets another laugh.

"I do have more gags," I say to her, ad-libbing. *"...Maybe your boyfriend can fit you with one later."*

A pause.

I panic, wondering if I've gone too far, if the joke is insulting or sexist or... *God knows what?* But I'm saved by shocked laughter and applause. Once the audience has died down, I continue. This is the best reaction I've ever had and, for the first time on stage, the terror leaves me. I'm actually really enjoying it.

"Sorry about that. But friends are always telling me that I've got a bad attitude. It's not my fault…

I pause, and count to three.

"…My inner-child just wants to bitch-slap people."

I see Maz at the back, he raises his thumb at me as the room erupts again. The crowd doubling over in laughter.

"I have a girlfriend," I say very seriously to unbelieving giggles. *"I recently took her for a romantic drive in the countryside… I wanted to show her the true joy of nature.*

"She got to see a badger. She stroked a fox. She even held a little squirrel in the palm of her hand. Tears were streaming down her face…"

This time I leave a longer pause. I see faces waiting expectantly. Hanging on my every word.

"…I found them dead at the side of the road."

This is my marmite joke, the one that divides the audience. Christ, even I think it's near the edge. I only keep it in my set because Jozee loves it so much. The room groans… groans that turn into peals of laughter.

"They do say that women like a man with a good sense of humour, don't they?" I continue, pushing the laugh.

"But I also suffer from what scientists call 'Tourette's Syndrome By Proxy'…

"…All my girlfriends call me, *wanker!*

I'm absolutely smashing it for the very first time. I feel vindicated, elated, god-like. I carry on, loving the sound of the laughs and applause. The giggles and guffaws. Everything forgotten except this wonderful, glorious moment. If only Jozee was here to see me…

And as her name flits into my mind, I catch a glimpse of her at the other side of the pub, heading for the door. Her blonde hair shining.

"Jozee!" I shout to more laughter. *"Jozee! Wait!"*

I walk forwards and misjudge the end of the stage, falling over the first row, piling into the red-haired girl and her boyfriend, knocking pints and people over.

"Jozee!" I scream, getting to my feet and pushing through the

confused audience. I rush to the doorway, past the bouncer and outside. I see Jozee standing with a group of girls, smoking.

"Jozee?" I say, wondering what she's doing with a cigarette. I grab her shoulder and spin her around.

13

IT'S NOT her. Not Jozee. Of course it's not.

Shit!

The girl is the right height and build with the same hair colouring, but nothing like her. She's also wearing lot of makeup. Jozee never wore anything other than a bit of eyeliner.

"Get your hands off me!" she shrieks.

I let go immediately, raising my hands. "I'm sorry," I say. "I thought… I thought you were someone else."

The other girls round on me, their made-up faces twisting in disgust. Sneering lipstick and flicking false eye-lashes. "Get away from her you creep!"

I back away, repeating my apology. The girls are a little drunk and very aggressive. I wonder if they are going to start kicking me with their impressive high heels.

"I said I was sorr—"

Rough hands grab me from behind and drag me back inside the pub—the bouncer. He sits me down at a table near the door and stands guard like I'm some criminal. I notice the couple from the first-row standing at the bar, staring angrily at me. The sharp guy's suit is wet from spilled lager and the redhead's green dress stained almost black from, I'm guessing, contact with the dirty floor.

I'm not keen on talking to them and decide it's time to leave. Jozee isn't coming. The whole night has been a bust and I want to go home.

"Easy, tiger," says a deep voice and the bouncer pushes me back down into my seat. "You're not going anywhere, just yet."

I hear Maz introducing Billy Belter in the background. He comes off stage and goes to chat with the couple at the bar. All three of them stare at me. None of them look particularly pleased.

"What the hell was that?" Maz says, coming over. "I've got two irate punters who are demanding I pay for their drinks and a cleaning bill. You can see why."

"I'm sorry," I say, feeling a little dazed. "I just thought—"

"Shut up!" Gone is the affable promotor and in his place, someone much more thug-like and aggressive. "I put you on in good faith. You were smashing it until… what was that anyway?"

I draw breath to reply.

"Forget it," Maz says. "Those two want compensation. Fifty quid. I knocked them down to thirty and you're gonna have to pay up. Understand?"

"But I don't have thirty quid on me," I protest. I gave twenty to Vinnie and the rest was spent on getting here and drinks.

"You've got cards I take it?"

I nod sullenly.

Maz turns his attention to the bouncer. "Jezza, please escort this gentleman to the nearest cash machine and make sure he comes back with the cash."

Jezza nods.

Fifteen minutes later I give Maz the money, which he snatches off me. An annoyed looking Billy Belter stands at the bar. I'm guessing his set didn't go as well as he'd hoped.

"You, and that no show girlfriend of yours are banned from playing here and any other of my gigs," Maz says with venom. "And I'll make sure everyone knows about what went down tonight. Same goes for that unfunny twat as well," he adds, flicking his thumb in the direction of Billy. "What a disaster. Now get out!"

I feel the need to explain, but the expression on Maz's face convinces me otherwise. It's not important, I realise. Jozee was a no show. I can't help but be worried for her now. Properly. Beyond my own stupid irrationality. I walk out, quickly followed by Billy Belter.

"You were smashing it, mate," Billy says in my ear. "Then you blew it big time. Totally ruined the vibe. It ruined my first headline spot. I had no chance after that idiotic stunt. I hope you and Jozee are pleased with yourselves. I would offer you a lift to Brighton, but sod that."

He stomps off into the night and I make my way back to the tube station and Victoria.

14

I ARRIVE at Victoria Station only to find the next train is cancelled. I shouldn't be surprised—the trains between London and Brighton are always so gloriously shit. I don't care. Instead, I go and sit in one of those 'pretend pubs' that squat inside London train stations. They look like traditional pubs, with the same cheesy decor and sticky carpets, but they sure don't have pub prices. They can charge what they like for their badly kept, warm lager and soft crisps when they have a captive audience trapped by the almost continually malfunctioning train system.

But fuck it. I'm out of pocket as it is. I order a bottle of cider—they can't mess that up—and a bag of peanuts, settling myself at a small table. A barmaid arrives to squirt cleaning fluid in my general direction in a half-hearted attempt to clean my table. I gag on the spray. She doesn't notice. Not her fault, I suppose. It's probably an awful job with even worse wages.

From where I'm sitting, I can keep an eye on the information board, waiting for the next train. The cider goes down quickly, and I have another. With fifteen minutes to go, I order yet a further cider, but the fizziness becomes overpowering and I can only drink half of it. The information display finally reveals the platform number for the next Hove train—'Littlehampton and Ore'—and off I go, leaving my half-drunk cider behind. An offering to the station gods for a quick and safe journey. I laugh at the thought and stumble towards my train.

"I am quite pished," I say out loud. I am, I realise, very, very pished. Two nights in a row now. But I needed to celebrate and commiserate. The gig was both a breakthrough and a bust. I thought I'd found Jozee, but I hadn't.

"Jozee! Where the hell are you?" I shout into the station vastness, the roof so high that my words are swallowed. A few heads turn to stare, but I don't care.

I locate my train and find myself a seat at an empty table. After a fifteen-minute delay, the train finally lurches out of Victoria and I'm on my way back to Hove.

I phone Jozee again. And again, it goes to answerphone.

This is Jozee, it says jovially. *Leave me a fucking message or, if you don't fancy that, you can piss off. Beep.*

"Hi, Jozee," I say, realising that my mouth is no longer functioning as expected. "Pleass come home. Pleass! Thish is driving me mad. I love you. I'm sorry I wass such a prick. But thish is too much to bear. Juss come home!"

Afterwards, I finish the text I started yesterday, struggling with thumbs that find every other letter than the one I'm trying to press. Finally, after many *fucks, shits* and *for fuck sakes,* I send the message to everyone in my phone book.

> **Jozee Jackson has been missing for over 24 hours! If you've seen her in the last day or know where she is, please get in touch. I need to know she's okay. Adam H.**

The train makes its slow rattling progress out of London and stops at East Croydon. Or as I call it, *The Well Of Lost Commuter Souls.* I can't count the number of times I've been stranded here after yet another train failure.

A group of noisy teenagers, thugs in dirty, worn sportswear, get aboard and sit at a table a few rows down from me. *Track-suited Trouble.* Poor kids who never had a chance in life. They crack open lagers and chat loudly about porn, weed and joyriding.

Don't they realise what a cliché they are?

I glance up to find one of the thugs looking at me, a sneer on his face, tattoos poking out from under his grubby shirt. I'm boozed up and impervious. I glare back with a 'who do you think you're looking at' face. And he returns to his dull conversation.

Soon, we pull away and I let myself be rocked into sleep by the steady motion of the train. Consciousness is too wearing, I'm tired and properly boozed.

I'm awoken by something—I don't know what—and open my eyes to find one of the track-suited kids standing over me, a ginger-haired thug with love bites, cheap tattoos and too many spots, his hand outstretched towards my phone.

"Hey!" I shout, grabbing my phone and stuffing it into my pocket.

"What's a matter, Grandad?" he says belligerently. "I was only gonna take a look. Nice phone that."

I see the other thugs staring at me from behind him. They're cocky, but unsure. I wonder if they dared the ginger kid to come steal my phone.

"You thief!" I shout, surprised by the venom in my voice. The booze and all the stress I've been through today suddenly comes to a head. I jump to my feet, pleased to find I'm taller than the kid. It baulks him. But there's five of them. If they decide to turn on me, I'd be done for. "I'm gonna find the guard! You can't go around stealing people's stuff and think you can get away with it."

"Get lost, Grandad!" he shouts. "I ain't done nothin' wrong. Your word against ours."

The rest of his gang join in with the name-calling.

I push past the ginger kid and head into the next carriage, just as Hove station is announced. I must have slept nearly all the way home. Lucky that thug woke me up, otherwise I might've ended up in Littlehampton again. I go to the door and wait until the train screeches to a stop. I get out, and further down the platform the kids also alight. They see me, and I see them.

Shit...

Luckily, I'm not alone. A few others are also alighting from the train. I feign indifference and walk to the exit, making sure to stay close to a couple as I go through the barriers. There's no train staff at this time of night. Of course, not... there never is when you need them. I quickly exit the station. The couple get into a taxi and it drives away. I look behind them for another one, but the taxi rank is empty.

The Station pub, which sits outside Hove station, is closed. No lights, no one inside. I check my phone. It's past 12am. I've no choice but to walk down the hill towards George Street on my own. The kids follow. I hear them talking amongst themselves. A low, threatening dirge.

"Oi, Grandad!" One of them finally shouts. "We wanna see your phone."

I quicken my pace, looking around for anybody else to walk with. No one. There's a small set of steps to the right of the Station pub. I decide to take a detour and jump down them. I'm at the bottom and out of sight before the thugs get there. They start shouting and I've no choice but to leg it, moving as fast as I can, darting through another alleyway under some flats onto Clarendon Road. I hear running and angry scowls behind me.

My feet are stamping as quick as my heart is hammering. More shouts and I think they're gaining on me. I dart down Goldstone Street and then along Livingston Road to cross Sackville Road into the maze of streets above Portland Road, taking a left, a right, another left, before coming to a stop, unable to run any more. I crouch down behind a parked car to catch my breath, my chest heaving. I hear someone running, footsteps slapping past, disappearing into the distance.

I look up gingerly to see a jogger. What are they doing out at this time of night? Then again, joggers are a strange breed.

I'm still freaked out and a little nervous and half-run, half-walk the rest of the way home.

I arrive at Eaton Palace Gardens totally out of breath. I can hardly hold my keys as I put them in the lock. The stairs up to my floor nearly kill me. But I'm soon inside my darkened flat with the door closed.

"Jozee," I gasp, my voice nothing but a breathy wheeze. "Jozee!" But, of course, she's not here.

The room starts to spin, and I rush, retching to the bathroom. I throw up the remains of the cider, sickly sweet and sour, hugging the toilet like I'm worried someone will come and take it away, throwing up until I'm just dry-retching. A terrible, whimpering sound matching the hollow emptiness of my soul.

After I'm done, I fall onto my bed fully clothed and begin to sob.

A dreadful, body-wracking lament that only ends when I drift into troubled, nightmarish sleep.

THURSDAY MORNING

I AWAKE with sun streaming through my open curtains, my mouth dry and my tongue sore. There's something terribly wrong… and then I remember.

Jozee!

Her no-show at the gig, the scene I caused onstage and those stupid kid-thugs chasing me home. I was lucky, I realise. Very lucky to not have seven bells kicked out of me.

I check the time on my phone. 10.20am. I'm late for work, but more importantly, I notice over twenty messages.

Jozee? Trying to get back in contact with me!

I quickly open them, filled with a dull urgency, knowing that I'm forgetting something very important, but unsure what that important thing is.

The texts are all replies to the message I sent last night, and in a similar vein. I scroll through them.

> *Sorry, Ad, I haven't seen Jozee since that awful bust up. Hope you didn't do her in!*

> *Fraid not. I'm so sorry to hear she's missing. I'm sure she's okay. You know Jozee! She can be such a drama queen.*

> *I know you worry ever so much, but she'll turn up.*

> *Hugs xxx*

> *Etc.*

No reply from Jim Laker or Shirley Sands. That is suspicious. I decide to bite the bullet and call Laker, mentally preparing myself to talk to the self-important git, but I get a *number not recognised.*

I call Shirley Sands, and it goes to voice-mail again.

Odd and perplexing.

There are also two emails and a ton of WhatsApp messages from the Gannet. All asking the same thing, *where the hell was I?*

"At home, hungover, and in a bit of a state," I say to myself, answering her questions. "Properly in a state."

I type a simple five word reply to the Gannet—*I'm taking some personal days*—and leave it at that.

I feel terrible. My mouth tastes like a herd of sheep have slept in it and then used it for a toilet. I stumble, bleary-eyed into the kitchen, put on the kettle and delve into the fridge. A single can of lager sits on the top shelf, glistening with condensation. I take it out on a whim, thinking, *hair of the dog,* and crack it open, swigging it down.

The lager drops into my stomach like a heavy stone and I barely have time to lurch to the sink before I throw it back up again. Retching abominably and grabbing onto the worktop as a series of little stars flash and twinkle across my vision. And while I'm vomiting, I remember the important thing that has been niggling at me. Jozee's shift at ASDA started at 10am!

I wash the recently reappeared lager down the plughole, wipe my face and dry my hands before looking at my recent call lists. One unknown number sits at the top. Vinnie, from yesterday. I add his name to my contacts and call him.

Another voicemail message!

I text him.

Is Jozee there?

It takes an immeasurable amount of time for him to reply. While I wait, I make myself a cup of tea and a single slice of toast both of which, thankfully stay down. And I start feeling a little better. In truth, I'm more centred than I was yesterday. I'm hungover with a head like a jackhammer, and yet I'm calmer.

Vinnie replies with a two-word text a short time after I've finished eating.

No show

And those two words tell me this is more than a silly argument. Something is seriously wrong. I dig out the number for the local police in Hove and get put through to a desk sergeant.

"I'd like to report a missing person."

My voice sounds detached, but the words blare loudly in my mind.

Jozee is now properly missing…

I tell her Jozee's name, the time she went missing and my contact details.

"As this is a missing person, you will need to come in and make a formal statement and sign a few forms before this can become official," the sergeant says, her voice efficient but bored. "I can schedule you for tomorrow morning at Brighton Police Station. When is the earliest you can come in?"

"Tomorrow morning? That's a whole extra bloody day!" I'm almost shouting, evidenced by quite a long pause on the other side of the call.

"We aim to expedite our cases as quickly as possible, Mr Hanson. However, I cannot progress this inquiry any further unless you are able to contain your anger. Do you understand me?"

I take a deep breath. "Yes, I'm sorry. I'm just upset. I can be there as early as is possible."

"8am tomorrow. Ask for DC Marley."

"Just a detective constable?" I say, aware of anger creeping back into my voice.

"If you are unsatisfied with the level of service you have received today, you can visit our website and leave your feedback. You can also take our online questionnaire which you will also find on our website. Would you like the address?"

"No thanks," I reply. "You've been very helpful, goodbye."

"Goodbye, Mr Hanson. I hope your girlfriend turns up very soon. Please remember that most missing people come back home within a few days."

"Thanks."

I off the phone with an angry stab of my thumb.

"Another day before I can officially report her missing!"

I shout some more, raging at the unfairness of it all, and start to feel a little better. But I can't wait around all day, doing nothing other than shouting into an empty flat. Jozee missed her gig and now work. This is serious. What can have happened to her? I've already checked hospitals and news websites all to no avail. I decide to make another list. Positive and negative reasons for her disappearance. I start with the 'positives'.

> PROS
> 1. She's stopping with Shirley Sands or Jim Laker
> 2. She's with an ex.
> 3. She's taken a break from everything for a few days, a holiday of sorts.

On the face of it, the positives are not that encouraging. But in these scenarios, she is in charge of her destiny and *safe*. However, they are, in my estimation, unlikely, simply because Jozee knows me, knows how much I will fret. How much her disappearing will freak me out.

The worst-case scenario from the above is that she's left me—something I don't believe for a moment—but even if I have misread everything about her and our relationship, she'd at least put me out of my misery. I'm positive about that more than anything else.

The logic scares me. But I won't let myself panic like I did yesterday.

The fact I can't get in contact with Shirley Sands or Laker is also perplexing. I know next to nothing about them, other than they are comedians and where they will be gigging next…

Brainwave. I check out Shirley Sands and Laker on Facebook—they are both playing the Comedy Gods in Hove tonight! The regular weekly night hosted by my favourite, all-time compere, Donnie Coogan. I'll go there myself and grill them.

With a feeling of nervousness, I move onto the negatives.

CONS
1. She's dead!

These words pop straight into my mind, but I ignore them. She's not dead, she can't be.

1. She's been abducted.

This is a possibility. The woman at the Argus mentioned dismembered female bodies washing up on Sussex beaches. The police are suppressing the story, making me wonder… *why?* Then again, the victims were all illegal immigrants, which means Jozee doesn't fit the pattern. There's one other thing… they ended up dead and Jozee is still alive, so it can't be that.

It can't be!

Could someone else have abducted her? The notion belongs to the realm of schlock mystery novels and scraping-the-barrel TV detective shows. You can't flick on the TV these days without accidentally watching a program about serial killers.

If not serial killers, what other reason would Jozee have for being kidnapped?

2. Ransom.

Jozee is skint and I've not yet received a ransom note—not that I have that much money either. It's also in the realm of TV make-believe. I discount it.

3. Revenge.

For what? Jozee was the warmest, kindest person I've ever met. I suppose she might've annoyed somebody in her past. An ex, maybe? If this is the case, I've absolutely nothing to go on.

4. Jozee has suffered a 'mental episode' and has forgotten who she is.

She could be hundreds of miles away, still driving her mini. Or wandering around lost. This is far-fetched, and unlikely. Jozee is down to earth. If anyone was going to have a psychotic episode, that *anyone* is most likely to be neurotic old me.

Nevertheless, I still must consider it as a possibility. Tomorrow, I'm seeing the police. Once the missing person forms are made official, they will be looking out for her across the country. Which is more than I can do.

5. A road accident.

I've checked all the hospitals and the news. Nothing. Unless…

I remember one of my first panicky thoughts that Jozee could've crashed her car and be lying undiscovered in a ditch somewhere. It had seemed a little silly at the time, but it's more likely than the other possibilities I've listed and it's something I can go and check for myself.

I need to retrace her steps back to the Dog and Duck. And there's only one way I can do this. I call Stevo and he answers within a single ring. Good old dependable Stevo.

"Yellow…"

"You at work?"

"Yeah. I've got a pile of shit to go through that you won't bleedin' believe, so you better be quick."

"Did you get my message about Jozee?"

"What bloody message?"

"About Jozee being missing and—"

"She's what? Missin'? Why didn't you tell me?"

"I did, I sent you a text last night."

"Hang on…"

A pause. I hear impressive hi-tech machinery humming in the background, and the click and rattle of multiple keyboards.

"…Shit! You texted me last night!"

"Yeah, I just told you that. What were you doing? You normally live on that phone of yours."

"That's not important is it? D'ya know where she's gone?"

"She wouldn't be missing if I knew that. She disappeared into thin air." I give Stevo a run down of what's been happening over the last thirty-six hours.

"She really is missin'?" he says. "You should've told me straightaway! The first few hours are the most important."

"I texted you, it's not my fault you didn't get the message," I say, wondering why Stevo is so upset, although I've often thought he likes Jozee, possibly as much as I do. He's making me feel nervous. "I need your car, mate. I'm worried she may have had an accident on the way back from Burgess Hill. I want to check all the roads for her mini."

"Sure, yeah, right. Course you do. I'll be at your place in thirty mins. Forty at the most."

16

I'M ITCHING to get started. To do something. To do anything. I watch the minutes tick by, prowling around my flat like a wolf trapped in a cage.

"C'mon Stevo, where are you?"

I'm never very good at waiting. I decide to power up my laptop and check Jozee's social media again. Nothing. Although a few comedy friends have posted on Facebook—pretty much the same messages they sent me via text. But at least the knowledge she is missing is now out there. More people than just myself will be looking for her. And if Jozee sees their messages, she'll be compelled to let them know she's okay… won't she?

A thought pings into my brain. *The Cackle Comedy Forum.* I stay away from Cackle due to the serious amount of trolling that goes on between comics. Usually comics no one has ever heard of. Comics can be *funny people,* and not in the humorous way you'd think.

Not everyone stays away like me, however—a lot of comics use the Cackle Comedy Forum to share info on gigs and promotors, etc. I login with an old account, after requesting a new password because I'd forgotten the old one, and go to the 'News' forum and post a thread.

HAVE YOU SEEN JOZEE JACKSON?

Jozee Jackson, from Brighton, has not been seen since the night of Tuesday the 3rd July. If anybody has any information about where she is, please contact me.

All the very best,

Adam Hanson

I hit 'send' and I'm pleased to see it appear at the top as the latest post. While I'm here, I go over to Jozee's profile to add an extra message on her personal noticeboard. I'm shocked at what I find. There's a single post with multiple replies.

FOR YOUR INFORMATION!

I recently went to see this so-called comedian, Jozee Jackson at a Brighton gig and I was appalled to find out that she'd stolen half of my set, fifteen of my jokes, word for word.

I tried to talk to her afterwards and she brazenly told me she'd written them months ago. And that new comics like myself, sometimes accidentally copied material from comics they'd seen.

I didn't believe her for a second.

I warn all comics and promoters to stay well clear of her or she may steal your material as well.

I'm staying anonymous, because… well you know what this forum is like, but I couldn't keep quiet about this any longer.

She may have been around longer than I have, but that doesn't give her the right to steal my gags.

I'm sick to the guts with this, it's almost made me give up.

Yours, faithfully,

Anon2069.

If I knew one thing… Jozee never stole gags. Never. No self-respecting comedian would do that. Yet the post was, I have to admit, *believable*. If only because it was well-written and sounded reasonable.

Gag stealing is the very worst thing a comic can do. Jozee's set was daft, idiocentric and character-based which meant copying another comedian's gags word for word, didn't ring true for her. Plus, it was also common for comedic minds to come up with the same connection or subconsciously write material they may have heard from another comedian as their own. Most comics sorted it out, coming to an arrangement—usually to do with who used the gag first and who can prove it.

Could this have anything to do with her disappearance? Could another comic have attacked or… killed Jozee because of this? I doubt it. But it still isn't very pleasant. Some of the comments underneath were horrible.

> *NO ONE likes a thief!*

> *Gag steeling bitch!*

> *Don't you dare think about copying any of my gags!*

> *This stinks!*

> *Who is Jozee Jackson anyway? Never heard of her*

> *Etc.*

And one last comment that piques my interest:

> *After what Jozee Jackson did to Tom, she should be ashamed of herself.*

Tom? Who the hell is Tom? And what did Jozee do to him? Steal his gags? Was he even a comedian? I check the name under the comment.

> *FunnyIsFunny77*

Another anonymous account.

I reply to FunnyIsFunny77, asking for more information about Tom, and for them to private message or email me if they want to keep it off the forum.

I wait, refreshing the page. It's unlikely they'll get back to me straightaway on a Thursday morning when most people will be at work. They'll probably wait till the evening or weekend to visit the

Cackle Comedy Forum. It seems like a dreadfully long time. At least I'll be able to ask Laker about Tom when I see him at the Comedy Gods tonight. And Shirley. Maybe they know about him and, more importantly, where Jozee is.

A car horn. I glance at my phone. It's an hour and a half since I phoned Stevo. What took him so long?

Stevo's elegant Rover P5 Mark 3 saloon, a monster of a car and a classic of its time, is parked outside. Maroon and chrome glints in the blazing noon sunshine. This was the vehicle to own in the early sixties, especially if you didn't hold with all that E-Type Jag nonsense and couldn't afford a Rolls Royce. He'd bought the Rover at auction a few years ago and lovingly restored it himself, or so the expression goes. For Stevo, this car is an obsession.

I make sure my flat keys are in my pocket and go outside to meet him. The mid-morning sun is already fierce, and my skin is smarting from the heat as I pull open the heavy car door and slide in onto the luxurious red-leather seating. All the windows are down, but it's an oven in here. I thought the heatwave was yesterday? If anything, today is looking to be even hotter.

Stevo hits me with a full-on frown, his jaw clenched behind an immense beard, his worried brown eyes framed by bushy eyebrows. He's thickset, possessing a massive bull-neck, massive chest and massive arms, hands, legs and feet. Everything is massive where Stevo is concerned. He wears his customary ensemble—purple shirt, purple tie and purple, corduroy trousers. The guy is colour-blind, not enough to stop him getting his driving licence, but just enough for him to not register the colour purple. And because he's never seen this colour, he is convinced it is something special. To everyone else, he looked like a gorilla with a purple fetish.

"You alright, mate?" he says, switching on the powerful engine that purrs loudly. "Jozee disappearin'… that's got to be a shitter. A big un. How you holdin' up?"

His words are a little shaky. I can tell the news of Jozee's disappearance has hit him hard, harder than I would've thought.

"That's why you're here, Stevo. We're going to search for her. Why are you so late?"

He shrugs, his arms vast tree-trunks. "You know how it is? Shit and bollocks croppin' up. Soz about that. But I'm here now though, yeah? So where're we goin' in Burgess Hill?"

"The Dog and Duck. I'll bring up the destination on my phone and—"

"No need," Stevo says, tapping at his head. "It's all in here, innit? I'll get us to Burgess Hill and you can do the rest. I don't do that satnav shitola."

I'm sitting on a folded paper. I pull it free to discover a completed Times Crossword.

"You did this?" I ask, knowing the answer as I recognise Stevo's spidery writing. "That's impressive. Very Inspector Morse. You even have a classic car."

"I just like a puzzle is all. And it passes a few minutes."

"A few minutes?"

"Yeah, if it's tricky. C'mon, let's go."

We pull away, heading towards the other side of Brighton via the A27. I lift my feet up to place them on the dash, but Stevo wags a finger at me. "No way! I've just had the interior steam-cleaned. I don't want any more of your scuff marks all over my pride and joy. And by the look of you, you could do with a clean as well. You're a mess."

"Steam-cleaned?"

"Yeah, it's the only way to keep the leather pristine."

17
THURSDAY AFTERNOON

IT'S SUNNY and the roads are mostly clear of traffic. This would be a pleasant drive if not for the reason we are taking it. Within thirty-five minutes, we park outside the Dog and Duck. A nice enough pub, although modern in design and a little tacky. During the drive up, we gave the hedgerows and fences a quick onceover, hoping to spot any sign of damage indicating that a car might have crashed out of sight, but there was nothing obvious.

"I suppose we trace the route back now," Stevo says.

He'd been uncharacteristically quiet. Normally, he was ebullient—if you called swearing and making off-colour remarks verbose.

"Yes," I reply earnestly. "And slow enough to make sure we don't miss anything."

"That's gonna irritate the other drivers."

"Jozee's missing. That's all that matters."

"You're right, sure you are but…"

"But what?"

"You sure she didn't leave you a message and you missed it?"

"Of course! I'm positive. And Jozee wouldn't disappear without saying something. You know her. It's not who she is."

"No, it's not. I believe you."

"What do you mean by that?"

"Nothin'. She's considerate, that girl. Very considerate, but…"

"But what?" I almost shout, feeling annoyed at where Stevo is going with this.

"Well, let's face it. You can be a bit of an idiot sometimes."

I often marvel at Stevo's direct way of speaking. It is one of the reasons why I think he's on the autistic spectrum. He is obsessive about some things, like his purple attire, this fabulous car, and his fishing trips, but his house is a mess, he swears like a trooper and is apt to say what was on his mind without any attempt at censorship or self-control.

"I suppose you're right, Stevo. But we're happy together."

"Sure you are," he replies, like he's not convinced. "Jozee's one in a million. She'd have to be, puttin' up with all your self-centred nonsense."

"Let's get on," I say, feeling annoyed.

I'm sure Stevo has a thing for Jozee. I've seen him talk to a lot of people, but only in the presence of Jozee did he moderate himself. And after a drink or two, he always tells me what a lucky guy I am. But in that resentful way that guys sometimes get when they wish it was them who was with your girlfriend. Nevertheless, Stevo is the epitome of 'the gentle giant'. All that muscle and power and yet somehow childlike and simple-minded. Not that he is anything other than fiercely intelligent, as proven by his prowess with the Times Crossword, and his work as a numbers man for some national financial firm that he is vague about. I've never properly understood what he does for a living, but he has enough cash to own a house, to go on many fishing holidays around the world and to buy an extensive wardrobe of purple-themed clothing. And he isn't unattractive—he has a look that a lot of women go for, and some men—which made me wonder why he was perpetually single. He quite obviously prefers the female sex, as his interest in Jozee proves, and yet he does nothing about his romantic life. He is an enigma, but most of all, a firm and dedicated friend, and I love him for it.

"You're a cunt," Stevo says, gunning the engine. "But you're not all bad."

18

THE NEXT two hours go slowly. We crawl at twenty miles an hour down A-roads where the speed limit is fifty, creating ire and rage behind us, but it has to be done. We pull over whenever possible to let people pass, but that doesn't stop them beeping their horns and shouting abuse at us. We check alternative routes and side roads, driving through small villages and past impressive houses and mansions.

I'm looking for tyre tracks, broken fences and smashed bushes or trees. We stop numerous times to explore further, but to no avail. I notice CCTV cameras at one of the mansions we drive past. It makes me wonder about Tuesday night. My next-door neighbour, Clive, said he hadn't seen Jozee come home, but perhaps there would be CCTV cameras outside our flat or on neighbouring properties that might've captured her arrival—although I doubt she came home that night. I'm clutching at straws, I realise that, but what else can I do?

As far as we can tell, there is no evidence of a recent accident and no sign of Jozee's mini.

"A dead end," Stevo says as we give up the search close to Brighton. "Did she say anythin' before she left?"

"Something has been bothering her from before we started going out together. Not sure what. I just assumed she'd tell me when she was ready. She's also been a bit distant for a couple of weeks. Distracted."

"What happened, you two have a falling out?"

I shake my head. "It was nothing to do with me, at least that's what I think. Whatever it was, I'm convinced she was going to tell me the night she disappeared."

"She's the secretive type, that much is for sure."

I give Stevo a sideways glance. "What do you mean by that?"

He shrugs. "I always thought there was a lot more goin' on under the surface with her, that's all."

I can't argue with him. Jozee was certainly unforthcoming about her past. "I wondered if she'd gone up to North London instead of coming home, but she wasn't at the gig last night. I'm worried sick."

"London?" Stevo says, repeating the name as if it held some special kind of significance.

"Yeah, but like I said, she did a no show. And we can't check all the different routes she could've taken to drive there, especially if she was avoiding the M25. It'd take us days. I'm visiting the police tomorrow, they'll then be on the lookout for her and her mini."

"You should've gone to the rozzers straightaway."

"I know that now," I reply, "but I thought… I thought she'd come home. I still do. I suppose it's possible she's stopping with a friend somewhere. Her only friends are Shirley Sands and Jim Laker."

"I never liked him, although that Shirley Sands is a bit of alright."

"I'm seeing them both tonight," I say. "They're playing at the Comedy Gods. If Laker knows anything, I'll get it out of him."

"I can come along with you if you want," Stevo says, his massive hands squeezing tightly upon the driving wheel.

The thought of having Stevo's muscle as back-up is appealing but I don't want him blowing his mouth off. He seems agitated—not the relaxed, happy-go-lucky guy I'm used to. Jozee's disappearance has unnerved him.

"Nah. But thanks for the offer." I remember the Cackle Comedy Forum and the name that cropped up. "Did Jozee ever talk to you about a guy called, Tom?"

"Tom?" Stevo mumbles. "Never heard of him."

19

THURSDAY EVENING

AFTER AN uncomfortable drive back into Hove, Stevo drops me off at my flat, and drives away, his engine roaring.

I check outside for CCTV cameras but can't see any. The block next door is called Blenheim Towers, a more modern and aesthetically pleasing building with an underground garage. It has two cameras—one for the garage shutter and one for the main entrance. Neither are pointing at the road. The other houses and buildings in the area don't appear to cover the road either.

Another dead end.

Frustrated and annoyed, I go back to my flat and knock on my neighbour's door. Clive answers in moments, as if he is expecting me.

"Hello, Adam. I hope you've come to apologise for your harsh words, yesterday."

My harsh words! The man has quite some nerve saying that after the names he'd called Jozee. I ignore his question. "I just want to let you know that Jozee still hasn't come home," I say, "and that the police will be soon formally treating her as a missing person."

"Oh," Clive replies taking a step back. "Of course, I never liked the girl, but that sounds serious. You're *that* convinced she hasn't run off with another dog?"

I feel my hackles begin to rise. "Just let me know if you see Jozee, so that I can tell the police she is okay. Yeah?"

"Why me?" he asks, his milky green eyes glittering from behind his gold-rimmed glasses.

"Because, if Jozee is to be believed, you are obsessed with her comings and goings. I can't be in all the time, especially when I'm trying to find her. But if she turns up, I need to know about it. You have my number?"

Clive says nothing for a few moments. "You are a very rude young man," he says. "Very rude."

"Just let me know if you see—"

Clive retreats into his flat and slams the door.

"—if you see Jozee!" I shout.

I stand outside my door, not wanting to go inside. My flat is no longer the welcoming home it was when Jozee was with me. I begrudgingly enter and do my customary search again. Jozee's still not here. Not that I expected her to be hiding under my bed or in the wardrobe.

I pop a frozen meal into the microwave—if I don't eat, I won't be of use to anyone. While the microwave hums and whirs, I check the Cackle Comedy Forum on my laptop.

My post has been read over twenty times, but no one has replied.

And no reply from the mysterious FunnyIsFunny77, although there is a new message on Jozee's comedy profile page.

I hope Jozee Jackson dies!

I know they are alluding to dying on stage, not in real life, typical troll stuff, but it sends a chill through me.

Can Jozee really be dead?

It's a thought I've not wanted to entertain, but it remains a possibility. A dreadful, scary possibility.

Sudden images of Jozee's funeral pop into my head. A coffin sitting under one of her promo shots. The comedians sad-faced. Some god-bothering priest banging on about Jesus Christ and how we can all meet again in heaven—milking the grief in some vile advert for his particular brand of self-delusion. I see myself walking up to give the eulogy. Feeling the horror of it... The vision is so real that I can almost smell the flowers.

I shake my head, forcing different images into my mind. Of me and Jozee sitting in a pub, chatting, laughing about the last few days.

Alive and well and back with me. We raise our drinks to make a toast, and—

The flat buzzer bursts into my thoughts, trilling loudly.

20

"PIZZA DELIVERY."

"Huh?" I say into the phone I use to communicate with the downstairs outside door.

"You ordered pizzas."

"I did no such thing."

A rustle of paper. "Flat 5, Eaton Palace Gardens, Hove?"

"That's my flat, but I didn't order pizzas. Sorry, you've made a mistake."

"They were ordered by a Miss Jackson. Is she not in?"

I'm so shocked that I drop the phone.

Jozee ordered pizza?

I grab the phone again. "One second, I'm coming down."

I race outside, leaving my flat door open, aware of Clive's door opening as I go. I jump down the stairs and find the pizza guy waiting outside.

"You say these were ordered by Jozee Jackson?"

"That's what it says on the ticket," the man answers. "Three ham and pineapple pizzas. Thin crust. That'll be twenty-eight, fifty-nine."

Ham and pineapple? Our favourite topping!

What does this mean? Is Jozee on her way home? Is she coming here to join me for a pizza dinner in apology? I'm confused, but also elated. I scrabble around in my pockets for my debit card and pay contactlessly. The man gives me the pizza and I go back upstairs. I check all the boxes. Like the man said—three ham and pineapple pizzas. The one thing me and Jozee share is a liking for the most unpopular pizza topping.

I flip out my phone and ring Jozee, hoping she will answer this time. But it still goes straight to answerphone.

Dammit!

The doorbell buzzes again. I pick up the phone. "Jozee!"

"Pizza delivery."

"What? You've just been."

"Sorry mate. Don't know what you mean, I've three pizzas for you."

Confused and a little irritated, I go back down to the main entrance. A different man stands outside holding a pizza bag. Behind him another pizza delivery scooter turns up. And also a car.

"What the hell is going on?"

"Pizza," the man answers, as if I'm some kind of simpleton.

The other two pizza delivery people come up to the door and look at each other. All carrying three pizzas each. Meanwhile, a further scooter stops.

"I'm sorry," I say, feeling sick to my guts. "But I didn't order any of these. It's a prank. It has to be."

I close the door and walk back upstairs. The smell of pizza suffuses my flat, making me retch. The last thing I want to do now is eat. I grab the pizzas and throw them outside on the balcony. I sit at the kitchen table, my head in my hands. Someone is deliberately pranking me. A low trick. Someone who knows our favourite pizza topping. Could it be Jozee? Could she be behind this? It doesn't bear thinking about. The door buzzer rings again, trilling multiple times, but I ignore it. Then somebody is knocking on my door. "Open up, young man. Open up now!"

I sigh, it's Clive.

"What is going on outside?" he says when I finally answer. "Why are all those delivery people buzzing my flat?"

"I don't know," I reply. "I'm sorry."

"You need to go downstairs and sort this out."

"Right, I'll do that now." I slam the door in his face.

I disconnect the buzzer and go and sit in the bathroom with the door locked. Clive knocks a few more times and then thankfully gives up.

I can't take much more of this. I just can't.

Ten minutes later, I hear Clive knocking again, but I stay where I am. Slowly, the clock moves towards 7.30pm. I emerge from the bathroom and gingerly check my window. No more delivery people outside. Time to go to the Comedy Gods and talk to Jim Laker and Shirley Sands.

21

I WALK into Hove, trying to clear my head. I've been mostly on top of things today, on top of my panic. But the incident with the pizzas has sent me spiralling. I'm walking hunched again, occasionally bumping into people who curse and shout at me. The air is warm and balmy. The heatwave giving everyone a gleam of sweat. The temperature has dropped only fractionally, the late evening sun still hot and bright. At any other time, I'd find this pleasant. *At any other time…*

I finally arrive at the pub of my destination. The Cathedral Tavern perches on the Brighton and Hove border on Western Road. Tables full of early evening drinkers spill out onto the street. The pub doors and windows are open, a cacophony of shrieks, chatter and laughing coming from within. I can't face going inside, not yet. Not in my present state.

I hate being like this, anxious, stressed and freaked out. I'm only popping into a pub to ask people some questions, and yet it feels like I'm on the way to my execution. It's ridiculous, self-centred, and totally self-involved. But that doesn't make it any less debilitating or real. I just want it to stop! I've been relying on Jozee for too long I realise. Without her, I'm such a useless mess. I feel tears welling behind my eyes.

"No, dammit!"

A few people sitting outside the pub look up and stare.

"This isn't about me. It's for Jozee," I say to them, as they hastily turn back to their drinks.

I cross the road and find a bench on Norfolk Square. A concrete and grassy area shared by an uneasy alliance of the homeless, picnickers and its main residents, Brighton seagulls. I ignore a group of drunks sprawled on the sun-yellowed grass and try to calm myself, taking deep breaths. Counting to six and breathing out. Repeating the same process until my heart stops its frantic beating and the tight knot in my stomach recedes.

A seagull waddles towards me, its beady, yellow-ringed eyes regarding me with disdain, rebuking me for having the audacity to come here without bringing food. It throws back its head and gull-shrieks in a deafening cacophony that is repeated by the other seagulls. A seemingly vocalised frustration at the unfairness of it all.

"Me and you both," I say.

I return to the Cathedral Tavern and walk inside, pushing through the tightly-packed revellers, who, even at this early hour, seem pissed-up to the gills.

The Comedy Gods is run in a function room at the back of this noisy bar, its name coming from the name of the pub. I always marvel at the inventive names of the various comedy clubs I've gigged at, such as *The Comedy Cooler, The Filthy Gigdog Club* and the rather profane *C U Next Tuesday.*

Tonight, I'm not interested in comedy. To be honest, after what I read on the Cackle Comedy Forum today, I'm sick of it.

I push through and enter a large backroom with a balcony stage, known as 'the pulpit', half-way up the far wall accessed by a spiral staircase. A microphone stands on this elevated stage, lit by a single light. Tables and chairs, mostly full of punters, fan out to fill the room below. A small bar sells drinks, including the potent *Comedy Gods Cocktail,* which I've vowed never to drink again. Most of the audience are new comedians, I notice, even newer than myself.

The Brighton comedy scene is a monster that feeds and entertains itself. And I'm a living, breathing part of it.

Tonight's comedians are congregated in a cordoned off 'green room' area. Inside I spot the impressive frame of Jim Laker, and my heart lurches. There's no sign of Shirley Sands.

Before I can enter, I must pass security. In this case, a small box-office table at which sits a stalwart of the comedy scene, Pari Chabra, a posh English, somewhat overweight lady in her late sixties with a penchant for weed and very blue jokes. She has impressive grey dreadlocks tied with beads and other hippie paraphernalia, all stuffed underneath a voluminous, brightly-coloured sari. Her real name is not Pari Chabra. She changed it years ago after living in India for ten years.

Comedy is Pari's social life, a way to get out and about, although her mobility is reduced by a series of unspecified ailments and the reason why she smokes so much cannabis—as she often takes great pains to explain. Not that anyone minds her little indulgences. She is a warm and generous older lady who regularly does door duty, mainly to get out of an evening and chat to the punters. Onstage, she is very funny and quite rude. It's a shame that she can never be on at the Comedy Gods again. The spiral staircase to the stage is now beyond her capabilities.

"Oh Adam," Pari says, pulling a sad smile.

Her voice is false-posh and overblown, like a grand old duchess in a BBC costume drama.

"I read your message about Jozee. Has she still not turned up?" she continues, her face a mask of concern behind thick, theatrical-like makeup.

"No, not yet."

"I did my bit, you know, emailing and Facebooking everyone. And I also mentioned it on the Twitter. I don't have that many followers, but I did get a retweet."

Pari is very proud of her social media skills, which I'm sure makes her quite the star amongst her age group.

"Thanks," I say.

"Poor Donnie is going spare. Jozee was supposed to be headlining tonight. I don't think he's heard anything from her either. We're all very worried."

"Jozee was on tonight?"

"Yes, didn't she tell you?"

"Jozee doesn't tell me about every gig she plays," I say, feeling left-footed. "It wasn't on her website."

"Oh yes, Donnie organised it a while ago. You know how he likes to be ahead of things."

"Ticket for one," I say.

"Don't be silly. Donnie won't mind me giving you a freebie under the circumstances."

22

BREATHING DEEPLY, I walk through the thronging crowd, the chairs and tables, and step into the Green Room, a cordoned off area with a few sofas and chairs. My heart is thudding again, my temples tight and a little painful. I walk up to Jim Laker, who is sitting with his gag-book open on his lap. Nat Naylor sits opposite him, looking nervous and a little tired, her normally glossy black bob greasy and unkempt.

Laker ignores me, like I'm not even there.

"Oi, Laker!" I shout over the chatter and background music.

I try to snatch his gag-book off him, but he grips it tightly.

"What has gotten into you?" he spits.

"Jozee's missing. Your phone says *number not recognised*. Have you heard from her?"

"You should know better than coming to talk to me before a gig. This is the comedian's area. If you're not on tonight, you shouldn't be here. If you don't piss off, I'll go get Donnie to throw you out."

The threat is an empty one, Donnie and Laker don't get on, that is well-known.

"Don't make me laugh," I say. "Not that *you* ever do."

Laker lurches to his feet so that we're face-to-face. He's as tall as me, but with a naturally bigger frame. Thickset and bullish. "Laugh?" he says in rich tones honed from years of stand up. "You're the one who dies night after night. At least I'm value for money, you jumped up newbie turd. I'm not surprised Jozee walked out on you. She probably got sick to death with your neurotic puppy-dog act."

Laker hasn't talked to me like this before, it's a vindication of everything I've ever thought about him.

Nat jumps up and grabs Laker's arm, doll-like and ineffectual. "Hey guys, calm down," she says in her baby-girl voice.

I ignore her, realising that I'm quite happy to tussle with Laker right here, right now. I don't care if he's bigger or stronger than I am, someone needs to stand up to him for once.

"Jozee hasn't been seen for nearly forty-eight hours and she never misses a gig!" I shout, my heart jackhammering. "If you've heard from her, you better tell me, understand?"

I grit my teeth and push my face into his, almost willing him to have a go, but instead, he backs down. "I haven't heard shit from her."

"How do I know you're not lying?"

"Why would I lie? You think she's hiding back at my place? My fiancée wouldn't be too pleased. She's never been into threesomes, more's the pity. I'm sorry Jozee has left you, but it was only a matter of time."

"Hey, lay off him," Nat says. "Can't you see Adam is upset? What if it was Ruth, your fiancée, who was missing? You'd be distraught."

Laker flicks his eyebrows up and down. "Would I?"

Nat turns to me. "We were chatting about Jozee earlier. Jim is very concerned, despite his silly attitude. Everyone is."

"You listening, newbie?" Laker says, letting his eyes drop down to stare at Nat's pert backside. "Laker doesn't lie! He's as straight as a die."

"Have you contacted the police?" Nat asks me.

I look at Laker and reply. "Yes, I have."

Nat seems genuinely surprised. "You're *that* worried? What did they say?"

"To come in and make her disappearance official. So they can begin an investigation."

"I really hope nothing bad has happened to her."

"Adam is worrying about nothing," Laker says with a knowing nod of his head. "Jozee will turn up, she's a bad penny that one."

"There's one more thing," I ask, remembering the Cackle Comedy Forum post. "Does anyone know someone called Tom?"

Nat and Laker glance at one another.

"That's enough!" Laker says. "You're putting me off. I'm opening soon, and I need to get my head together."

23

AFTER THE confrontation with Laker, my legs go wobbly and I feel weak. I need a drink and head to the bar. I know I shouldn't, especially after last night, and the night before, but I have to control my nerves. And alcohol is the most effective sedative out there.

The barman offers me the Comedy Gods Cocktail deal, which I seriously consider for a few moments before ordering a pint of lager instead.

Someone pokes me in the ribs while I'm waiting. I turn to look into the grizzled, red face of Donnie Coogan. The guy is in his mid-fifties, slightly rotund and wearing his famous pink shirt and silver suit combo. His full head of hair is curly and greying. But he's young for his age, although I've often wondered if he'd had some work done.

"How you holding up?" he asks in his comical-sounding, Irish accent, a look of concern creasing his ruddy features. He's from Northern Ireland and, even though that accent can sometimes sound harsh, his has a lyrical tone to it, softening out the sharp consonants and extending the cramped vowels. "I take it there's still no sign?"

"No, nothing at all. I'm going spare. I suppose she didn't contact you about tonight either?"

"Yes and no," he answers enigmatically.

"What does that mean?"

"I received a text, supposedly from her, but on a different number."

"You did?" I reply, wondering if this was it, if this was the proof Jozee was alive and well. "What did she say?"

"I don't think it's from her." He takes out his phone, the size of a mini-iPad and shows it to me.

This iz Jozee. Your a old fat gay cunt. Juss saying.

Jozee was an intelligent, well-read woman. And yet she revelled in misspelled texts and posts. 'Dumbspeak' she called it.

"It's certainly in her style," I say, my heart sinking, "but she'd never be so rude. Especially to a cool guy like you, Donnie."

"But I am an old fat gay cunt," he replies, sticking out his gut, pursing his lips and pulling a camp face. "Something I pride myself on, young man. And a right funny fecker!"

I chuckle. It's good to laugh, even though my insides are so whipped up and crazy right now.

"It must be a joke," Donnie continues, relaxing his pose. "You know how comedians like to play? It could be any one of them."

"Maybe it's malicious?" I say. "Jozee has been getting a lot of flak about joke-stealing on the Cackle Comedy Forum."

"Jozee? Stealing gags? No fecking way."

"That's what I thought. But it's odd. Give me the number. I'll see if I can find out where it came from."

Donnie reads it out and I copy it into my phone.

"I'm very worried about Jozee," Donnie continues. "It's not like her to miss a gig, nor to not let me know."

He puts his hand on my shoulder and tenderly rubs it. "People disappearing can put a lot of strain and stress on those left behind."

I don't know much about Donnie, but he's of an age to have lived through *the Troubles,* as the horrific situation in Northern Ireland was known back in the 70s and 80s. Disappearances were rife, as were shootings and bombings. I wonder if he's had personal experience of this.

"Yeah, you're right," I say. "I've been going mental."

"You think she may have run off because of what happened the other night? Your argument in Burgess Hill?"

I'm reminded again of that awful scene in the Dog and Duck. *Does everyone know about it?*

"Possibly," I say, feeling myself flush. "But it's unlikely. All this is just not Jozee's style."

"I'm more of a man's man," Donnie says, his hand falling from my shoulder. "So I can't say that I know women that well, but I've noticed they can sometimes be flighty creatures. She's probably kicking her heels somewhere, enjoying making us suffer."

I forgive Donnie his old-fashioned views. On top of everything else, being gay in 70s Ireland must've been quite a trial for him. He is a survivor though, that much is for sure.

"However," he continues, a jokey grimace creasing his face, "the little minx was supposed to headline tonight, and you know how uptight I can get about comedians not turning up?"

I nod. Acts dropping out at the last moment was a real problem. Even I'd done it before due to a sudden attack of my killer nerves or being stuck at work in one of the Gannet's pointless meetings.

"Shirley Sands is also a no show."

"She's not here either?"

"Apparently," Donnie continues, lowering his voice, "and I'm not sure how much of a secret this is, but Shirley Sands has hung up the microphone. I was shocked. I love her man-hating act."

"She's retired?"

He shrugs. "Keep it under your hat for now. Comedians are always giving up and coming back. She did sound pretty adamant though, and a little upset."

"Why would she do that?" I ask, wondering if her retirement had anything to do with Jozee's disappearance.

"To say I was miffed is an understatement. Being a promoter is no fun, I can tell you. I don't know why I put myself through it. I really don't. Still, everything has worked out brilliantly. I contacted Scott Wong on the off-chance he might fancy a Comedy Gods' headline and Bob's your horny aunt's live in lover, the fecker only said yes. That was quite a coup. Between you and me, Wong has just signed with Blowback, he'll be on the telly soon earning the big bucks. The lucky bastard."

I whistle. Blowback is the biggest comedian agency in the country. Signing with them is every comic's dream.

"I was stuck for another replacement and had to ask Nat Naylor." He lowers his voice. "But needs must when the Devil pisses in your soup. The girl just isn't funny anymore. No new material in over a year. Of course, you won't say anything, this is all between you and me, yeah?"

I nod. "Sure, of course."

Donnie is right. When I first saw Nat, she was mesmerising, but recently… not so much. Comedians have these low patches, or so I'm told—so far, my comedy hasn't escaped the doldrums—but Nat Naylor is a star that has fallen and failed to shine again.

"Do you know where Shirley lives? All I've got is a number."

The rotund Irishman shrugs. "No. She's a secretive sort. You must've noticed that? Keeps herself very much to herself."

"Yeah, I have, but I really need to talk to her."

"I'll ask around for you, and also enquire about Jozee, although I'm abroad for the next few days and incommunicado." Donnie checks his watch, a heavy, gold affair and expensive. "I'm on soon, I suppose I'd better go and think up some gags. Hang on in there, laddo."

He squeezes my shoulder again, winks, and disappears into the crowd.

I watch him nodding and pointing to punters and comedians, wishing that I shared his easy sociability. Talking to Donnie has been the best thing that's happened since this nightmare started.

My lager waits on the bar for me. I'm feeling a helluva lot more relaxed, but I knock it back anyway. Why not? I've got nowhere with Laker and Shirley Sands is a no show.

"Oi, wanker!"

I turn around to see Billy Belter standing next to a tall, elegant, well-dressed 50-something woman with fantastic cheekbones and a killer smile.

"How you doing, kid?" Billy says in a friendly way, as if what he said to me last night in the Lord Horatio had been forgotten.

"Jozee is still missing," I reply feebly, feeling like a stuck record, suddenly aware of lager on my chin, and wiping it away.

"This is Cheryl, my other half," Billy says proudly. "My girlfriend this time, not the mistress, wahey!"

Cheryl laughs as if this is a terrific joke.

"And this is Adam Hanson, a new comic I've been helping along the way," Billy continues. "Mainly to stay off the booze by the look of him, not that it's working."

"Hi," Cheryl says, chuckling, her accent pleasant but posh, her head framed by styled blond hair, like she'd just stepped out of a salon. "I'm usually too busy to come and indulge Billy's hobby, but tonight I thought I'd push the boat out. All work and no play is no good for anyone is it?"

"Nice to meet you," I reply, realising I'm not that interested in Billy or his stuck-up girlfriend, annoyed that I'm forced to now do the *dreaded small talk,* especially after the way Billy talked to me last night.

"It's so good of Billy to help out other, newer comics, don't you think? He's very generous like that. It can be such a cutthroat profession, or so he tells me."

I stifle a laugh. "Yes, he's a real boon is Billy. One of the best."

"And, I don't know if you heard, but Billy did his first headline last night. A great success, wasn't it? He brought the place down. Pretty soon, he'll be the breadwinner and I can stay at home." She laughs as if this is quite hilarious and I'm unable to tell if she's being sarcastic. "I'm so pleased for him."

Billy gives me a 'don't say anything' look and I comply.

"He's a very funny, wonderful man," I say. "No one laughs at his jokes, of course, not at first, but once he's explained them to the audience two or three times, with diagrams and a few notes, they just can't stop tittering."

"I can see that you've also got a funny bone!" Cheryl says, giggling. "Are you on tonight?" She pulls out a fifty-pound note from her purse and gives it to Billy.

I shake my head. "Just here as a punter," I reply, wondering what I'm still doing in this place, but I suppose I've got to stay in case Jozee turns up, although I very much doubt it.

"Why don't you go and find us some seats, luv," Billy says to Cheryl, "and I'll get drinks. G and T?"

She nods. "Double. Nice to meet you, Adam."

"Nice to meet you too."

"Thanks," Billy says once Cheryl is out of earshot. "And sorry for last night. I was in a foul mood. Water under the bridge. Okay?"

"The less I think about that, the better," I say, remembering falling off the stage and screaming for Jozee like a madman before shouting at some poor unsuspecting girl and her mates on a night out. "Cheryl seems nice. And rather posh."

"Not what you were expecting, huh?" Billy says, proudly. "Took a lot of effort to bag that one. Well, a couple of G and Ts and a quick squeeze of my money-maker. Wahey! But joking aside, I'm as happy as a pig in shit." He waves the fifty-pound note in my face. "And Cheryl sure has a lot of shit! Want another pint to make up for last night and for saving my blushes in front of the girlfriend?"

I've got half a pint left but I nod anyway. "Go on then."

24

I GO find a seat near the back of the room, my limbs suddenly feeling like lead, the booze having a different effect on me than I was expecting. And thinking about it, I've not had the healthiest few days. I've hardly eaten or slept, I've drunk too much and last night I was forced to run all the way home. I'm knackered and not in the mood for comedy, yet I can't face going back to an empty flat. I decide to have one or three more pints and pass out again. I'll get no sleep otherwise, I'm sure of it. And maybe… just maybe… when I wake up, Jozee will be there, in bed with me, snuggling up to me like always.

After a short wait, the stage lights dim and music blares from the impressive sound system. Donnie ascends the spiral staircase and pauses at the top to theatrically catch his breath. Finally, he gets to the microphone and draws his finger across his throat, but the music keeps playing and getting louder. It shouldn't be funny, but it is. The music stops. He goes to speak, and the music starts again. The crowd roar with laughter, and despite everything that's been going on over the last two days, I join in with them.

Donnie does an opening routine about growing up gay in Ireland, I've heard it before, but it's still hilarious. Like going to a gig to see a band and they play a list of your favourite songs. Even though I know the gags backwards, I love to hear them over and over.

And then Jim Laker is introduced. I can't stand the man, but I have to begrudgingly admit, he's funny. His gags are weak, but it's how he sells them to the audience that works for him. I force myself to remain stone-faced, closing my eyes so I don't have to look at the git.

I'm awoken by a massive laugh, and realise I've slept through almost the entire first half of the show.

The last act leaves the stage and Donnie comes on to close the first half. I take this opportunity before the interval to go to the bar. I decide to have a final pint and go home. I'm still tired and another drink should keep me comatose enough to enable me to pass out.

Out of nowhere, a smartly-dressed man appears next to me. "Hello," he says loudly. "I'm David Gentry, pleased to meet you."

I take his hand before I've realised what I'm doing. His palm is clammy, and he holds on longer than is comfortable, his grip limp and off-putting. The guy wears a tight-fitting brown suit, white shirt and red tie. His face is lugubrious, emerging from a tight collar like a bulldog. I immediately dislike him, especially his chummy smile. The man is disagreeable, but in a friendly way.

"Are you on tonight?" I ask, thinking that by the look of him, he must be a comedian.

"Me? Good God no!" he says. "I'm what you call a fanatic."

"Huh?" I reply a little belligerently, wishing the guy would let go of my hand.

"A fan. Of comedy. I think what you guys do is amazing. Quite amazing. I'm in absolute awe of you all."

"What're you doing here?" I ask, realising it's a dumb question, but I'm still half-asleep.

"I came to see Jozee Jackson."

"You did what?"

"You're her boyfriend, aren't you?"

"Yes, yes I am," I say, forcibly pulling my hand out of his. "What of it?"

"Like I said, I'm just a fan. Perhaps you can tell me where she is. She was supposed to be headlining. I really love her. As a comic, I mean, nothing else—although you're a lucky fella!"

"Oh, I see. She's um… she's not coming tonight. Didn't you hear the compere announce her replacement, Scott Wong?"

"No, I only just got here. I was really hoping to see Jozee. That's a real shame. Under the weather, is she? I came down from London to see her."

"London?"

"Well not *just* to see her, that would be weird. I'm here for a few days on business and thought, why not catch some local comedy? I've seen Jozee many times in the Smoke. But I never get bored with her. Such a shame she's not on tonight. It's nothing to do with the argument she had the other night, is it?"

"What damn argument?" I almost shout, rounding on him, wondering how he knows about my altercation with Jozee at the Dog and Duck and why the hell he thought it appropriate to talk to me about it.

"They were going at it hammer and tongs."

"*They?*"

"Yeah, Jozee and another girl who was screaming at her. She practically chased your girlfriend down the street."

"When was this?"

A thoughtful expression crosses his fat face. "I arrived Monday… it was that night. Yeah, definitely Monday."

The night before Jozee disappeared!

"What did she look like?"

"The girl? Mad-looking, but kind of hot. And scary. Hang on," he says, pointing at the wall behind me. "That's her, that's her right there."

I turn to see tonight's Comedy God's poster and a picture of Shirley Sands.

25

ACCORDING TO David Gentry, Shirley Sands' altercation with Jozee happened nearby.

"I can take you there, if that will help?" Gentry says eagerly. "It's just a street away. I remember it very well because it's close to where my hotel is located. The mad girl came out of this quite expensive looking building with a large blue door. You can't miss it."

"Yeah, sure," I reply, necking the rest of my pint and waking up.

We leave the Comedy Gods and walk the short way to where Gentry says he saw the argument. The balmy, night air hits me hard and I feel a little woozy from the quickly consumed lager and my quickly beating heart. The guy doesn't share my eagerness to get on. He ambles along without a care in the world, chatting about comedy and comedians. I suppose at any other time, I'd enjoy the adoration, but tonight it's just irritating, and I find myself getting frustrated with him.

Finally, we reach a large, mansion-like house converted into flats, like so many old buildings in Hove.

"This is it," Gentry says excitedly, pointing to an impressive, blue door. "I didn't know at the time that the other woman was also a comedian," he continues, babbling on.

"I don't suppose you know the flat number?"

Gentry shakes his head. "No, but after Jozee Jackson drove away, the Shirley Sands girl went back into this building."

"Thanks," I say, with a heavy hint, wanting him to leave. "You've been very helpful."

"Oh, right… you sure you don't need a wingman?"

"Positive. If you hurry, you can get back to see the second half of the show. Scott Wong is headlining. You don't want to miss him."

"Yeah, sure," he says, but I can tell he'd rather stay.

I wait till he walks out of sight and go up to the door, aware I'm a little worse the wear for booze, although my nerves are thankful for it.

Three buzzers with flat numbers and no names. Not like the old days, when ID fraud wasn't such a problem. I raise my hand and pause, my finger hovering. What were Jozee and Shirley Sands arguing about? And why has Shirley retired from comedy? Are those two things connected? Is Shirley the reason why Jozee ran away? Or could she be involved in her disappearance? There's only one way to find out…

I take a deep breath, burp, and hit the buzzer for the top flat. A few seconds wait, and my choice is rewarded by the inquisitive, if not defensive voice of Shirley Sands.

"Who… who is it?"

"It's Adam, let me in."

A long pause.

"No, I don't want to talk to you. Please go."

"You've got to see me. It's about Jozee. Is she up there with you? Is that why you won't speak to me?"

"Just go, Adam!"

I ring her buzzer again, but it's ignored. I then ring one of the other flats.

"Yeah?" The voice sounds young and more than a bit stoned.

"I forgot my keys," I say drunkenly. "Let me in."

"Sure man."

The door buzzes and I push into the communal entrance hall.

I race up the stairs to Shirley's flat and bang on the door. "I'm not going anywhere until you speak to me!" I shout, aware that I'm sounding more than a little boozy. But I don't care. "Jozee, are you in there? Jozee!"

"Jozee isn't here! Go away!"

"I'm staying right here until you talk to me." I bang on the door again.

"Okay, okay! Give me a few moments. Just stop your damn knocking."

Five minutes later, Shirley opens the door, wearing almost exactly the same gear she wears on stage. Miniskirt, fishnets and long brown, high-heeled boots. I push past her and run into the flat.

"Jozee!"

I drunkenly search Shirley's apartment. Bedroom, study and toilet. It's bigger than I was expecting. Well-to-do. Not that all comics were struggling or came from poor backgrounds—the profession attracted screw-ups from all walks of life.

Jozee isn't here and there's no sign that she ever was.

"What do you think you're doing?" Shirley says angrily when I return to the living room. "Look at the state of you. You're drunk!"

"Just tell me what happened!"

Her features crease in confusion. "You're making no sense, Adam."

"You were seen arguing with Jozee the night before she disappeared."

Shirley seems taken aback by this, although she crosses her arms and says, "Like you did on the night she actually disappeared? I heard all about that, Adam. You drank too much and acted like a twat. Like you're doing right now."

"Did you have something to do with her disappearance?"

Shirley goes suddenly quiet and the mood changes. "She's still not turned up?"

"No, she hasn't. Now explain to me what the argument was about."

"Nothing. Just stupid girl stuff."

"Something to do with Laker?"

"Laker? No. Why on earth would you think that?"

"I dunno, I was… Jozee's missing… I don't know where she is."

"You need to go."

"Not until I know what you were arguing about."

"I don't have to tell you nada."

"You're right. But I'm worried sick, okay? If you had anything to do with her disappearance, then I need to know about it." Sudden tears fill my eyes and stream down my face. "I'm sorry," I say, trying to wipe them away, but the sobs keep on coming.

"Here," Shirley says, softening and handing me a box of tissues. "I know you're in a bit of a state, but you can't come drunkenly barging into my place like this."

"I lost it. I'm sorry. I thought—"

"Thought what? That I'd abducted your girlfriend? That she moved in with me to get away from you? Listen to yourself. Jozee told me how you overthink everything in that overactive mind of yours. You've got to calm down."

"I can't, not while she's missing. It's driving me mad. And it will do until I know what you were arguing about."

Shirley nudges aside a large cardboard box and slides gracefully onto her sofa, pushing her miniskirt down her well-formed thighs. "Jozee had something on her mind," she says, pursing her full-lips. "She decided to tell me about it. I suppose after Laker and you, I'm her best friend. It was something… *something very horrible.*"

"About who? Laker?"

"What is this obsession you've got with him? Jim is one of the few guys who has never hit on me—and when you look like I do, that goes a long way."

"I've never hit on you."

"That's true. I've always enjoyed your company. Until tonight."

"If it wasn't Laker… who did Jozee talk about?"

"I'm not going to tell you that."

"Why not?"

Shirley's face hardens although her eyes are full of sadness. "It's private. Something I'll never reveal. So, stop asking me."

"Sounds serious."

"It was…. It is. I was angry, distraught. I kicked Jozee out and even ran after her into the street. I totally lost it for a while. When she turns up, tell her I'm sorry, okay?"

"And that's everything that happened?"

"She got in that death-trap of a mini and drove off. I haven't seen or heard from her since."

"And you won't tell me any more?"

Shirley gives me an adamant shake of her head.

"Even if I promise to keep it a secret? Just between us?"

"Who do you think you are, Adam? You drunkenly barge into my flat, you accuse me of having something to do with your girlfriend's disappearance and now you expect me to reveal personal secrets to you? You've got a goddamn nerve!"

"I'm sorry."

"You should be."

"I hear you're retiring from comedy. Is that something to do with what Jozee told you?"

Shirley clenches her jaw. "I think you should go now." She stands up and walks to the door, and I'm compelled to follow.

"You're sure that what went on between you and Jozee has got nothing to do with her disappearance?" I ask.

"I'm positive." Shirley opens the door and steps back to let me pass. "Now get out."

I walk into the hallway. "I'll find out," I say to her. "One way or another."

"Just go."

She slams the door and I make a sad way home, a route that takes me past the Cathedral Bar. I hear Scott Wong singing one of his hilarious songs, the crowd laughing uproariously.

The smell of cooking meat is pervasive along this part of Western Road and all I've eaten today is a slice of toast. It's probably a bad idea, but I feel an overwhelming urge to consume.

Twenty minutes later I'm walking home with my face in a lamb kebab smothered in yoghurt and chilli sauce. I've a vague feeling that I'm being followed. I glance over my shoulder, bits of slimy salad dripping off my chin, but the street is full of people. I'm becoming paranoid. I decide to add it to my growing list of psychiatric ailments at the first available opportunity.

I'm perplexed by Shirley Sands. What could Jozee possibly tell her to make Shirley give up comedy? And why chase Jozee into the street? It made no sense. But as I told Shirley Sands, I'm making it my mission to find out.

I take another bite of kebab. It's greasier than I like, and I'm suddenly very queasy. It's probably the booze sitting on a mostly empty stomach that's the problem. I come to the drunken conclusion that the only way to stop the feeling is to finish eating.

Mistake. I swallow the last mouthful and throw the bag into a nearby bin, which I then lean onto.

"I'm gonna be fine," I say, stifling a burp. "I'm gonna be fine."

I stumble along the road for another twenty or so feet, but it's no good. Despite all my desires to the contrary, it would appear that the kebab has made a startling, if not disturbing decision to soon re-emerge, spluttering and shouting back into the world. Whether I want it to or not. I find an alleyway and jog inside, retching and burping—looking for a suitable place to let the contents of my stomach run free.

My phone beeps. I take it out and glance at the message, bile reaching the back of my throat, my mouth filling with saliva

> *You were asking for information on Tom. I know all about him. If—*

A shout behind me and the sound of pounding footsteps.

"Hey, Grandad! Think you could get away from us that easy!"

Shit! the track-suited thugs from the train! How the hell did they find me?

26

I RUN as fast as I can up the darkened alleyway, but I'm nauseous and shagged out from the last few days, and they're gaining on me. If I'm caught, they'll beat me up and rob me, taking my phone.

I can't let that happen. My phone is my only connection to Jozee. And there was that text message about Tom. Without thinking, I toss it over a wall hearing it thud on the other side, probably landing in someone's garden. But I'm desperate.

Suddenly the lads are on me, pushing me into the alley wall. I look up to see the ginger kid and another one of the thugs. Just two of them.

Damn! I shouldn't have run, I should've stood my ground.

The kid takes out a knife. "Hand everything over, Grandad."

My stomach spasms and I can't resist the kebab's demands for freedom any longer. I puke up over myself, the alleyway floor and all over the trainers of the two thugs, who jump backwards in alarm.

I throw up again, this time, the vomit emerges from my mouth in a steady stream, loudly splashing, and accompanied by my best Chewbacca impression.

The kids jump even further back. But I haven't finished. I retch again and again, lager and chewed kebab going everywhere.

"You disgusting bastard!" the ginger kid shouts. "You disgusting…"

I take a step towards them, coughing and spluttering.

The kids look at each other and, shrugging, run away, shouting curses and insults. I watch them go, vomiting now in relief. But still vomiting.

Finally, the retching comes to an end, my insides are like jelly, but I'm feeling clear-headed and relieved. That's the first time a technicolour yawn has saved me from a beating. The ginger kid had a knife. Things could've gone badly for me.

I head back to the wall to retrieve my phone. It's a lot higher than I thought. I find a handhold and pull myself up within arm's reach of the top. I try another handhold and sudden pain blooms in my fingers. I slip, twist and slam down on the alley floor, landing awkwardly on my side, my face smacking concrete.

I come to sometime later. My head is throbbing, and my lip swollen and bloody. My hand cut. Someone had concreted glass into the top of the wall to stop burglars.

Great.

I stumble down to Western Road, trying to flag down a taxi. None are stopping. I guess they don't want some puke and blood-covered passenger stinking up their cabs. Twenty-five minutes later, I arrive at Eaton Palace Gardens, glancing up disappointedly at my darkened flat. It doesn't look like Jozee has come home. And once inside, I realise I'm right.

Stripping off my clothes, I take a shower. I've a long cut on the palm of my hand, but it's not deep. Afterwards, I wash the wound with cold water, swathe it in antiseptic cream and wrap it in a bandage. I look at myself in the mirror. Bruises have bloomed on my side where I landed after the fall. My unshaven face is also bruised and scraped, and my lip is swollen.

I'm an utter mess.

And yet, I don't feel any pain. Externally that is. My inner hurt will only end when I find Jozee. I'm worried that she may be trying to call me. But my phone is still somewhere in that alleyway. I'll have to go back at first light to retrieve it.

After glugging half a bottle of Gaviscon, I power up my laptop and PM Jozee on Facebook and Twitter.

> *Phone temporarily lost. Getting it back tomorrow. If you need to contact me, PM me here or on Twitter.*

I remember the text I received just before the lads attacked me. Someone knew about the mysterious Tom. But who?

I go over to Jozee's Facebook page and check out her extensive list of friends, searching for 'Tom'. There are five of them. One of them is a deceased account.

Remembering Tom Blunt

Straightaway I can tell Tom Blunt was a comedian. I see photos of him with Jim Laker, Nat Naylor, Donnie Coogan, Billy Belter and *Jozee*. Lots and lots of photos of him and Jozee. Arm in arm. Holding hands. Kissing.

I check his relationship status.

In a relationship with Jozee Jackson. Status: it's complicated

What?

I spend the next hour researching Tom Blunt on the internet. He was a comedian like me. He was in a relationship with Jozee, like me. And I find out one other thing.

Tom Blunt killed himself…

FRIDAY MORNING

I JERK awake at 7.18am, sitting on the sofa, my laptop open on my lap still showing Jozee's Cackle Comedy profile. I re-read the last message in the post about her supposed gag-stealing.

And after what Jozee Jackson did to Tom, she should be ashamed of herself.

Is this the secret she was keeping from me?

After finding out about Tom Blunt's suicide, I researched him further. Apparently, the normally clean-living comedian took an overdose of heroin a year and a half ago.

I don't have time to ponder. It's light outside and I need to go get my phone. I shave and pull on some decent clothes—I want to look as presentable as possible for my interview with DC Marley—and get a taxi straight to the alleyway.

At this time on Friday morning, the alleyway is busy, used as a shortcut. I feel somewhat self-conscious lurking in there trying to retrace my steps. The pool of sick is easy to find. The half-digested kebab is an even uglier sight in the light of day. I locate the wall and can now clearly see the jagged glass embedded in its top. It's illegal to do such a thing these days, and the glass has been mostly broken off. But just enough remains to catch out the unwary climber.

After waiting self-consciously for the alley to empty, I make a second ascent, this time taking an alternate route. I clamber up and crouch on top of the thin wall of bricks. On the other side is a small, enclosed space full of rubbish and discarded metal and a square of overgrown garden used by smokers, judging by the number of cigarette butts that litter the place. I drop down and locate my phone, covered in a sheen of early morning condensation. I'm pleased to find it's still working, although the screen is cracked. I have a joke in my routine about that one clumsy friend who always has a broken phone screen. I am now that friend.

I check for messages and missed calls—nothing new—and then scroll to the message that arrived just before I was attacked, reading it in full for the first time.

> *You were asking for information on Tom. I know all about him and Jozee. Meet me at 11am in the Robin Hood xxx*

The Robin Hood is a small pub—a stone's throw away from this alleyway on Norfolk Place. The number is not recognised by my phone. And I wonder who sent it. The kisses signify that they know me, but why hide their identity?

I clamber back over the wall, startling a middle-aged woman on her way to work, and check the time. 7.50am. I'm going to be late for my appointment with the police.

The reception area of Brighton Police Station is like any other reception area I've been in, except that the policewoman, who looks like an old school dinner-lady of mine, is in uniform and is sitting behind a barricade, tapping at a computer with a bored expression on her face. I feel suddenly vulnerable on this side of the glass with all the felons.

I go and sit on a series of chairs by a wall. Others also wait here, although I have no idea why. An overweight man with greasy hair, acne and an ill-fitting greasy suit is accompanied by a skinny, hard-faced woman angrily rummaging through an immense handbag. Two teenage boys stare zombie-like at their phones. A well-dressed old man sucks loudly at a sweet, his head in a large, hardback book whose cover features a bikini-clad woman from the fifties. Two obviously gay men in immaculate t-shirts and chinos whisper to one another conspiratorially, while a twenty-something, podgy woman in a tracksuit reads a magazine, chewing gum with her mouth wide open.

The walls are a mess of public information posters that I idly stare at feeling very pleased with myself when I spot the odd grammatical mistake. I have a very enjoyable habit of subbing posters, menus, and everything else in the public domain that offends me. Actually scribbling corrections onto them with a red biro that I keep in my pocket just for this purpose. I decide against doing this inside a police station, although I'm still tempted.

I wait for twenty minutes, trying to control my growing irritation with the non-appearance of DC Marley. My phone battery is low, and I switch off all non-essential functions, and refrain from constantly looking at it, deciding to turn it off completely while I'm chatting to the police.

After forty minutes pass, I go back to the reception to be informed DC Marley will be with me soon.

I'm not convinced she's telling the truth. I remember I'm in a police station—kicking off about their terrible service isn't a good idea and go silently back to my seat. After another ten minutes, a policewoman enters through a private door holding a clipboard. An attractive black woman with dark, golden skin and warm eyes sitting above a pinched nose.

"Adam Hanson?" she says.

I stand up and she beckons me to follow her back through the door and down a series of corridors past offices in which uniformed officers stare intently at computers, drinking from coffee mugs. Others dart past carrying files or fiddling with radios, like they know a member of the public is in their midst and are trying their best to impress.

We arrive at a small office-like room.

"I'm Detective Constable Ella Marley," the officer begins in quiet, relaxing tones, her eyes roving over my discoloured face.

I guess my split lip, bruises and bandaged hand look a little suspicious.

"And no, I'm not related to Bob," she continues, her lips parting into a wide smile, revealing an array of flashing teeth, seemingly too large for her mouth.

This must be all part of the routine to calm down panicked relatives and spouses like myself. "I wouldn't have made that connection," I say. "I was thinking of the dog."

Marley's eyes narrow, a confused, slightly annoyed expression crossing her smooth features. "Dog?" she says, her relaxed tones now sharpened.

"I mean, *Marley and Me,* the movie," I say hastily. "The dog was called Marley. But there's also Jacob Marley from *Scrooge* and—"

"Let's get on, shall we?" she asks, the smile gone, sitting down and opening up a battered laptop.

I nod and sit opposite, cursing my stupid mind and my stupid small talk in equal measure.

"What is the full name of the missing person?"

"Josephine Margaret Jackson. Although she prefers to be called Jozee."

"Age?"

"Thirty-one."

I give her the details she asks for, which she diligently and efficiently taps into her laptop, including a recent photograph sent from my phone, Jozee's job details at ASDA, and confirming that, as far as I know, she doesn't have any medical problems. I also give Marley a description of Jozee's car, number plate and mention the missing wing mirror that some vandal broke off the week before. And then comes the difficult part. The argument.

"Can you tell me what it was about?"

"Not really. I wasn't driving, so after my gig—which bombed—I started drinking."

"This is the comedy night hosted by the Dog and Duck in Burgess Hill, yes? Where you both performed as comedians?"

"Yes," I reply, feeling like a fraud, remembering the silence that met my jokes.

"Go on."

"Jozee had been off with me for a couple of weeks."

"Off with you? Can you be more specific?"

"Something had changed between us. A distance had developed."

"Did this bother you?"

"Yeah, it did a bit. And that night she'd wanted to have a talk. But I messed up by drinking too much and generally making an idiot of myself, which didn't go down well. The argument carried over into the car park and… You can imagine how it played out. I acted like a prat and she drove off. I was forced to make my own way back home."

"And when you arrived home, Josephine wasn't there as you expected. Is that correct?"

"Yes. And there was no sign of her mini."

"Do you have any idea where she might have gone?"

I shake my head. "I checked everyone she knows."

"Have you talked to Josephine's family?"

"As far as I'm aware, they are all dead. If she has brothers or sisters, she's never told me."

"Are any of her personal things missing. Shoes, clothes, toiletries… sanitary products."

"Nothing."

"And you say she also hasn't turned up for work?"

"That's right. I'm in contact with one of her work colleagues. She was scheduled to come in yesterday morning at 10am but did a no show."

"Facebook? Instagram? Twitter?"

"No updates."

"How long have you been together?"

"Six or so months."

"How would you describe your relationship? Did you argue a lot?"

I'm reminded of my neighbour, Clive, and his negative thoughts on this matter. "We had pretend arguments. A lot of shouting, but no real substance. We were very happy."

"Until recently, when you say there was something on her mind."

"Yes."

"And you have no idea as to what this was?"

"No, I just wish I hadn't drank that night. I would've gone home with her and all would be okay."

Marley looks up from her screen and straight into my eyes. "You don't have to answer my next question, but it will help to get an insight into Josephine's mental state at the time she disappeared. Was everything alright sexually?"

"Everything was dynamite," I say. "Until a week or two ago."

"You stopped sleeping together?"

"Not stopped exactly, but Jozee couldn't find the time. She's been very busy gigging and working."

"Did you have sex at all in the two-week period before she disappeared?"

"No," I admit. "No we didn't."

"Any other men or women in the picture?"

The image of Jim Laker flashes into my mind. "No."

"Sure?"

"Who can ever be one hundred percent sure? I don't think so."

"If she was sleeping with someone else, how would that make you feel?"

"Is this a necessary question?"

"You don't have to answer, if it makes you uncomfortable, but as I said, it helps to get as full a picture of Jozee's mental state as possible."

"I would be very, very unhappy," I admit. "Let down. Hurt. She's special to me. Very special. The most special person I've ever met. But a lack of fidelity isn't the end of the world. I'd forgive her. People fuck up… I mean, people make mistakes. I make mistakes. We all do. So, you can't judge others too harshly."

Her stare stays on me longer than I care for, but finally, she nods and taps what I'm guessing is my reply, or at least her thoughts on my reply, into her laptop. "Thank you. We're done."

"Is that it?"

"After you leave, I'll make a few more notes before officially processing a Missing Person Report. Josephine Margaret Jackson will be added to the Missing Person's Register, accessed electronically by all national police forces. I'd like to remind you that Jozee is an adult. She is independent. With a bank account and means. The most likely scenario is that she has disappeared of her own accord and will turn up when she's ready. Which means she is perfectly safe. However, we know this is a difficult time. Here are some leaflets that will help you to process what's happening, and places and groups where you can discuss your experiences with others who have gone through, and who are also going through, what you are going through.”

The words are rehearsed, and I guess she's said them quite a few times. I take the leaflets, knowing I'm not going to read them. Leaflets and support are the last thing I need. I have to find Jozee, that's the only thing that will help.

“What about those dead women?” I say. “Murdered, cut up and found on Sussex beaches?”

Marley's eyes narrow. “How do you know about that?”

“Twitter and a few phone calls to local news organisations. I was freaked out until I heard they were illegal immigrants—which is awful just the same—but with Jozee missing, it is still worrisome.”

She sits back in her chair. “All I can say of those killings is that they're gang-related. Foreign mafia and some nasty homegrown criminals. The girls were trafficked, forced to take drugs and used as prostitutes. It's very unlikely your girlfriend is involved with them.”

“I know. You're right. But I just needed you to tell me that.”

“In the meantime, Adam, rest assured we will be on the lookout for Josephine Jackson. And if you hear from her, or find out anything more, please let me know.”

She stands up, straightens her trousers and hands me her card.

“Contact me at any time. It has my phone and email.”

I take the card and slip it into my wallet. “So what is your next step?”

The question seems to perplex her. “If Jozee turns up anywhere, at a police station or a hospital, we will be alerted. Similarly, if her car is involved in an accident or traffic violation.”

“That sounds a little passive.”

“It may seem like that, but it's the very best way to locate her. You must also remember that even if she is found, it doesn't follow on that she will want to see or have anything to do with you. However, if she is safe and well, we will pass that information on to you.”

I suppose I knew this would be the police response. They are not mobilising any extra personnel to find Jozee. Shit! But it's better than nothing.

“Is there anything else I can do?”

"Just do what you've been doing. And, above everything else, don't give up hope."

28

MY MEETING with DC Marley has had a sobering effect upon me. It's now official. I'm not looking for Jozee on my own. Not that the police are actively doing anything, but at least if she is wandering around lost in some mental state, it's now a lot more likely she will be found.

My phone beeps after I switch it back on again, shocked that I've spent so much time at the police station. I no longer expect to hear from Jozee. And I'm right. It's another text from the mystery number.

You coming to meet me?

Who the hell is this? I suppose I'll find out real soon.

On my way now.

I make my way from the police station through Churchill Square and toward the Robin Hood public house. It's a minute's walk away from the Cathedral Bar, and yet, just that short distance from Western Road, the main thoroughfare through Brighton and Hove, is enough to give the pub a relaxed, welcoming and quiet air. Every year the pub seems to be painted with a new bright colour. It was previously a garish pink. Now it's an iridescent blue. I step inside and mosey up to the bar. It's not even the afternoon, but I find myself ordering a pint. I'm weak-willed at the best of times and using alcohol to stem my everyday anxiety is a habit I've gotten into. Now that I'm engulfed with real anxiety, the need feels visceral. I snatch a gulp and finish a third of the pint before I sit down on one of the comfortable sofas by the door.

I check the time. 11.12am. Maybe they're gonna be a no show. A short time later, a taxi pulls up outside, the door opens, and Pari

Chabra enters. She sees me and smiles—cherry-red, badly painted lips creasing amongst the white of her overblown makeup. Today her sari is an LGBT rainbow, from which long, grey dreadlocks spill over her shoulders.

"You?" I say, pleased to see a friendly face. I had no idea who was going to turn up, but Pari would've been at the bottom of my list.

"Of course, it's me, who else would it be?"

"You used an unknown number."

"Did I?" Pari pushes her weight over to the sofa opposite and sits down heavily.

She takes out an iPhone from a voluminous handbag and stares at the screen confusedly through thick spectacles, which she holds up to her eyes in a mimicry of pince-nez.

I notice her text is three times the size it is on my phone, then again, Pari's eyesight is not the best.

"I'm sure I sent everyone an email about my new number. Didn't you get it?" she says, jabbing a beringed, wrinkled finger at her phone's screen.

"I must have missed it," I reply guiltily. Pari was always sending emails about this, that and the other. Helpful stuff, or so she believed. I have to admit to never having the patience to read them, which is probably why her number isn't updated on my phone.

"What do you know about Tom?" I ask eagerly.

"Be a good boy and get me a neat gin, will you? Helps dull the pain from my stupid ailments. Double. And then we can talk."

I quickly do as she says and a few minutes later I'm sitting opposite her again.

"About Tom?" I ask.

Pari squeezes her gin in a stubby hand, her elegantly painted fingernails tapping against the glass. "I know all about him, Adam. Everything."

29

"TOM WAS a funny, funny guy. One of the very best comedians I've ever seen. In a totally different class, even funnier than the brilliant Scott Wong. I'm shocked you don't already know about what happened to him… from Jozee."

Pari takes a gentle sip of gin, her cherry-red lips puckering over the rim of the glass, revealing a filigree of wrinkles and lines.

"She told me nothing about Tom," I admit.

"Which puts me in a delicate position. I don't want to get myself in trouble with Jozee when she turns up again. I'd hate to be in her bad books."

I take a gulp of lager, it goes down very well, even on my abused stomach.

"Your secret is safe with me," I reply.

"Thank you, Adam, you're a good man. And thanks for the gin. What do you know about Tom?"

"Not much. Most of it I found out last night. He used to be Jozee's boyfriend and that he took an overdose, but that's all."

"Tom, wonderful, charming Tom."

"You knew him well then?"

"Oh yes. We started comedy together. A very special time, before my health gave way." She gazes into the distance, her focus looking into the past.

"About Tom?" I urge as gently as I can.

Pari smiles and comes back to herself. "Tom fell for Jozee hard. And, if you will forgive me, they were very well-suited to one another. Or so everyone thought."

"That sounds ominous."

"They were happy for a short time, certainly, but Tom changed. Became withdrawn. All was not well in paradise. I tried to talk to him about it, but he was the silent type. A bit like Jozee in that respect. Being infirm and a little older means that I get to notice things that others don't. Jozee had fallen out of love with him, that much was obvious. They used to be very lovey-dovey, all hugs and kisses but that stopped abruptly. Their relationship was obviously in trouble. A few weeks later it all came out in a bust-up at the Wagon and Horses."

The Wagon and Horses is Brighton's post-comedy go-to pub. I've spent many evenings there after gigging. It's where comedians hang out, drinking to the early hours of the morning.

"Jozee dumped Tom in front of everyone else. She didn't plan it, I'm sure of it. But drink was involved. It was all so dreadfully public."

"You mean Tom took an overdose because Jozee left him?"

"There was that and… the video."

"What video?"

"Someone filmed their argument and put it online. I think that was what pushed him over the edge. I didn't see the video myself, I didn't have to. I was there. Tom and Jozee were huddling away from the rest of us. Having one of those nasty, whispered arguments. I guess Tom was trying to save the relationship, trying to get Jozee to stop what she was about to do. That's when it happened."

Pari takes another slurp of gin, her pink tongue flicking in and out of the spirit.

"She dumped him. Right there. Loudly and publicly. Told him she wanted nothing more to do with him. Shouted it to his face. Tom was pleading with her. Crying. Tears running all over his poor face. Quite a scene."

"That's not the Jozee I know," I say. "She'd never do anything so heartless."

"Oh, of course not. It was fuelled by drink, plain and simple. And when there are problems in a relationship, drinking heavily is a bad move."

Pari's words cut into me. I feel like she's talking about my argument with Jozee, rather than the one with Tom.

"Everyone saw the video. Everyone. The day after it was posted, we heard the news about Tom's overdose. Poor Jozee, she was heartbroken. To all and sundry who saw that tape, it looked like Jozee was the cause of Tom trying to take his own life."

"Trying? Tom's dead, isn't he?"

"Oh no, of course not… but he might as well be."

30

"NOT DEAD? But the papers said he was. That's what it says on Facebook. Is that where Jozee is then, back with her ex? Back with Tom?"

Pari raises a stubby hand, a look of alarm crossing the wrinkled, makeup-plastered skin of her face. "God forbid, no. You don't know the real horror of what happened to Tom. He's not dead, but not properly alive either. He's in a dreadful limbo, hospitalised at some care facility near Haywards Heath. A vegetable. Nothing more. Poor, poor Tom. Jim Laker was Tom's best friend. He found him just in time. Kept him going until the paramedics arrived."

"Laker?"

Pari nods sagely. "Yes. He was a real hero that night. Although it changed him. He's not always been such a disagreeable individual."

I'm not liking what I'm hearing from Pari, but it does make dreadful sense. Maybe Laker resents me for going out with Jozee because Tom was his best friend?

"Of course, Jozee was distraught," Pari continues. "I suppose she didn't expect Tom to do what he did, no one did."

"Poor Jozee," I say, taking a gulp of my pint. "I knew she was keeping something from me. That she was holding something back. What an awful, awful thing to happen."

"She blamed herself for what Tom did. But we, Jozee's friends, rallied around her. Especially Laker. He protected her from the flak that came her way. Jozee owes Laker for that, she will owe him forever. But it changed Jozee. It was soon after Tom's suicide attempt that she threw everything into her comedy. A way to forget, I suppose."

"Why did no one tell me about this?"

Pari shrugs. "Why rake up the past? Jozee was happy again with you. No one was going to spoil that. And why shouldn't she have a little bit of happiness?"

It's a lot to take in, but it makes sense. If I had a similar secret to Jozee's in my past, would I want to tell her? No. Of course not. But it would have to come out sooner or later. I can't help feeling sorry for her. No one deserves to go through what she did. I can't see how Tom's suicide attempt could've led to Jozee's disappearance, but it's good to know about it.

"Thanks, Pari," I say, finishing my pint. "Do you have any idea of where Jozee may be or what has happened to her?"

"If I hear anything, you will be the first to know."

31

FRIDAY AFTERNOON

BACK HOME, I plug in my phone to recharge, and do some more in-depth research on Tom Blunt. I find that what Pari told me was the truth. He is still alive. Not that I doubted her.

Part of me wants to search online for that video Pari mentioned. But I decide against it. It will not tell me anything I don't already know. To watch it would be some dreadful kind of rubber-necking. And I don't want to judge Jozee. What happened was over a year before I met her. And for whatever reason she dumped Tom, she would have no idea he'd try to kill himself. I also hate to admit it, but what Laker did was pretty damn heroic, protecting Jozee like he did—especially as Tom was his best friend.

No wonder Jozee and Laker were so close.

Maybe he's not the heartless git I've made him out to be. He did a good thing. And, according to Pari, he was also damaged by Tom's attempted suicide.

This news is not palatable, and I find myself at a loose end. It's early Friday afternoon. Normally I'd be out at work, and a part of me wishes I was there. At least I could keep my mind busy.

Is this what it's going to be like from now on? Will I have to accept Jozee has gone and be forced to go back to my everyday life? I can't imagine what that would be like. Back in the office with Ollie and the Gannet. Horrific. No, I must keep myself busy. I decide to find Tom and go visit him. I have no idea what that will achieve, probably nothing, but at least it's a plan.

Pari said Tom was in a care home in Haywards Heath, a small town on the north side of the South Downs. And the more I think about it, the more I realise that this care home must be a specialist institution, caring for Tom and others like him.

I google local care homes and find three possible places, and, without any preamble, I start phoning, amazed at my lack of nerves. Phoning strangers is usually a sweaty experience for me at the best of times.

Firstly, I'm met with an automated menu and realise this is a transplant recovery clinic. The second is for psychiatric referrals. The third is answered by an efficient male voice. "Good afternoon. This is the Haywards Heath Long-Term Care and Rehabilitation Clinic."

"Good afternoon, I was wondering when it would be possible to come and visit Tom Blunt, who I believe is a resident in your facility," I say with surprising calm.

"Ah yes, Tom Blunt is one of our newer clients. Family visiting hours are between 2pm and 4pm weekdays and 10am-6pm weekends. Although special visits can also be arranged."

I check the time on my phone. "Thank you. Can I make an appointment to visit today after 2pm? I'm in the Haywards Heath area and thought I might drop in to see how he's um… doing."

"And your relationship to Mr Blunt is?"

"I'm his brother. Mr Adam Blunt."

"I will tell his private nurse you are expected. Please report to reception on arrival."

I off the phone and ring Stevo. It rings a few times then goes to voicemail.

"Mate," I begin. "I need a lift to Haywards Heath ASAP. A care centre where one of Jozee's exes is now living. Can you let me know when you get this? Ta."

I sit by the phone while it's still charging, willing Stevo to get back to me. I wait twenty minutes and leave him a few more messages.

Where is the he? Stevo and his phone are never separated. He's never off the damn thing.

After half an hour, I realise I must make my own way to Haywards Heath. I check the trains, but a bus route stops almost outside the care centre. Looks like I'll have to bite the bullet on this one. The bus it is.

I'm about to leave when my flat buzzer rings.

"Who is it?" I ask over the phone to the front door.

A pause.

"Hello? Who's there?"

"Is this Jozee's flat?" asks an uncertain-sounding cockney male voice.

"Yes, it is… who are you?"

32

THE MAN won't say any more other than he wants to talk to Jozee. I'm leaving anyway, so quickly jog downstairs. I open the main door and come face to face with a seedy looking, skinny guy with a 70s mullet, beady eyes and a wispy beard giving him a rat-like demeanour. He's in his late 30s, early 40s and clutches a sheaf of printouts.

"Are you the guy I just talked to?" he says aggressively.

"Yeah, who are you and why do you want Jozee?"

"What the fuck is this? Some kind of set up? I don't do fellas, understand? I came here for Jozee. Where is she?"

He holds up his printouts, one of them is a blown-up, sexy photo of Jozee that I recognize from one of her early posters.

"What are you doing with that?"

"I've come a long way to meet her, not you!" he says. "Is she up there?" He jabs at my flat buzzer again.

I grab his arm, pulling it away.

"Hey, don't be greedy," he says. "She likes to share it out. Let someone else have some."

"What do you mean by that?"

He quickly shows me the printouts which appear to have come from the internet.

"She arranged it for today. A hook-up. I'm sorry if that treads on your toes, but a horny bitch like that ain't gonna be satisfied by a single fella. That's what she told me anyway." The man punches the buzzer again.

Clive speaks over the door intercom. "Who is this?"

"Stop that!" I shout to the guy, pulling his arm away from the buzzer and suddenly we're in a tussle.

"Adam is that you? What is going on down there?"

The man is wiry, but strong—yet his heart isn't in the fight. He pulls away. Shouting. "This is disgusting! She gets me all the way down here for this! I'll make sure everyone else knows what a prick-teaser your little slut is!" He thrusts the printouts into my face and stalks off, shouting and swearing.

"Adam! Adam, are you okay? Shall I call the police?"

I go over to the intercom. "I'm alright, Clive," I say, breathing heavily and feeling shaken. "Just some nutter."

"Are you sure? You sound very upset."

"Yeah. Sorry for the disturbance."

"This is not good enough, Adam. First all this pizza delivery nonsense, buzzing mine and the other flats and now this!"

The flats are sound-proofed, but it is still possible to hear the door buzzers in adjoining flats when someone buzzes them. And Clive has a nosey habit of listening in to their intercom conversations and complaining if anybody pushes the buzzer more than once.

"We really need to talk about all this recent disturbance, Adam."

"We will do, but now I've got to go. I'm sorry."

Clive says something else but I'm not listening. My eye is taken by the top printout the creepy guy left behind. It's a private message thread printed out from a website.

From: *FunnyBrightonBitch*
To: *BigManInYorFace*

Subject: RE: Hot Hove Sex

33

WALKING TOWARDS the bus stop, I feel sick to my guts, still clutching the printouts, unable to bring myself to look at them. It's another boiling day. The heatwave is showing no signs of abating.

What was that messed up shit? The guy was a total creep. And he'd come to my flat to meet Jozee. To have sex with her.

To have sex!

And where would I normally be at this time of day? Safely at work, that's where.

The bus arrives, and I get on, making my way to the back seat. I can't ignore the printouts any longer and begin to read. They come from a website I've never heard of before.

http://www.instanthookup.co.uk/

It's a profile page of a girl called *FunnyBrightonBitch,* with a picture of Jozee. One that I've seen before—a sexy promo photograph in a revealing, off the shoulder low top. The one she used a couple of years back. The one that made all the comics wolf-whistle her as a joke. She'd been so embarrassed that she'd never used it again—or so she told me. But it was here. And cropped, to make it look like she was naked.

Name: *Funny Brighton Bitch* **Age:** *26*

Looking for: Casual hook-ups, couples, threesomes and sex on the beach!

Likes: Boys and girls. Cumming on your cock, strapon or tongue. Bondage, pissing, threesomes (MMF, FFM), dogging, public displays of sex. Will fuck first and ask questions later!

Doesn't like: Comedians and timewasters

I can't quite believe what I'm reading, but it looks like Jozee had arranged for this guy to come visit her while she was at home and I was out at work.

A cheap hook-up with a creep like that.

Do I know Jozee at all? I never question her whereabouts, but she's out most evenings and also in the daytime. A workaholic… or so I thought. I assumed she was gigging, but was she meeting up with other guys, for dogging and other weird stuff? And in our flat? Was that why Clive despised her so much? Because he knew what she was doing behind my back?

I think of the many evenings when Jozee would arrive home late. I'd ask her where she'd been and what she'd been up to. 'Writing comedy in my favourite little café', is what she usually said, although, now I think about it, she could've been anywhere.

Fucking with strangers.

Did she do that the night she disappeared? Was she angry about our argument and met some weirdo for sex?

I'd always assumed I was enough for her. Our sex-life was normal as far as I knew. A few times in the week and lots of fun at the weekend. She didn't appear to be highly-sexed. Although once she got started in bed…

Could Jozee's interest in this sordid underworld of sex be the reason why she's gone missing? No, I can't believe it. I don't want to.

I should phone up DC Marley and let her know what I've found… but I can't. I just can't. This is too much to process.

I want to believe that the guy who turned up was mistaken, but the printouts tell another story.

There're no dates on the messages, so I don't know when they were written. They are explicit and hard for me to read, but I force myself. A series of disgusting exchanges, culminating in today's arrangement. All in black and white.

I'm not sure if I'm angry or heartbroken. More than anything, I feel numb.

The bus, which has meandered through the countryside, stops outside the clinic of my destination and I stumble off in a daze. People stare at me and I realise that I'm crying. Tears streaming down my face. I fold the printouts and thrust them into my jeans, sitting down on a nearby public bench that is thankfully out of the burning sun. I call Stevo again, needing to chat to someone—*to anyone*—but he's still not answering.

Where is he?

The time is 2pm. I wonder what I'm doing here, on the outskirts of this grey little town.

"Visiting Tom Blunt. Another of Jozee's sap boyfriends," I say to myself, although it now seems utterly pointless.

I suddenly feel sorry for Tom. He seemed such a vibrant, alive chap in his Facebook photos. Maybe I *should* visit him. To show him some respect. After all, we have the same person in common... Jozee. Perhaps he also found out about Jozee's secret life, a secret that ultimately split them up and led to him choosing to do what he did. One thing is for sure though, Tom won't be able to tell me himself.

34

"I'M ADAM, Adam Blunt," I say to the sterile receptionist at the Haywards Heath Long-Term Care and Rehabilitation Clinic, a rather severe woman with her hair pulled back and no makeup, wearing a badge printed with, 'Receptionist Naomi' in an unnecessarily large font. "Of course, I am," I add, to make myself sound even less believable.

Receptionist Naomi gives me a look, like she's found something nasty on her shoe, glancing up from a book of Sudoku that she obviously finds more interesting than talking to me. "Is this your first visit?" she asks, her eyes roving over my bruised face and split lip. "I don't think I've seen you before."

"Yes, I phoned earlier."

She tilts her head to one side and frowns, before punching irritable fingers at her PC.

We wait patiently for the computer system to upload the much-needed answers required for the receptionist to resolve this complicated situation.

"Finally!" she says after thirty seconds that feel more like an hour. She picks up a phone and punches the dial with equal vigour.

"Nurse Sally, a Mr Adam Blunt is here to see his brother. If you can find time out of your busy schedule to come and collect him, that would be wonderful."

The mention of an actual nurse jolts me back to my senses. This is a stupid idea. I shouldn't be here.

Receptionist Naomi gives me a tight smile, picks up a pencil—that she jabs into the corner of her thin-lipped mouth—and returns to her Sudoku.

Before I can think of a clever way to get out of here, without actually turning around and going back through the doors I've just entered, a very attractive amber-skinned Asian woman, with far too many pleasing curves, saunters into the reception area to smile at me with big, wide eyes and full lips.

I'm quite taken by her nurse's uniform that appears to be something you'd try and get your girlfriend to wear for fun and games on a Friday evening, rather than an official outfit. It seems dreadfully inappropriate, then again, I'm not a member of the medical profession—the closest I've ever gotten to it was attending A&E in a series of rather clumsy accidents that have mostly involved overuse of alcohol.

I turn to face her.

"This is Nurse Sally," the receptionist says behind me with a hint of disapproval.

"Mr Blunt," Sally says. "It's very nice to see you."

She takes my hand and gives it a firm shake. "Your first visit? Come with me."

Nurse Sally ambles down a corridor lined with prints of famous paintings and iconic photographs, including Marilyn Monroe with her dress blown above her head and that awful Vietnam image of a napalmed child, mixed in with Van Gogh's *Sunflowers* and even a Mondrian. The result is disarming to say the least. The carpet is also a jarring yellow set against bright blue walls.

What on earth is this place?

"We like to keep the clinic as sensorially challenging for our clients as possible," Sally says, as if she can read my thoughts, her swaying hips certainly challenging my senses.

I follow her, deciding to make this a quick in-and-out visit.

I shouldn't be here, I say to myself again.

"Mr Blunt is one of our most popular clients," Sally continues.

"He is?" I reply, wondering why she's calling someone in a coma a 'client'. It makes it sound like he wanted to be here and was paying for the privilege. It is a private clinic though, that much is obvious. And, I'm guessing, very expensive.

"Oh yes. He gets visitors every week. Unlike some of our other clients. But regular visits can sometimes be hard on the relatives."

We enter a large, airy room with a window looking over a well-kept inner courtyard. The room is full of flowers and the cloying smell of scent. In the centre stands a single bed in which Tom Blunt lies, inert and deathly-looking. Pale, shrunken, surrounded by machines and drips.

"Hello Tom," Sally says to him in a loud, childish voice. "You have a visitor." She grabs a remote control and Tom's bed buzzes and whirs, lifting him up into a sitting position. I can see him more clearly now. His eyes are shut and his mouth open. His hair seems dark next to the whitened skin of his face, like a dreadful old actor with bad hair dye.

A ghoul.

Although, if anyone is worthy of that description, that someone is me.

"Can he hear us? Does he know we're here?" I say nervously.

Sally pauses. "All the tests indicate that your brother is not fully brain-dead, but he's in a deep coma, a coma it is predicted he will never recover from. I guess you know that already. But where there's life, there's always hope."

"He's not my brother," I hear myself saying. "I shouldn't have come here. I'm an idiot."

Sally turns to me, a frown on her face. "It is supposed to be family visitors only, unless they give you special permission, but…"

"But what?"

She shrugs, her professional tone disappearing to be replaced by something infinitely slyer. "I won't tell if you won't."

"You don't… *you don't mind?*"

"I don't make the rules and they don't pay enough for me to always follow them. And, you're not the only non-family member who visits. The way I look at it, the more visitors he gets the better. Isn't that right, Tom?"

"Who else comes to see him?"

"There's his sister, Charlotte. She comes every weekend and sometimes mid-week. Charlotte is the one who brings all these wonderful flowers. She's devoted to him, poor girl. I certainly wouldn't do the same for any of my brothers." She shakes her head adamantly. "The girl needs to move on. Charlotte still hopes Tom is gonna come back to her. But that ain't ever gonna happen."

"But you said *non-family.*"

"That's right. Tom also has another visitor. Don't you Tom?"

"Who is that?"

"Maybe you know her? A Miss Jozee Jackson?"

"Jozee comes here?"

"Yes, once, sometimes twice a week. She was his girlfriend, apparently. She reads to him and tells him jokes. Does a whole comedy routine. Tom is popular. Very popular. Shame he will never know it."

"But if she's not family, how does she get in?"

Sally smiles at me, her big eyes staring straight into mine. Normally I don't like eye-contact, but it doesn't bother me. The confidence, however, comes entirely from her.

"Just between you and me," she says, "we have a little arrangement."

"You do? With Jozee?"

"Ms Jackson texts me when she wants to visit, to find out when I'm on my shift, and I let her in via another entrance."

"That's very… um… nice of you."

She winks. "She pays me to come and see Tom on the quiet."

"I see."

"It's not illegal, but the bosses wouldn't be pleased if they knew. Especially that snotty cow on reception. And we all have to make a living, don't we?"

"So why tell me?" I ask, the realisation suddenly dawning. "Because I shouldn't be here either, right?"

"That's it. Which means we can also make the same arrangement… if you like?"

I'm both shocked and impressed by the girl's candour. "Let me be honest with you. I don't really know Tom at all. I'm Jozee's boyfriend. Well, the latest one."

"Oh," Sally says. "That's a bit stalker-like, don't you think?"

I was expecting Sally to be more alarmed but finding this out seems to please her.

"I'm no stalker."

"Then why are you here?" she continues. "Are you jealous of Tom? He's just a vegetable. Nothing to see here."

"This was a mistake. A big one. I should go," I say. "But before I do, can you tell me one thing? When was the last time Jozee visited?"

Sally seems disappointed that I'm leaving. "Tuesday afternoon. Is that important? You sure you're not stalking her?"

Tuesday was the day Jozee disappeared. I remember her coming home late. She told me she'd been out writing comedy and the time had gotten away from her. We'd then had to rush out to the comedy in Burgess Hill. Jozee must've driven all the way back home from here just to pick me up.

"Jozee is missing. I'm trying to find her," I say, quickly putting the fact she lied to me out of my mind. "Can you do me a favour, if you hear from her again, or can think of anything that will help, can you get in touch?"

Sally takes a step toward me, standing very close, looking up at me with her big eyes, and despite everything that's going on, I feel a tingle. "I can do anything you want, for a price," she says.

This experience is turning surreal. I'm confused and a little irritated.

"I don't want to be rude," I reply. "But this isn't the behaviour I'd expect from a trained professional. I'm surprised."

Sally snorts. "I'm no professional. I'm not even a proper nurse. The in-house doctor takes care of all the medical stuff. Not that she has much to do. I'm more 'front of house'. Someone pleasing to look at to keep the visitors happy."

"Well… um… thanks. But I'm only interested in information on Jozee. She's missing. I'm trying to find her."

"Fair enough," Sally says taking a step back, her coquettish behaviour disappearing. "Shame though… you're kinda cute. Especially with those bruises."

I shake my head, trying to refocus. "Is there anything you can tell me about Jozee, anything at all?"

"Nothing. Other than she always pays up front."

"You don't know anything about her secret life?" I ask, wondering if this flirty girl is also on the same hook-up website. She sure seems to be the type.

"Secret life?" she repeats. "The girl comes here on the quiet and tells jokes to her vegetable ex. She pays for the privilege. That's all I know about her. But if you want me to keep a look out for her, it will cost you twenty pounds."

"Really?"

"Unless you want some of those extras I mentioned?"

I take out my wallet and hand her the money.

"Thanks. Give me your number and if she turns up I'll let you know, okay?"

On the way out, I spot a willowy girl in her early twenties walking towards the clinic. Long blonde hair and sunglasses. Before I realise what I'm doing, I catch myself eyeing her up and down. The encounter with Nurse Sally has certainly had an effect. And not one I was expecting or enjoying. Jozee could be dead or dying somewhere and all I can do is ogle women?

I stalk quickly away, both angry with myself and with Jozee.

35

I WANDER back to the bus stop, feeling soiled. My experience at the Haywards Heath Long-Term Care and Rehabilitation Clinic has left a bad taste in my mouth. I want to get away from here as soon as possible. Thankfully, the bus arrives promptly, and I get on, presenting my all-day-ticket to the driver who makes a show of inspecting it closely. I dump myself on to the back seat, warm from the heat of the engine and the blistering sunshine streaming through the windows, and gently start to cook.

What the hell was going on inside Jozee's head?

Was she punishing herself for what she did to Tom by sleeping with those creeps on that hook-up website? Was that it? If so, why do that to me? Why even go out with me in the first place? Unless I was part of her punishment?

No, that couldn't be true. I know I don't sense things like others, but I just can't believe Jozee could be that heartless.

None of this adds up. None of it.

I shake my head, trying to get my thoughts into some semblance of order. It doesn't work. No matter how I look at it, it's like there are two Jozee's. The one I know, the one I love, the one who I thought loved me back—the Jozee I'd lived with for the last four or so months… and this *other Jozee*. The one with secrets and vices.

My phone rings and I fully expect it to be Stevo, apologising for missing my calls, but instead it's the Haywards Heath Long-Term Care and Rehabilitation Clinic.

I answer. "Hello, um… Adam… um Blunt speaking."

"Hello."

It's the Receptionist Naomi and her tone is severe to say the least.

"Regarding our client, Tom Blunt," she continues coldly. "It has come to our attention, that you are not his brother, but instead a rather nasty impostor. Be forewarned that you will not be allowed to visit this centre again. If you attempt to do so, you will be escorted off the premises and the police will be called. Do you understand?"

"Yes," I reply meekly, wondering how the hell they found out about me so quickly. Did Sally rat me out even after I paid her? It seemed unlikely.

"Good bye."

She puts the phone down and I'm left suitably chastised. I should never have gone there. It was an insult to Tom. I didn't know the guy, but to end up like that… it was a sad end for him.

Would Tom still have taken an overdose, if he'd known what would happen?

I have no idea. My mind starts to buzz with flashes of Tom, of Sally. Of that perv who turned up at the flat and of Jozce. It's all too much.

I start my breathing exercises, concentrating on the outside world and not what is going on inside my head. My thoughts still race, but, thankfully, they become a background noise. The bus travels through country lanes, taking a route joining up villages and hamlets. I decide to employ a favourite technique to try to calm my overactive mind.

Naming things.

A way of distracting myself and irritating others by vocalising everything I see like some annoying toddler.

"Crow, tractor, two women on horses," I whisper. "Saddles and bridles. Hooves. Swishing tails. Hedges. Rusted fence. Pothole. Magpie. Cows. Sheep. Bicycles. Dog on a lead. A grey four by four. Jim Laker. Nat Naylor. A white mansion. A large, never-ending field of yellow. Corn or some other crop. More fields in the distance…"

I do a double take. Jim Laker? Nat Naylor? What are they doing out here?

36

I GET off the bus at the next stop and jog back to the four-by-four, an impressive BMW parked outside an equally impressive mansion sitting in an overgrown, untended garden.

I arrive out of breath, concluding that myself and jogging are not made for one another, and that any future relationship we might have is doomed to failure. Clutching at my side, I edge around the vehicle to take a closer look at the house I just saw Nat and Laker entering. It sits alone next to a range of arable fields. Isolated. In the middle of nowhere… wherever *here* is. I don't even have a phone signal.

What are Laker and Nat doing?

The question has been on my mind ever since I saw them together. They had no connection with one another outside of comedy. Nat was very much into her boyfriend, and Laker was engaged to his fiancée, Ruth. So why? My mind gives me the only possible answer.

Jozee.

I'm filled with the sudden desire to run up to the front door and hit the doorbell. Yet, I do nothing, and not because I'm still shagged out from jogging. No. Jozee may be inside of her own free will or maybe Laker and Nat are somehow involved in her disappearance. Either way, ringing the doorbell will get me nowhere. It might even endanger her.

I skirt around the house, checking the windows and doors, but all are curtained and locked. On a summer's day like today, this indicates the house is empty or at least, not lived in. The back garden is overgrown and untended, a vast hedge between it and fields behind. I'm surprised to see an impressive satellite dish, that seems newer than the surroundings, although bits of it are rusted and covered in spider webs. I try the back door, but it's locked as I expected.

I examine the upper floors and spot a half-open sash-window high above.

I can't… *I can't break in, can I?"*

I listen to my thoughts. Am I being rational? A silly question that I've never properly been able to answer all my adult life…

It's hard to tell.

But I can't call the police, because I don't know where I am and, more importantly, there's no phone signal. What would I tell them? No. I'm on my own and climbing is one of the things I'm good at. I'm doing the right thing, I'm sure of it.

Before I can change my mind, I grab hold of a sturdy drainpipe and pull myself upwards. I've always been a climber, even as a kid I used to freak out my parents by climbing to the top of trees and anywhere else I fancied. Sure, I fell a lot. I was a clumsy kid, which only added to their tensions. But, in those days, I had rubber bones, or so I believed. I was a strange child, granted. Never popular at school, but I gained a certain notoriety for my climbing antics.

Breaking into a house is an entirely different matter from climbing onto the school roof and getting a two-week detention. But I'm on a mission. A mission to save Jozee, or that's what I tell myself.

I scamper up to the first level, along a ledge to the back of the mansion and onto a small roof, realising that I'm already half way up. Ornate brickwork gives me enough foot and handholds to scale the next section until I reach the eaves and I'm onto the roof. I edge around until I find the open window and drop down, dangling my feet until they find the window sill. I fall into a crouch, push the window open and slip inside.

I'm in a fusty-smelling attic room, empty apart from a few boxes and cobwebs, the walls bare, yellowed paint cracking and flaking. Somewhere down below I hear voices. I find a landing and creep, as quietly as I can, down a flight of carpeted steps. Another landing, larger this time. Jim Laker and Nat Naylor's voices come from a room with an open door. And I'm shocked at what I'm hearing.

"…from behind. I'll edit out any shots of your face—so don't mind if you want to turn around to look at me."

The voice is unmistakably Jim Laker.

"No way!"

"Come on, Nat. I've filmed other girls. It turns them on. You'll love it. And you've a great ass, why not show it off?"

"No effing way."

"What's a matter, won't your boyfriend approve?"

"Stop going on about him! You know the pig left me for someone else."

"I do. And your comedy act is the saddest thing I've ever seen. Why do you do that to yourself night after night?"

"Eff off!"

"I'll tell you what, if you let me film you, I'll give you an extra few lines of coke."

"Make it a bag and yeah, why not?"

"A bag?"

"Yeah."

"You ain't that good a lay."

"You effing creep. Just let's get it over with, okay?"

I listen, shocked. Nat is having sex with Jim Laker for coke? And the creep wanted to film her? Is this what this is then? Another seedy hook-up?

I broke into this house to find Jozee and instead I've stumbled into a bizarre world of drugs, sex, and also porn, if Laker got his way.

They go silent apart from the slap, slap, slap of sex. I feel like a voyeur, except this isn't turning me on, quite the opposite. I feel sick to my stomach. A short time later, Laker grunts and I guess it's over.

"You done?" Nat asks.

"Yeah."

"Good, now give me my coke and let's get out of here."

I hear the clink of a belt buckle and the stumble of feet coming towards the door. I've no choice but to retrace my steps back upstairs. I turn quickly, brushing against a picture. It twists and bangs on the wall with a loud clatter.

"What was that?" Nat says. "You said we'd be on our own."

"We should be. This place is empty. It's probably only a rat."

"Don't effing say that! I hate rodents."

"Oh relax. C'mon."

I take the steps two at a time, reaching the higher landing where I first arrived, hearing Laker prowling below. Three doors. I can't remember which door I came in through and choose one at random. It's full of chairs and bits of furniture—the wrong room! On the far side is another door. I slide past the furniture and twist the doorknob, it opens to reveal a closet and I slip inside.

A moment later, I hear someone enter the room next door.

A voice muffled by the walls. "The stupid idiot. He's left the window wide open up here. Anyone could get in… not that there's anything to steal, but still…"

"He? Who does this house belong to anyway?"

"Now there's a long story. It's presently owned by a consortium as an investment and I've got a spare set of keys."

"You think someone got inside?" Nat asks. "You think they were spying on us?"

"I dunno. No one could get in through this window. It's too high up."

"Let's get out of here."

"Yeah, let's."

37

I HEAR them go downstairs and, a few seconds later, the front door bangs. I relax but stay hidden until the four-by-four starts up and drives away, before coming out, thinking about what I've just overheard. Laker getting a leg over in return for a line of coke. Of him wanting to film it.

What a creep… and he was just back in my good books.

The guy is a controller. Using coke to sleep with women. It's cheap and nasty but seemingly effective. I have to admit to myself that I'm a lot happier thinking Laker is a bastard again, even if it does lend itself to the possibility Jozee was somehow involved in this seedy world of his.

Did she come here? Did she also sleep with Laker for a line of coke?

I'm appalled at my thoughts. I love Jozee. And yet there is a growing possibility that I'm in love with a lie. It's eating me up inside.

I go back downstairs and look into the room where Laker and Nat had sex. It's a bedroom with two old-fashioned chairs, a stained mattress on the floor and a used condom lying next to it on bare floorboards.

Classy.

A single window looks out onto the overgrown front garden and the road. The four-by-four is gone. I'm hit by how quiet this place is. Like a mausoleum. I'm not one to get spooked by an empty house, but it's giving me the creeps.

I want to leave, but I must make sure Jozee isn't here. I check all the upper floor rooms before going downstairs. I find nothing, apart from a pile of yellowed paper clippings from the 70s and early 80s in an old backroom. Stuff about UK riots, IRA bombings and Madonna.

The kitchen is on two levels, and older than the rest of the house, complete with an AGA cooker and an impressive stone fireplace. I'm about to leave when I spot a door in a hidden recess. I open it, expecting to find a walk-in larder. A flight of steps plunges down into darkness. It smells odd. Of chemicals.

I find a light-switch and flick it on. Instead of a single bulb throwing scary shadows into a dank, dark, spider-infested cellar where monsters lurk, the room bursts into bright, almost blinding light. I go down the steps into a large underground room with white-painted walls in which three impressive cameras stand, surrounded by wires and professional lighting rigs. A single chair, similar to the ones I saw in the upstairs bedroom, sits in the centre, a pile of used mattresses stacked against one wall. It's obvious what all this is for.

Pornography. Has to be.

And didn't Laker want to film Nat? He has to be involved with it. Why else would he have a key to this place?

I'm disgusted.

I'm no prude and more than aware that these things go on, that places like this exist and that a lot of us, including myself, regularly use porn for um… recreational purposes. But to see this nasty-smelling cellar dedicated to such a seedy side of life is galling. The equipment looks expensive though. This is a professional operation, not some homemade webcam POV from a student's bedroom. The location is soulless, but I guess they can dress it any way they like.

I switch off the lights, make an exit by the front door, and retrace my steps to the bus stop.

38
FRIDAY EVENING

THE NEXT bus takes over an hour and a half to arrive. I stand waiting, concentrating on the road. On the sound of approaching car engines. Doing anything to keep my mind occupied. I can't find a phone signal anywhere, so I'm unable to call a taxi. And after an unimaginable wait, the bus finally arrives.

While waiting, I was able to control the surge of thoughts that were threatening to erupt back into my mind. Breathing slowly, repeating phrases and naming things. The bus, on the other hand, is too much of a challenge—packed, noisy and hot with many sweaty bodies. Shouty teenagers, overly-pungent with perfume and aftershave, inhabit most of the seats, the rest are twenty-somethings and some well-dressed older people all on their way into Brighton for a Friday night out. Excited and full of life.

Everyone except me.

Today's events have taken their toll. The police station, Pari Chabra, the perv from the hook-up site, Tom Blunt and his dubious nurse and then Laker, Nat and the sex dungeon. Now, amidst the noise and chatter of this bus from hell, trapped between the beeping phones, the tinny teen music, the shouting, shrieking, and laughing, the flickering epileptic-inducing shadows of passing trees and the unending heat, it all gets on top of me. I'm the furthest away from the good times as it's possible to be.

I'm lost in a sea of conflicting emotions and confusion. I'm sick of it. Sick of these awful feelings, sick of the hopelessness of it all, sick to death of the painful thoughts that stab into my mind like burning daggers of ice. Sick of this bus and its horrors. But more than anything, I'm sick of Jozee.

I wish I'd never met her.

Finally, we reach Brighton. I stumble out of the bus, gasping for air, swearing to myself, and getting odd looks form the other passengers, but I don't care. I'm free!

I head straight for the nearest off-licence and buy a bottle of cheap whisky, grunting at the man and paying.

Oblivion is what I crave. I know it's a terrible solution to my feelings and woes, and that tomorrow everything will feel a hundred times worse than it is now, but I need it.

I just do!

I unscrew the cap and down a third of the bottle, ignoring my gagging throat and my stomach's desire to throw up.

I call Stevo again, but he still isn't answering.

"You're a useless tosser!" I yell down my phone as passers-by give me a wide berth. Already I can feel the booze hitting my system. I completely miss the merry stage and enter full-on intoxication. I take another gulp of the bitter spirit and head towards home to the empty flat I'm beginning to despise.

"Adam? Is that you?"

A familiar voice. Ollie!

"Hey!" I shout, pleased to see a friendly face.

"You look like death, man!"

I can tell he's been drinking. He always likes a Friday night tipple.

"The Gannet has gone nuclear on you after your no-show this last couple of days—"

"Here." I offer Ollie the bottle of whisky, but he declines it.

"You know I stay off the hard stuff."

I take another long swig while Ollie looks at me with a concerned expression on his face.

"Man, what has happened to you?"

"It's Jozee!" I blurt.

"You still not found her?"

"No."

"That's terrible, man. No wonder you're in such a state. You been to the police?"

"Yeah. Useless bastards."

"She'll turn up. I'm sure of it."

"How do you know that?" I ask aggressively. "What do you know about it?"

"That you're a lucky S.O.B. She's one hot babe."

"You what?"

"She's hot. Well hot."

I push Ollie against a wall, my elbow over his throat. "Did you sleep with her? Were you fucking her?"

"Get off me, you idiot!" He easily pushes me away, knocking me to the pavement by the roadside. I'm aware of the drone of traffic as it speeds past. The concrete is warm and inviting. I stifle the urge to close my eyes and go to sleep. To leave all this behind. It would be so easy. I put the whisky bottle to my lips, but Ollie snatches it away from my weak fingers.

"Of course, I didn't sleep with your girlfriend!" he shouts, standing over me. "If she's gone, you've probably only got yourself to blame!"

He marches angrily away, leaving me lying on the street.

I prise myself into a sitting position, my lips wet. I dab a hand at my face and it comes away bloody—my lip is bleeding again. All the fight has gone from me. Whatever anger I now have is pointed at myself. I drop my head and pull my arms around my legs and start sobbing.

Revellers walk past, ignoring me. Just another drunken nutter having a breakdown on a Friday evening. Nothing to see here.

Jozee is dead. I know it. Killed by one of her many lovers.

Dead and gone.

39

I'M IN the mansion's porn dungeon, tied to a chair in the dark and howling for Jozee. I'm aware of animals prowling around me, growling and hissing. Close enough for me to smell their foul breath on my face. With a jolt, a bright, insistent light snaps on, blinding me. The light flickers and burns, and I hear Jozee screaming in the distance, calling to me, pleading for me to find her. Her screams morph into tinny, echoing music playing far away. It's familiar, important, yet I can't place it. I struggle against my bonds, but I'm tied fast and unable to move. The music stops, the light winks out and I'm suddenly alone, sinking into a deep, inviting well of blackness—a blackness that I want to envelope me forever. But the music plays again. This time, louder and more insistent.

My eyes open, I take a deep breath and start hacking. A dreadful, dry, empty cough that shudders through me.

Where the hell am I?

It takes a few moments for my eyes to adjust. I'm lying between a toilet and a bath, my mouth and throat sore, my lips stinging. My phone lies on the floor behind me, buzzing with an incoming call. The music loud in my ears. I push myself up onto all fours, and reach for it, crying out at the sudden cramp that engulfs my neck and back.

I'm at home. On the floor in my bathroom and, judging by the smell, I'm covered in vomit. I crawl to my phone, its cracked screen shining like a portal into another dimension, spinning, blurred and somehow arcane. I can't read the time or the name. It could be anybody calling me. I slam it into my ear.

"Jozee?" I say hopefully, my voice nothing more than a rasp.

"Thank god you've answered! I've been phoning you for hours," says a male voice I can't quite place. "Where've you been?"

"Who… who is this?" I say in between coughs and retches.

"It's Vinnie, innit? From ASDA. I know where Jozee is. But it's gonna cost you."

39

40

"WHERE IS she?

"Didn't you hear me? This ain't free information, geddit? I want paying."

"What?"

"You unnerstand what I mean. Meet me at the Sea Life Centre."

"At the what? Huh?"

"And bring a hundred quid. That's how much it's gonna cost you."

"A hundred quid?"

"Like I said. The Brighton Sea Life Centre as soon as you can get here. Bring the cashola."

Vinnie ends the call.

The phone winks off and I'm plunged into darkness. I stumble up to legs that feel like they belong to someone else and switch on the bathroom light, the harsh white of its naked bulb blinding me. When my bleary eyes finally adjust, I'm able to see myself in the mirror. A godawful mess. I'm covered in the chucked up remains of whisky and whatever else was in my stomach yesterday. I can remember getting off the bus, buying a bottle of whisky and… shit! A fight with Ollie.

And after that? Nothing. Another booze-induced blackout. At least I somehow managed to get home.

I pull off my vomit-covered clothes, leaving them on the bathroom floor and step into the shower, blasting myself with cold water. It does the trick. I'm shocked into wide-eyed wakefulness—well, as wide-awake as I can be after all that whisky I necked. Thankfully, Ollie took the bottle off me. Judging by how I feel—still drunk and only just able to function—that was a good thing. I'll have to smooth it over with him later. Hopefully, he'll understand. I towel myself down and get quickly dressed. I check the time, 3.20am.

Won't the Sea Life Centre be closed?

I don't care. Vinnie knows where Jozee is and I need that information. Having something to do focuses my mind. Stops the ever-present swirl of thoughts. I wonder if I should call the police, but I want to hear from Vinnie myself. I want to hear what he has to say, what he knows. Waiting on the cops is not going to help my mental state. Not one bit.

I order a taxi, pick up my vomity clothes and decide to throw them away. I exit the flat, closing my door as quietly as I can—I've no idea how much noise I made when I came in, but I'm guessing I wasn't quiet. I'm sure Clive will tell me the next time I see him.

I'm still dizzy but manage to get down the stairs to the outside communal bin with no injury. I throw in my clothes and close the lid just as the taxi arrives. I tell the driver my destination—the Sea Life Centre.

"You going to that sit-in, huh?" he asks.

"Sit in?"

"Yeah, an all-nighter to raise awareness about the danger of plastic to ocean life."

He drops me off near a cashpoint in Central Brighton and I withdraw one-hundred pounds. I don't have savings to speak of—who does?—and this will create a sizable dent in my already flagging finances, but I'll pay anything to find Jozee.

The Sea Life Centre is situated off the roundabout in front of the Palace Pier and down a serious set of wide steps. I'm greeted at the entrance by some enthusiastic types with buckets and t-shirts, although they look at each other with alarm when they see the state of me. Hair still wet, lip swollen, covered in bruises and stinking of whisky. I shrug, drop them a fiver and go inside, entering an underground complex.

The air is refreshingly cool down here and I soon start shivering. Fish tanks line one side of an impressive entrance hall at the end of which is a brightly lit wider area. I walk towards it, my eyes flicking around for any sign of Vinnie. The wider area is full of displays highlighting the dangers of plastic in the ocean. A hundred or so children are with their parents and minders. Some are asleep in sleeping bags, while others are singing songs. An open, shallow pool sits on one side in which manta rays splash.

The place is strewn with banners—turtles befouled with plastic bags, a dead whale with its stomach contents showing intestines full of plastic items, and close-ups of the dreaded microbeads.

I still can't see any sign of Vinnie.

I walk past the kids, who give me sideways looks, and go further into the complex. The centre is enormous and not at all what I was expecting. I've lived in Brighton for years and never visited. It's amazing. I make a mental note to bring Jozee here once this madness is behind us. She'd love it… I catch my thoughts. After everything I've found out about her, the likelihood of us being together seems more and more doubtful.

I quickly go through a few of the rooms—a tour of sorts. One with giant red crabs, another with a starfish display. There are jellyfish, sea horses, and hundreds and hundreds of other fish. Some enormous, staring at me with big sad eyes.

I enter an underwater section. A tunnel running below a vast marine tank. Here are sharks, manta rays, turtles and more fish, swimming above.

"Oi!" says a voice behind me. "You deaf as well as blind?"

I turn to see an agitated-looking Vinnie wearing a bright blue Sea Life Centre volunteer t-shirt. "Huh?"

"I was calling to you. You walked straight past me."

I shrug. "Where's Jozee?"

He comes closer, his nose wincing. "What have you been drinking? Whisky? You know that stuff rots your liver, don't you?"

"Where is she?" I say, raising my voice, wondering why he's being so judgemental.

"Well that's the rub, isn't it?"

"Just tell me."

"She's left you mate. Done a runner."

"I Iuh?"

"I liked Jozee. She was always very friendly to me. But don't worry, she's not my type."

"What do you mean, she's done a runner?" I say, my dull-head under attack from a sudden jolt of adrenaline.

"She's left Brighton ain't she? Gone to live in London with a friend."

"No… that's not possible. It's not true."

"Jozee left a forwarding address with one of the other ASDA girls. One of my bitches, if you know what I mean?" He cockily pulls back his shoulders and I stifle the urge to punch him. Even so, his words cut into me.

"She really was leaving me?" I say, my voice breaking, finding it hard to process.

"Don't start blubbing on me, okay? Cos I don't give a rat's ass. Now pay up. I'm skint. I thought if I could get you to turn up here in the middle of the night, then I'd know just how important the information was to you. And here you are. So… if you want Jozee's address this badly, it's now gonna cost two-hundred quid. I'll unnerstand if you ain't got it on you, but I don't mind waiting until you find a cash point. I've got plenty of time and—"

I lunge at him, knocking him into the plastic, underwater walls, startling a shoal of fish. The attack is instinctual, visceral—a response to everything that's been going on over the last few days. I've finally had enough. And there's no way I'm letting this vile teenager extort my hard-earned cash. No way.

I punch him once, twice, three times, and, for good measure, I knee him hard in the groin.

"You want some more?" I shout, but the knee to his happy sacks has done all the damage I need.

Vinnie crumples to the floor, grabbing his groin with both hands and groaning. And suddenly I feel guilty. He's just a kid. Cocky, irritating and seedy, but just a kid.

A quick search through his pockets produces a piece of paper with an address in North London near Wood Green and the word 'Jozee' scribbled above.

"I'm sorry," I say, "but you need to learn not to push desperate people. *Unnerstand?*"

If my words have any effect on him, I can't tell. I leave him crumpled on the floor, silently watched by the sharks and turtles. I stalk out of the Sea Life Centre and into the balmy night, heading past the Old Steine up to Brighton Station and the first train to London.

41

SATURDAY MORNING

SLEEPING OUTSIDE Brighton station is not possible, I realise, as I'm moved on by an over-friendly policeman. I make my way to the back of the station to an over-ground car park, where I catch a couple of hours kip in a stairwell before the first train to London departs at 6.23am.

The station opens long before then. I get myself a coffee and a croissant and find a hopefully quiet seat on the unfortunately-named *Gatwick Express.*

After the shocks of the past two days, I find I'm becoming immune to the revelations about Jozee. If Vinnie is to be believed, Jozee was planning to leave me.

Has left me, I correct myself. It's very likely she has moved to the address I've got in my pocket.

The information grates. But it doesn't change what's been bugging me ever since this thing started… *Jozee wouldn't leave without telling me, without letting me know.*

Sure, she could've left the Dog and Duck in Burgess Hill and driven straight to London. But Jozee would've at least called the next day to dump me over the phone. For her to stay silent, and to also miss gigs without contacting promotors to apologise, was not like her at all. Jozee wouldn't do any of that… *would she?* I see a vision of that creep, *BigManInYorFace* and his printouts from the hook-up site. If Jozee was capable of sleeping with other guys behind my back, what else was this other Jozee capable of?

These thoughts spin around dizzily in my head. Jozee good, Jozee bad. Jozee evil and cruel.

My phone is almost out of charge again. I should call DC Marley to tell her about the address. But if Jozee is in London, I want to talk to her face to face, without the police alerting her.

I text Ollie, apologising to him.

Sorry mate. I messed up. Big-time. I'll make it up to you.

It is too early for a reply, but I feel better knowing I've at least tried to put things right. Ollie looked up to me, although I doubt he will do so from now on.

The train is sparsely populated, mostly people travelling to Gatwick Airport, judging by their travel bags. I catch some sleep, waking up as the train pulls into Victoria. The last time I was here was only two days ago, but it already feels like a lifetime. I check Vinnie's address again. The nearest tube station is Turnpike Lane, North London, on the Piccadilly Line. Twenty minutes later I emerge from the Tube into another bright, sunny morning. The time is 7.52am, and even at this early hour, the sun burns.

The address is on Boundary Road, a short walk away. I arrive to find a pleasant-looking house with two floors and bay windows. Feeling sick, and also a little relieved that this is nearly over, I ring the doorbell.

42

A SHORT, nervy wait and the door is answered, a sturdy chain preventing it opening further than a few inches. A young woman in her early thirties, rotund, chubby-faced with no makeup and an untidy blonde bob—like she'd just woken up—sticks her head into the gap.

"Yeah?"

Her voice reminds me of Jozee's North London accent, although she sounds a lot sterner.

"Hello," I say, suddenly feeling weary. "I'm here to see Jozee Jackson. Can you tell her Adam is outside and that he'd desperately like to talk to her."

Her eyebrows furrow and her jaw clenches. "Adam, her boyfriend?"

I nod.

"She's not here, goodbye." The woman tries to close the door, but I block it with my foot. "Remove yourself, or I'm phoning the police!"

"Just tell me if Jozee is here, safe and well, and I'll go."

"Get out!"

She pushes her considerable weight against the heavy door, crushing my foot, making me wince.

"Okay, okay, I'll go," I say through the pain. "I've made a police report about her disappearance. Ring Brighton police and ask for DC Marley. Just tell her Jozee is here, safe and okay."

"Go!"

"I can't, you're trapping my foot."

She releases the pressure just enough for me to pull my foot free and slams the door.

I put my mouth to the letter box. "If she's here, tell her to come to the coffee house on the main street. I'll wait there until I either hear from the police or... or Jozee can come and talk to me herself. If she wants."

"Go away!" the woman shouts.

"I'll be waiting at the coffee shop."

43

THE COFFEE has a nasty taste to it, probably due to my last remaining taste-bud after two consecutive nights of vomiting. The café is a Polish place and, other than the vile coffee, it is warm and inviting. Not what I was expecting from 'cold London'. Metal-rimmed, cheap tables sit on equally cheap red and yellow lino, the walls are hung with jarring blue and white, thick-brush paintings of rural scenes and in a corner sits an umbrella rack stuffed with tree branches covered in pink ribbons and fairy lights. Somehow it works. Maybe there's a Polish equivalent of Feng Shui I know nothing about? Anything is possible, I suppose. A more traditional chalkboard lists various foods and drinks, although a few spelling errors and a host of errant apostrophes preclude me from ever eating here. And as for the *Hacked Meat Fingers,* the less said the better.

A few people sit on the mostly empty tables, but the place is still busy with a steady stream of punters queueing for take-out coffee.

My phone sits on the table in front of me, attached to a charger, courtesy of the waitress, to whom I'm very much grateful. DC Marley might phone at any time and I need the battery. I can't stop staring at its cracked screen. Willing it to ring. Trying to use some previously unknown power of coercion to make the thing light up and buzz. To end this living hell I find myself in.

A message arrives. It's from Vinnie.

> *No one messes with me. I'm gonna do you for what you did!*
> *You owe me and I'm gonna get my money. I'm coming for you!*

I dismiss his threats for what they are, the empty bleating of some stupid kid, although my inner Neanderthal almost wishes that he would try and have a go at me. There was something pleasing about beating up on the kid, despite wanting to think otherwise.

Was it justice being righteously served on an extortionist scumbag or something more visceral? At this point, I don't care.

I'm sitting by the plug socket on a far wall and, from this position, I'm unable to see the door. I told myself this would calm me, but it's put me even more on edge.

I hear the door open for the umpteenth time. I've been here nearly forty minutes, and my heart still flutters at the jingle of its old-fashioned bell.

The footsteps of someone approaching, coming closer. Heavy footsteps, not Jozee. I glance up to see the woman I met at Jozee's address—her hair is no longer unkempt, her face made-up.

"You still here, huh?" she says, nodding to the waitress and ordering a coffee.

I say nothing, hoping that she is going to tell me Jozee is okay. That she's around the corner, working on gags and watching TV. Safe in this woman's house.

"You're right," she says finally, sitting down opposite me. "I've been phoning around. Jozee hasn't been seen for a few days. I'm Angela, by the way. One of Jozee's school-friends. Angela Phillips."

"What!" I say, raising my voice. "She's not living with you? She has to be… unless you're lying."

Her coffee arrives. She takes a sip, froth coating her upper lip, but she doesn't notice.

"Jozee told me you were highly strung, she wasn't wrong."

"But—"

"If Jozee was at my flat, I'd tell you," Angela says matter-of-factly. "I wouldn't mess you about. No way. My sister disappeared years ago. Not knowing where she had gotten to was the worst thing that ever happened to me and my family. She'd run off to some cult. And you know what they can be like? She's back with us now. But not the same. That's why if Jozee had moved in a few days earlier than we'd arranged, I wouldn't lie or let Jozee lie about this to you. Okay?"

My world shifts. Jozee was actually leaving me to come and live here with Angela Phillips in North London. It's true then… *I don't know Jozee at all.* How could that have happened? I loved her, or I thought I did. I was hoping Vinnie had lied to me. Was making the whole thing up for a bit of cash. A slim hope, that I never consciously considered, now dashed.

"She loves you very much," Angela continues. "But with everything that happened a couple of years ago—"

"You mean with Tom? Tom Blunt?"

Angela nods, her impressive jowls wobbling. "Jozee said she'd made a mistake. Moving in with you happened too fast. She wasn't over all those dreadful events. You can imagine? Dumping Tom like she did on that awful video and the next day… just horrible. I think she felt trapped."

Trapped? I can't believe what I'm hearing.

"The way she told it to me was that she needed a bit of space to process things. But I got the impression that she was hoping you'd still be there for her afterwards."

I shake my head, wanting to shut her out. Wanting to scream and shout that this was all wrong. That she was lying. To pick up her coffee mug and throw it at the wall. But… I do nothing.

"Jozee is still in shock about what happened with Tom. Unable to get over it, although she said going out with you helped. Until, well, I suppose you being here means you know all about what happened? Her terrible mistake?"

I say nothing, just giving her the barest nod of my head.

"Sleeping with someone she shouldn't have… it made Jozee realise that she wasn't ready for another relationship. She couldn't bear hurting you. That's why she was leaving. To live here in London for a month or two to sort her head out once and for all."

Of course, I know Jozee is sleeping with other people, the ones on that seedy www.instanthookup.co.uk website, but hearing this from Angela somehow makes it more real. "Just the one mistake?" I reply with a sneer.

"What do you mean by that?" she says pulling back.

"I mean that she's been sleeping with more than this one person you mention. God knows how many other people she's been seeing behind my back."

"What are you talking about?"

"It doesn't matter," I say sullenly.

Up to now, Angela has been supportive, but her face becomes suddenly hard. "Do you know where Jozee is?"

"Huh? Why would you say that? Of course I don't. I'm trying to find her."

She shrugs. "Jozee was leaving you. She told me it was because she'd made the mistake of sleeping with someone she should have stayed a long way away from. That it made her rethink her life and her relationship. And that she was going to come clean and tell you all about it. And yet here you are telling me Jozee has gone missing. Don't you think that sounds a little suspicious?"

I can't properly take in her words. "What?"

"I wasn't born yesterday, Adam. Isn't this the kind of thing a guilty boyfriend would do? Kill their girlfriend, and then do everything to cover their tracks, including coming here to give me a bullshit story about trying to find her?"

Her words are accusing, but they are spoken flatly, her eyes staring into mine as if trying to divine the answer.

"I'm no murderer!" I blurt and everyone in the coffee shop looks up. "You shouldn't go around accusing people like that. It's slander. You'll be telling me next that you read too many mystery novels."

Her sudden flush of embarrassment tells me that I've hit the mark.

"This is no cheesy mystery," I say. "This is Jozee and she isn't dead, she can't be."

"Well, I for one think this very suspicious."

"I don't care what you think, okay? Maybe whoever she slept with has something to do with her disappearance. Isn't that just as likely?" I'm clutching at straws, but I can see doubt crossing her face. "Did she tell you who this mystery person was? Jim Laker? Vinnie? *BigManInYorface?* Or was it a woman?"

Angela says nothing for a few moments, before continuing. "Jozee doesn't call me very often, so it didn't bother me that I'd not heard from her for a few days, but let me tell you, Adam Hanson, regardless of my interest in mysteries, I'm now very worried about her safety. About what you may have done to her."

"You can't be serious? I'm trying to find her! I'm the only one trying to find her! No one else gives a damn. Besides, Jozee is not all black and white. She has dark secrets. She meets men on pick-up sites. Pervs who come around to our flat when I'm out. Has sex with them. That's the kind of girl she really is." I reach into my jeans for the printouts that creep *BigManInYorFace* thrust into my face yesterday to show Angie and prove my point, realising that I've left them in my other, vomited-covered, jeans. The ones I threw out before my meeting with Vinnie.

Dammit!

It's obvious Angela doesn't believe me. And I understand why. I sound like a mad, possessive boyfriend who's convinced himself his girlfriend is sleeping with every other guy. Just like all the murderous lovers in her cheap mystery novels.

Angela pushes her substantial bulk up onto her feet. "You told me to phone DC Marley at Brighton police station. And believe me, if Jozee doesn't turn up soon, I will certainly be in contact. Goodbye, Adam."

She stomps out of the coffee shop, while everyone else stares at me.

"What?" I say belligerently.

A few moments later, the waitress unplugs her charger from my phone and nods towards the door.

"I'm no murderer!" I shout as I leave.

44

I MAKE my way back to Victoria Station in an angry daze and get on the next available train to Hove, grabbing a sandwich and a bottle of water on the way.

I eat mechanically, hardly tasting the 'Gourmet Chicken'—not that there's that much to taste. Flavour is not high on the station sandwich priorities list—unlike impenetrable plastic wrapping, a list of preservatives as long as my arm and exorbitant pricing. But my body needs fuel. I've not been eating properly since Jozee went missing. Hell, I've not been doing anything properly.

I shouldn't be surprised that Angela found me a suspicious character, turning up at her house unannounced. Bruised and with a cut lip. The boyfriend Jozee had cheated on. And on top of that, for her to then discover Jozee was missing.

At least she's as worried about Jozee as I am, even if that worry seems to come from her interest in mystery novels and her belief I'm some kind of murderer. I wonder how many others are wondering if I had anything to do with Jozee's disappearance? Boyfriends and spouses were usually to blame when their other halves went missing.

And I don't have an alibi.

No one saw Jozee drive off on her own. I was too embarrassed to go back into the Dog and Duck. Instead, I made my own way home. The events are a little hazy, due to the booze. I only came back to my senses when I found myself hanging onto the wall outside my flat and nearly falling.

Who would believe that as an alibi? No one, that's who.

I'm halfway to Hove when my phone rings. The battery is still very low, but it should last until I get home, and I need to be connected. I'm hoping it's Stevo, or even Jozee, but instead, it's Sally, Tom's enterprising and morally dubious nurse.

"Is that Adam Blunt," Nurse Sally says. "You never did give me your proper name."

"Yeah, it's Adam," I say, thinking that to give this girl my full name is a bad idea. "Have you heard from Jozee?"

"No. I haven't I'm afraid, but I did remember something about her visits."

"You did?"

"She normally arrived in a tiny white mini, but sometimes she got a lift in this fantastic old car. Maroon in colour, like a Rolls Royce."

"What did you say?"

"A posh old car. A beautiful thing."

"Stevo's Rover P5!"

"Huh? Who's Stevo? The ape in the driving seat?"

"Ape?"

"Yeah, a humongous guy. And sexy. You know what I mean?"

And again, I'm reeling. Stevo? What is he doing giving lifts to Jozee? He must've known about Tom all the time. And why do that behind my back? I know he's always had a thing for Jozee, but I was his friend long before Jozee came on the scene. Could he be involved in her disappearance? It seems a ridiculous idea—the guy is harmless, isn't he?

"You still there?"

"Yeah. Sorry. Did you see or find out anything else?"

"No. But if you want to come and visit Tom again, I'll be happy to let you in."

"Didn't you hear? I've been banned by the family."

"Yeah. But don't let that worry you."

"I don't think I'll be going back, but thanks for the offer."

"Okay, but if you want anything else, I am—"

I off the phone and sit back in my train seat.

Shit!

45

THOUGHTS REGARDING Stevo's involvement with Jozee play on my mind all the way to Hove station. Phoning him gets the same response I've had for two days now—his mobile rings out until I get his answering service.

My battery is down to 3% which means that it could blink off at any time. Even so, I decide to phone Stevo's work number—the one he gave me for emergencies only. It's Saturday, but he regularly works weekends. His office is one of those twenty-four seven operations. After a rather long and overly-convoluted process of locating him via the company switchboard, I'm finally put in contact with his line manager.

"Hello, may I ask who's speaking?"

"Adam. I'm wondering if—"

"Your full name please."

"Is that important?"

"Yes. I'm afraid we don't reply to anonymous calls. Your full name is…?"

"Adam Hanson. I'm the best mate of one of your employees, Stevo. I mean Stephen Stevens. Is he there? I'd like to speak to him."

A long pause. "Mr Stevens hasn't been in the office since Thursday afternoon. He's disappeared. We can't get in touch with him either."

"Isn't that a little odd? Stevo, I mean, Mr Stevens, taking time off work? He's always telling me he's never missed a single day."

"It is especially out of character, as this is a very… um… busy time for us. Which is why I let this call through, normally personal calls are not allowed."

"What is it you do again?"

"Mr Stevens didn't tell you?"

"Data or finance or some-such."

"If you find Mr Stevens, can you please tell him to contact us ASAP. Thank you."

A click. "You still there? Hello?" The line is dead.

Stevo is missing as well? Feeling angrier than I am concerned, I phone Stevo again, using the last few drops of phone battery to leave him a message.

"I know all about you and Jozee, and your secret trips to Haywards Heath to visit Tom. If you have any idea where Jozee is, you need to get in contact with me now. Oh, and your boss is looking for you as well. But, Stevo, what you've done, going behind my back, it's…" I take a deep breath, unsure what I'm going to say next, and my phone finally dies.

I exit Hove station and take a quick walk home. It's a warm and sunny day. Glorious in fact. The days have been getting steadily hotter and hotter. The sun is shining brightly, the sky an iridescent blue, and yet I can't enjoy any of it. The storm clouds that have dogged me for the last few days will not go away. They crowd inside my head, black and threatening. Rumbling. Regardless of the heatwave.

I arrive back at the flat at around noon, increasing my pace as I get closer. I need to get my phone on charge. With it dead and blank in my pocket, I feel cut off from the world. I jog up the stairs and stop in my tracks when I reach the top floor.

A bouquet of elegantly wrapped, but dead flowers lies outside my flat door. The flowers are brown and decaying. I pick them up, my nose wincing at the smell. Rotten and like someone had urinated on them. A card falls out. I pick it up and read the printed note.

Watchin out for you hun xxx

Jozee? I run into my flat, throwing the flowers into my bin, before completing my now customary search of rooms, cupboards and under my bed. Jozee isn't here, of course she isn't.

I look for my phone charger, but it's not where I normally keep it plugged in. With growing frustration, I check the bedroom and the other places where I sometimes leave it. The thing has disappeared. It makes no sense. I even check the bin, lifting out the stinking dead flowers.

Not there.

I resist the urge to run around my flat, ranting and screaming about the unfair, totally screwed-up mental-ness of it all—which I've done far too many times—and decide, alternatively, to forego all the shouting and kicking of inanimate objects, and try to look for a rational explanation.

I came home last night paralytic after drinking two-thirds of a bottle of whisky. Who knew what I did before I woke up passed out in the toilet? I've had the occasional drunken blackout and found out that, during that time, I've acted quite rationally, if not very oddly. It was very possible I had something to do with its whereabouts.

I decide to make myself a cup of tea and to logically work out where the charger might have gotten to and…

The cord to the kettle is also missing!

"What the bollocks!" I shout, slamming the kettle down so hard that I think I may have broken it and then slamming it down again to make doubly sure that's what I have done.

I methodically check the flat after that, finding that all my power cables and lap top chargers are missing. Either I was so drunk last night that I decided on getting rid of them all—for a reason I can't possibly fathom—or…

Someone has been inside my flat.

If anyone would notice someone entering my flat, that anyone is Clive, my nosey next-door neighbour. I go and bang on his door.

No answer.

"Clive! Are you in there?" I shout, knocking even more loudly.

He hardly ever leaves his flat. Especially on a weekend. He doesn't like the crowds, preferring early morning walks down the beach and off-peak shopping.

"Clive!"

Nothing.

A memory slips into my mind. When I first moved in here, two years ago, it was Clive who let me in. Clive who had a set of keys to my flat. He was acting as the landlord's agent. Did he still have a set of keys? Could he let himself into my flat anytime he wanted? Could he have done this in a fit of pique? It seemed dreadfully passive-aggressive, then again, that was Clive all over.

I bang on his door a few more times, loudly shouting his name. Someone from the floor below shouts up the stairs, a concerned male voice. "Is everything okay up there?"

I ignore him, returning to my flat and slamming the door, hit by the stink of those disgusting flowers. I pick them up and take them downstairs to the outside communal rubbish bin, lifting the large lid and throwing them inside. And as the lid drops back into place, I notice my vomit-covered clothes. I must've been still half-cut when I threw them away this morning, those jeans are new and expensive. They just need a wash. I reach in to fish them out and, stuffed down the back of the bin, is a bag full of my missing cables and laptop chargers. Not thrown in casually, but deliberately hidden.

I return to my flat, turn out the contents of the cable bag onto my kitchen top and jump back in alarm. Three dead sparrows drop out, the ones I put in my trash days ago, except that someone has ripped their wings off.

Huh?

I can't imagine that in my drunken state last night that I efficiently hunted down all my power cables, put them in a bag and stuffed them down the back of the rubbish skip, adding a few dead mutilated sparrows as some psychotic artistic touch. There's no way I'd cut myself off from Jozee, drunk or not. *Is there?*

I've done some very odd things in my time, especially when drunk, but never anything like this.

I'm guessing the person who hid my chargers is the same person who left those flowers outside. I read the note again.

Watchin out for you hun xxx

Jozee liked her pranks, but this isn't funny. It is 'malicious'. Like those pizzas that turned up the other night. Despite everything I've found out about Jozee, I can't believe it's her who has done this. *I just can't.*

I wrap up the dead birds in clingfilm and throw them back in my bin and plug in my phone, watching it keenly until it finally bursts into life. I give it a few minutes to update with any new messages or missed calls, but it remains depressingly silent.

It's now I could really do with a cup of tea and a ponder, but having killed my kettle earlier, this is no longer an option.

If Jozee didn't do this, then who? Clive? He's melodramatic and passive-aggressive. But I can't imagine him touching those dead birds or those flowers. I'll still need to have a word with my nosey neighbour, to see if he saw or heard anything, and to ask him if he still has a set of keys to my flat. After that… there's no one else I can think of. The whole thing is just too bizarre.

Stevo?

I have a mental image of him quietly entering my flat, searching for all my cables and chargers. The image doesn't gel with the big lumbering oaf at all. But what do I really know anymore?

There is one thing left to do. I search my vomit-covered jeans rescued from the skip for the card DC Marley gave me at the station yesterday. It's wet and a little manky, but serviceable. The printouts that that perv left aren't there. I must've dropped them sometime yesterday. I don't care, it's not something I want to be reminded about.

I tap the number into my phone and I'm surprised when it's immediately answered by DC Marley.

"Someone has broken into my flat," I tell her. "And they left flowers!"

"Who is this?"

"Adam Hanson. My girlfriend, Jozee Jackson, is missing. Remember? You told me to phone if anything came up."

"Oh right. Adam. You say you've been broken into, burgled, and they left you… *flowers?*"

"Dead ones."

"How did they get in?"

"I don't know."

"Wasn't the door jimmied or broken?"

"No, but they've been inside."

"Did they ransack the place?"

"No, no. Nothing was disturbed."

A short pause. "What items did they steal?"

"All my wires and chargers… why would they do that? Although I found them again. And why the flowers? It's like a threat, a threat I don't understand. They were dead and bad-smelling. Like someone had pissed on them. You need to send someone over to dust the place for prints."

Another pause, this one significantly longer, long enough for me to realise how lame I sound.

"This seems more like a prank, don't you think? Or… and I want you to think about this very carefully… it could be your missing girlfriend, Jozee Jackson, messing with you. You told me she was a comedian. If anything, this suggests to me she's alive and well, which is good news."

"No, it can't be. It's not her. She wouldn't do this to me. She's missing. This is the work of the person who abducted her. I'm sure of it."

"Does Jozee have a set of keys?"

"Yes, of course."

"Then you must consider the possibility that it was her. The missing person report is now official, if you do hear from her, please make sure you let me know. Have you found out anything else?"

"She… she was leaving me," I blurt down the phone in frustration. This wasn't the way this conversation was meant to be going. "I talked to her friend in London. Angela Phillips. Someone she knew from school. Jozee was going to move there in a day or two, after talking to me. She's not heard from Jozee either. Angela told me she was thinking about phoning you."

"Angela Phillips hasn't contacted me so far. I'm afraid that in this situation, unless more information is unearthed, or… a body is found, there is nothing more I can do for you. If you want to report this as an illegal entry to a property I can put you through to the appropriate department. But this will, most likely, not result in a visit to your residence and will be given low priority as nothing was stolen. Would you like me to do that for you?"

"No."

"Is there anything else you want to tell me?"

"Jozee had an argument with a comedian friend, Shirley Sands, the night before she disappeared."

"What was that about?"

"I… I don't know. She wouldn't tell me. Said it wasn't relevant."

"If you think she might know something, I suggest you go and talk to her again. Sometimes people can hold clues without realising it."

"I'll do that ASAP."

"Good. It's still early days. Hang on in there."

I sit back on my sofa, resisting the urge to throw my still recharging phone against the wall. But DC Marley is right, I don't know anything concrete. I should've pushed Shirley Sands harder for the truth.

46

SATURDAY AFTERNOON

I OPEN my eyes and yawn. I must've nodded off. I check my phone. Forty minutes later and 100% battery.

I unplug it and stand up. It was only a short snooze, but I feel refreshed.

I'm keen to go and see Shirley Sands again but, I decide she can wait. I have a more important concern.

Myself.

I've let things go these last few days. Becoming a dishevelled, drunken mess. I can't go on like this anymore. *I just can't.*

I shave, shower and re-dress my cut hand. Afterwards, I take another look at myself in the mirror, rubbing away the condensation with the palm of my hand. My lip is still swollen, I have a few large bruises from where I fell off that alley wall, and my foot hurts from Angela's front door, but I'm almost presentable.

My head is calm, calmer than it's been for a while. Change is hard for us Aspies. It's challenging. Finding out Jozee was in the process of leaving me, and that she was sleeping with other people behind my back, is hard to accept. I'm not without emotion, if anything, I'm over-sensitive. But, as I often say to myself, *it is what it is.* I haven't spent a lifetime suffering from this condition without learning to adapt. Some might say, an Aspie's life is only that—adapting to a world we don't fit into. Or at least trying our best not to stick out too much.

I don't like what I've found out about Jozee, and the inevitable change it has wrought upon my life… but I can't do anything about it. I'll just have to live with it, like I do with all the other shit. But, believe me, it doesn't make me happy.

I still love Jozee. It's that love that has kept me going this far. Mistaken or misguided it may be, but it's what I feel. And I feel my emotions ever so intensely. The love belongs to me and me alone. Jozee's lovers, ex-boyfriends and even Jozee herself can never take that away from me. It's love that is driving me now, pushing me ever forward to get to the bottom of this. But I won't do it on an empty stomach. I need to eat, even if I'm not feeling hungry. I make myself a cheese and mushroom omelette with a side-salad of the remaining vegetables that are not presently composting in my fridge, glancing again at Jozee's goat's milk, my bottom lip trembling.

"And I'm stopping drinking," I say out loud. This time, when I see Shirley Sands, I'm going to be stone cold sober.

I arrive at Shirley Sands' building after a short bus ride. The outer door is propped open, allowing me to walk inside and up to her flat door… which is also propped open.

"Shirley?" I say, walking inside. "Shirley? You there?"

I'm surprised by Billy Belter who walks out of the kitchen area holding a clipboard.

"Shirley?" He says with a smirk. "*Shirley* you're mistaken."

47

"WHAT ARE you doing here?"

"I could ask you the same question," Billy replies. "This is one of Cheryl's flats. She has quite a wide-ranging property portfolio, don't you know. Quite the property magnate. I'm more of a fridge magnet, myself, ha-ha! I'm her handyman so to speak."

I give him a confused stare.

"I look after all of her properties," Billy explains. "Organise plumbers, painting, other stuff she doesn't want to deal with. It's how I keep myself in her good books. I'm just checking this vacated flat for any damage, etc. Now let me ask you the same question? What are you doing here? And what happened to your face? Ouch!"

"You say the flat was recently vacated?" I reply, ignoring him. "This is where Shirley Sands lived."

"Shirley Sands? The hot comic with the devastatingly long legs? She lived here?" Billy winks at me. "Wish I'd known. I have a spare set of keys!" He guffaws at his own joke. "She's a mad one, her. Bonkers. I love that in a young woman."

I'm a little bemused. This is not what I was expecting and already I can feel my newly acquired calmness retreating. Why has Shirley felt the need to also disappear? Just what is she hiding?

"Not very PC, I admit," Billy continues. "And of course, I never use my keys to enter one of Cheryl's flats without arranging with the occupant first. If they want me to enter them afterwards, then it's all above board. Wahey! As long as Cheryl doesn't get to hear about it," he adds conspiratorially, "otherwise she'd wear my guts for garters."

"You didn't know Shirley Sands lived here?"

"Nope. I'm responsible for all the bricks and mortar, Cheryl is the one who deals with the paperwork and the money—which she keeps a tight hold of. She won't let me go near it, tight-fisted cow! …Only joking of course. I love my Cheryl."

"Don't you think Shirley leaving like this, seems a little sudden?"

He shrugs. "The keys were handed in this morning by the tenant who voluntarily terminated the tenancy. I'm just here to do a quick check for damage and the like. Her personal belongings were picked up by some guy before you arrived."

"Some guy? Who?"

"Dunno, *just some guy.*"

"You know where he was taking her things? Her new address?"

"I couldn't give you those details, even if I wanted to."

"But you could find out, couldn't you, as a special favour? I covered for you the other night with Cheryl, remember?"

Billy gives me a pitying smile. "Okay, I'll take a look as soon as I get back home—but promise to keep it schtum, okay? I'm not joking about Cheryl. She has a temper that one."

"Thanks."

"And if I do find Shirley's address, don't tell her. I don't want that crazy bitch on my back… I'd much prefer her on my front, if you know what I mean? Wahey!"

"This isn't funny," I say with more than a little irritation. "Jozee's still missing!"

"Sorry mate. Just my way. You know that. Billy Belter… always belting them out. Can't help myself. Still no word from Jozee, then? That's gotta be rough. Especially after that argument you had."

"I'm worried, Billy, very worried."

"I can see you're upset. I'm almost done here, you want to go for a drink? It's the afternoon, so no foul."

I don't like Billy, I never have. I'm not sure why. He's always mostly friendly, if not crass, and unintentionally rude, but I've already had enough of him and his 'banter'. "Thanks, but no. Do you mind if I look around?"

"No problem, but I think Shirley's taken all her dirty knickers, more's the pity!"

I leave Billy behind to get on with whatever he's doing. The flat is very much as it was when I came here before. Almost as if Shirley wasn't actually living here at all.

And then I remember. Shirley sitting on her sofa after moving a large box.

Was she packing to leave? She must've been. Why didn't I notice?

I enter her bedroom, feeling like a trespasser. A double bed complete with bedclothes sits against the far wall. I remember barging in here the other night looking for Jozee. I'd acted like a fool. I should've stayed and got Shirley to tell me everything when I had the chance instead of freaking her out.

I call Billy. "She's left her bedclothes. That's odd isn't it?" I say to him when he pokes his head through the doorway.

"In this game, nothing's odd. You should hear about some of the things I've found. Worse than a vibrator or two, I can tell you. But we always get a new bed in when a tenant moves out. Cheryl's orders." His phone buzzes. "I gotta go. Can you pull the doors shut before you leave? And don't shit in the bed… not unless you film it!" He winks and leaves.

I wander around the bedroom. All scrupulously clean. No dust. I check the two bedside cabinets. Nothing. I'm about to go when I spot the corner of something sticking out from under the bed.

I grab it, unable to process what I'm seeing, but there can be no mistake. It's an old photograph of Jozee and Tom hugging each other. Jozee has her face crossed out by something sharp.

48

I HOLD onto my calm all the way back home, although the extraordinary photograph is playing on my mind. Why would Shirley Sands have crossed out Jozee's face? It smacked of a weird obsession. Even hatred.

I know next to nothing about Shirley Sands. About any of the comics. For instance, I thought Nat Naylor was a sweet, monogamous girl very much devoted to and in love with her boyfriend. A pretence that extended beyond her stage act. But what I'd heard from her and Jim Laker in that deserted Sussex mansion, had shown her in a totally different light. No boyfriend, taking drugs, and screwing Jim Laker for a few lines of cocaine.

I suppose it's true what they say, below the smiles and the jokes, comedians are all a bunch of desperate-to-be-loved fuck-ups with secrets to hide.

What secrets does Shirley Sands have? I need to find out soon. I will go and ask her when Billy gets me her new address. In the meantime, there's nothing I can do. I decide to use this time to go over everything I've learned.

I put on my brand-new kettle that I bought on the way back to the flat and brew myself a pot of tea. I sit on my sofa, staring at the teapot, hot air gently rattling the lid, hissing and sputtering. Tea is a ritual for many. For me, it's a way to relax, a form of meditation. Shirley Sands' photo agitates me but, for now, I put it out of my mind.

Since Jozee has gone missing from my life those few days ago, I've found out almost too much about her.

Jozee had been responsible for the suicide attempt of her ex-boyfriend who she was regularly visiting behind my back. She'd been possibly punishing herself for this by picking up internet strangers for sex. And, if using a hook-up site wasn't enough, according to Angela, she'd also recently slept with someone 'who she shouldn't have'—I'm guessing it's someone I know, very probably Jim Laker or, if her hook-up profile was to be believed, possibly Shirley Sands or even Nat Naylor. An event that had pushed her over the edge—after which she became cold towards me. She'd reassessed her life and had decided to leave Brighton and… *to leave me.* To tell me everything, before running away to London to sort herself out.

It was obvious going out with me was something she regretted. Was she frightened she'd do the same to me as she did to Tom? It seemed very likely.

If I'd only stayed sober on the night of that gig, none of this would've happened!

I shake my head. *What ifs* will not help. They never do. Only cool logic.

Jozee missed two gigs. One of them for Donnie Coogan, Brighton's biggest amateur promotor. She missed her shift at work. And, most importantly, she didn't contact me to let me know where she was, and that she was safe.

I pour tea into my favourite mug, adding my preferred quantity of milk that I'm guessing is just about to turn sour, and take a sip, a disturbing thought flashing into my mind.

Maybe Jozee did want to hurt me? Maybe I did something so awful that Jozee is punishing me. But what?

Its unpalatable, but logically, I can't ignore the possibility. I've upset people hundreds of times in the past and been blissfully unaware of it, thinking that I was being witty, clever or even misguidedly sympathetic, only to have the wrath of the world dumped on my shoulders. My social faux pas were a constant source of horror and depression that took months and sometimes years to get over. Not that anyone would ever guess. To them, I was crass and unfeeling. Some loud-mouth whose only job on this planet was to annoy everybody. Someone they could self-righteously shout at like they were living in some pathetic TV soap.

But Jozee saw through all that. She was one of the few people who understood that this strange, sometimes crass, loud man, was actually okay. That he was loyal, nice and caring. The kind of guy who would do anything for his friends, even if he unintentionally insulted them while helping out.

I take another sip of tea, pushing away the familiar soft blanket of my own woes. I can't forever look at my social relationships through the prism of my disability. Everything bad that happens can't be related to that. It just can't. No matter how much it may seem that way.

"For the sake of argument," I say out loud, "let's say that I did or said something so unbelievably stupid and upsetting that Jozee turned against me. That Jozee is punishing me, like DC Marley suggested. Jozee could've let herself into the flat and stolen all the power cables, while leaving those awful flowers outside. It could've been her who ordered the pizzas, with our favourite but unpopular ham and pineapple topping. She could've even arranged for that perv to come around from the hook-up site, leading him on to confront me at home."

I must admit, it makes logical sense, filling me with dark hope. In this scenario, Jozee is safe and alive and punishing me. Even if this is the case, I won't stop searching for her.

The only lead I now have is Shirley Sands. I research her online. First, I check Facebook, pleased to find she hasn't unfriended me. She was active until the night before Jozee disappeared. Just the normal stuff. Gig dates, replies to invitations and photographs of her on stage. Very few text updates. But lots of photos. Most of them of... Jozee. That is odd. I've never noticed that before—although I am not in the habit of looking at Shirley's Facebook profile.

Is there more to Jozee's relationship with her? Could Shirley be the person Jozee slept with? Jozee's hook-up profile said she liked women. Although she'd never mentioned that to me—not that I'd judge her for it. I'd be turned on like every other pathetic boyfriend hoping for a threesome. Jozee has always seemed straight, but you never know. And yet, why would Shirley cross out Jozee's face in that photo I found? Is she a jilted lover, pretending to be Jozee's friend until—

My phone rings, blasting into my thoughts.

Stevo!

"Where have you been, you lying bastard?" I shout, jumping to my feet, noticing his Rover P5 parked out front, unusually muddied and dirty.

"Adam, mate, I'm so, so bloody sorry."

49

"WHAT ON earth were you doing, going behind my back with Jozee like that?" I shout at Stevo, getting into the passenger seat of the Rover. "And where the hell have you been these last few days?"

"I was lookin' for her. Had to. Couldn't get it out of my mind."

"Huh?"

"That she'd crashed somewhere on the way to London. Was in a ditch. You know. Trapped. Searchin' for her, like we did the other day. I became obsessed that she'd maybe taken another route. I've been out checkin' all the possible roads she may've driven."

"Including going to that clinic in Haywards Heath?"

Stevo nods guiltily. "I created a map. Found all the backroads and routes, I checked 'em all."

I understand the Aspie mind very well. Obsessive, single-minded behaviour was sometimes a negative as well as a positive aspect of the condition. And Stevo was first and foremost an obsessive.

"Okay," I say, "and I suppose that explains why your car is so muddy, but why the radio silence? Why ignore me and all my messages?"

"I slunk off work. Never done it before. That's why I left my phone at home. I couldn't take the guilt of my boss, Jeffers, phonin' me up. I only just went through my messages this mornin'. I was shittin' myself."

"Why didn't you phone in sick and save yourself the hassle?"

"Lie to Jeffers? I could never do that. He's a marvel. I love that man."

I'm not sure I believe him. "When I asked if you knew anything about Tom, you lied to me, didn't you?"

The big ape squirms in the leather seat of his Rover. "Jozee's car wasn't that reliable, so I gave her a lift whenever she needed one."

"You lied to my face! You were taking Jozee to go see Tom, her ex, and you didn't think about mentioning this to me?"

"What could I do?" he shrugs, enormous shoulders stretching the fabric of his bright purple T-shirt. "She swore me to keep schtum, didn't she? It was Jozee. I'd never let her down. She's one in a million. I love Jozee."

"You what?"

"You know what I mean," he replies a little too quickly, turning a lurid shade of crimson. "I love her as a friend. Of course, I do."

I stare at him and he squirms some more. "What did she tell you about Tom?"

"Everythin'. Nasty business that. Broke her heart."

I can't believe what I'm hearing. How can Stevo know all about this when Jozee told me nothing?

"Jozee had to pay to see Tom," he babbles on, "a secret arrangement with one of the nurses that look after him. You know he's a vegetable, right? Just lies there. The lights are on, but no one is home. Nasty."

"Yeah, I've been there and seen him," I reply, sure that Stevo is holding something back.

"You have?"

"It wasn't one of the greatest moments of my life," I say. "Did she tell you anything else? Any other secrets?"

He gives me a hopeless look. "Nope," he says after a long pause, his face turning crimson again. "Only that Tom had a sister, Charlotte. She was the reason why Jozee was forced to sneak into the clinic to see Tom. She banned her from visiting."

"The nurse mentioned Charlotte to me as well. I think we should go and pay her a visit."

"You know where she lives?"

"Nope, but I know someone who does."

Stevo frowns.

I take out my phone and ring Nurse Sally.

Getting Charlotte Blunt's address from nurse Sally wasn't difficult. I threatened to reveal her business dealings with Jozee. She phoned back a short time later, and sullenly gave me an address in Fulking—a small village nestled on the north slopes of the Sussex Downs, roughly nine or so miles away.

Twenty minutes later, after a convoluted drive past Devils Dyke, the windows wide open to let in air on this stiflingly hot day, we arrive on the outskirts of the village. Stevo remained silent for the entire journey. And I catch myself wondering how much I can trust him. Did he really spend the last two days searching the roads for Jozee's car? It seems a little far-fetched to say the least. But how much do we know about anybody? Or what they're capable of doing?

I've been to Fulking many times before. There's a popular five-mile walk, beginning and ending at the famous Shepherd and Dog public house that sits next to a spring. The village owes its existence to this natural water source, although I'm sure the only spring water the residents now drink is bottled and imported from miles away.

"This is Fulking?" Stevo asks.

"Yeah."

I wait for him to make a joke about the name. Stevo is just about the most sweary person I know, but instead of a mouthful of expletives, he gives an impressed whistle.

We drive past thatched roofs, timber-framed buildings and stately-looking mansions. The place is beautiful. Glinting cobbled streets and flint walls, the downs rising protectively above, like a curved, velvety-green giant's arm.

The main road through the village is narrow, cars are parked on each side making it impossible for two-way traffic. The house numbers are difficult to spot, and we are forced to drive up and down the road a few times, avoiding other cars, tractors and pedestrians. At this time of year, it's very busy.

"There it is," I say, jerking forward in my seat as Stevo roughly stabs the brakes. A small van emerges from a gravelled driveway of the house we're looking for and nearly crashes into us.

"Bleedin' imbecile!" Stevo yells. "Can't he see this ain't no modern piece of shit but a decent motor? Wanker!" He sticks his head out of the window. "You dangerous twat!"

Two passers-by turn to face us.

"Didn't you see what that stupid bugger just did!" Stevo shouts at them, gesticulating wildly through the window. The passers-by turn quickly away and carry on walking.

I'm a little taken aback. I've never seen this side of Stevo before.

He slumps back down into the driver's seat. "Snobs!"

"I'm not sure they are snobs these days. Just the well-to-do," I reply, wishing I could afford to live around here. This place is magnificent… apart from the constant stream of traffic down this impossibly narrow road and the backpackers and Sussex Downs-walkers for whom this is a popular route.

Shaken, but not quite stirred from the near miss, we park outside and knock on the door of Charlotte Blunt's rather imposing house. White-fronted and stretching a long way backwards into what I guess is a large garden. An elegantly-dressed old lady answers.

"We've come to see Charlotte," I say under the judgemental gaze of a rather smart and polished woman, feeling pleased I made the effort to wash, shave and dress myself properly.

"And who the hell was drivin' that van?" Stevo asks, his arm flailing in the direction of the offending vehicle. "Do you know how much my car cost to restore? Thousands. It's almost akin to vandalism. If he'd hit us I mean. The bastard missed us by inches, but that's not—"

"What do you want to see Charlotte about?" the woman interjects, her voice painfully posh. Like she'd been following a YouTube course on 'How To Talk Down To Plebs'. Maybe Stevo is right. Perhaps this place *is* full of snobs.

"It's, um… a personal matter," I say. Out of the corner of my eye I spot Stevo winding up for another tirade.

"And you are?" The woman asks.

"Um… I'm a friend."

"And if I'd not reacted as quickly as I did—" Stevo tries to continue, but I put a finger onto his lips.

"I mean," the woman continues with growing irritation, "what is your name?"

"Oh right. That."

I hadn't thought this far ahead. I'm tempted to lie, but when it comes down to it, Charlotte doesn't know me from *Adam*.

"I'm Adam Hanson," I reply, somewhat weakly. "Pleased to meet you," I add as an afterthought, offering my hand.

The old lady stares at me and at my hand for a few moments, and then replies, her tone harsh and not to be messed with. "I'm afraid Charlotte is not home at the moment. She told me who you are, Adam. The boyfriend of that awful comedian, Jozee Jackson. I hear she's gone missing. Good riddance!"

She tries to close the door and, before I can advise him against this course of action, Stevo jams his foot in it and squeals in pain.

"You know me?" I say, wondering how that was possible.

"My foot!" Stevo says through gritted teeth. The woman is small in stature, but the door is heavy.

"If you don't leave now, I will call the police," the woman says, pulling back and slamming the door onto Stevo's foot. He grunts in pain and hops away cursing.

"Now get off my property." She closes the door with a bang.

"My bloody foot!" Stevo groans. "That was an assault! Plain and simple. You saw it. You saw what that old harridan did to me!"

I ignore him. A taxi has pulled up, out of which steps a tall, leggy blonde with flowing hair, sunglasses and a summer skirt. The same girl I'd seen outside Tom's care home.

Charlotte Blunt!

50

CHARLOTTE SPOTS me and a literally hopping-mad Stevo and stops dead in her tracks.

"You think that's her," Stevo blurts, pointing. "Charlotte Blunt? Bloody hell! She's a looker though. Those legs!"

"Yes," I reply. "I've seen her before outside Tom's clinic." It must've been Charlotte who banned me from seeing Tom. The clinic phoned me only a short while afterwards. But how had her mum heard about me and Jozee?

Charlotte takes a deep breath, shoulders her bag, and strides purposely towards me.

"Charlotte?" I say. "I'm Adam Hanson, I'd like to talk to you if I may."

The girl says nothing, instead she walks past me and towards the door.

"Please. I'm looking for my missing girlfriend and… and I think you may know something about her disappearance."

No reaction from the girl.

"Charlotte!" I grab her elbow.

Charlotte twists out of my grasp, punches me in the throat, sticks out a leg and elbows me roughly to the floor where I lie squeaking and gasping.

"She's a bleedin' ninja!" Stevo shouts, backing away. "Is everyone in this family dangerous?"

Charlotte fumbles with her keys and I see her face in profile, the image of the van that almost hit us as we arrived flashing into my mind. And like some arcane, weird magic, my brain puts these two bits of information together and comes to an astounding conclusion.

Charlotte opens the door and glides inside, closing it behind her.

I lurch to my feet, still winded and hold up the photo I found in

Shirley Sands' flat. I press it against the glass of a window by the door.

"I know who you are and if you don't talk to me, I'm going straight to the police!" I croak, rubbing at my injured throat with my other hand.

"I mean it!"

The door opens to frame Charlotte standing there, her sunglasses now removed. "The police? Don't make me fucking laugh," she says. "But… I suppose we do need to talk."

"That's no way for a lady to speak," the old lady says from somewhere behind her.

"Oh, piss off, mum."

"What?" Stevo says dazedly behind me. "How come she knows who you are?"

"Shall you tell him or shall I?" I reply.

Charlotte shrugs.

"Charlotte Blunt… *is Shirley Sands!*"

51

AN ASTOUNDED and now very quiet Stevo, drives us all to Tottingtons, a small bistro restaurant nestling under the South Downs. We park, get drinks and go sit in the pub garden. A beautiful place full of flowers wilting in the intense heat of this burningly hot summer's day. A pond tinkles with running water within which swim large, ponderous goldfish. On a hot day like this, it's a relaxing place to be, but I'm unable to feel uplifted. I'm keen to hear what Charlotte has to say. Yet, if I'm honest, she doesn't appear guilty. If anything, she seems relieved.

Nearly all the tables are occupied. Couples and families, and a small afternoon party of smart-looking couples, worse the wear for booze, with many empty bottles of prosecco filling their table.

I get a text from Billy Belter.

> *Shirley Sands didn't give a forwarding address, but her parents live in Fulking - nice place if you can afford it! I'm sure you can find them if you go to the local pub and ask around. Good luck!*
>
> *Billy Belter*

"I still can't get over it," Stevo blurts, sipping at his preferred sparkling water and lime. "Shirley Sands, that man-hatin' leggy comic everyone drools over? That's you? Fuuuuck! How did you work it out, Adam?"

I shrug. "Even though Shirley wore that black wig and all that make-up, she couldn't hide her profile, but it was the van that did it."

"That idiot who nearly hit us?"

"Yeah, Shirley Sands moved out of her house this morning. I put two and two together and made two-hundred and sixty-eight.

Charlotte and Shirley are the same person."

"The driver is a handyman from the village," Charlotte says. "I'm glad that my possessions survived the journey, although he was in a lot more danger from the Full English Breakfast Mum cooked for him in payment."

A wasp buzzes into Stevo's face and he frantically tries to bat it away.

"Yes," Charlotte says, sipping at a large rosé and leaning back in her chair. "I'm Shirley Sands… but, as I told you before, I have nothing to do with Jozee's disappearance."

A loud Aston Martin roars past, and the wasp is forgotten while Stevo's eyes follow the noisy car powering along the small country road.

"But why the whole act with Shirley Sands? Why pretend to be someone else?" I ask.

Charlotte rubs long fingers over her chin and shakes her head. "I wanted to get close to her. Close to the woman who ruined my brother's life."

"By living a double life as a comedian? By doing actual gigs?"

"I know it seems I'm messed up, but…" Charlotte sighs. "Tom is my older brother. I look… I looked up to him. Dad died years ago, and Tom was like a father to me. He took care of me. Helped me sneak boyfriends in and out the house under my snobby mother's nose. Bought me my first drink. Let me be me. I know it's a dreadful cliché, but when he nearly died… a part of me also died."

"Okay," I say. "I get that. And you blamed Jozee didn't you? For what happened. You became Shirley Sands not just to get to know her but to do her harm? Am I right?" I hold up the photo. "And don't lie. You crossed out Jozee's face. If that's not a sign of what you planned to do, I don't know what is."

"Yes, maybe… I dunno." Charlotte takes a large swig of her rosé. "I was angry at her. I was convinced it was Jozee's fault that Tom tried to kill himself, especially after I saw that dreadful video. I wanted to… *I don't know what I wanted to do.* But the more I found out about Jozee… the more *I liked her.* She was warm, forgiving and helpful. The kind of girl Tom would go for."

"That's right," I hear myself saying, realising that I'm hungry for any information that backs up what I know about Jozee. That she's kind-hearted and not the kind of girl to pull a series of nasty stunts just to make me miserable.

"The last month or two I've been very confused," Charlotte continues. "I wanted to be angry with Jozee, but I couldn't. She obviously loved Tom, very much, and when I pressed her about what happened the night she dumped him, I could tell there was something more. That it just wasn't a simple break-up."

"Is that what she revealed to you, the night before her disappearance? The real reason why she dumped him? Is that why you were so angry and chased her out into the street?"

She nods.

I take a deep breath. "Well, what was it?"

She shakes her head. "I can't... I won't tell you."

"You have to. I'm sure it's got something to do with her disappearance. Unless... you're the reason she disappeared."

"I'm not. Like I said, I was spying on her, sure, but I had no real idea what I was going to do."

"Kill her?" Stevo blurts. "You sure have the motive. What you did was mad enough."

"I didn't... I wouldn't... that wasn't my plan."

"You need to tell me," I say coldly. "Jozee is missing. And if you are not responsible, then someone else is."

Charlotte takes another gulp of rosé and shakes her head.

"Do you think this is a game?" I ask, raising my voice, not caring that others in the garden turn to stare. "Don't you get how much trouble you are in? You pretended to be someone else to get close to Jozee—and you were seen arguing by some guy called David Gentry. I'm sure I can find him again to make a statement. I was contacted by the police today—they are taking Jozee's disappearance very seriously and want me to give them any information I find. Billy Belter was in your flat when I found this photo." I hold it up to show her again. "He will vouch for me and make a statement that it was found under your bed."

I'm lying, but I need to put pressure on her. Charlotte is a fruit loop, no doubt about it. But my guess is that she's as scared of the police as anyone else.

"Billy Belter?" Charlotte says. "What was that creep doing in my flat?"

"He was there in his official capacity as your landlord's agent. Understand? This isn't hearsay. This is evidence in a missing person case. Unless you tell me what you know now, Stevo will drive me straight to Brighton Police Station and I'll give this to them."

"I will," Stevo says with a nod of his mammoth head.

"Don't do that," Charlotte says, removing her sunglasses. I see flashes of Shirley Sands in her face, but it appears Charlotte doesn't share the cold-heart of her double. Tears appear in her eyes and stream down her impressive cheekbones.

"Oh hell… it's the waterworks!" Stevo says, raising his bushy eyebrows and pulling a face.

"I had nothing to do with Jozee's disappearance, I swear it!" Charlotte hisses through her sobs.

A concerned, smart-looking guy in expensive sunglasses, golden bling and too many cheesy tattoos saunters over from the party table.

"You okay over here, love?" he says to Charlotte, his voice slurring. "These guys bothering you? Come and join us if you want."

"Fuck off!" Charlotte says suddenly. Her voice sharp and piercing, directly channelling Shirley Sands.

"I was only asking if you were okay, you stupid cow!"

"Johnny!" shouts what I assume is the guy's girlfriend. "Stop causing trouble and come back and sit down at once!"

The guy stands his ground, but not for long.

Stevo pulls himself out his seat and stands up. "Watch your lip when talkin' to a lady," he says threateningly.

It's a side of Stevo I've not seen before. The Stevo I know wouldn't raise a fist or a finger to anyone, or so I thought.

The guy looks Stevo up and down, thinks better of the exchange and staggers back to his table, where his friends wave apologies at us.

"I suppose it doesn't look good, us fellas making this beauty cry," Stevo says, squeezing himself back into his seat.

"I mean it," I carry on, pointing to the photo and ignoring the exchange. "I'll take this to the police if you don't tell me what you know. Don't make me do it."

"Okay!" Charlotte says quietly. "Okay, you win. But you can't tell anyone else."

"I can't promise that," I say leaning over the table and staring straight into her face. "What did Tom do to make Jozee dump him?"

"It was this time two years ago," Charlotte begins, draining her rosé as more tears stream down her face.

"What was?"

"When it happened."

52

"A NASTY hit and run. Two teenage girls were killed—"

"Bloody hell!" Stevo shouts so loudly that everyone turns to look at us again. He raises his hands and mouths *sorry*. "I remember it well," he says, lowering his voice. "Nasty. They never caught who did it. But that was… *that was your brother Tom?* What a bastard!"

Charlotte nods, and I see desolation behind her eyes. I now realise why Shirley Sands was so angry with Jozee that night. Jozee had told her an unimaginable truth about Tom. The brother she idolised. A most awful, vile truth. Tom was the culprit in a nasty hit and run that left two teenagers dead. No wonder Shirley had freaked out. Now Charlotte had left Shirley behind, literally. And with it any motive for killing Jozee.

"You see?" Charlotte says angrily. "What Tom did has nothing to do with why she's gone missing. Jozee didn't dump Tom because she was a heartless cruel bitch, but because Tom told her what he'd done. That's why their relationship fell apart, that's why he took the overdose. She couldn't love him anymore and he couldn't live with such a dreadful secret."

"I can deffo understand that," Stevo says. "Those young lasses knocked out of existence by something your brother did. The guilt would eat him alive."

"That's why I'm sure others were involved," Charlotte says. "I don't think he was alone. Someone else was in that car with him that night. Someone who stopped him going to the police."

"Who? Who was it?"

Charlotte went quiet after that. I asked her about the hook-up website Jozee had signed up to, but she didn't believe Jozee was into such things, although it was obvious her trust in human nature had been dented by what Tom had done. In the end, we took her home.

"I need to know more about this hit and run, I don't remember it at all," I say to Stevo on the journey back home.

"It was around this time of the year," Stevo begins. "Two years ago. In the late evening. Dusk is statistically one of the most dangerous times for pedestrians and motorcyclists. The human eye doesn't function well in low light. Now if we'd evolved from cats, from felines, this wouldn't be a problem because unlike us humans the cat eye is specially adapted to—"

"Try and stick to the issue, Stevo. Sodding cat's eyes are the last thing I want to hear about."

Stevo grips the steering wheel tightly, as if trying to concentrate his mind, and stares blankly ahead. "The teens were walkin' down a Sussex country lane late at night somewhere near Pulborough. A couple of girls. Very attractive. And you know what the press are like with that kind of thing? If it had been a couple of tramps or an old ugly bloke, it wouldn't have caused half the furore. But that's the problem with the press these days. If I had my way, I'd—"

"Focus!"

"Sorry, yeah, right. The car was never found. No evidence at the scene to give the police any ideas about make or model. As a result, no one was ever arrested or questioned. Tom got off scot free. The lucky bastard."

"What do mean lucky? He killed two people."

"Wrong choice of words is all. You know me. Always sayin' the wrong thing."

"You and me both."

"How come you missed it? The hit and run was the top story that summer, plastered all over the papers."

I shrug in answer. "Everything I've found out about Tom has told me he was a nice guy. Not the type to run over two teenagers and leave them dying in the road. No way. Imagine if that was you or me, we'd have stopped, wouldn't we?"

"Depends," Stevo says in reply.

"Depends on what?" I ask, feeling increasingly irritated by my friend.

"Well, if they were dead and you couldn't do anythin' about it, what's the point in reportin' it to the rozzers? What's done is done."

"You're telling me that you'd calmly get back into your car and carry on with your life after doing something like that?"

"No. Of course not. That's the bastard thing to do."

"Good," I reply, not sure if I'm convinced by his answer.

"I'm jus' sayin' I can see the logic of the situation," Stevo continues, "puttin' myself in the mind of a git who'd do somethin' like that. Havin' to live with that decision, with the guilt of what you did? Well, it's a whole different thing."

"You're right, Stevo. Which means we agree with Charlotte… that someone else was in Tom's car. Someone who convinced him to do what he did."

"A passenger you mean?"

I nod. "Yeah."

"But why? If Tom was drivin', it was his fault. Why not let him take the blame?"

"Maybe Tom wasn't driving that night?"

"It's possible, I suppose."

"I think it's more than possible. If Tom was half the guy everyone said he was, he'd be too remorseful to do anything else but walk into the nearest police station the next day and hand himself in. And even if he didn't, there's no way he could've lived with that on his conscience—in fact we know he couldn't. Someone else put pressure on him."

"So, you trust Charlotte's story then?"

"Are you saying that you don't?"

"All that Shirley Sands secret identity shit seems fishy to me," Stevo says. "She could be a psychopath, lyin' about the whole thing. And you know what they're like, hidin' in plain sight. She could've killed Jozee and spun us a line."

"Don't say that! Jozee is alive, of course she is."

"I'm jus' sayin' that she's obviously an all-round, calculatin' full-on nutter. She has to be, to live a double life for all that time. To become a stand-up comic and Jozee's best friend jus' so she could bump her off."

"Stop saying that!"

"Well if you can't read between the lines, I can. Why else do what she did? She had to be plannin' murder. Had to be."

Stevo is irritating me, but his logic is spot on. "Maybe you're right."

"Of course I'm bleedin' right."

"Okay. Let's say she was planning to… to hurt Jozee. That changed when she found out about Tom. When she realised Jozee wasn't the cause of his suicide attempt. Charlotte left her flat and her secret identity behind."

"Unless she'd already silenced her. To stop it comin' out. Maybe Jozee was goin' to the police to rat Tom out? That would be motive for murder."

"Then why tell us what Tom did?"

"Yeah, you're right," Stevo admits begrudgingly as if he wants Charlotte Blunt to be guilty of harming Jozee. "But Charlotte or Shirley Sands or whoever she is," Stevo continues, "is a fruit-loop though. You have to admit that. A fruit-loop with fantastic legs. I always loved those high-heeled boots she wore on stage. Magic. *The Kinky Boot Killer* is what the press would probably have called her. The papers would drool over a story like that."

I ignore him, and the car returns to an uncomfortable silence.

"So, what are we doin' next?" Stevo asks as we crest the hill above Hove, the sea stretching to the horizon below us.

"I'm going to find out as much as I can about that hit and run and discover who was in the car with Tom."

"Okay, it's a plan. What do you want me to do?"

"Nothing. You lied to me, remember?"

"Jozee made me promise, what else could I do? I thought we were okay."

"We are. I'm just not in my right head. Things will be okay when Jozee turns up."

"If she turns up."

"Shut up and take me home."

"I don't want her to be dead either you know? I'm just as cut up about it as you are. I want her to be alive, I really do. But I've always expected the worst. Ever since my family were killed."

"You what? Your family… *they were what?*"

"Gas explosion. I was out at a party that night. I was fifteen or so. I sort of knew something was wrong when Dad didn't pick me up. I waited for ages. Until I got a lift home and saw all the fire engines. That's when the rozzers told me the news."

"Mate, I'm sorry."

"It's alright. The inheritance was absolutely fantastic. I got everything. Only child you see. I still miss them. I suppose I always expect the worst."

"Not this time. Jozee's coming back. She has to."

53

STEVO DROPS me off at my flat just after 2.30pm and drives away sullenly. He doesn't like being in my bad books, that's for sure. But the guy shouldn't have lied to me. Although, if I'm honest, the fault lies with Jozee, making him promise to keep her visits to see Tom a secret and god knows what else he isn't telling me.

The day has been a long one and it's only just the afternoon. I make my way up to the flat, pausing to knock on Clive's door again. And again, there is no answer, although I can smell an overpowering scent of Lavender that appears to be emanating from his flat. Flummoxed and a little angry, I make myself a cup of tea, power up my laptop and begin searching.

Two teenagers on 'fun night out' killed in Pulborough horrific hit and run

The victims were walking down a country road close to Pulborough when they were mown down by a car travelling at 'excessive speed' late last night.

The two teenagers, who friends and family described as 'the best of friends' were on a fun night out to celebrate one of the girls' birthdays. They were making their way between pubs along a dimly lit road when the incident occurred.

Police have launched a search for the vehicle and are calling for the driver to come forward.

It is believed the car that hit the victims either did not see them or deliberately ran them down.

"We found no evidence that the car attempted to brake before this horrific incident," a traffic police spokesman said, adding,

"I've seen many hit and runs, but this has to be one of the most disturbing."

Police issue an appeal to track down a vehicle with 'extensive' damage' after horrific hit and run

Mid Sussex Police issued an appeal last night to find a vehicle involved in Thursday's hit and run that left two Pulborough teenagers dead.

"The vehicle hit the victims at considerable speed and must have suffered extensive damage," a police spokesman said, adding, "if anyone knows who did this, a friend or family member, I urge you to contact the police straightaway.

Police appeal to driver of fatal Pulborough hit and run

After an extensive vehicle search that involved CCTV, local garages and a police recreation of last week's fatal hit and run that killed two local teenagers, the police are now making a direct appeal to the driver to come forward.

Police no closer to finding driver in tragic hit and run

The investigation into the fatal hit and run incident that took place last month on Thursday 9th July close to Pulborough, Mid Sussex, is no closer to finding the driver.

"This was a very serious incident," police said, "involving the deaths of two bright, up and coming teenagers who were just starting out in life.

The driver of the car must've had help from friends or family to conceal their damaged vehicle. I appeal to them now. Please get in touch. Your information will be treated in the strictest confidence."

Reward offered to help find driver of fatal hit and run

Fundraising efforts by friends and families, including a fun run, and donations from local Pulborough businesses and

others in the community, have raised £10,000 as a reward for information on the driver involved in July's fatal hit and run that claimed the lives of two popular teenagers.
A spokesperson for the parents of the dead teens, said, "This has been a terrible time for everyone who knew those beautiful girls who were taken from us in such cruel circumstances.

We thank everyone who has donated to this cause. No one should suffer as we have done and still do. Please help to end our suffering now. If anyone has any information about what happened on that tragic evening three months ago—please come forward."

A memorial service is to be held for victims of the Pulborough hit and run

Pulborough hit and run: A year on and still no answers

The grief of not knowing. The parents of Pulborough fatal hit and run, speak out

I scroll through the timeline of the accident and get as much information as I can, but the most important information is the date.

9th of July two years ago. Almost to the day.

If Tom had been driving that night, it's likely he was coming back from a gig. If so, he'd delete any reference to it on social media, but I have to check. I go back to Tom's Facebook pages and search through his photos and posts, scrolling laboriously down his timeline.

No photos, no events. A dead end as expected.

I try a different tack. I look at Jozee's Facebook pages and scroll back two years. Also nothing. No reference to any gig.

Dammit.

If he was at a gig, any number of comedians could've been on with him. I can't go through every comedian's web pages in the hope of finding it. It would take forever.

I shake my head. I'm being too specific. There's another way to find out. I go to Google and type in the date followed by the word 'comedy'—a whole host of event websites pop-up, referencing a comedy night held at a small pub in a place called Petworth.

I bring up the details.

*A night of comedy hosted by Brighton's most accomplished
local compere, Donnie Coogan, with special guests:*

Tom Blunt
Nat Naylor
Jim Laker
Billy Belter
Pari Chabra
and newbie: Scott Wong

I look at the list of names. One of them was in Tom's car the night
of the hit and run. I'm sure of it. One name sticks out though.
Scott Wong

As far as I know, Wong only started recently. A meteoric rise, by
all accounts, but here he is on a comedy bill two years ago. That's
suspicious in itself.

I take out my mobile and I'm pleased to see him in my contacts
list. Comics are always swapping numbers and emails and following
each other on social media. I press his number and wait.

It goes straight to voicemail.

*"Hi, this is Scott Wong, if you want to contact me about any possible
bookings please get in touch with the Blowback Comedy Agency on…"*

Does no one ever answer their damn phones these days? But I
suppose he's happy to let his phone trip to voicemail, especially when
he can brag about Blowback in his message. That's quite some result.

I visit his website. For an amateur, it's impressive. A banner at the
top says, 'Under new management - watch this space!' I click through
to his upcoming gigs list and find out he's playing at the Hove Lawns
Chilli Festival this afternoon. I check the time… he's on now!

54

I LIVE minutes away from the seafront and head out of my flat to be hit by a wave of heat. The weather is glorious. The best for decades, apparently.

I pound down the packed promenade, feeling the heat of the patchwork concrete through the soles of my shoes, stomping past the multitudinous hoards who have come out this weekend to enjoy beer, books, bodies, booze and the beach. It is loud and frustratingly busy. People mill around as if they have no idea where they are going or what they are doing and I'm constantly swerving to avoid crashing into them. Kids run screaming under beach showers, dogs slink panting in the shadow of the promenade wall, while self-important groups of scantily-dressead young men and women stumble drunkenly, buying cheap wares from the many stalls selling hats, t-shirts, jewellery, sunglasses and anything else that takes their fancy. Bicycles whizz past, skateboards clatter and somewhere in the distance I can hear the pounding of drums and various competing musical instruments.

The heat is oppressive. I'm sweltering under a harsh and unremitting sun burning alone in a blue sky absent of the normal sea breeze. I lift my head to spy an array of white tents shimmering in the distance upon Hove Lawns, my hand shading my eyes.

Hove Lawns are exactly what they sound like. Vast lawns sitting a stone's throw from the sea behind the promenade's iconic, brightly-coloured beach huts—the grass now yellowed from the near constant beating of the sun. The lawns are used all year round for various outdoor activities like yoga, sports training and illegal BBQs—and a safe place for locals and visitors to engage in any number of recreational drugs.

In the summer, the lawns are host to regular weekend festivals and events. This weekend it's the annual Chilli Festival. There's no entry price, most of the festivals are open to anyone and everyone, which includes drunks, religious weirdos and pickpockets—not that you can always tell the difference. I'm met by a sea of white tents in the midst of a thronging hoard. A typical Brighton and Hove festival crowd—hippy couples well into their 70s and 80s, dogs of all shapes and sizes, men holding hands with men, women draped drunkenly over their girlfriends, chairs and tables full of friends and families, eating and drinking, jugglers, clowns, people in fancy dress, stag and hen dos. There's a BMX bike display, a small skateboarding exhibition rink and various rides for all the screaming, braying children who are seemingly having a lot more fun running around playing a game of annoying the fuck out of everybody. A public address system drones with the excited, but indistinct tones of the compere, drowned out by the sheer volume of all these squawking humans.

It's the kind of situation that I normally stay away from. Just the idea of walking amongst all these people is making me sweat even more than I am already. But I don't have a choice and push on through.

It's at times like this—jostled, pushed, assailed by the smell of sweat, smoke, perfume and the screams of babies screeching above the never-ending noise and jabber of packed humanity—that I seriously wonder if I belong to the human race. I feel so utterly different to them. I wouldn't be surprised if I was some alien sleeper, a spy awaiting the invasion, where I'm transformed into my true self to achieve dominion over this irrational, messy world and its petty inhabitants—a common, if not stupid, fantasy of mine.

I wish.

I head towards the tents, hit by the smell of various exotic foods. Thai, Caribbean, Malaysian, Vietnamese, and any other cuisine you can mention, all containing that one special ingredient… *Chilli.* Guaranteed to not only burn a hole in your stomach, but also in your wallet. I'm tempted to go and try the chilli-infused fare, more than tempted—a visceral urge that starts with a rush of saliva in my mouth and turns into a Neanderthal grunt for food—but I decide against it, I've more important concerns than my stomach and its slutty ways.

A bearded steward with a face as red as his t-shirt bearing the slogan 'Put something hot into your mouth!' directs me to the event tent. A large open canopy under which I can hear muffled words coming from a sound system—a voice I recognise. *Nat Naylor.*

I pass out of the sunlight and enter the slightly less frenetic but infinitely warmer awning-covered stage area, sweat dripping off me. The orange-coloured cavernous tent is swelteringly hot and gives everything a sickly yellow tinge.

My phone beeps. A text from an unknown number:

> *Your gf is a mean liddle biiiitch whos gonna get slapped.*

I recognise the number at once. The one Donnie gave me back at the Comedy Gods. I'd forgotten all about it!

How could I have been so stupid? I text back, my fingers slippery with sweat.

> Who is this?

> *Where is ur bitch? Why wont she reply?*

> Answer the question? Who are you? How do you know Jozee?

> *Wassup man? U didnt no you gf was a hor? I fucked her behin ur back*

Before I can reply again, my phone is hit with a tidal wave of disgusting texts from the same number.

> *I filled yor bitches ass with cum an gave her aids and hurpees ur gonna get deseesed*

> *Fucking hor! Hiding her cunt from me*

> *Why won she anser? Why she ignore me? Bitch fuckin bitch*

> *I will find her an do her propurly*

My phone is beeping almost constantly, and people are getting annoyed. I off the sound. Watching my screen as the texts keep coming, one after the other, shuddering at the angry, vitriolic wave of hate.

Why did I forget about this number? I should've chased it up. Could it be one of those guys Jozee had met on that sex site? Someone she'd upset? The thought appalls me. How could Jozee be seeing such low-lifes? And how did they get my number?

I see Scott Wong sitting at a table by the side of the stage, sipping at an iced water with a slice of lime in the top and tapping vigorously into his phone.

Could it be him? Could it be Wong?

I put my phone in my pocket, which continues to vibrate against my thigh and go over to talk to him.

55

I WALK past the stage that is at least four feet high. Nat Naylor stands in the middle, a diminutive, insignificant figure in a skimpy t-shirt and shorts, holding the microphone pressed to her chin, her eyes wide and manic. It amazes me how different she is from that first time I saw her on that magical night. The same night I saw Jozee's set. Then, Nat Naylor was a comedy powerhouse.

Now?

She is broken. Her jokes have become desperate and empty. And I can't help but feel a little sorry for her.

"My boyfriend is a metro-sexual. He's got more shoes than I have…

"…I call him a shoe-sexual."

No laughs and I feel myself cringing. This is the first new stuff I've heard from Nat Naylor in ages and it isn't good.

"He says I never notice when he buys new clothes.

"…So, I bought him some camouflage trousers."

Nothing again from the audience of about two-hundred. Not even a titter. She's dying but is refusing to leave the stage. I've seen it before, comedians who just won't accept the inevitable and drone on and on, trying to get that one elusive laugh.

The best advice when you're dying is… *to get off stage as quickly as possible.* To forego the rest of your set and hit the room with your closing joke, usually your best, killer line, to thank the audience for having you and to slink off to the toilets for a little cry and a deep and detailed examination about what the fuck you're doing with your life.

Not so Nat Naylor. She looks desperate and her desperation has lost the crowd. She's got zero chance of getting them back

I go over to Wong and sit next to him. He hastily offs his phone and I'm disturbed to find that my phone stops vibrating.

Even though the tent is boiling, Wong is wearing chinos, a bright blue, open-necked shirt, and he isn't even sweating. His thick black hair is swept back behind his ears, framing a warm, symmetrical face of mixed European and Asian origin. The melding of races gives him an attractive demeanour. He looks calm, at ease and professional. He is made for TV and I can't help but feel a little jealous.

I don't begrudge success, it's simply that the guy is just too good. Someone who makes everyone look sub-standard. He's the kind of comedian who sometimes unexpectedly turns up on a bill forcing the headliner to convince the promoter to put Wong on last instead. The reason? Who'd want to go on after Wong?

I realise I don't know him that well. I've only ever talked to him a few times before, mainly due to the fact he's one of the local comedy grandees and I'm a lowly newbie.

"Hi Adam," Wong says in his clear, penetrating tones and I'm surprised he knows my name. "How's it going? Any sign of Jozee?"

He seems genuinely concerned.

I shake my head. "No, nada."

"She's still missing? Shit, man, that must be a bitch to live with. I hope she turns up soon. I love her. She's one of the funniest women comics on the scene. Her and stunning Shirley Sands." His dark brown eyes flash towards the stage. "Unlike some others I might mention."

I say nothing. It's dreadfully bad etiquette to bad-mouth other comics to other comics—not that it doesn't go on. I suppose Wong is leaving us, and gigs like this, far behind. He can say what he wants. I find myself nodding in agreement.

"Are you on?" he asks.

"No, no, I've come here to talk to you."

"To me?" He's a little taken aback. "Sure, I'm on after Nat though, so I might be called away at any minute. For the sake of this crowd, let's hope so, eh?" He chuckles, his face splitting into a winning smile.

"You're on next? Sorry. I can come back when you're done."

"No worries, man. I'm easy. And it looks like Nat won't be off-stage for some time yet." He grimaces. "I'm off up to London with my new agent when I'm finished here."

"I want to ask you about a gig. A gig from two years ago."

Wong's eyebrows furrow. "What gig?" he asks, his eyes narrowing, as if he knows what I'm talking about.

"It was at a place outside Pulborough. You were on with a guy called Tom Blunt as well as Jim Laker, Billy Belter, Donnie Coogan, Pari Chabra and… Nat Naylor."

He nods. "I thought that's what you meant. Man, I tried to forget that night. To put it out of my mind, but you know what? That night changed me. Made me who I am today."

"It did?"

Wong nods and I can see I've piqued his interest. "I'll never forget it."

"Why was that your last gig for almost a year?"

I'm being direct, but Wong doesn't seem to mind. He takes a sip of his water and hunches over the table, his head close to mine.

"I died," he says conspiratorially. "And I mean…" he flicks a thumb towards the stage, "I totally bombed."

"*You* died?"

He smiles at my compliment.

"Yeah. I was overconfident. One hundred percent sure I was the next big thing. And more than a little arrogant. You've seen it before. That cocky kid doing his first gig, convinced he's gonna smash it just because he can make his mates laugh, bragging backstage to the seasoned comedians, thinking that all he needs is a few nob-jokes and a bucketload of confidence, before dying a well-deserved death." He chuckles again. "Admit it, it's kinda enjoyable watching guys like that taken down a peg or two, isn't it?"

"Yeah, I suppose it is," I reply. I never like to see people fall, especially in such a public way, but he's right.

"That night, the over-confident cocky kid was me. I paid the price and, man, did it burn. But it taught me a lot. I decided to take time out and learn my trade properly. I went to every gig I could. Worked on my set day and night. Took part in try-out and new material nights and started adding songs. It was the songs that brought everything together for me—something to hang my set around. After six or so months, I started playing a few out of town venues under a different name. And this time, I didn't die. The rest is history, ha-ha. And now here I am, about to leave this all behind… I'll be honest, Adam, I'm not going to miss it."

"Can you tell me anything else about that particular night?"

"It was goddamn awful. All of it. I wasn't the only one to die, although my set was a complete and utter bust." He cringes at the memory.

I can't imagine Wong being anything other than brilliant, then again, he was one of the hardest working comedians I knew, gigging nearly every night of the week.

"The bright light that night was Donnie Coogan," Wong continues. "That guy's a natural compere. "He even got the audience to applaud me. You know the kind of thing? Telling them that it was my first ever gig and how much guts it took for me to get up there. I'll always be thankful to him for that."

"What about Jim Laker? What was he like that night?"

"Laker?" he replies, his eyes widening. "The guy was as high as a kite. Just terrible. Doing this chummy, cliquey shit with one of the other comics while on stage. Like he was performing just for him. Lost the audience. Just an awful, awful night. I'd stuck around cos I had to wait for my lift back home."

Again, I'm surprised by his candour. But like he said, he's leaving all this behind. I suppose he can now finally say what he thinks. I decide not to ask him about my comedy set.

"Laker was high?"

"Yeah, man. You know what I mean…" he sniffs at the air and pulls an 'out-of-it' face.

"Coke?"

Wong nods.

Coke, like Laker was doing with Nat.

"He'll get nowhere doing that stuff. None of them will."

"Who else?"

"There was a clique of them. It was a lot more prevalent back then. Or they were less discreet. Laker was handing out coke like candy. Everyone was partaking, and things got messy." He takes a nervous sip of his drink.

Wong is straitlaced. I've never seen him smoke or even drink. "And you?" I ask incredulously.

"It's poison, yeah? That's all I'm gonna say about it."

I decide to change tack. "Who was the comedian Laker was playing up to?"

"Tom Blunt, you know, Jozee's ex, the dead comic. He was usually bloody marvellous. An inspiration. Although…"

"Although what?"

"He was also awful that night. All over the place."

"You think he was on the um… nose candy as well?"

He shrugs. "Like I said, it was messy. That night nearly put me off comedy for good."

"Who gave you the lift to the gig?"

"Billy Belter. Told me how funny he was. How he'd help me. You know? The whole knowing-the-ropes speech. Until I saw him that is. What a douche. He stank the place out." He lowers his voice. "He always does."

"Who else was with you in the car? Any other comics?"

"Just Nat Naylor. I had to wait for Billy to drive me back to Brighton, otherwise I would've left a long time before. Man! I had to watch the whole awful show."

"You went home with Billy Belter?"

"Yep, that was a long journey, let me tell you."

"And Laker, how did he get back to Brighton?"

"I don't know. I was distraught after dying a total and utter death and didn't take much in. Except that the whole thing was a shit-fest. It put me off for a long time, but I finally cleaned up my shit, made my come back… and here I am." He smiles at someone over my shoulder and waves. "Sorry man, my new agent is here. Gotta go," he says full of pride, offering me his hand. We shake. "I hope Jozee turns up real soon."

I watch him walk over to one of the most powerful agents in the business, wondering if I'll ever be as successful.

Probably not.

"Hello?" I look up to see a familiar lugubrious face staring at me.

56

THE FACE belongs to David Gentry. He's still wearing his brown suit complete with white shirt and red tie. He's also ripe with the smell of unwashed sweat. His armpits are wet as is his hair, plastered to his greasy forehead.

"You're looking sorry for yourself, anything up?"

I say nothing. Gentry's body odour is a full-blown attack on my senses. Smells have that effect on me. Not as much as sound, but a close second.

"I can't wait to see Scott Wong," Gentry says. "You were right the other night—the guy is fantastic. Unlike this slut on stage. Not funny."

The word 'slut' focuses my attention. "Huh? What do you mean by that?"

"Nat Naylor. Didn't you just hear her new 'slut' routine? Bombed and, if I may say, a little misogynistic. Can women be misogynistic?"

"What do you want?" I ask testily, pulling back, wanting to get my nose as far away from this olfactory nightmare as possible. This only seems to encourage him to lean in closer.

"Just to say hello is all," he replies. "And to ask you about Jozee Jackson."

"Huh? Why would you be interested in her?"

"I'm a fan, remember? Is she on anywhere today? I saw you in the crowd and assumed you'd come to support your lovely girlfriend."

"No, no. Jozee's not turned up yet."

"Not turned up?" The news seems to confuse him. "Where is she?"

"I dunno."

"Did something spook her?"

The hairs on my neck suddenly prickle. "What do you know about that?" I snarl.

"How about I get you a drink?" Gentry says unfazed. "I really am a big fan of you comedians. What you do is so brave." His smile widens.

At that moment, Nat Naylor finally leaves the stage to a round of muted applause.

"Thanks for the offer," I say to Gentry, "but I've got to go and chat with my friend."

"No worries," he replies, offering me his hand.

I pretend not to notice.

"See you later," I say and push through the crowd to talk to Nat Naylor. She was also there at that gig two years ago and I'm keen to find out what she remembers or knows.

57

I GRAB Nat by the shoulder, my normal-sized hand enormous against her tiny frame. I try and imagine her standing next to Stevo. The size difference would be quite something. "Can I talk to you?"

"Huh? What?" Nat replies with irritation, before she realises it's me. "Oh, hi Adam. I hope you didn't just see that. I stank the place out." She smiles, but her eyes are full of dread. I've seen that look way too often in my comedy career. Mostly in the mirror.

She's wearing a tiny pair of shorts that leave nothing to the imagination and a loose t-shirt with no bra, her nipples are fat, rounded bullets that point in different directions like two lazy eyes.

Behind her, the compere introduces Scott Wong to an unenthusiastic crowd who are expecting more of the same after Nat Naylor's recent stage death. Part of me hopes Wong will die as well, but I'm not betting on it.

Nat is agitated, a chemically sweet smell of sweat emanates from behind her cheap perfume, but it's better than the rank smell of David Gentry.

"Oh poo! I was terrible. That was my big effing chance. I heard Wong's agent was coming in and thought I'd try some new stuff. Blast it!"

"It's a difficult crowd," I say, over the sudden roar of laughter greeting Wong's first joke. "C'mon, let me buy you a drink."

We leave the stage awning area that is now uproarious with laughter and go to one of the many beer tents dotted about the festival. I'm served after a short wait. Two lagers in flimsy plastic glasses, ordered on autopilot before I realised I'm not drinking.

"Let's get away from the crowd."

"Thanks Adam," Nat says, grabbing a hold of my arm.

If I didn't know any better, I'd guess she was coming onto me. But

I'm not the best judge of these things. It seems unlikely though, with Jozee still missing.

"Let's go down to the beach," she says, dragging me thankfully away from the maelstrom of the Chilli Festival, although the beach is also quite full. "My boyfriend would be jealous if he knew I was taking sexy men down to the beach in just my skimpy shorts," she giggles coquettishly.

"Sure."

We leave the lawns, cross the wide, concreted promenade and walk down more concreted steps to the beach, pebbles crunching underfoot.

"I hate these bloody stones," Nat says, struggling to walk in a thin pair of plimsoles.

We sit down with our backs to the scorching hot concrete of the promenade and look out towards the sea. Today it is becalmed, the waves that lap below us are weak shadows of themselves. Kids, dogs, teenagers and adults of all ages potter, swim and lark about in the water. I seriously consider joining them.

"Good call, Adam," Nat says, taking a gulp of her pint. "This is the hottest day for years although tomorrow is gonna be even hotter."

I'm also tempted to down my pint, but I've made up my mind to stay sober and I'm sticking to it.

"Any news of Jozee?" Nat asks, taking another gulp of lager, some of it spilling down her chin and onto her t-shirt, although she doesn't seem to care.

"I don't want to talk about that. Instead, I'm interested in a gig from a couple of years ago."

"Huh?"

"A place outside Pulborough. You'll remember it because it was Scott Wong's first gig. He died, you can't forget that. You travelled there with Billy Belter and Wong, remember?"

Nat looks confused for a moment, as if she wasn't expecting to be interrogated, but answers. "Actually, yeah, I do! Billy was being his normal pompous self. I felt sorry for Wong. Not now though. He's on the fast track to TV. And his agent saw me dying the effing slow death. I kept thinking, *I'll get a big laugh and get off stage...* Oh effing hell!" She downs the rest of her pint and I offer her my own, which she takes without comment.

"Forget Wong," I say. "I'm interested in who took a lift with Tom Blunt."

"Tom? You've found out about him, yeah, Jozee's ex?"

I nod and say nothing, letting her speak.

A fly is crawling down the side of Nat's face, although she doesn't seem to notice. "That was sad. I loved Tom, he was a great guy. After he died, nothing was quite the same."

"Why would you say that?"

Nat shrugs. "I dunno. Things were different somehow. Not as much fun. Why you asking about him and that night in particular?"

"It's important."

She shrugs. "I can't really remember. A lot of water…" she holds up her lager. "…and a lot of booze has passed under the bridge since then."

"Try and think back. Did Laker travel with Tom? Was he in Tom's car that night?"

"Laker? I dunno. It's possible I suppose. But it was maybe two years ago. Why is it important?"

"Do you remember anything about Tom's car around that time?"

"What are you getting at?"

"Tom's car? Was it damaged?"

"Damaged? I don't know what you—" Nat's eyes widen. "His car wasn't damaged, it was stolen. Tom was distraught, but he always did feel things a lot more keenly than everyone else. He missed quite a few gigs after that. Until the insurance company paid up and he got a new car. Quite some policy. It was brand new as far as I remember."

"He got a new car?"

"Yeah, very plush. Some kind of four-by-four. A BMW I think, but I'm not very good with cars. They all look the same to me."

My heart flutters. Laker was driving a four-by-four BMW when I found him and Nat at that weird country house. Could it be the same vehicle?

"Sounds great. He must've been quite happy then?" I venture.

"Funny you should say that, but he was the opposite. Down. I think he was having problems with Jozee. Those two were tight." Nat sounds resentful. "It was soon after that they split and…"

"He took an overdose."

"Yeah, that was messed up. Tom was no druggie. Not like the rest of…" She closes her eyes and takes a mouthful of lager.

"I read online that Laker was there when Tom took the overdose? He was a hero by all accounts, trying to save his friend. Although I've heard other stories. Apparently, he likes a line of coke every now and then."

Nat stops halfway through a gulp of lager and swallows noisily. "He's a complex guy. But what Laker does with his life or his nose, is not my problem," she says defensively, and I can tell this is not how she was expecting this conversation to go.

"Isn't it? From what I hear, you have quite a cocaine problem yourself."

Nat's eyes widen in her face as if she can't believe I'm saying these things to her.

"Don't pretend otherwise. You've got bigger problems than dying in front of an agent, especially if you're secretly sleeping with Laker for a line of coke."

"You bloody bastard… How dare you!"

She tries to stand up and leave, but I grab her arm and easily pull her back down. Nat hardly has any weight to her and I feel guilty, man-handling her like this. But I can't let her go just yet.

"Watch yourself, Adam," she says. "I might be small, but my boyfriend will—"

"Don't give me that nonsense, Nat. I know he left you, so cut the crap."

Back in that empty mansion when I'd heard Laker and Nat together, I hadn't thought it was anything other than a low-level, nasty little fuck. But now a more sinister idea pops into my mind.

"Is Laker a drug-dealer? Is he *your* drug-dealer? Did he give drugs to Tom the night of the hit and run?"

"Hit and run? What are you talking about?"

"Who else does Laker deal coke to? Who else fucks him and lets him film it in payment? Jozee?"

"Get off me!"

"Do you know where Jozee is? Is she with him? Are they messing me around for some kind of joke? What the hell is going on?"

"I said get off me!" she shouts, throwing the lager at me.

Other people on the beach are staring at us, and I'm forced to let her go.

Nat storms off, fumbling for her phone.

Dammit!

58

I LEAN my back against the promenade, my lager-soaked clothing cooling me in the unremitting heat of this fearsomely hot Saturday afternoon. The time is just past 4.30pm, but, if anything, it's getting hotter. I stare out to the new wind farm sitting on the horizon, the sun catching glints off the ocean. If it wasn't for all the people and the noise, and the fact Jozee has now been missing for three and a half days, this would be relaxing.

A drunken bloke wearing only a pair of red shorts, his body, thin and sun-browned, and smoking a spliff wanders past. "Woman trouble, huh?" he says.

I must look pretty upset.

"Sort of," I reply.

"Complicated?"

"Yeah, more than you could possibly know."

The man shakes his head, and crunches away across the pebbles.

Things are complicated, but I now know something I didn't before, Laker was high on the night of Tom Blunt's hit and run. And so, I guess, was Tom Blunt. I don't know Tom, but everybody so far has told me he was pretty much as straight as a die. If anyone was in a position to influence Tom to do stupid things like take coke and drive, that someone had to be Laker.

I'm sure he was in the car with Tom, sure of it.

I try to imagine the events of that night. Laker coercing Tom to take coke. He's never done it before. It feels great. He can do anything, but his set suffers. He drives home and, on the way, kills two teenagers. Laker panics—they are both high on drugs. He convinces Tom to leave the scene. Laker, with his drug-land connections, knows how to hide the car, and has the money to bribe Tom with a four-by-four BMW, using the cover story that his other car was stolen. If Laker was a full-on drug-dealer, selling to other comics, and possibly comedy club promoters and punters—who knew how much money Laker had stashed away? Enough money to bribe Tom with a brand-new motor? *Very possibly.* Especially if it was to keep Tom quiet.

The hit and run was big news two years ago. And once they were committed, it would become harder and harder for Tom to come clean.

But it doesn't make sense. Why would Laker help Tom out with a replacement car? What reason would he have to bribe Tom at all? Tom told Jozee he was the driver, so if anyone was to go down, that someone would be Tom. And besides, Tom could tell the police he was alone that night. Laker wouldn't have to be involved at all.

But that BMW came from somewhere, and certainly not from an insurance pay-out, which means there was more to this, there had to be. Was Laker in the driving seat for the hit and run, perhaps? That makes sort of sense, but it doesn't explain why Tom would tell Jozee he was the driver. Why lie about something as awful as that to your girlfriend? No. Something else was going on that night, something more than a simple hit and run. But what?

I look at the facts again. Tom told Jozee about what he did, and she dumped him, leading to his overdose, unless…

…unless Tom had decided to go to the police.

A new, chilling thought pops into my mind.

Who was it that found Tom after his overdose?

Jim Laker.

That was suspicious right there. If anyone was able to get their hands on heroin, it would be a drug dealer. And who was better placed to administer an overdose to Tom other than his supposed best friend? Especially after Tom blabbed to Jozee about the hit and run.

Could it be possible? Did Laker do the unthinkable?

I shudder at my logic. If Laker was that cold-blooded—capable of trying to overdose his friend to save his own neck—what else would he be capable of doing? Of killing Jozee? Of making her disappear?

Jozee and Laker were close. She'd go straight to the police if she thought he was involved and not sit there letting him paw at her. No,

Jozee was in the dark about Laker. She had to be. Unless she'd made the same deductions I have, or worse still, confided in Laker about Tom, not realising that Laker was in the car with him.

I place my head against my knees, the sun is so hot on the back of my neck it's making me dizzy.

Should I phone PC Ella Marley and tell her what I've found out? That would make sense wouldn't it? I remember our last conversation. She was not exactly laughing at me, but unbelieving and dismissive.

No, I need more concrete information before I talk to her again. Evidence is all that the police care about. I must first find out more about Laker, what else he's into, where he lives and who he visits.

I take out my phone, shocked to discover over a hundred messages and emails. It looks like someone has been signing me up to spam websites. There are emails for hair regrowth, Viagra, get-rich-quick schemes, diet tablets, and more. There's a ton of verification messages, intermingled with emails from someone with a nonsensical email address, *dhdhriebdhrhr@dgrhdhdk.com* giving me the same abuse as all the texts. The same messed-up guy or girl who was texting me earlier, is my guess.

I pop over to Jim Laker's Instagram page. The guy is an Instagram nut.

> *Enjoying summer sun at the Chilli Festival on Hove Lawns with the future missus*

A selfie of Laker and his overtly blonde, trophy-girlfriend. And in the background... David Gentry. Not exactly photo-bombing, but part of the shot. Does he know Laker? Or was he caught passing?

It's not important, Laker is somewhere here at the chilli festival. As I examine his feed, another photo appears.

> *Waiting in the queue for the i360... Gonna be awesome!*

A dizzying shot of the i360, a tall observation tower at the top of which is a moveable glass donut viewing platform. Brighton's newest tourist attraction, allowing 360-degree views across Brighton, the South Downs and the English Channel.

I look down the beach towards the old pier, where the i360 is located on the landward side, just above the beach. The capsule is descending, which means Laker and his girlfriend will be up next.

It's time me and Laker had another chat. I jump to my feet and race towards it.

59

BY THE time I reach the i360, it's already ascending up its pole. The promenade is crowded, as is everywhere today. A massive queue waits for their turn on this attraction, which has had a rocky start. This heatwave should certainly help with their profit projections. I should've saved my breath. Running in this heat was stupid.

The experience lasts roughly an hour, which means that I'll have to wait. Part of me is relieved. Just what would I say to Laker once I caught up with him anyway?

Did you try and kill Tom Blunt?

Are you a drug dealer?

What have you done to Jozee?

I can't imagine him answering those questions. No. I need to be more circumspect. I decide to follow him home, to find out where he lives—or maybe he'll do something or go somewhere that will give me a clue. The guy lives in Brighton, maybe in walkable distance of the seafront.

It's still damn hot. I cross Kingsway, Brighton and Hove's coastal road that is seemingly always jammed with cars, towards Regency Square and a large café sitting on the lower corner. After a long wait, I manage to get a bottle of water, a cup of milky tea and a seat outside— stealing an empty chair from an excited table of Chinese tourists.

I down the ice-cold water from the bottle, sip at the refreshingly strong tea, and check my emails again. Over a hundred of them, mostly from the same nonsensical email address and still as abusive.

I ignore them. Instead, I go through and try and unsubscribe and block as much of the spam as possible. Deleting all these emails individually on my phone will take forever, so I decide to wait until I'm back home on my laptop. I check the Cackle Comedy Forum again, but there's no new posts.

I try phoning the number that is sending the texts, but it goes to a 'number not recognised'. I search the number online—a little trick I've used in the past to check out missed calls or what I think may be spam. The number is not picked up by any of the websites dedicated to this kind of thing.

It's odd and perplexing. Whoever it is, Jozee sure pissed them off. Maybe she was supposed to meet one of those creeps from that nasty hook-up site and did a no-show. That guy I'd met outside the flat, *BigManInYorFace,* was also very angry about being 'led on' and said he'd make sure everyone else knew Jozee was a prick-teaser. This was very probably the fallout from that. Somehow, they'd gotten my phone number and email address.

I should phone DC Marley and tell her about the hook-up website. I go to my phone's contacts, my thumb hovering over her phone number, but what am I going to do? Talk about this in front of all these people? Informing Marley would make the seedy side of Jozee all too real. I know it's selfish, but what would that make me look like? Some sad sap boyfriend being messed around by his user girlfriend, especially after Marley believed it was Jozee who had broken into my flat to steal my chargers in some prank. No, I need to find out more about Jim Laker. I'm sure he's involved somewhere in this. Positive of it.

From where I am sitting, I can watch the glinting i360 capsule rise to the top of its four-hundred and fifty-foot pole before slowly descending again.

I can't imagine a more loathsome experience, other than flying, which I refuse to do on the simple principle that if man was meant to fly he wouldn't have been given crippling anxiety syndromes.

I regularly check Laker's Instagram feed, but he's not posting anything, which is odd. He's an Instagram nut. The guy likes to keep a record of everything, as his desire to film Nat Naylor *in flagrante delicto* proved. This is very unlike him.

I finish my tea and make my way back to the i360 disembarkation point, waiting patiently for Laker and his girlfriend to appear.

Finally, he emerges, but something is wrong, he's angry. Ruth walks behind him, looking let down. He gives her a quick kiss and storms away, crossing Kingsway and walking through Regency Square, his phone jammed into his face. He's trying to phone somebody and, judging by his reaction, that somebody isn't answering.

I follow him through the maze of backstreets up to Western Road. He waits for a bus and a short while later, gets aboard the Number 1 to Whitehawk, jogging up the stairs to the top deck. I run from my hiding place and also get on the bus, sitting at the back. The bus makes a slow, hot, sweaty journey towards Churchill Square and up St James Street where Laker disembarks, with me in close pursuit. St James Street is a tightly packed hilly road on the eastern side of Brighton, bustling with restaurants, coffee houses and a host of lifestyle-friendly pubs. Today it is heaving with people and, annoyingly, I lose sight of my prey. I step out in to the one-way street, wide enough for only one line of traffic but he has disappeared.

I'm about to give up on my search when I see the white chinos and blue shirt of Scott Wong.

Didn't he tell me he was off to London with his agent? What's he doing here?

Maybe I'm being overly suspicious, but the fact he lied to me about where he was going bothers me. Could he possibly be here to meet Laker? A host of possibilities fly through my head. Perhaps Wong was in that car with Tom and Laker. That could explain why Laker was so pissed off when he came off the i360. Maybe Wong had got in touch, told him I was onto them?

Wong walks up to the top of St James Street, taking a left into a side-street cluttered with parked cars from a local garage. The buildings here are varied, but mostly used for business, including an acting school and what looks like a web company. He stops at one of these buildings towards the sea-end, hits a door buzzer and waits. A few seconds later he pushes himself inside.

I go and take a look. This is a business building, the companies and organisations are all non-descript, apart from one called *Brighton Rock Drug and Rehabilitation Clinic.*

60

I PRESS the buzzer and a few seconds later, it's answered by an efficient sounding female voice.

"Yes?"

"I was wondering if there was a… um… meeting today?"

A pause. "Yes, Cocaine Addicts Anonymous. Is this your first time?"

"Um… yeah."

The door buzzes to let me in, but instead, I guiltily walk away, finding a spot to wait out of the sun. Time passes slowly, piquing the interest of two mechanics working in an open-fronted garage. I suppose they are wondering what I'm up to, standing here on a hot day like this. And so am I…

I'm hoping to see both Laker and Wong emerge. Then again, have I actually seen Laker take coke?

No.

He may still be dealing it, I suppose—and using it to get a quick leg-over—while coming here for rehab. According to Wong, Laker had a problem two years ago. Maybe Laker was trying to get off the stuff.

Finally, people start to emerge. Men and women of all types and ages—I shouldn't be shocked that this pernicious drug affects the lives of so many, but these guys are the antithesis of what I envision when I think of the word 'addict'. They are 'normal'—whatever that is.

I tried coke once many years ago. For someone with an overactive mind, it wasn't the most pleasant of experiences, although at the time I thought I'd made some wonderful discovery about myself, only later to realise that this discovery was linked to the almost superhuman amount of shit I was filled with.

Wong emerges with another guy, tall with greying hair in a ponytail, wearing hippie pants and a loose shirt. Not someone I'd associate with the clean-cut Wong, but who am I to judge?

I take a few steps back just as Wong glances in my direction.

Did he see me?

I wait a few moments and follow him and his friend back to St James Street where they enter a small coffeehouse and have a heart to heart over twin cappuccinos in a window-seat. Wong sits with his back to the street. The conversation seems intense and more cappuccinos are ordered.

I wonder if this is what the life of a private detective is like—forever standing around, spying on people. Apart from the mind-numbing boredom, the sense I'm invading someone's privacy is disconcerting. Wong may be entirely innocent in any of this. Sure, he lied about going to London, but what was he going to say? 'You can't talk to me after the gig because I'm going off to my regular addicts anonymous session'. I suppose not.

Before I realise what's happening, a taxi pulls up outside. Wong jumps up, shakes hands with the ponytail guy and exits the café, before opening the taxi door and getting inside. The car pulls away, leaving me behind on the street. I'm not sure if I'm annoyed or relieved. I'm not made for following people like this, that much is for sure. Yet Wong being involved with drugs... with cocaine, docs make me suspect him. Then again, if he was somehow involved with Tom's hit and run, or with Laker, why tell me he remembered that night at all? And Nat Naylor corroborated his story... unless they are all involved somehow?

I shake my head. No. That is unlikely... but I still need to be sure.

The man with the ponytail isn't showing any signs of leaving the café just yet. I go inside and sit opposite him.

He's mid-way through rolling a cigarette and seems startled by my appearance.

"Can we chat?" I ask.

He gives me the onceover, raises his eyebrows and nods. "Sure, why not." His voice is northern, his tones warm and friendly. This close, I notice faded musical note tattoos poking from the neck of his shirt.

He also wears a guitar-shaped earring and a skull and crossbones ring on his pinky finger.

"I think you might have caught the sun. You're looking a little red my friend."

"Am I?" I reply, feeling left-footed. "I burn easily and forgot my sun-block."

"You need to be careful in weather like this."

"Yeah, it's hot out there."

"So what do you want?" he says after the pleasantries have finished. "I saw you watching over the road. If you're into men, I'm not your guy. I'm fully butter-side up, if you know what I mean?"

I smile and shake my head. "I saw you leave the rehab clinic."

A knowing look passes over his face. "Right. I didn't see you in there. First-timer with cold feet?"

"Yeah."

"It's nothing to be ashamed of. But you're taking the right steps. First is realising you've got a problem. What's your name?"

"Um… Stevo."

"Well done, *Um Stevo*. I'm Martin. Pleased to meet you."

He offers his hand over the table and we shake.

"A friend recommended it to me. I don't know if you've heard of him. Jim Laker, the comic."

A quick shake of his head. "No. But coke affects a lot of people in the entertainment industry." He flicks a finger at his guitar-shaped earring. "Although it's not restricted to us alone. The problem is far wider."

"So how do these sessions work?"

"First off, you need to get signed up and assigned a sponsor. That's what I am. Someone to help guide you through your addiction. A friendly, supportive voice at the end of the phone should you be tempted."

"Do you talk about… personal things?"

"Sure. But be assured that everything that is said, never leaves the meeting. We are a supportive group. We do not condemn. We've all done things we regret."

"But what if that thing was something illegal?"

"You mean like buying or selling coke? Pimping? Assault? Domestic abuse? I could go on. The list is endless. We don't judge in the group, we listen and lend support."

"What if someone was involved in the deaths of people."

Martin sits back and contemplates me again. "Sure, some in our group have admitted how their actions have resulted in the deaths of others. Addiction can lead to harmful behaviours. Is this… is this something you may have done? Just a yes or no will suffice, you don't need to go into detail."

"Me?" I shake my head. "Has anyone in your group been involved in a hit or run?"

"Just what are you getting at?"

"Has anyone in the group admitted to such a thing?"

"I can't divulge anything in particular, but no. Nothing like that. Is this what you did? Was this your crime?"

"No one?" I ask. "Not even Scott Wong, who you were just talking to?"

"Who the hell are you?"

"Someone looking for the truth."

"I thought it was odd, you standing there watching us like that. What are you? A bloody reporter?"

Before I can respond, he snatches his roll-up off the table, stands up and pushes his chair back noisily. "You're a parasite," he says. "Of the vilest kind. A parasite!"

He leaves the café and walks angrily away.

For the second time today, people in a café turn to stare at me. I'm rapidly becoming a pariah. I'm expecting to feel guilt at what I just did, but instead there's nothing. An empty hole. Martin made no reaction when I mentioned the hit and run. Another dead end.

One thing is for sure though, it's now early evening and I'm no closer to finding Jozee. The thought makes me feel glum and sad for myself. I order a coffee and sit back, changing my position to also stare out of the window. Maybe Jim Laker will walk past. Unlikely, but what else can I do?

61
SATURDAY NIGHT

I WALK home after the café, only stopping to get myself a burger and fries that I almost inhale, ignoring the pain from my split lip. I've hardly eaten since Jozee disappeared and, unlike the other night's disastrous kebab, the burger thankfully stays down. The early evening temperature drops only fractionally as the sun makes its slow, ponderous way below the horizon, lengthening shadows and making me squint as I head back towards Hove, sweat dropping off me like a melting ice-cream, my skin hot and clammy.

Back at the flat, I'm hit by a wave of tiredness. A quick inspection in my bathroom mirror reveals Martin was right about the sun. My face is bright red, a blush that stretches down my neck to form a perfect V-shape that matches my open-necked shirt. My arms are also similarly-coloured and beginning to sting. I slather myself in moisturiser, too tired to rub it in, and drop, fully-clothed onto my bed and into a deep, deep sleep.

Sometime later I'm awoken by what I think is the sound of my flat buzzer. I lie half-awake for a few moments unsure if the sound was in my dreams or reality. I hear a sound like a squeak—it is my buzzer, but not the normal, loud, insistent trilling, but more of a bleep. As if the battery is going, or there is a short in the mechanism. I see a vision of Jozee outside Eaton Palace Gardens, weak, trying to press the buzzer and failing.

I'm up, out of my bed and at the door in seconds. "Jozee!" I blurt over the com. "Jozee? Is that you?"

There's no reply… and is that the sound of someone breathing?

I tear down the stairwell to the front door, flinging it open to find nothing. No one is here. No Jozee, no anybody.

I take out my phone. It's just past 3am. No messages. No phone calls.

"Is anyone here?" I shout impotently into the hot, sweaty night, feeling the stretch of painful, sun-burned skin around my mouth.

Sudden movement out the corner of my eye. Before I can turn to see what it is, I'm hit by an explosion of white and then blackness.

62

MY HEAD is throbbing and my throat dry—my tongue stuck to the roof of my mouth. Something is dreadfully wrong, but I can't put my finger on what it is. I try to move my hands, but they're paralysed, as are my legs.

What's happened? Where am I?

I push open my eyes to a thin slit and harsh light sears into my brain.

"So, you've finally come round?" says a familiar voice that I can't quite place. "I wondered if I'd hit you a little too hard. But something tells me you've got quite a thick skull around that annoying brain of yours."

The words are confident, but the tone belies nervousness and a little fear. They are also slurred and quickly spat out.

I turn my head towards the voice and try and focus, but my eyes refuse to adjust. The air around me is smoky, and I smell the ripe, cloying aroma of cannabis.

"A little bird tells me you've been nosing around. Asking questions about Tom. About that hit and run."

"Tom?" I reply. And everything comes rushing back to me. Jozee missing, the hit and run, going to see who was at my flat door and… *someone hitting me over the head!*

"Don't play the innocent, Adam," the voice continues, sneering my name. A voice I now recognise.

"Laker!" I spit back, my eyes finally focussing to see him sitting back on a chair, a large spliff held in shaking fingers, his eyes glittering and manic, like he's also coked up. Twitching, fidgeting and freaked out. He's wearing a loose white shirt and shorts and sweating hard, his collar-length hair matted and sticking to his neck and reddened face.

"The one and the same."

I'm sitting in a chair opposite him, in the same room in the isolated mansion Laker and Nat were in yesterday. The used condom still lies on the floor next to the grubby mattress. My hands are gaffer-taped to the armrests, my legs to the legs of the chair. A single, harsh bulb shines brightly from an unshaded light-fitting.

"So, it *was* you!" I croak from a dry, painful throat. The air is clammy, sweat running down my back. "I knew it all along. I was wrong about so many things, but I was right about you."

I'm elated for the barest of seconds before I realise my predicament. This house is in the middle of nowhere and I'm at the mercy of this drugged up lunatic comedian. But I can't think about my own personal woes at this time. I have bigger concerns.

"Where's Jozee? If you've done anything to hurt her, I'm gonna make you pay, understand?" I struggle against the gaffer-tape, but I'm held fast, the chair creaking under me.

"Jozee?" Laker replies in surprise. "I've no idea where that stupid little bitch has got to. She's left you, if she has any sense. And is never coming back."

"Don't lie to me!"

Laker sits back in his chair and takes a long toke on his spliff, before blowing out thick smoke in my direction. "Like I told you, I know squat about her disappearance."

"You really don't know where she is?"

"Nope."

"But you must've had something to do with it. Look at what you're doing… you've kidnapped and tied me up for fuck's sake!"

"She's not why I brought you here. She's got nothing to do with it."

"Why then? What is this about?"

"Nat tells me you've been nosing around asking questions about me and that awful night of the hit and run." And then I spotted you following me. Did you think I wouldn't notice?"

"You really don't know where Jozee is?" I ask, ignoring him. Unable to fully comprehend what he's telling me.

"Forget her!" he replies, visibly irritated. "This has nothing to do with that bitch."

"I don't believe you. It's not hard to put two and two together. Tom didn't drive home alone on the night of the hit and run. You were in the car with him. And Tom told Jozee, didn't he? Except that he kept your name out of it. Took all the blame himself. That's why Jozee dumped him."

Laker shrugs. "You were gonna find out I was in the car with Tom on that night, sooner or later. Why else do you think you're here? But Jozee never guessed about that. To her, I am a hero. Saving poor old Tom after his attempted overdose. Why else do you think she treats me like one of her besties? Not that I'm complaining, I always love how jealous you get whenever she's around me."

"So, you didn't sleep with her?"

"Chance would be a fine thing," he replies. "It's what I wanted to do—and to tell you all about it afterwards—but I was ordered to leave it alone. Although a quick-leg over was certainly on the cards before you came along. Jozee is easy and…" He looks me up and down and sneers, "…she is not very discriminating. If you know what I mean."

I'm tied up and at his mercy. Laker has no reason to lie and, even though I don't want to, I find myself believing him. "What do you mean 'ordered'?"

"You'll find out soon enough."

A chill goes through me. Who is he talking about?

"Okay," I say, "it makes sense Jozee didn't know you were in the car at the time of the hit and run, otherwise she would've been as upset with you as she was with Tom. But you were involved in the cover up, you had to be."

Laker shrugs again.

"It was you who convinced Tom to keep quiet about the hit and run wasn't it? Something to do with drugs is my guess. Scott Wong told me there is quite a coke scene amongst some Brighton comics. And I know you've been supplying Nat." I nod at the condom on the floor. "And giving her a helluva lot more. I'm thinking you're the dealer. And someone had to give Tom the heroin for the overdose… or overdosed him on purpose."

"You what!" Laker bellows, raising his fists.

"I'm saying that it was very convenient for you that Tom did what he did."

"It's not my fault that Tom took the easy way out to spend the rest of his life as a vegetable. You can't put that on me. No way."

The bang of the front door closing and slow, purposeful footsteps on the stairs getting louder until they reach the landing outside. The door creaks open, I strain to see who it is, but my chair is facing away.

"Laker, you little prick! What the feck do you think you're playing at?"

63

DONNIE COOGAN! I can't believe my ears or my eyes.

"What the balls is this," Donnie says, ignoring me and going over to Laker. "Why in tarnation did you bring him here? I told you, this house is out of bounds."

"He's been asking about the hit and run. About who was in the car that night."

"And you thought that was reason enough to kidnap him, you fecking eejit!"

Donnie hits Laker in the face with the back of his hand, knocking his spliff onto the floor, where it smoulders.

Laker pulls an expression like a wounded dog. "I'm sorry, Don," he squeaks. "I only did what I thought was for the best."

"'Sorry' doesn't cut it with me, laddie. I told you, we're in the clear. You've fecked up this time, good and proper."

"But he knows!"

Donnie turns his attention back to me. Gone is the affable, buffoonish comic and in his place, someone infinitely more calculating and sinister. "So, Adam, what exactly do you know?"

It is evident who is in charge here. Laker is too disorganised and too damn high. No, he has an accomplice, a mastermind of sorts. I make the obvious conclusion. "Laker wasn't the only one taking a lift home with Tom that night. You were also in the car, weren't you?"

"Was I?" Donnie replies with a gentle shrug of his shoulders. "What evidence do you have to support your accusation?"

"Nothing, so far. But connect the fact that Laker is dealing drugs and Tom's supposed overdose, and you've got a reason for attempted murder. Tom was going to the police, wasn't he?"

Donnie shrugs. "It makes no difference what Tom was going to do. The guy is a vegetable, or didn't you notice that when you visited him?"

"You know about that? What am I thinking, of course you do. Nurse Sally!"

"I have an arrangement with her," Donnie continues. "The bent tart has been keeping a watch on the lad, should he ever show any signs of waking up. Which he hasn't done." He turns to Laker. "Adam has nothing on us, couldn't you see that?"

I take a deep breath. "Maybe on the face of it, but put everything I've found out all together and—"

"And what?" Donnie blurts, his Irish accent taking on a more forceful, threatening tone. "The hit and run investigation is still open," he continues dismissively, "but with no suspects or a car, there's nothing for the police to go on. And I can guarantee you that Tom's car isn't going to magically reappear. And if Jozee ever turns up, all she knows is that Tom was driving the car that night. I made sure Laker kept close to her, just in case she twigged, but she knows nada."

My heart lurches at the mention of Jozee's name. Is it possible— are these lunatics uninvolved in her disappearance?

I struggle against the gaffer-tape. "So it was you who bought Tom a replacement car to shut him up. The four-by-four Laker now drives. And all along I thought it was him who was the big deal here, the drug dealer. But it's you, Donnie, isn't it?"

Donnie shrugs. "Don't make me laugh. I own many properties and businesses and have many fingers in many pies. All legit and above board. There's nothing guilty about being a business man. I can account for every damn penny—or my accountant can. But your accusations are getting tiresome. You've got nothing on me or Laker, just make-believe. And as for Tom's overdose? That investigation is closed. Suicide. We didn't know he was going to try and kill himself. How could we? The guy was cut up about your lass dumping him so horribly in public, not helped by that video posted on social media. But Tom was always weak. It pushed him over the edge."

"As far as I know, Tom was no druggie," I say. "Especially after the hit and run. So where did he get the heroin from?"

"Desperate people do desperate things, Adam," Donnie says, but I know I've touched a nerve. "And this is Brighton," Donnie continues, giving a casual wave of his hand. "You want heroin? You can find it on the right street corner. Go to the police if you want, tell them everything and anything you know. But where's your evidence? You've got feck all, laddie. Although I would strongly advise against involving them."

"No evidence? You've kidnapped me, don't forget. How's that gonna play out?"

A frown creases Donnie's face. "Yeah, I'm sorry about that." He turns to Laker. "You weren't stupid enough to get yerself caught on CCTV, were you?"

Laker shakes his head, rubbing at his face where Donnie backhanded him. "No. There's nothing covering the street outside Adam's flat."

Annoyingly, Laker is right. I checked for CCTV the day after Jozee's disappearance. Just those cameras next door, and they were pointing the wrong way.

Laker retrieves his spliff off the floor, puts it out with a pinch of his fingers and slides it into his pocket. "It was 3am. No one was about, I made sure of it."

"In Hove?" Donnie's tone was incredulous. "There's always some fecker about. That was risky, you stupid wee cunt. There're cameras everywhere these days. You've made a difficult situation worse. You at least offed his phone, I hope?"

"Sure, I'm not stupid." He pulls out my phone and waves it at Donnie. "There's no way it can be tracked back here, and this area has little or no signal."

"Good. At least you did one thing right."

"I'm sorry, Don. Really sorry."

"Now listen to me," Donnie says. "And listen good. You're gonna drop this prick back home, okay? And if anyone reports this stupid stunt to the police, you'll tell them it was a prank."

"But what if Adam says different, or goes to the police himself?"

"I think I can convince him to keep his mouth shut," Donnie says with a considered raise of his eyebrows.

With all the talk, I've forgotten my predicament, that I am their prisoner, trussed up and at their mercy. Laker doesn't worry me, but Donnie? He is a totally different proposition. There's steel behind his eyes. As far as I can tell, he's going to let me go, although I doubt he will just untie me, open the door and send me on my way. I decide to try and negotiate a way out of this with minimal pain and suffering.

"Consider me already convinced, okay? I won't say anything. I was only trying to find Jozee. I thought that… well, that she'd found out about the hit and run, and you silenced her, but I'm back to sodding square one."

Donnie's face softens, his chubby frame seeming massive as he towers above me, lit by the single harsh bulb hanging in the middle of the room. "I'm sorry, lad, I have no idea of Jozee's whereabouts. Where she's gone to is a mystery to me. It's you that's my main concern. You and your blabby mouth. I don't want to hurt you—you're in quite a state as it is—but I will if I have to, believe me. I just need your word that you'll keep schtum and we can put this behind us, you understand?"

I draw breath to speak, but Donnie raises a single finger.

"Be warned, Adam. You break your word with me and I'll break every bone in your body… one at a time."

Even though this is the first time I've seen this different, harder Donnie, I take his threat very seriously. I have no doubt he will hurt me and hurt me bad. "I'm only interested in finding Jozee. I give you my word to say nothing about the hit and run, or this dumb kidnapping. I won't even mention the porn dungeon."

Donnie's eyes narrow. "Porn? What the feck are you talking about?"

"I followed Nat and Laker here yesterday," I say, seeing an opportunity to get Laker into more trouble with Donnie. "He was dealing coke in return for sex."

"You sneaky little shit!" Laker blurts.

Donnie whirls onto Laker. "Is this right?" he asks, his tone full of ice. "You were fecking that wee floozie here?"

Laker baulks. "Yeah, sure. I sometimes bring girls to this place. Every now and then." He turns to me. "I knew I heard something yesterday. Was that you then, Adam, hiding upstairs? You pervy little creep. How did you know about this place and how did you get in?"

I say nothing.

Donnie is livid, and I smile inside.

"You led him here? When I gave you strict instructions to stay away from this place?"

Laker shrugs, but I can see he's scared. "It was just a line of coke and a screw."

"Then why ask Nat if you could film it?" I interject, enjoying watching Laker squirm. "I saw those cameras down in the basement. You're the pervy creep not me. Is that what you do? Fill girls with drugs and make cheap nasty porn?"

Laker appears to be genuinely confused. "Cameras? What the heck are you talking about? I film on my phone," he says, pulling out his mobile. "POV. The full personal experience. You'd be surprised to find out who I've got on here. It's quite the show-reel."

Donnie's eyes sparkle coldly. "Get out," he says to Laker. "Get out of my sight and out of this house, you understand?"

"What? I thought you wanted me to drop this twat off back home?"

Donnie shakes his head in a way that means his order isn't up for discussion. "Just leave. I'll deal with Adam. I want to continue our chat in private. Give me the house keys and Adam's phone. Oh, and don't ever come back here."

Laker stands up, looking relieved—he's terrified of Donnie, that much is for sure. "Okay, Don, I'm outta here." He tosses my phone at me. It bounces off my chest and scuttles away along the floor. He pulls out a set of impressive keys from his pocket and hands them to Donnie, before leaning in close to my ear.

"You better listen to Don," he says. "He ain't the type you want as an enemy, that's for sure. And you can forget doing any more comedy gigs in this town, I'm gonna bad-mouth you to every promoter and comic. Not that you were funny, anyway. You got that, you nosey little prick?"

"Just go!" Donnie's voice is a rough growl.

Laker exits down the stairs and slams the front door with a bang.

Being alone with Donnie feels more dangerous than when Laker was here. "So, what's the plan?" I ask as jovially as I can muster under the circumstances. "It's late. I hope you're still going to give me a lift back home."

Donnie remains standing where he is, rock still and says nothing.

"I'm only interested in finding Jozee. I don't care about Laker, drugs, porn… or the damn hit and run. We can forget what Laker did. He's coked up to the eyeballs. Just a silly prank, yeah?" I'm rambling. Something isn't quite right and I'm suddenly very, very scared.

Donnie takes a breath and comes back to life. "If things were only that simple, laddie."

His tone is as cold as ice.

"I'll keep quiet," I say, my voice high-pitched and full of unconscious fear. "I gave you my word, remember?"

Donnie shakes his head. "I'm afraid things have progressed in a way that I'm not comfortable with. You've become a problem, Adam. A problem I'm now forced to make go away."

"What… what do you mean by that?"

He takes out a small, old-fashioned mobile phone—an outdated model from years ago and taps out a number with his pudgy fingers. Those older phones always did have better reception. It hardly seems to ring before he speaks.

"Hi. It's me. Yeah, I'm back already, landed a couple of hours ago. But there's a problem. We need to clean up… Yeah, straightaway. Come over now. There is also a candidate waiting for you. Yeah. He won't be any trouble. I'll make sure of that." Donnie looks at me and pulls a sad smile. "A disposal job. Just someone who needs to be silenced. Don't worry, I'll make sure he's pliant."

My heart is now hammering in my ears. I'm unable to believe what I'm hearing.

He's going to have me killed, but why? What happened to make him change his mind?

Donnie offs his phone, returns it to the pocket of his elegantly tailored silver-grey suit and sighs. "I'm sorry Adam. Despite what's going to happen next, I've always liked you. I thought that, with a little more experience, you'd one day be very funny."

"Why are you doing this? I told you I wasn't going to talk to the police. I gave you my word!"

Donnie doesn't answer.

"Speak to me, Donnie! What are these people going to do with me?"

"It's the business I'm in, you understand? Nothing personal. Just *business*. I'm afraid it's over for you, Adam. That's how it goes sometimes. I've seen it many times before. Unfortunate when it happens, but absolutely necessary in the circumstances. And I can't possibly allow any loose ends." He looks at the used condom on the floor next to the mattress. "No loose ends at all. I'm afraid Laker has also compromised himself, if that's any consolation to you. Then again, he was always gonna be a problem sooner or later."

He leaves the room, goes down the stairs and I hear the front door slam.

Is he leaving me here? I can't believe it. Here's my chance to escape! I wiggle in the chair, trying to break free. The chair is weak and creaky. I hear something crack and I try to twist against it, trying to pull the chair apart. Something else snaps, but I'm still held fast.

The front door opens and closes again. Methodical footsteps on the stairs.

Shit! He's coming back!

Donnie returns, holding a length of thin rubber tubing. I struggle even more, but he sits on me. I hear the chair creaking beneath our conjoined weight, willing it to collapse.

He yanks up my sleeve and ties the rubber tubing around my upper arm, pulling a full syringe out of his pocket.

"Another overdose? Won't that be suspicious?" I say, my heart punching a hole through my ribcage.

"I'm just giving you a slightly higher dose than we give to the gals. Helps with their work, if you know what I mean?"

"What girls? What else are you involved in?"

He chuckles. "This isn't gonna kill you, boy. No, no, laddie. Not like I tried with Tom."

"So, it was you who gave Tom the overdose!" I say, feeling like I'm in the midst of some fantastical dream. But this is here, now and happening to me.

"Tom was going to the police," Donnie explains. "I couldn't let that happen. And he would've died if that idiot Laker hadn't found him. But fortunately, he was too late."

"If you're not trying to kill me," I say, glancing sideways at the syringe and the needle poised over my arm, "what are you doing?"

"Making you pliant for when my associates arrive. Professionals you might call them. I don't get my hands dirty anymore. And I have to be off. More business to attend to. Oh, and just to let you know about Tom and that hit and run. I had a big bag of coke that night, too big to be caught with by the police. It's not often that I partake, but we all need to unwind sometimes. I was slap-happy dishing it out, via Laker of course. I'm no eejit. On the way home, when we hit those stupid teen gals—who ran out blitzed drunk in front of us on a dark country lane like a pair of suicidal twats—the bag of coke exploded. Went everywhere. Sent us all a bit manic. I didn't think straight. But I knew enough to realise that with two dead girls and ten grand's worth of coke in the car, we were all going down. It would've been game over for all three of us. Keeping Tom quiet was always going to be a problem though. He was the sensitive type. Unable to put things behind him. He came to tell me he was going to the police the night of his unfortunate overdose. As you may imagine, that was the worst mistake of his short wee life." He sighs at the memory. "Now, laddie… are you ready?"

"Don't do it, Donnie, don't!"

"See this as a little goodbye treat."

He jabs the needle into the crook of my arm and slowly squeezes the plunger. "Sweet dreams."

64

I FEEL a warm rush surging through my body like a tidal bore, and I'm hit with an instantaneous wave of euphoria. I sink into the chair, falling through it into the floor, sucked down into a place of no cares or worries.

I hear Donnie say something, but his words are indistinct, far away and dreamy.

I've only smoked weed a few times, to unsuccessfully try and relax. Heroin is a hundred times more intense. Am-a-zing. Wonderful. I'm fully disconnected from the world for the first time in my life. A floating, dream-like state free of all worry and concern, like I'm cocooned in cotton wool. I no longer care what Donnie has planned for me, or what's going to happen when those people he phoned arrive. I'm aware of him moving around, but he no longer frightens me. Nothing frightens me anymore. I wish I could feel like this forever.

Is this how Tom felt? It doesn't seem such a bad way to go after all.

I open my mouth to try and speak and feel suddenly nauseous, but the sensation passes, my mind slipping into an indecipherable haze. I'm unable to think, just to enjoy, smiling and laughing at myself and all those silly worries that seem like nothing more than wispy clouds in a blue summer sky. Trivial concerns. Nothing.

I want to feel like this forever.

But I can't.

Something niggles at me. A name. It floats around in my mind, bouncing off my sensibilities, jarring them… and it won't go away.

Jozee.

It chides against my euphoria, and it won't let itself be ignored. And slowly, my mind begins to focus, centring on that name. Allowing it to grow and flourish. I don't care about myself, I realise, not anymore… but I do care about Jozee.

I love her.

She's missing and needs me.

I have to escape. I must…

My brain wants to do things, to get up, to try and free myself from the chair, but my body won't move. I'm not paralysed, I just don't have the strength, like my muscles have turned to sponge.

But I have to! I can't stay here!

I wriggle my toes and fingers, getting life back into them. Willing them to move, but I keep dropping into unconsciousness and coming back seconds or minutes later—slow-motion waves crashing against a faraway island shore. And with each ponderous wave, I become more lucid. I wriggle and jerk, breathe as deeply as I can, forcing my ribs to move. And sluggishly, I come back to myself.

I open my eyes and force myself to keep them open, staring at the single harsh lightbulb. Focussing on it. The room is empty. The house quiet. I twist and writhe life back into my limbs, fighting against the dragon that inhabits my veins. Trying to mentally force it out of my system. Screaming at myself to recover.

C'mon, Adam! Do this! For Jozee!

I spy my phone on the other side of the room. It concentrates my mind and, even though I keep zoning out, I work my body against the chair, grinding and pushing. After what seems like an age, I hear it creak and, with another snap, it half-collapses under me, jerking me sideways, although I'm still sitting, but at an angle. I notice my right leg is free. I try and stand up but fall back on myself, the chair crunching below me. I repeat the movement until the left armrest breaks in two. I zone out with the effort, before coming back to myself some unknown time later. I take as many deep breaths as I can and half-whining, half-screaming, force myself up on one leg and hop towards the wall, throwing myself at it. I hear the crash and snap of broken wood, but I don't feel the impact. Instead, I fall into the wall, dropping down through it, into the dungeon below, and further down into a black pit of nothingness.

My eyes flicker open. I'm disorientated, unsure of who or where I am. I stare, unable to comprehend what's in front of me, trying to make sense of it for long minutes until, like a camera that comes into sudden focus, I see a grubby carpet and broken bits of furniture. I'm lying, crumpled on the floor. And then I remember. Donnie. The chair. Jozee and… *escape!*

I'm able, with pathetic half-movements, to wrench myself free of the broken chair, kicking its remains away with my feet. I crawl over to my phone just as I hear vehicles pull up outside, the sounds of doors being opened and closed and the thud of boots.

Am I imagining it?

I scramble to unsteady feet that feel disconnected from my legs, like they belong to someone else, and lurch out of the bedroom. A key goes into the lock downstairs and I'm forced to clamber on all fours up to the next landing and the room with the window. The room I climbed into an age ago.

Many people enter the house, I hear foreign voices and the tramp of purposeful, booted feet.

If they find me, I'm dead.

Commotion from below. I guess they've found the broken chair and now know I've escaped. The booted feet thump around, rushed and angry, running up the stairs. They will find me any second…

I push open the window, clamber out onto the ledge, and slide it shut behind me. A bright light illuminates me from inside the room. I sidle sideways, nearly falling, knowing that they must have seen me.

SUNDAY MORNING

I PERCH on the windowsill, bathed in the light from the room. Knowing that I've been found, knowing that these dangerous men will open the window, drag me inside and kill me. Time passes interminably, even the scudding beat of my heart seems to slow down. But, after what I assume is cursing in a foreign language, the light goes off and I'm plunged into darkness. I'm guessing they saw their own reflection in the glass and not me perching outside.

I'm still not yet over the heroin and I wobble on the windowsill, momentarily losing my sense of where I am. If I fall now, I'll be dead or seriously injured. Not that that would matter when those guys found me. I push back into the glass, giving myself a point of reference. I stand up, running my hands over the bricks that surround the window frame, my fingers finding their outlines, rubbing against the rough mortar. Cracks, fissures and cobwebs. I think of the history of these bricks. When and where they were made. Of the person who laid them probably fifty or so years before. What he was thinking. Where he was now. Alive or dead. Not knowing that one day these bricks would save someone's life. And slowly, my eyes adjust to the dark, and I find myself again.

I'm tired, not only from the opioids in my system, but from the intensity of the last few days. I so want to drift away. But that word comes back and starts to shout at me.

Jozee! It says. *JOZEE!*

I force myself to stay awake and become aware of angry voices and the flash of torches below. A bright light shines right at me and I instinctively close my eyes, thinking that this will somehow protect me. And somehow it does. I can't believe it, they didn't see me.

The voices go back inside. I stay where I am, keeping myself awake—my stupid overactive brain is actually useful for the very first time. Although most of my thoughts are concerned with discovery and what these guys might do to me.

The sun is rising. It must be sometime past 5.30am. Even at this early hour, the sun on my face and neck stings. But I have more important concerns. If the men come out again and stare up, they will see me. I hear the front door opening and a flurry of voices and the tramp of boots. I pull myself up onto the roof, clambering up to the chimney. Hiding behind the thick stack of bricks, the sun is now fully up. But even if they come around to the back of the house, I'm hidden.

I hear the men going back and forth for another fifteen minutes. Then, the slamming of car doors and the sound of gunning engines.

I poke my head around the chimney stack and see a white van followed by an impressively massive black pick-up truck. Its cargo area full and covered with a green tarpaulin. They go off in different directions, powering down the country road. In the distance, the morning sky looms huge and blue over yellow fields.

I stay on the roof for the next few hours, occasionally snoozing, too afraid to come down, wondering if anyone else is in the house, waiting for me to show myself. Aware of my body metabolising the opioids in my system, feeling increasingly thirsty in the growing heat of another oppressively hot day. Slowly, I emerge from the fug. My memories of the last few hours are nightmarish. Like a dream, but I know they are real.

I periodically check my phone, but there's no signal. I have no way to call the police to get them here. I'm on my own and I can't stay here forever. Behind the house is the impressive hedge I saw yesterday. And behind it are fields. I decide to climb down and take my chances. It's not what I want to do, but I can't see any other way out. If anyone is left behind, I'm sure I would've heard them searching the house or garden. But it's also likely they are down there, silently waiting.

I move as cautiously and as quietly as I can. Catlike and agile.

Although my head and body are still not right. I'm whacked out and distant. And, if I'm honest, missing the euphoric feel of heroin.

I've always been anti-drug, but not in that blind, *all-drugs-are-evil* way popularised by hypocritical coke-snorting politicians. No. I'm actually in favour of full legalisation of all drugs for lots of sensible reasons. But I've never really liked the idea myself. Cannabis makes me paranoid and the only time I took speed, my heart beat so fast and so long that I thought I might have a heart attack, although I managed a lot of midnight cleaning and other domestic work I'd been putting off for weeks.

Heroin was different. The wonderful oblivion was something I didn't expect. A way of leaving my life—*of leaving me, behind*. I know a lot of people see heroin users as just druggies and losers. But I now realise they may have a deeper story. I understand why damaged people are so susceptible to it. The drug offers them escape. A way to leave the horrors of everyday life behind. A way to shut everything out. The memories, the abuse, the life they are now trapped in.

Such wonderful, bliss-like oblivion.

Avoiding all the windows, I climb silently down into the back garden, my heart thumping so loudly that it makes me worry that someone lurking in the house may be able to hear it.

My eye is taken by a yellowed indentation in the grass. Something has been removed. The satellite dish I saw the other day. Did those guys take it? They must've done, but why?

I don't have time to ponder. I push myself through the hedge and into the field beyond, crouching low and run along its length, getting as far away from the house and its nightmares as possible.

66

AS THE distance between myself and the mansion increases, so does my elation.

I escaped. I made it.

After a mile or two, skirting the road, I come to another house and my phone beeps into life.

I crouch down and check my messages, hoping for a word from Jozee. There's nothing from her, other than a long apology from Stevo and more of those abusive emails. Some of them have large attachments and are taking ages to download and suck at my battery and my data allowance, which must be pretty close to the edge. I ignore them all, and instead bring up Google Maps to find my location.

I phone 999. When asked for the nature of my emergency, I tell them 'attempted murder'. They ask if I want to stay on the phone while a police car is despatched, but I decline.

Twenty or so minutes later, a police car followed by a police van arrive and I burst from my hiding place, surprised to see DC Marley getting out of the lead car.

What's she doing here?

"Adam Hanson," she says grabbing my wrists, a pleased look on her face, turning me efficiently around and handcuffing me. "I am formally arresting you on suspicion of being involved in the disappearance of Josephine Margaret Jackson."

"What?" I blurt, flabbergasted, unable to process what's happening.

I'm bustled away and thrown into the back of the van, the doors loudly slamming.

67

SUNDAY AFTERNOON

I'M FINALLY brought up from Brighton Police Station cells and ushered to an 'interview room'. I notice it's very different from the one in which I met DC Marley Friday morning. The strip-lighting seems deliberately bright and the decor is anything but welcoming, as is the smell.

Since my arrest, I've not seen Marley or found out the reasons behind why I was arrested, only that it was in connection to the disappearance of Jozee... *not her murder*, which means a body hasn't been found. Thank God.

Jozee could still be alive.

But I'm her boyfriend and, as these things tend to go, the likeliest person to have caused Jozee harm. I know I'm not guilty and as soon as I can establish this fact, the sooner I can get out of here and the sooner they can start looking for Jozee. I'm pleased that the police are now taking all of this seriously but being treated like a criminal is a sobering experience.

I was taken to the station and thoroughly searched. My clothes were removed, and I was given slip-on pumps, sweatpants and a t-shirt. Afterwards, I was met by a custody sergeant, a rather intimidating woman who clearly enjoyed her job of *banging up perps*. I was assigned a duty solicitor and given a notice explaining my rights under the Police and Criminal Evidence Act. They took my fingerprints and a DNA swab. I complained about that, but apparently, they have the right, as explained in my handy leaflet.

The things you learn when you're suspected of murder...

A doctor was also summoned to give me the once-over. I told

her about the heroin Donnie gave me, after which a blood sample was requested. Apparently, I didn't have to give blood unless I was arrested for drink or drug-driving, but I gave her permission anyway, especially as I didn't want Donnie to get away with what he did. Even so, it was obvious the doctor didn't believe my story of abduction and near murder, that much was for sure. She asked me about any pre-existing conditions and I grudgingly admitted my autism, which she took a note of. Finally, after I was given some cream to help with my sunburn, I was passed as 'fit'.

After a few other basic tests, I was taken to a vomit and urine-smelling cell, consisting of a toilet and a single bench with a thin mattress—although it was more like a yoga-mat and just as comfortable. Before the door was banged shut, the custody sergeant warned me not to graffiti or 'mark' the cell walls otherwise I'd be charged with criminal damage. And then I was left to my own devices for the next few hours.

The time did not pass easily. The aircon was set too high and I was almost freezing. I tried to sleep, yet my dreams were full of Donnie Coogan's leering face, of being chased, hiding from some nameless terror and falling. Forever falling. So, when they came for me, I was somewhat relieved, if not anxious to put DC Marley and her fellow officers straight.

I'm welcomed into the interview room by a scruffy looking overweight man in an open-necked shirt wearing a cheap suit, with a mop of balding curling hair and thick glasses. He gives me his hand and we shake.

"Hi Adam, I'm Adeep Singh, today's duty solicitor," he says with a jollity I find off-putting. He shows me to a seat and sits down. "My job is to give representation to people in custody, which in this instance is yourself. And to arrange bail should it be offered. However, in your situation, that's going to be unlikely. I'm here to sit through your interview to make sure your rights are not violated. You understand?"

"I didn't do it. I didn't hurt Jozee," I say.

"That's all good and well, but it won't be enough to satisfy DCI Evans, I'm afraid."

"DCI Evans?"

"He's in charge of the investigation into the disappearance of Josephine Jackson. Now before we continue, and I have to ask, do you understand my role here?"

"To represent me, I suppose," I venture feebly.

"I'm a temporary solicitor. If your stay is longer than twenty-four hours, which is likely in a case like this, then the next duty solicitor on the roster will be assigned to you. Okay?"

I nod. "How long can they hold me here?"

Adeep Singh shrugs. "Suspicion of murder is treated very much like actual murder. And for murder and all serious crimes, you may be kept in custody for up to ninety-six hours."

"Ninety-six bloody hours!"

"Please calm down, Mr Hanson. I've read the doctor's report. Autism tends to play badly with cops, you understand? Anything that's not normal… well, they might see that as acting guiltily. They will also be briefed on your condition, and its possible they may try and use it, and your recent opioid use, against you. However, I will be here to make sure they don't do that. How you feeling?"

"Anxious. Properly anxious."

"Okay, let me try and calm some of those nerves. Firstly, do not answer any questions you are unsure about without asking for my advice. I will also be on hand to make sure questions asked of you are fair. Remember to be polite and, if possible, try not to swear. The interview will be digitally recorded and filmed on CCTV. The days of tape recordings have long gone. The interview may also become confrontational on occasion, just remember that they are only trying to do their job, the same as I'm doing my job now. So, no matter how irate or annoyed you may feel, try not to fall out with them—try to treat them with the same respect with which you expect to be treated, okay?"

"And that is supposed to calm me down?"

The solicitor shrugs.

The interview room door opens and in walks DC Ella Marley, carrying a sheaf of papers and some folders that she places on the desk in front of us, followed by a competent, dull looking man with prematurely receding, closely trimmed ginger hair. He sits down and presses a tab of what I'm guessing is a digital recorder, built into the wall. A long tone and the recording equipment kicks in.

"Interview begins," DCI Evans says. "The time is 12.43pm on Sunday the eighth of July. In attendance, myself, DCI Evans, DC Marley, duty solicitor, Adeep Singh, and suspect, Adam John Hanson. Adam, you are here to answer questions regarding the disappearance of Josephine Margaret Jackson."

"Disappearance? Then you still haven't found a body then?" I say, showing my relief with an unconscious smile, which I soon realise makes me look and sound guilty as hell.

"Mr Hanson," DCI Evans continues, giving me a 'pleased-with-himself' look. "Can you tell me your whereabouts on the evening of Tuesday the third of July?"

"I know you think I had something to do with Jozee's disappearance," I say. "But I didn't. At least you are taking this seriously now."

DCI Evans leans forwards. "Just answer the question."

"I was at a gig in Burgess Hill. The Dog and Duck public house. I'm a stand-up. New to the scene. We have to do a lot of these gigs for experience. Jozee drove us both there in her mini earlier that evening."

"For the record, this was a white 1974 Mini Cooper," DC Marley interjects. "Registration RNU 471M. A car that has not been seen since that night."

"Were you angry with your girlfriend that evening, Adam?" Evans continues. "Were you annoyed with the missing person known as Josephine Margaret Jackson, who also goes by the name of Jozee Jackson?"

"I've seen these things on the telly," I reply. "So, let me be as open about this as possible. I'm not going to lie. I'm going to tell you everything I know. Hopefully, you will be able to rule me out of your investigation."

"This will go a lot faster if you just answer the questions," Evans says testily.

"Yes, I was annoyed with Jozee. Angrier than I realised. She'd been distant for a couple of weeks and it had gotten to me."

"When you say 'distant', what do you mean?"

"We'd not slept together for nearly a fortnight... we shared the same bed, but nothing, um… sexual. She wanted to talk to me that night. But I got drunk and made a fool of myself."

"And this anger spilt over into an argument, is that right?"

I nod. "Yeah. A bit of a shouting match if I'm honest. My set didn't go down well. I died. A miserable experience. My timing was all over the place. Afterwards, I had a few too many drinks. A bad combination."

"We have witnesses who say they saw you arguing with your girlfriend at the bar. You were verbally abusive to her, accusing her of being over-friendly with another comic, before throwing your drink over her. Josephine Jackson then stormed out and you followed her. Is that what happened?"

I take a long breath, imagining what the scene must've looked like to everyone else in the pub—wondering who it was they'd interviewed to get this evidence, not that it matters. I want to disagree, but, as horrible as this is, I'm forced to nod again.

"For the tape, Adam Hanson is nodding in the affirmative."

"And what happened in the car park?"

"I completely lost it. I was… I dunno. A bit aggressive and said some stupid things."

"Did you hit her?"

"No!"

"Have you ever hit or harmed your girlfriend?"

"No, of course not. Never."

DCI Evans pushes a series of stapled pages towards me. "This is a statement from your neighbour. A Mr Clive Walsh. You know him?"

"Yes, yes I do. The man is always sticking his nose into my business. We were friends once, but not since Jozee moved in. He despises her. And now me."

"In Mr Walsh's statement, he says that you and Josephine Jackson, your girlfriend who moved in six months ago, argued pretty much all of the time. Was that the case?"

"No. He thought we were arguing, but it was the way we both let off steam. Shouting and ranting at one another. It was… I dunno… fun. I used to be embarrassed about my ranting, but Jozee didn't mind. She joined in. She made everything better." Sudden tears well up in my eyes and I wipe them away.

DCI Evans is unconvinced. "But it was more than just arguing wasn't it? You and Josephine Jackson had a violent relationship. Isn't that correct?"

"No. No way. And I told you, they were not arguments."

DCI Evans nods towards the statement. "Mr Walsh disagrees. He says that on the tenth of May this year, after a loud argument, he saw you 'aggressively slam the front door of your flat on the arm of Miss Jackson as she attempted to exit your flat'. Is this correct?"

"What are you talking about?"

I have a vague memory of something to do with the door—and then it comes to me. It was nothing but a minor accident. What the deuce was Clive doing?

"Please answer the question. Did you or did you not violently slam your girlfriend's arm in your flat's front door?"

"No. I mean yes. It wasn't like that."

"Perhaps you can explain to us what happened?"

I sigh, knowing how this must look. "We were leaving the flat, I went to close the door, just as Jozee realised she'd forgotten something and lurched back inside—or tried to. I pinched her arm with the door. She squealed in pain, but it was just a minor injury. I don't think it even bruised."

"We have a statement that this was part of a violent argument between yourself and the missing woman. That she was attempting to leave and that you prevented her from doing so by violently slamming the door on her."

I shake my head. "I'd never hurt her on purpose. We laughed about it afterwards, at how clumsy we both are. There was no argument and no violence. We occasionally argue, sure we do, like most couples. I know Clive dislikes Jozee and would be happier with us both out of the building, but his statement is pure exaggeration. He said we were too noisy. Not that that stopped him playing his awful classical music full blast at 2am in the morning."

The solicitor puts a hand on my wrist. He doesn't say anything, but the meaning is clear: *Calm down*. I take a few deep breaths.

"So, you admit to harming the missing woman, Josephine Jackson?"

"Yes, but unintentionally. How was I to know she was going to lurch back into the flat just as I closed the door?"

"So, we have determined you have a history of harming your girlfriend, the missing woman."

"No. That was a one-off incident. I've never raised my hand against her. I'm not the violent type. The opposite in fact."

"Let us go back to the scene that night in the car park outside the Dog and Duck. You say you *completely lost it.* Does that mean you hit her?"

"No! You don't understand. Jozee means everything to me. *I love her.* When she came into my life, everything was dull. Safe, *but dull.* I started doing stand-up to try and do something about that and it was then that I met her. I knew she was the one for me there and then. I couldn't believe my luck when Jozee fell for me too. We were happy, very happy and very close, despite that stupid argument…"

My voice dries as I listen to what I'm saying. In reality, Jozee was leaving me. That's what she was going to tell me the night she went missing. I know I should tell them this, but it makes no difference to the actual events of that night.

"I said something stupid and she drove off. I've not seen her since."

"If that is the case, how did you get home?"

I shrug, trying to think back. But after Jozee drove off, everything was a bit of a fog. "When I drink, I sometimes have problems remembering things."

"Are you actually telling us you don't remember?"

I look at the solicitor. He has a concerned expression on his face. An expression that tells me what I already know. I'm convincing nobody here.

"I have a vague recollection of walking in a rainstorm and getting on a train."

"You're saying you caught a train back to Hove?"

"I think so. I'm not a hundred-percent sure. But I'm guessing that's what happened. Unless someone else gave me a lift."

"I'm afraid that after you left the Dog and Duck to follow your girlfriend, nothing was seen or heard of you. And you were not picked up by a taxi, we checked."

"Then the train it was. I must've gone to Burgess Hill Station."

"How did you pay for a ticket?"

"I can't remember. I would've paid with my card I suppose. That's what I usually do with those bloody machines—you can't put cash in them without losing your money."

Marley opens her folder and pulls out a list of transactions from my bank, and I realise they have been very busy while I languished in the cells. "There is no record of a card payment for a ticket on the Tuesday night in question," she says.

I flush. "Maybe the barriers were open, and I just walked onto the train?"

"Do you regularly travel on public transport without paying?"

I shake my head. "No… no I don't, but I'd drank too much and maybe I just—"

"Don't you think this story about booze-induced forgetfulness sounds a little too convenient?"

"I'm just being honest, like I said I would be. Is there no CCTV footage from Burgess Hill station?"

"Inconclusive, it was raining particularly heavily that night."

"Yeah. But if I walked home to the flat from Hove Station, there would be other CCTV of me along the way, surely?"

"Very possibly, Mr Hanson. But that will only prove you arrived home by other means than travelling with Miss Josephine Jackson."

"What do you mean by that?"

"I mean, Adam, that the argument that started in the Dog and Duck in Burgess Hill, could've been easily continued after you arrived home. Regardless how you arrived there. No doubt angered that you were left to make your own way home."

"No. Jozee wasn't there when I got back. No car, nothing. I'd forgotten my keys and was forced to climb up to my balcony and let myself in. Didn't Clive tell you that?"

DCI Evans gives me a knowing look. "Yes he did. And that you made enough noise, cursing and shouting, to wake him up. You told him, quote, 'I had an argument with Jozee'."

"That's right," I reply, wondering why this filled Evans with so much glee. "I'd gotten stuck and thought I was going to fall."

"But after this conversation you were able to climb the remaining few feet to your flat without a problem, correct?"

"Yeah, I was lucky."

"And now that your neighbour had been woken up, he was also able to then hear you thumping and banging around your flat shouting for Jozee, is that not also correct?"

"I doubt I woke him up, but, yes, that's what happened."

"You don't think that that sounds a little convenient, Adam? I put it to you, Mr Hanson, that after you arrived home—either together with your girlfriend or sometime after she had arrived on her own— that you killed Josephine Jackson in your flat by a method that will soon be established. Most likely strangulation or blunt force trauma. You disposed of her body and her car, and then created this cock and bull story about forgetting your keys to fool your neighbour, intentionally waking him to support your assertion that you arrived alone and that your girlfriend was not there waiting for you."

"That's preposterous," I say, my voice a whisper, unable to properly take in the reality of Evans' words. "I didn't kill Jozee. She's still alive, she has to be. I'd never hurt her. I love her."

Evans holds my eyes with his for a few seconds before continuing. "For the recording, I am now showing the suspect, evidence 43451 C. A photograph of the missing woman, Josephine Jackson with her arms around another man. However, Miss Jackson's face has been scratched out with a sharp instrument. Adam… how do you account for this photograph being found on the bedside table in your flat?"

68

"YOU SEARCHED my flat?"

"Yes, Adam," DCI Evans says knowingly and with more than a little threat. "SOCO have been through it with a fine-tooth comb early this morning. I am convinced they will soon provide evidence that a murder was committed there."

SOCO? I've heard that term before, but I don't know what the initials stand for. They're to do with forensic investigation though, that much is for sure. If I was guilty, this news would no doubt fill me with dread. Instead, I'm relieved that there's no way they can find anything to incriminate me. Unless someone else was in the flat with Jozee before I came home—but I don't believe that for one moment. Instead, I take solace in the fact that the police are trying to scare a confession out of me.

"Now, Adam, tell me about the photograph."

"I found it."

"You found it where?"

"It belonged to a comic named Shirley Sands, real name Charlotte Blunt. I thought she had something against Jozee… and I was right. The guy in that photo is her brother. Tom Blunt, another comic and Jozee's ex-boyfriend. Charlotte blamed Jozee for Tom's attempted suicide after Jozee dumped him. That's why Charlotte was masquerading as Shirley Sands, to get close to Jozee. I thought she might be involved in Jozee's disappearance. But, as far as I know, Charlotte had nothing to do with it."

"That sounds a little far-fetched, don't you think?"

I shrug again, bile from my stomach crawling into my mouth. "Ask her and see what she says. She lives in Fulking with her mother."

DCI Evans scribbles this information onto a small pad with a flashy looking pen and continues. "Will she back up this story of yours?"

I think back to her telling me to keep quiet about Tom. "Probably not."

"Things are not looking good for you Adam. You might want to reconsider some of your answers."

"No. No way. I'm telling you the truth. Everything I know."

DCI Evans lets out a long breath, blown through pursed lips. "Let's move on. Item 43451 D. Printouts of a dating profile named *FunnyBrightonBitch* belonging to Josephine Jackson, indicating the missing woman had quite an interesting personal life. This profile is for a 'hook-up' site where members arrange casual sex with one another. For the record, the messaging system on this website indicates Josephine Jackson was arranging sexual liaisons with strangers who she had met online. When did you find out about your girlfriend's secret and sordid sex life?"

"Where did you get those?" I ask. "As far as I knew, they were lost."

"They were found in the outside rubbish skip at your flats, as you well know. Now please answer the question," Evans continues, "when did you find out about this?"

"I'd forgotten about the printouts," I say weakly, realising how this must look. "Somehow, I put them out of my mind. You can understand why. It came as a complete surprise to me."

"You forgot that your girlfriend was seeing other men and women behind your back? I find that difficult to believe, especially when you've just told us that your sexual relationship with the missing woman had ended."

"That's not what I said… she was just… we didn't… It wasn't about that!"

"You can change your statement at any time Adam. Come on. Tell us the truth about what happened that night?"

"I didn't know anything about…" I point at the printouts. "… about this until some bloke turned up on Friday. *BigManInYorFace* he called himself on the site. Those are his printouts. I had a brief altercation with him and he dropped them."

"You are really telling us that this only came to light *after* the disappearance of your girlfriend?"

"Yes. Very much so."

"How very convenient. But let's say I believe you. How did finding out your girlfriend was prostituting herself out to creeps and perverts make you feel?"

I can see what Evans is trying to do. To get a rise out of me. I take another calming breath. "I felt disgusted. Let down. Like I didn't know who she was any more."

"Were you angry?"

I say nothing.

"Answer the question. Did this make you angry with her?"

"Yes, yes it did."

PC Ella Marley clears her throat. "On the morning of Saturday, the seventh of July, yesterday, you phoned me directly, using the number I gave you should you hear from Jozee or if extra information came to light. Do you remember that phone call?"

"I do."

"You were agitated, were you not?"

"Yes, I was."

"And you told me, quote…" Ella raised her pocket book and began to read. "'She [Josephine Jackson] was leaving me. I talked to her friend in London, Angela Phillips. An old friend from school. She was going to move there in a day or two.'"

"Just for the record," Evans says smiling, "is the statement read out by DC Marley correct?"

"Yes, but—"

"Your girlfriend was in the process of leaving you, Mr Hanson," DCI Evans says forcefully. "And Angela Phillips confirmed that Josephine Jackson never turned up. In fact, Josephine Jackson has not been heard from since the night she disappeared. The same night as your argument with her."

"Stop calling her that! She hated the name Josephine. Despised it."

"Angela Phillips also went on record to say that around two weeks ago, Josephine Jackson, your girlfriend, slept with another comedian. Is that also correct?"

I drop my head, staring at the table, at the printout of Jozee looking beautiful. "Yes."

"When did you learn of this?"

"From Angela, from Angela Phillips. She told me yesterday. That's the first I heard of it."

"I put it to you, Mr Hanson, that on Tuesday night, the night Josephine Jackson disappeared, she did indeed tell you about this other man and her intention to leave you. I also believe that you knew of her secret life—or she also informed you about it. Incensed and angry, you killed her and hid the body, before fabricating a fantastical story about a kidnapping, including arranging a meeting with Angela Phillips to help establish your story as a concerned boyfriend."

"I don't get it," I say. "I've been after you to take Jozee's disappearance seriously for days and you've done bugger all. Why the sudden interest? Why am I now the suspect?"

"My client has the right to know all the evidence that you have against him, Inspector," the duty solicitor says. "It's a valid question."

DCI Evans is obviously annoyed and rearranges the papers in front of him before answering. "It was an anonymous tip off. Someone who said they saw you putting something, likely a body, into a white mini outside your block of flats and driving away. Leading to—"

"That's a bloody lie!" I shout. "An anonymous tip-off? That could be from the person who really abducted Jozee! Do you have their number?"

A pause.

"Well do you?"

"It was a tip-off, *leading to…*" Evans continues loudly, "…the search of your flat and the interviewing of Jozee's friends and other witnesses, revealing strong evidence that points to you as the main suspect in her disappearance."

"No way! No bloody way!"

The solicitor puts his hand on my arm again and I force myself to stop shouting. But it's hard. This is unfair. All of it. I bite down my anger and frustration and speak through gritted teeth. "I've told you time and time again, and I'll never tell you anything different. The last time I saw Jozee was in the car park of the Dog and Duck. I'm not the person who did this."

A long pause. "Okay, Mr Hanson. Let's chat about why we have a blood report that indicates you've ingested an opioid, very probably, heroin, in the last twelve hours."

"I told the doctor all about it," I say belligerently. "I was kidnapped and forcibly injected with heroin."

DCI Evans and DC Marley share a knowing look.

The duty solicitor leans towards me. "Adam, you are here on suspicion of being involved in the disappearance of Josephine Jackson. If DCI Evans wants to talk to you about this matter, he must formally charge you. However, a blood test is not enough to incriminate you, unless you've been caught drug-driving. I advise you not to answer this line of questioning."

"But I want to talk about it," I reply.

The solicitor blows out a sigh. "It's your choice, Mr Hanson."

DCI Evans smiles. "Okay, Mr Hanson. Let's chat about your 999 call and the heroin that ended up in your system."

69

"I WAS abducted… kidnapped by another comedian. He took me to a house where another comic turned up. A friend of mine, or so I thought."

"Kidnapped?" DCI Evans says, not bothering to hide the incredulity in his voice.

"Yes, yes I was."

"By a comedian? Would you say comedians are in the habit of kidnapping one another?" Before I can answer, DCI Evans leans forward. "What was his name?"

"It was a guy called Jim Laker, but he's not important."

"The guy who kidnapped you isn't important? Adam, this is not making any sense."

"Someone else turned up. Another comedian. A guy called Donnie Coogan."

"Donnie Coogan?" Evans repeats, giving DC Marley another sideways glance. "You don't mean Sean Coogan… do you?"

"Who's that?"

"A career criminal we've been after for years. That's who."

"Actually, sir," Marley says. "Sean's second name is Donald. Sean Donald Coogan."

"You think it's the same guy?" he asks Marley who replies with a shrug. Evans turns his attention back to me. "What's your association with this Donnie Coogan?"

"Didn't you hear me? He kidnapped me, or his friend did. Then drugged me up with heroin and called some guys to *come and take care of me*. To kill me. I was terrified… until the heroin hit me."

Evans gives me a hard stare. "And this is how you're claiming the heroin got into your system?"

"Yes, Donnie injected me to make me more pliable."

"If he wanted you dead, why not give you an overdose there and then? Wouldn't that make more sense?"

"He wanted some other guys to do it. Said he doesn't get his hands dirty no more."

DC Marley brings up a picture of a younger looking Donnie on her police mobile phone. It's no comedy publication shot, that's for sure—more like the hard-eyed bastard who'd filled my veins with poison.

"For the record, DC Marley is showing the suspect a police photofit ID of Sean Donald Coogan."

"Is this Donnie Coogan?" Marley asks.

"Yes. That's him."

DCI Evan's eyes begin to glitter. "Let me get this straight. You are admitting to consorting with a known underworld criminal and you're telling me this has nothing to do with the disappearance of Josephine Jackson?"

"Are you deaf? I wasn't consorting with Donnie. I was kidnapped! I met him through my stand-up, I thought he was a funny guy. Nice even. I've known him for over a year, so all this came as a bit of a shock to me. I never would've suspected Donnie. Not in a million years. It's not the thing I expected to find in Brighton."

"Really?" DCI Evans says with an unbelieving shrug of his shoulders. "Brighton is like a bright light that attracts many moths. A perfect place for first-division criminals to ply their trade. There're two close major sea ports, an airport just a few miles away in Shoreham and miles of unguarded coastline. But I guess you know that, don't you?"

"I didn't know anything else about Donnie Coogan until this morning. Check him out on *www.donnie-the-lad-coogan.co.uk* if you want."

Evans nods to DC Marley who brings up the page on her phone. "For the tape, DC Marley is showing the suspect the web page *www. donnie-the-lad-coogan.co.uk*. Is this the website you were referring to?"

"Yes, that's it."

"So, you got to know Sean Coogan via his comedy alter-ego. Is this correct?"

"Yes, I just told you that."

DCI Evans sits back and crosses his arms, his glittering eyes becoming more slit-like—a snake about to strike. "Surely you can see how this looks, can't you Adam? Your girlfriend goes missing after a series of violent arguments. You find out she's been sleeping with other comedians behind your back, that she also regularly frequents hook-up websites for cheap sex with perverts and, on top of all of that, she is planning on leaving you. It's not a giant leap of imagination to wonder what happened next, is it? We have witness evidence and your own statement that your relationship was violent. You were drunk, angry and distraught. You confronted her didn't you, Adam? You wanted to make her pay for all the other guys, her secret life and for leaving you. And, either by design or by accident, you did just that and she died. We then get a report that you're seen putting a body into her car and driving away—where to? Your low-life friend and all-round bastard, Sean Donnie Coogan?"

"None of that is true," I say, staring back at him. "None of it."

"I don't believe you, Adam. You have now admitted to being associated with a career criminal who has a history of drug running, armed robbery and other violent crimes. You must see how that looks? Did you go to Sean Donald Coogan to sort out your little mess? Did he refuse? Is that why you're implicating him in this pathetic facade? To try and throw us off the scent. You may think you're being clever, Adam, but you're not fooling me."

"My client will only answer questions pertinent to the evidence you have against him," the duty solicitor says, raising his voice. "I strongly advise you, Adam, to not answer any questions pertaining to this line of inquiry until more or any evidence is shown."

I shake my head. "No. I want to make a formal charge of kidnapping and attempted murder against Jim Laker and Donnie Coogan."

"But why would they want to kidnap you?" Evans says incredulously. "Did you maybe promise to pay Coogan for disposing of your girlfriend's body and you couldn't come up with the cash? Is that it?"

"Adam," the solicitor interjected again. "I must advise you against answering any of these questions."

"The suspect has spoken on record that he is happy for this line of questioning to be followed. Isn't that right, Adam?"

"Yes," I reply.

"Adam Hanson has been assessed for his fitness to answer questions and no special treatment or facilities were deemed required. This interview is being recorded and your client will have an opportunity to review any given statement. Is that not correct?"

Singh nods. "Yes, but even so—"

"Donnie had nothing to do with Jozee's disappearance, I'm sure of it," I say, butting into their conversation. "He had no reason to lie to me. Especially as he thought I'd soon be dead." I spit out the words angrily, making DCI Evans jump. "But he was directly involved in a hit and run incident that took place two years ago. Two teenagers were killed. You must remember it? Big news at the time. The car was being driven by the comedian I mentioned earlier, Tom Blunt, with Jim Laker and Donnie Coogan as passengers. Coming back from a gig near Pulborough. Donnie told me they were all high on coke when it happened. The whole car was full of it after the accident, ten grand's worth according to him. Tom Blunt is the same guy in that crossed-out photo you found. The ex-boyfriend of Jozee."

"That unsolved hit and run?" Evans says hungrily. "Coogan was involved?"

"He disposed of the car involved in the incident and got Tom a replacement. And when Tom couldn't live with the guilt any longer and decided to go to the police, Donnie gave him an overdose of heroin to permanently shut him up. Tom Blunt is now a vegetable in a local care home in Haywards Heath. Brain dead. As far as I know, Laker wasn't involved with that. He's a creep but not a murderer. I thought Jozee had disappeared because she'd also found out about Donnie being in Tom's car and he'd decided to silence her. But I was wrong. Donnie knew nothing about her. In fact, he wasn't worried about the hit and run any more."

"What evidence do you have, Adam?"

I give an exasperated sigh. "Nothing."

"Then this is all hearsay," Evans says disappointedly. "Just your word against his. And if Coogan indeed thought he was safe from prosecution for this hit and run why even kidnap you in the first place? That doesn't sound like the Sean Coogan I know."

"I told you, *he* didn't kidnap me, it was Jim Laker, the other passenger in the car. He panicked when I started asking questions about that night. I was sure Jozee's disappearance was connected to Laker and Tom. It must've freaked him out, made him nervous. Made Laker do something stupid like kidnapping me. The guy is practically hooked on coke. I knew nothing about Coogan's involvement until later. Laker messed up though and made Donnie angry."

"But that's still no motive to kill you."

"That's right. Donnie was pretty much set on letting me go. Like you said, it was his word against mine. But, I dunno, something happened, I'm not sure what, and… that's when he decided to kill me."

"Something happened?" Evans repeated with disdain. "Sean Coogan isn't the kind of man to kill somebody on a whim. He's business-orientated through and through. There's no way he'd have you killed. Not unless he had good reason to."

"The only other thing I talked about were the cameras I found in the basement of the house. Some kind of porn set-up is my guess."

"Porn ain't illegal these days," Evans says quickly. "Or haven't you looked at the internet recently? No, I'm guessing you're either lying about your kidnap or not telling us the real reason why Coogan wanted you dead. Is that the case, Adam?"

"I'm telling you everything I know."

Evans sits back. "Let me ask you another question… if you were kidnapped and drugged up with smack, how did you escape? "

"I was lucky."

Another shared look between Evans and Marley. "Okay, Adam, my guess is that you're purposely wasting our time here. But I'm a kind-hearted guy. I'm going to offer you this once and only once… I want a full confession about how you murdered your girlfriend and hid her body. And any information on any part played in this by Sean Donald Coogan. In return, I will offer you police protection and make sure you end up in a jail-facility where it'd be impossible for one of Coogan's associates to get to you."

I shake my head forcefully. "I didn't have anything to do with Jozee's disappearance!" I shout. "So, I don't need any deal. And I've told you everything I know about Coogan."

"It's your funeral, Adam. I'm afraid I can do nothing other than treat this story of yours as an attempt to muddy the waters. Something you cooked up when you found out we were on to you. We were very surprised to get that 999 call. Did you think that was clever? You'll have to try harder to fool us, I can guarantee that."

"I don't care what you think. I still want to bring charges against Coogan and Laker."

"That is up to you, Adam, although I'm guessing that you'll soon change your mind. But I'll get the duty sergeant to come visit you after we're done. And bear in mind that if you're deemed to be seen wasting police time, I'll throw the damn book at you."

I take a deep breath. "I'm innocent, okay? Everything I've told you is true. Jozee's disappearance has thrown up too many questions and not one bloody answer. I only got into this mess because I was trying to find Jozee. It's been a strange few days. A whole load of weird shit has been happening." A thought pops into my head. "What about… about all those vile messages on my phone. What about them?"

DCI Evans smiles and searches through his folder to produce pages of printouts. "Are you referring to messages sent to you yesterday between 4.30 and 5.30pm?"

"Real creepy stuff. And emails too. Spam and shit."

"We have evidence that you sent them to yourself."

"What?" I reply in exasperation.

"Your location, as shown to us by your phone data tells us you were at Hove Lawns at the time the texts were sent."

"Yes, that's right."

"The unregistered, untraceable phone that sent those messages was also in the same location. It's a common trick that we see time and time again. A way to try and throw us off the scent. But people forget we can trace the location of unregistered phones, even if we don't know who they belong to."

My anger starts to rise again. "So where is this phone?"

Evans shrugged. "It was switched off and probably disposed of. It wasn't in your flat, because we searched for it."

"So, I spent all that time sending texts to myself, did I? I suppose

I also ordered all those ham and pineapple pizzas? Over thirty of the bloody things. And broke into my own flat to steal all my power cables and leads. And left those bloody awful, piss-smelling flowers and cut up birds."

"What did you say?" Evans asks, and for the first time in this interview he seems left-footed.

Marley picks up her notebook. "From the same phone conversation, I took notes from on Saturday morning, the seventh of July. The suspect said, 'Nothing was disturbed. But they took all my wires and chargers… and left dead, bad-smelling flowers on my doorstep'."

"Why didn't you tell me this before, Marley?" Evans asks accusingly.

"I didn't think it was pertinent to the interrogation, sir."

Evans sighs, looks at his watch and says, "Interview terminated at 1.38pm." Before angrily switching off the recorder.

"Is that it?" I ask, a little confused.

"For now!" Evans replies tetchily.

"Can I go?"

Evans shakes his head. "You are still under arrest for the possible murder of Josephine Margaret Jackson. For which I will be questioning you again later, when I'm sure more evidence will come to light."

He walks out of the room, leaving DC Marley to gather up all the documents, a bemused look on her face.

"I had nothing to do with Jozee's disappearance," I tell her. "I didn't."

70

"**THAT WAS** a bit odd," I say to the duty solicitor. "It's almost like I spooked them."

"I'm here to look out for your interests," he replies, ignoring me. "And I would strongly advise you to drop the accusations against Sean Coogan."

"And why should I do that?"

"I don't know how deep you are into this mess, but I do know Sean Coogan. A nasty piece of work if there ever was one. He's an Ex-IRA money man and gunrunner. He came over here after the Northern Ireland Peace Deal. Made a home for himself in Brighton. But he hasn't quite left his old life behind, or the IRA. I don't believe you ever can. The network still survives, and it's involved in all kinds of criminal activity, some of it international. But know this… bringing charges against him is not a good idea."

"You sound like you're working for him."

He laughs. "My job is to offer clients the best possible advice. You make any accusations against Coogan while you're in jail… you'd be a sitting target."

"You think I'm going to jail?"

"Adam, you are the main suspect in a missing person inquiry and the police have some compelling evidence against you. They are also actively trying to find more evidence. And, if they do, it's very unlikely you will get bail. Instead, you will be put on remand in prison. And prison is the last place you need to be if a man like Sean Coogan wants you silenced."

I swallow loudly. "I just want to find Jozee. I don't care enough about that bastard to get myself killed."

"I'm the duty solicitor, a stop-gap until you find a defence attorney. You may or may not want to answer my question, but it's in your best interest to tell me the truth. And, of course, we have client/attorney privilege. Did you kill Josephine Jackson?"

"No."

"Were you involved in any way with her disappearance?"

"No."

"Are you sure? If you come clean, and tell them everything that happened, including any incriminating evidence against Sean Coogan, the police will protect you from him, like DCI Evans offered. Otherwise, you'll be on your own."

"I'm very sure."

"Adam, I don't think you realise the serious amount of trouble you are in."

I fix him with my eyes. "Oh yes, yes I do."

71

I'M TAKEN back down to my cell where I'm left to ponder my predicament. Apart from the noise from the other inmates, which I hear only vaguely through the walls and the hefty, metal door, it's reasonably quiet down here—and cool. Which is a relief from the heatwave that is presently gripping the country. The lack of visual stimuli—blank, whitewashed walls, a grey, concrete floor, the single toilet and my bench, come bed—is somehow relaxing. I live in a certain amount of annoying clutter, most of it generated by myself. But since Jozee moved in with me, the clutter has gotten worse.

I find the minimalist cell calms me. My mind should be racing after the events of the last twenty-four hours, but instead it's quiet in there. As quiet and as empty as this cell. An after-effect of the heroin, perhaps?

I was shocked to be arrested, that much was for sure. I wonder who gave the 'anonymous' tip-off? Could it have been Donnie?

No. The police are the last place he'd want me to go. And I haven't forgotten the solicitor's warning. When the duty sergeant arrives, asking me if I want to make a statement, I refuse. Donnie, or Sean, as I now know him, has proved himself to be a resourceful and dangerous enemy. But I vow not to let him get away with what he did to Tom and me. And that vow includes Jim Laker.

If it wasn't Donnie who called the police on me, then who else would want me under the spotlight of a police investigation?

There can be only one possible answer—the person who abducted Jozee.

I'm using the word 'abducted' purposely, I realise. That word keeps Jozee alive in my mind. Not murdered, but alive and struggling to get herself free.

I keep dwelling on that anonymous report.

Someone saw you putting something, likely a body, into a white mini outside your block of flats and driving away.

This was either a complete fabrication, or—dare I think it?—they saw someone else and thought it was me? A black cloud descends upon me. Jozee could've arrived home before me and that's when… *when they struck.* It breaks me up to think like this, but I can't avoid it. Not anymore. Things are too serious.

If Jozee was killed who did it and why?

The beautiful face of Charlotte Blunt pops into my mind. No, it's not her. It can't be. She admitted her brother's involvement with the hit and run. If she had killed Jozee to keep her quiet, then why tell me and Stevo? No, she's out of the frame. The only other women are Nat Naylor and Pari Chabra. No matter how I look at it, they can't be involved. Nat is too tiny to be mistaken for me and unless her ailments are pure make-believe, it isn't physically possible for Pari to drag… *to drag a body.*

Which leaves Scott Wong, Billy Belter, Stevo and my next-door neighbour, Clive. They were all capable. I can't imagine any one of them being involved. But again, I never imagined Donnie to be a drugs and gun-running ex-terrorist lunatic, so what do I know? It could even be some random nutter no one's ever heard of from that hook-up site Jozee was on.

I try and visualise the scene. Somebody putting a body into Jozee's mini… but there's something wrong with the mental image. I sit up on my bunk. Of course!

How could anyone put a body into a two door 1974 Mini Cooper? The car is tiny. You couldn't put it in the boot. The only place would be the passenger seat. Now that I think about it, the whole idea is preposterous. Can't DCI Evans and DC Marley see that?

I decide to raise it with them at the next interview, whenever that will be. I may be in jail, but I'm now utterly convinced this so called 'tip-off' is a fabrication, which means Jozee is alive, she has to be.

Time passes slowly. Food arrives. Basic fare. Boiled vegetables, mash, gravy and dry-tasting chicken slices. My well-being is periodically checked upon. I should be morose, unhappy that I'm spending all this time under arrest, worrying about my fate, but the truth of the matter is that while I'm sitting here, DCI Evans and DC Marley and the rest of the Brighton Police Force are moving heaven and hell to find Jozee. Doing a far better job than I could do on my own.

I have faith in them to find me innocent and, more importantly, to find Jozee alive.

They have to!

SUNDAY EVENING

AFTER WHAT I guess is between ten and twelve hours later, I'm taken into the same interview room and sat down next to Adeep Singh, the duty solicitor. "You still here?" I ask.

"I was temporarily assigned to you. I was off-duty, but I wanted to be here for this."

"For what?"

The door opens and in walks a tired and sweaty-looking DCI Evans and DC Marley. Evans starts the digital recording, goes through the formalities and sits back, a perturbed expression on his face.

"You better have some more evidence or I'm walking out of here, I swear it!" I say as forcefully as I can muster without actually shouting. I expect Singh to tell me to calm down, but he appears happy to let me speak this way. "Jozee is missing. This is the fifth day since she disappeared and you lot are still mucking around trying to pin this shit on me. I'm innocent okay? And haven't you realised how small a 1974 Mini Cooper is yet? You can't hide a body in it, that's for damn sure. That anonymous tip-off is bollocks. The question you should be asking, is who sent it and why?"

"Adam," DCI Evans starts, ignoring my outburst. "We've had a busy few hours chasing up the story you gave us earlier."

"That was no story… it was the truth," I say through gritted teeth.

"We talked to Charlotte Blunt, sister of Tom Blunt. She confirmed that the photograph we found in your flat belonged to her. And that indeed, she had been masquerading as a comic called Shirley Sands in an attempt to get close to your missing girlfriend, Josephine Jackson. It was odd behaviour, and suspicious, but not against the law. That photograph has now been taken out of the evidence we have against you."

"That's what I told you. I wasn't lying."

"Do you know this man?" Evans pulls a photo out of a file and passes it to me.

I snatch it off him, wondering what new bollocks they have cooked up against me. A lugubrious face stares back at me. "That's… that's David Gentry."

"You are identifying the person in the photograph as 'David Gentry?'"

"Yes, I just told you that. What about him? Is he involved in all of this?"

Evans sighs. "The man in the photograph has many names. David Gentry being one of them. However, his real name, and the name associated with his extensive criminal record, is 'Simon Grenville'."

"Criminal record?" I blurt. "So why was he pretending to be someone else and what's he got to do with me or Jozee? Apart from being an annoying creep that is…" My mind makes a sudden connection. "You think he's involved in Jozee's disappearance?"

"David Gentry, as you know him, has many arrests for breaking and entering, burglary and… for stalking."

"It was the report about your missing power cables that led us to him," DC Marley says. "I wasn't aware of the significance of this until Grenville's MO was explained to me by DCI Evans."

"The man is a nasty customer," Evans continues. "He chooses a victim and then does everything to make their life an utter misery. He orders erroneous food deliveries—particularly ham and pineapple pizzas—sends obscene texts and emails. Signs his victim up to spam and porn sites to get them inundated with emails and nuisance calls. He is almost a savant at breaking into places unnoticed, where he likes to leave nasty little gifts like dead animals or flowers and… to remove power cords or cutlery. I know Grenville well. He's been out on bail for stalking another woman in the Roedean area of Sussex. Seems like he latched on your girlfriend after seeing one of her gigs. Became obsessed with her."

"You think he's got her?" I say, my heart racing.

DCI Evans shakes his head. "He's non-violent. He only injures his victims psychologically."

"Although there is compelling evidence that such behaviour can be worse than a physical attack," Marley intercedes. "Especially when it's inflicted from a man onto a woman."

I ignore her, my eyes staring into the cold grey eyes of Evans. "Can you be one hundred percent sure this creep hasn't abducted her, or done something worse?"

"I'm afraid we can. As I stated, Grenville was on bail—a decision we fought against, but with prison overcrowding... you know how it goes? He had an exclusion order keeping him off the internet and away from his last victim. On the evening of Josephine's disappearance, Grenville was picked up drunk in Worthing and spent the night in the cells. Cast iron. He's not the man we're looking for."

My inner calmness drains away like water down a plug hole. I'm relieved this creep had nothing to do with Jozee disappearing, but if he really wasn't involved, then where the hell was she? What had happened to Jozee?

"Josephine Jackson's hook-up profile, *FunnyBrightonBitch,*" Evans continues, "was in actuality created by Grenville on a burner phone he'd been using to access the internet."

"So Jozee didn't have a secret life..."

"It appears not."

"I knew that had to be bullshit, I just knew it!" I'm relieved, almost ecstatic.

"But, if her friend Angela Phillips is to be believed, she still slept with someone two weeks ago," Evans says.

My euphoria takes a sudden dive. Jozee may not have had a secret life, but she had still been unfaithful and was leaving me. "Like I explained, I found out when Angela told me."

DC Marley draws breath and says, "It appears Grenville was frustrated when Jozee ignored him. And so, he turned his attention on to you."

"How do you know all this?"

"We arrested Simon Grenville aka David Gentry this afternoon," DC Marley continues. "He had in his possession the phone that sent you all those anonymous texts and emails. He's downstairs in the cells. He won't get bail this time, you can be sure of it."

"He told us everything," Evans says. "I guess he knew he was going to go down for his activities sooner or later."

"And the anonymous tip-off?" I say, guessing the answer.

Evans sighs. "That was Grenville. From a burner phone found in a doss-house bin where he was sleeping."

"I knew it!"

"Let me get this right," my solicitor butts in. "All the hard evidence you have against Adam Hanson has now been discredited. What you have left is purely circumstantial. You have nothing to prove that Adam was involved in the disappearance of his girlfriend."

DCI Evans nervously plays with his shirt cuffs. "The SOCO report from Mr Hanson's flat found nothing that indicated a violent act had occurred. Nor any other evidence that pointed to any crime being committed there."

"Then Adam is free to return home, correct?"

DCI Evans grinds his teeth. "Yes. Although we reserve the right to question Mr Hanson again should any further evidence make itself known to us."

"Of course."

73

AFTER THE interview, I shake hands with Singh and thank him for helping me.

"It's my job. And normally thankless. But I enjoyed today."

"Enjoyed?"

"I suppose that's not quite the right word. What I mean is that it's usually drunks, domestic abusers and petty thieves who I represent. With not a single brain cell to rub together amongst them."

I'm taken aback by his candour and it must show in my face.

"Sorry," he says. "I haven't slept for over twenty-four hours. Good luck, Adam. And keep out of Sean Coogan's way. It's unlikely he'll try and harm you now, but watch out for him, okay?"

We shake hands and I'm escorted back to my cell to await official release.

As I'm taken down into the cell block, I hear a familiar sickly-sweet droning voice. I look up and see David Gentry—aka Simon Grenville—walking towards me, escorted by a woman police officer.

"Well if it isn't my friend, Adam Hanson!" Gentry says. "Finally caught you, did they? I should hope so, after what you did to poor Jozee Jackson."

"Piss off!" I growl in reply, wanting to punch the man in his stupid fat face.

"That's enough, Simon!" barks the female officer and drags Gentry past me.

"The little slut got what she deserved! Fucking your friends behind your back!"

I stop and the PC escorting me, bumps into my back.

"What do you mean by that?"

"Don't pretend you don't know what I'm talking about, you must've seen—"

"Shut up, Grenville," the woman PC says. "I'm not warning you again."

"Seen what?"

Gentry taps his nose as if we're sharing a secret.

"Seen what?" I ask.

He leers at me and says nothing.

I wait in my cell for another hour, stewing over Gentry's words. Did he know Jozee had slept with someone else? Or was the prick just trying to wind me up? The guy was a proven mentalist. A stalker who liked to mess with people's minds. I decide to forget about him. But it's hard, when all I want to do is punch the guy's lights out.

The duty sergeant, this time a middle-aged man with a prematurely lined face, finally arrives with some replacement clothes. My belongings are still in a lab somewhere. He escorts me out of my cell to be discharged.

DC Marley is waiting for me. "Here," she says, offering me my mobile phone in an evidence bag. "A peace offering. I'll make sure you get back everything we took from your flat as soon as we can."

"Thanks," I say sullenly.

"If it means anything," she continues, "I believe you about Jozee."

"What is this? Good cop or bad cop? Cos you can't seem to make up your mind."

"I'm just saying my gut has always told me you were innocent." She lowers her voice. "DCI Evans was too keen to accuse you."

"Believe me, from where I was sitting, the evidence was compelling. Terrifyingly so. You're really telling me you didn't think I was guilty for one moment? Even when you cuffed me?"

"I never thought that… I didn't think the evidence… we were more—"

"Forget it."

"I can get an unmarked car to take you home, if you want? There's some very bad, almost apocalyptic, weather expected tonight, if you can believe the meteorologists."

"No thanks," I say. "I've had enough of the police for one day."

"I also believe you about Sean Coogan," she says, lowering her voice. "You were really kidnapped by him, weren't you?"

"It's my word against his and Laker's and, according to the solicitor, it's best I keep quiet about that."

"That's good advice. The man has been beyond the law for too long. Has far too many fingers in far too many pies."

I'm startled by the same phrase Donnie used when talking about himself, but say nothing, removing my phone from the evidence bag and switching it on.

DC Marley puts a hand on my shoulder. "Be careful."

"I'll try my best."

She gives me a tight smile and leaves me to it.

My phone tells me it's 0.04am Monday morning. I've spent over half a full day in jail. My phone chirps. A voice message from Stevo.

"I've heard you're being released. I'm waiting for you outside. I'll wait as long as it takes. I've got things to tell you…"

74

I PUSH myself through the doors of Brighton Police Station feeling the need for some fresh air and I'm immediately hit by an oppressive heat. Hot and muggy. Sweat forms instantaneously on my exposed skin, my clothes becoming clammy. Even at this time in the middle of the night it feels as hot as being out in the noonday sun. Heat radiates from the pavement and from all around. I feel an urge to remove my shirt and trousers. Maybe that's what I should do? Streak home naked, screaming like a mad banshee. It's what I feel like doing, that much is for sure, especially after a whole day wasted in the police cells. But it's too damn hot. I wipe my forehead, my hand coming away drenched in sweat.

I walk down John Street towards the Olde Steine, the heat pressing in on me from all sides, making it difficult to breathe. A car pulls up alongside, Stevo's maroon Rover P5, looking deep black and shiny in the dark. It's had a clean since the last time I saw it.

Stevo leans over the passenger seat and sticks his head out of the window. "Get in, mate."

"I wanna walk."

"Just get in. We need to chat, okay."

"Leave me alone, Stevo. I've had enough shit today, okay?"

"Just get in! I need to tell you somethin'."

Sighing, I open the heavy door and slide into the passenger seat. Stevo wears shorts and a tight t-shirt revealing vast amounts of thick, curly body hair, making him look more like an ape than he does already. Although, not that many apes prefer the colour bright purple.

"There's a severe weather warnin'," he says as we drive off. "Thunderstorms and floods and shit. Bloody dangerous by all accounts."

The windows are down, but they give no relief from the heat. Hot air streams into the car in an unremitting wave, like it's being blown by a hairdryer.

"Is that really what you wanted to talk to me about?"

"It's serious. A once in a century type thing, they're sayin'. You need to get home before it hits. You must notice all this bleedin' heat. It's driving everyone mad. Myself included."

The car reaches the roundabout on which sits the Sealife Centre and the Brighton Pier, and heads for the sea front.

"I wasn't sure you were ever comin' out," Stevo says, as the large engine begins to roar down Kingsway towards Hove.

"Why the hell not?"

"I heard you were arrested, that the rozzers have been all over your place. I phoned on the off-chance to see what was happenin' and they told me you were bein' released. So I high-tailed it over here. I shouldn't have bothered rushin'. That was two bleedin' hours ago."

"Yeah. They messed up."

"Of course they did. I knew you didn't have anythin' to do with it."

"You didn't suspect me?"

"You?" Stevo says dismissively. "I dunna think so."

I'm not sure if I'm relieved or annoyed by Stevo's disdain.

Kingsway is unusually deserted, and we speed along the seafront, stopped only by a series of frustrating red lights.

"Seems like everyone has got the message," Stevo says as we are halted by more traffic lights at the junction between Kingsway and Hove Street.

"What message?"

"Aren't you listenin'? There's gonna be a massive fuck-off storm soon. Apocalyptic type weather. That's why the roads are empty."

"I don't care about the damn storm! Jozee is still missing. Don't you realise that?"

"Sure, I do, it's just that—"

"It's just what?" I shout. "She's disappeared into thin air! There's no trace of her. I thought it might be Laker and Donnie Coogan, then I was sure it had to be that twat David Gentry, or whatever the dickhead calls himself. I thought I was close to finding her, but she's nowhere, Stevo. No-bloody-where! Even the police haven't found

Clue Fucking One. So cut all this crap about a storm and tell me what you've got to tell me, or I'm getting out now."

Stevo says nothing. The lights turn to green and we turn into Hove Street, the engine roaring as Stevo negotiates a few side streets before arriving on Church Road.

"Well?" I ask in exasperation.

Stevo's ape hands squeeze and paw at the steering wheel as if he's suffering from some inner turmoil.

"Stevo! You're freaking me out."

We finally pull up outside Eaton Palace Gardens. A deep rumble greets our arrival, followed by a massive bang and the flash of faraway lightning. Inside the car is all silence, apart from the rasp of Stevo's breathing and the ticking over of the engine. The guy is struggling with something.

What on earth does he want to tell me?

An awful thought pops into my mind and it won't go away. "Don't tell me you have anything to do with Jozee's disappearance," I whisper, staring out into the muggy night, aware of a cloud of manic moths encircling a nearby streetlight. "You don't… *do you?*"

Stevo turns his big mop head towards me and I notice tears are running down his face.

"I love her," he says finally, his face creasing into sobs. "I always have. Ever since the first moment I saw her. And not jokin'-like. Proper love. But you went and blew it didn't you. Forcin' her to leave. Makin' her go away."

I'm finding it hard to take in… Stevo in love with Jozee? "You knew she was leaving? She told you that?"

"I was her special friend," he says. "I sorta hoped, you know, that one day she'd change her mind about you and maybe she'd see me as more than just a friend, more than just—"

"Have you done something stupid?" I ask, turning to stare at him. The big man seems broken, hunched in the front seat of his car. "Where is she? What have you done with her?"

Stevo says nothing, although I can hear the steering wheel creak under his now bulging, twin fists.

"Answer me, Stevo."

"Get out!" he barks, his face like an angry gorilla and, for the very first time since I've known Stevo, I'm scared of him.

He leans across me and flings open the passenger door, his weight crushing me. "I said, get out!"

An arm like a tree trunk pushes me roughly and I'm ejected from the car to land on the hot pavement. Stevo slams the door behind me and roars away.

"Stevo!" I shout after him, jumping to my feet. "Stevo!"

75

ANOTHER CRACK of thunder and I hear the thud, thud, thud of heavy raindrops, the air alive with static electricity. I whip out my phone to call the police just as the rain drops turn into a steady pitter-patter, increasing in volume and power. More thunder, behind which is a mechanical rumble. A cool-looking car with a rear spoiler, sits outside the underground garage next door at Blenheim Towers. The electric door slams shut and, with a squeal of tires, the car reverses away onto the road and drives away at speed. I suppose they want to get where they're going before this storm hits properly. Good luck to them.

Within seconds, the heavens open. I know it's an over-used phrase, but that's what they do. A humongous blast of thunder is quickly followed by a ballooning flash of lightning. I rush towards the communal entrance to Eaton Palace Gardens, all sound drowned by the terrific roar of rain, and let myself inside as more thunder booms and cracks outside, making the building rattle and shake. It sounds like a war is going on out there.

"Bloody hell," I whisper, but my words have nothing to do with the brewing storm. They instead have everything to do with Stevo. I can't believe what he told me, what he admitted. That he's in love with Jozee. Did Stevo tell her how he felt then? And she rejected him? I try to play out that scenario in my mind, but I can only see Stevo getting dreadfully embarrassed and disappearing himself, rather than doing something to Jozee. But what do I really know? What does anyone know about their friends, even if they aren't hamstrung by their stupid autism?

Stevo was uncharacteristically absent from work all week. That was a fact. He could've abducted Jozee to stop her leaving and took her somewhere. It's mental, utterly out there and ridiculous to think this, but it makes sense. If so, at least Jozee would still be alive. Stevo couldn't kill her, could he? I shake my head. This is Stevo… Daft bumbling Stevo!

This whole thing is one big mess, but I have no choice but to report him to the police. It feels like a betrayal, but what else can I do?

I sit dripping on the stairs, wipe my wet phone and ring DC Marley. It goes straight to answerphone.

"It's Adam Hanson," I say disappointedly, the storm booming and crackling outside. "I think I know who has abducted Jozee—"

A massive crack of thunder and simultaneous lightning directly above. The building shakes and the foyer lights blink off—like a bomb has just exploded—and the call ends before I can leave the full message.

Shit! No signal. It must be the damn storm interfering with communications. The lights flicker back on, although they are half as bright, and I stumble upstairs. Halfway, the lights go out again and this time do not return, and I'm forced to use the weak illumination from my phone.

My flat door is covered in police tape that I rip angrily aside. I fumble my key in the lock, just as the door to Clive's flat opens and he steps outside. He's carrying a torch with a bulb weaker than my phone screen. The smell of lavender with something nasty underneath bellows from his flat.

"What are you doing back?" he says in surprise, simultaneously wincing at an almighty crash of thunder. He's sweaty and agitated, and still wearing a smart shirt and cardigan in this unremitting heat.

"I was arrested!" I reply. "Why did you give that statement to the police? I'd never intentionally hurt Jozee, and you know that."

"I only did what any self-respecting citizen would've done. But why are you back here? I thought—"

"You thought what, exactly?"

"I knew you'd have a bad end after you started seeing that slut!"

"You what?"

Clive backs away.

"You never liked Jozee did you? In fact, before she moved in you were all over me like a bloody rash. Meals, film night, and inviting me around for drinks. But that all stopped after Jozee didn't it?"

"I don't know what you mean."

"Yes, you do. You wanted me all to yourself. You were oh so happy when I was a lonely singleton. What were you hoping from me? A pity leg-over?"

"You ungrateful little shit!"

A thought crosses my mind, maybe it wasn't Stevo who abducted Jozee, maybe it was Clive? I know next to nothing about him and he had a set of flat keys. Why else would he lie to incriminate me? I'm not sure, but I can't leave any stone unturned. And what have I got left to lose?

"You've always hated Jozee," I shout, rounding on him. "Did you do something to her? Did you use your keys to abduct her the night she disappeared? Is that why your flat smells so bad? Is she in there? Have you killed her?"

Clive steps back, raising his hands. I push past him and into his prissy little flat.

"What the heck do you think you're doing?"

His flat is a mirror image of mine. I enter the hallway, almost gagging on the cloying smell of lavender that I always politely ignored when I used to visit. This time it's mingled with air-freshener and a wall of damp heat, and something else… something nasty.

Clive charges in after me. "I'm going to call the police!"

"You do that!"

He follows me into his lounge, cluttered with ornaments, the garish, wallpaper-covered walls hung with gilt-framed paintings, novelty mirrors and a variety of cheap, wooden cuckoo clocks. The room is illuminated by two recently lit candles, sending crazy shadows amongst his collections of knick-knacks and other rubbish. Clive picks up a 70s style phone and punches angrily at the keypad.

I leave him behind to search both bedrooms and his bathroom—where I find the source of the smell. His toilet is backed up.

Jozee is not here. This doesn't mean he's innocent, though.

Is anyone? I ask myself, feeling even more angry and confused.

I return to the lounge to find the phone hanging off the hook. I guess the landlines are down as well. Outside the storm flashes and rumbles, rain pounding and smacking against Clive's balcony.

"Clive!" I shout. "Where are y—"

I'm hit on the head from behind, a hard whack on the same spot where Jim Laker clubbed me last night. It stings painfully. I whirl around to see Clive holding a long wooden antique ruler, he whacks at me again.

"Get out!" he screams. "Get out!"

I snatch the ruler from his fingers and snap it over my knee. "If I find you've had any part in Jozee's disappearance," I growl at him, "then—"

"Go!" He grabs at a hefty bronze bust and throws it at me. It clumps heavily on to the floor a few feet in front of him. "This is breaking and entering, criminal damage and personal attack!" he shouts as I stomp past him and outside, but I don't care.

"I'm going to call the police as soon as the phones are working again!" he squeals at me. "Do you hear me?"

I run into my flat, slam the door and deadbolt it behind me. A massive crash of thunder and the lights flicker back on. My flat is a mess from the police search. My books and DVDs lie on the floor in an untidy heap, their cases all opened. Drawers are left half-closed, chairs lie on their sides and black magnetic fingerprint powder covers most of the surfaces. A section of carpet where I once spilled a bottle of red wine has been removed, revealing ugly concrete beneath. Outside, the storm rages, pummelling my balcony and overwhelming it. Water is beginning to pour into my living room through a small gap by the open balcony door that I can never properly close. For the first time since I moved into the flat, I'm somehow able to push it shut, and mop up the water with some towels. I move the sofa back to its original position, sit down amongst the carnage and gently steam. I find the mess difficult to deal with, and yet, it reflects my own inner disarray.

What's happened to me? I've gone through so many emotions over the last few days, that it's like I don't know myself or anyone anymore. I put my head in my hands, tears arriving in a cascade to match the terrible storm outside.

I miss Jozee so much. I love her.

In the end, that's all I've got. Even if she did sleep with someone else and was leaving me.

I love her.

And that's my emotion, it belongs to me, no one else. Not even Jozee. And it's the one thing that hasn't changed throughout all of this. And I don't care how selfish it sounds. I pick up my phone and scroll to my photos looking for a picture of Jozee and immediately come across her smiling and looking beautiful. I'm bleary-eyed from the tears that refuse to stop, and it's like she's almost there with me. Wonderful, remarkable Jozee. I've never seen her look so pretty…

I sit up, wiping at my eyes and stare at the picture more closely.

What the…?

I didn't take this photograph… Where the hell did it come from?

76

I OPEN my phone's image folder. There are hundreds of thumbnails of photos I didn't take.

And then I realise. When the police checked out Gentry's emails and messages, they must've auto-saved to my phone's image folder. I tried to work out how to switch this function off as indiscreet stuff would often end up in there—comics sending embarrassing memes, especially the younger ones, cluttering up my images folder with their juvenile crap sent on Whatsapp and other platforms. Gentry must've sent me photos as well as all those abusive texts.

Was that what he was hinting at in the station? Has he not only seen something, but photographed it as well? The guy was a stalker, after all.

I open the photos and scroll back through time. There're pictures of me on the beach with Nat Naylor. Me chatting to Scott Wong. Me looking stressed out in the midst of hundreds of people at the Chilli Festival on Hove Lawns. I go further back in time. There's me at the Comedy Gods talking to Donnie. And even me at the Lord Horatio chatting to Billy Belter at the bar, the night after Jozee went missing. Was Gentry there then? I don't remember him.

There's a jump in time, probably when Gentry was banged up in Worthing, as the next photographs are taken on the street outside Shirley Sands' flat. The argument he told me about on the night before Jozee's disappearance. He captured it all, the stalkery creep.

I scroll further back in time. The date says roughly two weeks ago, and I feel my heart freezing. Jozee drinking outside the Wagon and Horses. The comedian's place to hang out. A Thursday two weeks ago. I'd gone home because of work and Jozee had gone on to the Wagon with the other comedy boozers. I remember waking up Friday morning and Jozee wasn't there. She hadn't come home, a text on my phone.

> *Made a night of it. Stayed up to watch sunrise on the beach.*

I'd laughed at that. Typical Jozee.

She's very drunk in the photos. Dancing, chatting and smoking—which she vowed she'd given up. Even in all these natural, un-posed moments, she's beautiful. More so. And I can see what fascinated Gentry so much.

Then it's later.

The tables outside the Wagon and Horses are almost empty. Just a few stragglers. Jozee sits on her own, huddled next to another man. Both of them are obviously drunk and sitting too close together for my liking. There are two more shots. Them getting in a taxi together. And… *and them kissing on the back seat.*

I stare at it for long moments. My Jozee with another man… *with that man!* The guy Jozee slept with. I can't believe it.

Lightening blooms outside my window, not just a single flash, but a continuous glow that lasts for many seconds.

"No way!" I shout. "It can't be!" And yet… it all makes dreadful sense. All of it."

I run out of my flat and bash on Clive's door. He doesn't answer but I know he can hear me.

"Clive!" I shout. "When the phones start working again, call the police, tell them I know who abducted Jozee. Tell them to come over right away. I'm going next door!"

I check my mobile again, but there's still no signal, not that I expected one.

I charge downstairs and into the Eaton Palace Gardens communal hallway. It's flooded by at least six inches of water. I slop through and push open the door to go outside, hit by a torrent of rainwater that momentarily staggers me. Worse than before, like I'm standing under a waterfall, making it hard for me to breathe. I'm drenched again in seconds.

This is like no storm I've ever experienced before. Winds batter me, blowing leaves and other debris into my face. I see trees bending and fallen signs. I climb over the partition to the Blenheim Towers block of flats and down the ramp to the closed shutter of the underground garage, sloshing through groundwater that's as high as my knees. The drainage system is being overwhelmed. Stevo was right, this is a once-in-a-century storm.

I need to get inside, but the garage is protected by an electronic pin. I don't know the number and I'm guessing that the electrics might be shot under all this rain.

I make my way up to the front door, which is normally protected by a small porch. The wind has totally destroyed it. Most of it has blown away, the rest is repeatedly battering against the building. The glass in the front door is splintered and cracked. Inside, all the lights are off. I try pressing at the buzzers, but they are dead, waterlogged.

Shit!

I wade around the side of the building and find two long horizontal windows a foot or two above my head. One of them is open a crack.

A way in!

I grab a large, communal bin from the side of the building and drag it over to below these windows, struggling against water that is high enough to cover its wheels. I climb up onto the bin and stare through the windows. I can't see anything. I slide my fingers into the gap and pull the window back far enough to stick my head through. It's dark inside, but I can hear the unmissable sound of water dropping into what sounds like a deep pool. I wait for another flash of lightning and the underground garage is revealed. It's a lot lower than where I'm standing and full of water, which is reaching halfway up the side of the cars parked in there.

I pull myself up onto the window ledge and kick at the glass, smashing both the window and bending the aluminium frame. It drops inside with a clatter and a splash, leaving a horizontal hole.

Holding onto the ledge, I push myself through legs first, dropping into the garage and land badly, my left foot catching something under the level of the water. Pain lances through me, and I fall headfirst into the freezing, underground pool. I emerge gasping and coughing, but at least I'm inside, out of the storm and can breathe properly. I take an experimental step on my injured leg and wince in pain. I can put my weight on it, even if it makes me cry out.

Lightening blasts through the broken window. The garage stretches the entire width and most of the breadth of the building—parked cars and a door on the far wall, next to what I'm guessing is a waterlogged elevator. The back of the garage area is taken up with electrical boxes, pipes and a half-submerged gas main. Various ladders are hung on the wall. And I glimpse the cars again. None of them are Jozee's mini. But in the far corner, a small car is hidden under a tarpaulin. I stumble over and pull the tarpaulin free, grabbing my phone from my sodden trousers and jabbing at its light function. The torch bursts into life and revealed before me, half hidden by the rising waters, is a white 1974 Mini Cooper.

77

I CAN'T quite take it in. It's Jozee's Mini. Here, next door! But it's been emptied. Where was her junk, her twenty pairs of shoes and her ironic furry dice? And all those stupid gum stickers she had all over the red-coloured dash? I shine my phone into the water. The registration is different, changed. But then I notice the broken wing mirror. The tape has been removed and someone has prepared the underlying paintwork ready for it to be repaired. It's Jozee's car alright. There's no mistaking that.

A cover up.

My elation at finding Jozee's mini is soon cut short. Jozee must've come back to the flat Wednesday night when something happened. Somebody intercepted her. And I now know who that was. This discovery means one thing though, Jozee could be dead. It's not something I've wanted to accept over these last few days, but the concept has been growing subconsciously. A self-protection mechanism preparing me for the possibility that…

No! I won't believe it, not until I see her body.

A small lull in the so far unremitting storm. I check my phone. Still no signal. I go to the shutter door and punch the open button… nothing. I spot a manual hand-crank and start turning it. It's loose at first but gets stiffer.

"C'mon!" I shout impotently, putting my whole weight against the lever, the pain in my foot somehow giving me the strength to push harder.

It suddenly gives. The shutter jerks upwards with a rattle and bang. A cascade of rainwater floods inside knocking me over, my head momentarily going under the surface. I emerge seconds later, panicked and gasping for air. Damn it! I lost my phone. I scrabble around for it, but it's gone, taken by the flood.

I stick my head out of the garage, shocked by what I see, the rain has become nothing more than a pitter patter. The main road has turned into a river. Summer trees and other vegetation that were full of green have been stripped of their leaves, branches hanging limp and broken. Road signs lie on the pavement, burst bin bags, and other rubbish litter the drowned landscape.

Is it over?

A distant sound, like a thousand hissing whispers growing in volume. Something splashes in the pool outside the garage, another splash and another. Hail. Slamming into the ground like machine gun pellets. Pummelling parked cars, smashing into what's left of the trees and rattling windows and gutters, some of the hailstones as large as my fist.

Like a scene out of an apocalyptic movie.

The hailstones stop as suddenly as they started to be replaced by the returning rain, not as strong as before, but falling in a steady, unremitting torrent. The underground garage will be submerged in minutes. Part of me wants to escape, to get out of here, but I'm not going anywhere. A flash of lightning reveals a painted sign on the wall above Jozee's mini. 'Caretaker' and underneath, in more recent letters is, 'FLAT 1A'.

Jozee's Mini is in the caretaker's parking spot. Or the flat that used to belong to the caretaker. Flat 1A.

Could she be inside?

78

MODERN FLATS don't have caretakers anymore, but Flat 1A must be what it's now called. I drag myself over to the elevator. It's waterlogged and locked by a dead-looking keypad. I turn my attention onto the door to the stairs. It is also locked by a similar keypad. I push against it. But it's solidly built, which is as it should be. No intruder into the garage should be able to get access to the flats above, that makes sense. Another flash of lightning and I notice a sign by the door.

Access To Flats 1B - 12

Huh? Where the hell is Flat 1A? If it's not upstairs then, logically, it must be down here somewhere. I wade through water that now reaches my upper thighs to the back of the garage, wincing with every step, putting the pain to the back of my mind. I stumble along the wall, feeling rather than looking, until I come to a recess and my searching hands find a Yale lock.

A series of lightning flashes, followed by a cascade of thunder rattling the garage shutter, reveals another sign.

Flat 1A

This is it.

I push my shoulder against the door. It's not as sturdy as the one leading up to the flats, but it still resists my efforts to barge it open.

"Jozee! Are you in there! Jozee!"

I remember the ladders and scrabbling along the wall like a mad man, I find a small step ladder. It's old and heavy. I struggle to lift it off its wall hooks, fighting against the water, the cold and my own weakening muscles. I ram it into the door, smashing it against the lock and, after five or so hefty thwacks, it splinters open and I fall inside a short corridor with a door at the other end lit weakly from above by what I'm guessing is emergency LED lighting.

I find my feet and slosh down to this door, dragging the step ladder with me. Again, I batter the lock repeatedly until it bursts open, revealing a hallway to a ground floor flat.

"Jozee!"

I walk forward, falling down a hidden step into the water. The rooms are on a lower level than the garage. When my feet find the floor, the water is up to my armpits. I wade through a large hallway leading to various empty, unfurnished rooms, lit by the eerie glow of more emergency LED lighting. I check the living room, bathroom, bedrooms and toilet. All are flooded.

Nothing here. No Jozee.

"For fuck's sake!" I scream impotently. It feels like I've been searching forever, all to no avail.

A bloom of sustained lightning reveals a garden behind the flats— or what was once a garden. The high walls surrounding it have trapped the stormwater creating a pool higher than the windows. I stare into an eerie submerged world lit by flashes from above. Water sprays inside though a ventilation grid and via cracks between the windows and the walls. I need to get out of here before the windows collapse inwards from the increasing water pressure.

I shake my head. There's nothing I can do other than return home, wait out the storm and to tell the police what I know.

I leave the old caretaker's flat and emerge back into the corridor, noticing a recessed door I'd missed earlier in my haste. A sign reads…

Belonging to Flat 1A

I turn the handle. It's unlocked. I open the door and see Jozee lying motionless, face down in the water.

79

I THROW myself into what is a small utility room and turn Jozee over. She's cold to the touch and unresponsive, her hands and feet bound with plastic ties, her mouth gagged with a black plastic bin-liner.

"No! Don't be dead! You can't be!" I shout, ripping the bag away and lifting Jozee up, perching her up on an old sink above the water line.

"C'mon Jozee. C'mon. Don't you dare be dead! Don't you dare!"

I check to see if she's breathing and notice a reddened burn mark on her neck. I ignore it for now, putting my ear next to her mouth. I can't hear anything, other than what sounds like a deep gurgling. I have no idea what that means, but I have some half-remembered memories from watching a lifetime of TV shows and movies. I prop her between the wall and the sink and give her an approximation of what I guess is CPR, pushing at her chest and blowing into her mouth, not sure if what I'm doing is the right thing or not.

"Jozee!" I shout at her. "Breathe!"

I compress her chest again, my cold lips touching hers. The panic in me rising like the freezing waters in this flooded underground nightmare.

"Breathe!"

A coughing sound and water ejects from Jozee's mouth. But she's still unconscious. I continue compressing her chest, willing Jozee to survive. Screaming at her. Another cough and more water appears. And then she's gagging and coughing her eyes flashing open in fear and shock.

"Adam!" she croaks.

"Jozee!" I hug her tightly, not wanting to ever let her go.

"You found me. I knew you would."

I can't say anything. There're too many emotions coursing through me.

Finally, I let her go and stare into her big eyes, although they are black-ringed and tired. She's had an ordeal, an ordeal that isn't yet over.

"I don't have time to untie you," I say, ignoring the tears spraying down my face. "I need a knife to cut those ties. I'll get you out of here and back to the flat." I lift her up, turn back to the door and stop. My neighbour Clive is standing in the doorway.

80

CLIVE HAS an empty look on his face, his eyes beady and cold, his clothes soaked, his cardigan sagging around his waist.

"Clive! Thank the stars. We need to get Jozee out of here."

Clive says nothing,

"I need your help! Don't be an idiot. Help me get Jozee out of here now."

My neighbour remains in the doorway, his cardigan floating around his belly like a deflated buoyancy ring.

"Snap out of it! I need your help."

Clive shakes his head, his jowls twitching like that of an agitated bird.

"Clive?"

From seemingly out of nowhere, an arm thrusts something into Clive's neck. There's a spark of electricity and he collapses facedown into the water.

A figure pushes himself into the doorway, holding a taser. "Well, well, well, Adam. I knew you little twat would put two and two together, I just knew it."

81

BILLY BELTER.

The person Jozee was kissing in Gentry's photos. The guy I'd just seen exiting the Blenheim Towers garage in a four door Audi TT, although I didn't recognize him or the car until I did indeed put two and two together after seeing Gentry's photos.

Billy told me he had driven up from Brighton for that gig at the Lord Horatio in his girlfriend's modded Audi with an ostentatious rear wing. It wasn't a leap of imagination to guess that Cheryl had an empty flat next door at Blenheim Towers, a flat where Billy was hiding Jozee and her car.

Billy of all people. No wonder Jozee was shamed into moving to London after sleeping with him. But I'm not angry. I've far more important concerns.

"I knew you were on to me," Billy continues. "Grabbing at your phone with that look on your face when you saw me driving away from here twenty minutes ago."

Billy mistakenly thinks he was the reason I took out my phone. He had no idea what had just happened between me and Stevo. At least the big ape was innocent.

"Up to then, I thought I was in the clear," Billy continues, his jokester persona now gone. "The pigs had nabbed you for Jozee's disappearance, or so I thought, but there you were, bold as day. Gave me quite a fright I can tell you. I thought it was game over for a while, until I came back to my senses."

I grab at Clive, who is bobbing unconsciously in the water. He has a burn mark on his throat. The same as Jozee. I guess that's how Billy incapacitated her. A handheld taser to the neck. Nasty. I turn him around to face me. His eyes are open, glassy.

"You've… you've killed him," I whisper.

"Well ain't this a situation," Billy says, staring through me as if I don't exist. "Ain't this a situ-fucking-ation."

"Is that all you can say?" I growl, wanting to jump up and attack him, but the water is now past my waist and I'm holding on to Jozee. Squeezing her closely to me. And Belter still has his taser. "Why are you doing any of this?"

"That stupid bitch of a girlfriend of mine," Belter replies without a second's thought. "If she knew… if she found out about what happened with Jozee…. That's me over and done with. Out on my ear. No job, nowhere to live and no pension. I've been working on Cheryl for months. Working on a way to get my hands on her money. She's a tight-fisted evil cow that one. But this week, I finally got her to say yes to marrying me. Can you believe that? In the middle of this bloody mess, she finally relents. And I wasn't even trying with her anymore. I had other things on my mind. Who would've guessed that the cold-shoulder treatment would've brought such a dividend? Women eh? You can't live with them…" He pauses.

This is a joke from Billy's set. Everyone is expecting the 'You can't live without them' line that never comes. I'm still not laughing.

"You did this all because of Cheryl?"

"For her money. Don't you get it? Jozee was gonna blab to all and sundry about what we did, wasn't she? Told me so to my face. Said she had to come clean. That she had to first tell you and then Cheryl, without any thought for how that would ruin everything for me. Can't a bloke get a crafty leg-over no more without ending up in the damn shithouse? I had to do something. I had to. I was panicking. After she drove off and left you behind the night you had the argument at the Dog and Duck… well, I saw my opportunity. I scooted off in the Audi and was waiting for her when she arrived, ready to taser the gobby bitch after she parked. Things were going the way I wanted, until now." Belter glances at Clive and frowns.

I can guess what he's thinking. Now that there was one body, two more wouldn't make that much difference.

"Clive was an accident," I say, trying to get my good leg under me. "And you kept Jozee alive. You didn't have to do that."

I don't mention that I arrived to find Jozee half-drowned, but Billy couldn't have guessed the extent of the storm that still thunders and rumbles outside.

"I just wanted to shut Jozee up. To stop her going to Cheryl," Billy replies. "And no one guessed it was me. I suppose I was waiting. Seeing what the police did. Carrying on as normal. That's why I turned up at the Lord Horatio that night. You didn't half give me a scare coming up to me like that at the bar. I had originally planned to be on the same bill with Jozee to try and get her to change her mind about telling you and everyone else about our little liaison. In the end, I used it as cover. I didn't want to change my behaviour and get caught. Billy Belter ain't stupid."

"But you kept Jozee alive," I say again. "Why?"

He shrugs. "I wanted to see what the police did. If they fingered me or not. Kidnapping ain't as bad as murder. So I held off."

"But Billy Belter isn't a killer," I say.

He nods to the dead body of Clive lying half submerged in the waters. "Not sure the stiff would agree," he says, some of the jovial Billy coming to the fore, but his eyes remain hard. "I suppose I knew it would come to this. It had to, didn't it? Once I kidnapped her, my hands were tied, which is ironic seeing that…" his voice dries. "I was gonna take Jozee away from here to one of my lockups, under cover of the storm. But you spotted me, and I panicked. I nearly lost it. But then I took a step back and thought, so what if Adam saw me? I was at one of Cheryl's flats. There's no reason why I shouldn't be there. So I came back to finish the job and found you'd broken in. A disaster, until this God-sent storm arrived, making it easy to cover my tracks." He sighs. "I've no idea who the dead chap is, but you know what they say… *in for a penny, in for a pound.*"

"You're really going to kill us? Are you capable of that?"

Billy takes a breath to answer and I lurch at him. It's a feeble attempt. I'm too cold, in too much pain from my injured leg, and the water is too buoyant, but there's nothing else I can do.

Billy knocks me aside and I'm forced to grab the still tied Jozee to stop her drowning.

"If that's the best you've got," Billy says, "this is gonna be easier than I thought."

He jabs the taser into my neck and the lights go out.

82

I'M AWOKEN by a cramp in my calf muscle. I straighten my leg, arching my foot up, aware that my arms are tied behind my back and my legs trussed tightly together. A sharp burning pain stings the side of my neck. I'm jostled from side to side, aware of a revving engine above the sound of thunder and the hammering of rain.

I push my head upwards and find myself in the rear seat of Billy's Audi TT. I see the back of his silver-haired head as he leans forwards staring out into the storm through the windscreen, wipers batting manically backwards and forwards against an overwhelming torrent.

I'm half-lying under Jozee. Her eyes wide with relief that I'm awake. After what happened to Clive, I suppose I could've died. I want to tell her everything will be okay, that we'll get out of this, but I'm gagged, and I'd be lying. We're both still alive, which means Billy chickened out of killing us. He must have another plan in mind. Whatever it is, the storm has given him the perfect cover. When all this is over, Brighton and Hove will be a disaster area and, I'm guessing, me and Jozee will be two of the storm's victims.

Above the batting wipers and the rain, I hear a single voice. Billy Belter, talking loudly to himself.

"You've got this, Billy," he says with determination. "Let the river wash them out to sea. Blame what happened at Cheryl's flat on storm damage. Dump the car and then back home. Job done. No one guesses it was you, Billy. You're gonna be in the clear. It's all gonna be okay, Billy. All okay. You can do it. You've got this."

The river? He must mean the River Adur or the Ouse. After a storm like this, they'd both be raging torrents. Our bodies so battered and beat up that it'd be impossible to tell who we were or how we died. If our bodies were ever found that is.

But why are we still alive? I'm guessing Billy isn't a murderer.

Otherwise Jozee would've died the night he abducted her. Clive was an accident. But now, Billy is forced to confront the results of his actions. He has to build himself up enough to actually do it. To kill us. To throw us into the deluge. I'm hoping he won't be able to do that… but what other option is he left with? He must've known it would come to this when he kidnapped Jozee. And now, tonight, he actually has to go through with it.

I put myself in his position. *In for a penny, in for a pound.*

I try not to think about our fate. Thrown into a raging river, battered and drowned. I suppose it will be quick.

Billy curses, his horn blaring and the car swerves, throwing us sideways. A massive bang and the world turns upside down. More bangs, crunching and the dreadful wrench of metal and the splinter and crack of shattering glass. Jozee and I are thrown around in the back of the car like rag-dolls, until we finally come to a dazed rest, lying in total darkness, rain still pounding in an unremitting deluge, drilling into my face. A flash of lightning reveals the car is on its side, smashed and in pieces. Jozee lies face down on the road a few feet away, next to the crumpled body of Clive. Another flash and I see Billy. He's halfway in and halfway out of the Audi's smashed and twisted windscreen, covered in blood streaming from his crushed head and mangled face. Dead. One of his arms missing, no doubt wrenched free by the force of the accident.

"Jozee," I say weakly. "Jozee?"

Beyond the broken, smashed windscreen and its dreadful victim, I see a lumbering shape. It stumbles into the still shining lights of the destroyed Audi.

The rain stops suddenly to be replaced by a ghostly silence.

The figure lumbers closer and I realise it's Stevo, his face and neck covered in blood. "I had to do it," he says. "I bloody had to!"

MONDAY AFTERNOON

"ADAM!"

Where is she? Where is Jozee?

That same question, over and over again, haunting me, never going away.

"Jozee?" I mutter.

"I'm here, silly."

And then I come back to myself. I'm in the Royal Sussex Hospital. In a ward side-room, slumped in a chair, light blinding me from a wide, low window showing Brighton spread out below, sunlight glinting off the sea. I'm next to a bed with Jozee sitting up and staring at me. I lurch to my feet, forgetting about my injured leg that is heavily bandaged and trip and fall onto her. She doesn't mind. She squeezes me hard and suddenly we're both sobbing. Tears soaking both our faces when we finally pull away.

Jozee lies propped up in bed, a bandage above her eye and her left hand in a cast for a broken wrist and fingers. Wonderful, amazing Jozee! Other than a concussion and a few cuts and bruises, she's okay.

"What happened?" she says, her big, dark-rimmed eyes staring into mine. "The last thing I remember was Billy putting me and you in the back of his car."

"It was Stevo," I reply. "The big ape drove Billy off the road. He was pretty upset about you going missing. More upset than I realised. He even took time off work to look for you. I thought he was maybe involved in your disappearance and we had an argument. He came back to apologise during that stupid storm and saw Billy Belter leaving Blenheim Towers."

"Blenheim Towers? You mean I was next door all that time?"

I nod.

"I remember parking outside our flat after coming home from Burgess Hill," Jozee says, "Billy appeared out of nowhere and put his hand through the car window and the next thing I knew, the lights went out."

"He hit you with his taser, like he did to me and… *and to poor Clive*. Then all he had to do was push you aside, jump in the driver's seat and park the mini in next door's underground car park. It probably only took a few seconds. All that time you were missing, you were literally next door, less than a hundred feet away. If not for Stevo, we'd be toast. He found the mini and put two and two together. He raced after us in his Rover, caught up with Billy and knocked him off the road. He didn't intend for such a big accident, or for Billy to be killed—"

"Billy is dead?"

I nod.

More tears fill Jozee's eyes. "No!"

"It was him or us, Jozee. Stevo saved our lives."

"But Billy as well? He…" her voice trails off.

"He got what was coming to him," I answer for her. "Sure, I didn't want him to die, but I'm not shedding any tears. Forget about Billy, okay? It's not your fault he did what he did. None of it."

Jozee says nothing for a few seconds, instead her large eyes stare back into mine. I can't fathom what she's thinking, but I sense she's not swayed by my words.

"You saved me, Adam, but I put your life in danger. And Clive was killed! I did that by my own stupidity. By my own selfishness. I asked myself over and over why I slept with Billy. Especially when I had you waiting at home for me. If I'd only gone home that night—"

"What's happened has happened. There's nothing much we can do about it now, except to put it behind us and get on with our lives together."

Jozee says nothing, although her eyes are full of pain.

"We all do stupid things from time to time, all of us," I continue.

"Me more than most… so I should know! It's the human condition to mess up. Drunkenly sleeping with someone you shouldn't is one of the mainstays of being homo sapiens. We all do it at some time. Everybody. If we didn't, there'd be something wrong with us—and no annoying soap programmes to tediously dissect the fallout. But deciding to kidnap someone and planning to murder them? That ain't normal human behaviour, Jozee. No way. So don't beat yourself up about Billy okay? He's responsible for his actions, not you."

She shakes her head. I can understand how she's feeling. Blaming herself for everything. But she didn't make Billy a murderer. No one did.

I grab her one good hand with both of mine. "I've been looking for you for days. You won't believe half of the stuff that's happened and what I discovered. And I know you were going to leave me to live in London with your school friend, Angela."

Jozee reddens, but I carry on. This needs to be said. "None of it matters now you're back with me and alive. None of it, you understand?"

Jozee pulls a strained smile. "I've been messed up for a long time. I wanted to talk to you about it, about my past. Some horrible things have happened. I think I've been subconsciously punishing myself for those things, although all I do is hurt everyone around me."

"If it's any consolation," I say, "Tom didn't take an overdose. It was attempted murder."

"What?" Jozee's eyes widen. "You know about Tom?"

"All of it. The hit and run. The overdose. That you've been secretly visiting him. Like I said, you won't believe half of the stuff I discovered."

I explain about Donnie overdosing her ex-boyfriend. That Donnie and Laker were also in the car when the hit and run happened, bribing Tom to keep quiet. And that it was Tom's decision to go to the police that had led to Donnie trying to kill him.

"Donnie? But—"

"But *Donnie is a nice guy?*"

"Well, yes."

"I thought so too. Donnie, real name, Sean Donald Coogan, is ex-

IRA and as dirty as they come."

"I can't believe it."

"I didn't at first. But I've seen another side of him. A dangerous side. If Donnie had been in Billy's shoes, he wouldn't have hesitated to kill us, that's for sure."

I think back to Donnie's business-like attitude regarding my own death, which he'd planned as if he was ordering a take-away curry. I shudder.

"But you were right about Laker," Jozee says, the guilty look returning to her face. "You never liked him, did you?"

"I can't pretend I wasn't mightily pleased he turned out to be the prick I always thought he was. But my jealousy was petty. I regret it. None of us is perfect."

"Have he and Donnie been arrested?"

"I wish. There's no evidence against them," I reply, deciding not to mention how Donnie planned to kill me. I don't want to upset Jozee any more than I have to. She's already punishing herself too much.

"But you said Donnie was dangerous, that he tried to kill Tom?"

"The police, who I've grown quite intimate with, don't have any evidence against him. Just my word against his. And he's too much of a tough nut to let a police interrogation get to him. But don't worry about Donnie. I'm going to make sure everyone knows what he did."

"Isn't that a bad idea? He sounds dangerous."

"Dangerous is an understatement, but he'll get what he deserves one way or another."

Jozee gives me a look—like she's seeing something new inside of me.

And maybe she's right.

Gaffa-taped to a chair in that Sussex mansion waiting for those guys to turn up to do me in should've filled me with some sort of post-anxiety stress syndrome. Especially as I've spent the entirety of my life in a constant state of worry. But instead, it's filled me with something akin to steel. When it came down to it, *I didn't give in.* I fought all the way, like I've fought my stupid anxiety all my stupid life. It somehow prepared me for that moment of real threat and terror. Donnie underestimated me. Hell, I underestimated me. And I escaped. My words to Jozee are not empty. I'm gonna bring Donnie down. I have to.

Jozee removes her hand from mine and squeezes my chin, breaking me out of my thoughts of revenge. Jozee is always good at knowing when I am overthinking.

"And you, are you alright?" she asks, rubbing her delicate fingers over my bruised, cut lip and down the side of my face.

"Just a few cuts, scratches and a broken heart. But they're all well on the mend now." I go to kiss her.

"No, don't," she says, pulling away.

I try and smile, although my heart is aching.

"I couldn't believe that you found me," Jozee says to cover the awkward moment. "When the water started coming into that horrible room I was trapped in, I couldn't move... I could hear someone breaking down the door thinking, *just hold on, Jozee, hold on for a second longer,* but then I was breathing water. Drowning."

Her face becomes a mask of terror and I want to hold her against me forever.

"How did you find me?"

I sigh, and then give Jozee a rundown of all the events leading up to breaking into the Blenheim Towers underground car park flat, unashamedly making myself sound heroic—and not mentioning some of the more stupid things I did.

Jozee takes it all in with nods of her head until I mention my arrest by DC Marley.

"The police arrested you? No way! I'm so very sorry, Adam. That must've been hell for you."

"To be honest, I didn't mind. I sort of enjoyed it... *in an odd way.* It was nothing like it was on telly. More mundane and, less competent. But I can't pretend it wasn't exciting. Me in a police cell. Me in an interview room. Me angrily protesting my innocence and swearing at coppers. Scary. But mostly exciting."

Jozee's fingers squeeze my chin again. "I'm glad you enjoyed it," she says.

"Retrospectively," I explain, making Jozee smile. "All that mattered was that they were taking your disappearance seriously. I've already had a personal apology from DCI Evans and DC Marley. That was probably the second most enjoyable experience of this whole thing. After finding you alive that is."

Jozee's eyes furrow and she sits back. "I'm feeling a little dizzy."

"They told me that's normal. You're to take it easy for a few days, due to the concussion you received in the accident. You were dehydrated, which is ironic, seeing that you nearly drowned. Hence the drip. You were also undernourished, but not seriously."

"I did need to lose a pound or two."

"No, you didn't!"

"You're such a liar, Adam. How long will I be in here?"

I shrug. "The doctor will tell you everything, but from what I've managed to get from the nurses, it's likely they will keep you in at least up to the weekend. You've been unconscious for quite some hours. They want to keep an eye on you and give you some tests. You're a celebrity now and that means VIP treatment."

Jozee perks up at this news.

"Yeah," I say, keen to steer the conversation into a happier area. "I can see the headlines now. 'Talented young comedienne saved from a fate worse than death by her dashingly attractive boyfriend'. Although it was Stevo who did the proper rescuing, if I'm honest. You never know, it might be the springboard you need to get noticed."

"I'm not sure what I'm going to do next," Jozee says. "I might give up the comedy. First Tom, now Billy and Clive dead. I'm a curse. No two ways about it."

"I wouldn't make any rash decisions after what you've been through. You need to get back home with me and spend a few days coming to terms with this. Then everything will make a lot more sense."

"Maybe it was the knock on the head," Jozee says, "but I'm thinking more clearly than I have in a very long time."

"That sounds ominous," I say with a quick smile. But it's not returned.

"I need a clean break. Away from everything."

"That's what I'm saying."

"You now know I was going to London. I don't think I've changed my mind. I'm still going to stay with Angie."

I had a feeling Jozee was going to say this. That the events of the last few days would only increase her resolve to leave Brighton and to leave me, so I'm ready for it. I'd already decided that if this is what she wants, I won't argue with her. She's alive and that's all that matters. Petty relationship shit comes second to that, even if I have to hold back the tears.

"Who's that?" Jozee says pointing past me and towards the doorway.

I turn to see Charlotte Blunt looking back at us, a nervous expression on her face.

"I'll let her explain," I say.

I lean in to give Jozee a kiss and this time she lets me, our lips touch. A terrific electricity comes from her, shooting inside of me. Filling me full of dizzying, all-encompassing love. Jozee is alive and everything is going to be okay.

I pull away and hobble outside to find a bandaged Stevo waiting for me. His head, hands and one leg are covered in dressings, like some failed, half-drunken attempt at mummification. I'm pleased he survived the collision, although his cherished Rover P5 was not so lucky.

"Jozee's awake," I say. "And thanks for what you did. I owe you big-time fella. How are you?"

"Fucked up like a bastard," he replies proudly, his mammoth chest inflating. "Just cuts and bruises. Unlike the Rover. I lived for that car. But it's just metal and chrome and shit."

He stares past me and into the room where Jozee and Charlotte are hugging.

"I love Jozee," Stevo says with a quick nod of his head. "I love her and you more than a stupid Rover P5… I'm sorry for what I said. For pushin' you out of the car like that and drivin' off. You were an idiot to suggest I'd hurt Jozee, you know that?"

"Yeah, I do. Things got a little crazy over the last few days."

"And that storm! They're sayin' it's the biggest Britain has ever seen. Trees ripped up. Power cables down. *Cats and dogs living together!*"

I laugh at the quote from one of our favourite movies. The newspapers always exaggerated things but the storm was a doozy, that much was for sure.

"You really upset me, Ad," Stevo continues. "And you know me. I don't get pissed off unless there's somethin' to get really pissed off about. The thought that I could hurt a hair on Jozee's head… *it made me bloody angry.*"

He pulls a face that is so far away from angry as to be comical.

"You were just as cut up about Jozee's disappearance as I was, weren't you?" I reply. "I didn't properly notice. I'm sorry."

"Yeah, you don't notice shit, do you, mate? You wander about in a bloody daze. Sometimes it's like you're not there at all. Lost inside that stupid head of yours. Sometimes I think you don't deserve Jozee, you know that?"

"Yeah, I do now."

Stevo sits back and I can tell he's still very upset. He killed Billy Belter and nearly killed himself, me and Jozee—as well as destroying the motor he loved so much. He has a lot to process and, if he's anything like me, it will take a bit of time and quite a few pints.

"Thanks for what you did, Stevo. I'm sorry we argued. It won't happen again. You're my best mate, you know that don't you?"

"I was only trying to save Jozee."

"I know mate. You love her too."

"Yeah, I do."

"But that's got to be awful, watching me and her together. Doesn't it bother you? Doesn't it make you hate me?"

"Hate you? I thought that maybe I did. But I was bein' stupid. You two are my all-time favourite people. I didn't realise it till now, but I'm happy as long as you're both happy."

Stevo is a remarkable person. I'm not sure I could be as big-hearted as he is. I'm very lucky to have him as a best friend. I'm not much of a hugger, but I grab the big ape and hug him hard.

"Alright," he says finally. "Don't make a scene. I only did what anyone else would do. I couldn't let Billy Belter, get away with it, especially after what he did to Jozee. Red mist and all that shit. But it's all over now isn't it?"

I say nothing.

"But it is, isn't it?"

NEXT THURSDAY AFTERNOON

I'M STANDING on Western Road outside the Cathedral Bar. It's another hot evening, but nothing like last week's heatwave.

It's four days since the famous storm. The promenade is still covered in washed up pebbles and stones that battered the seafront's iconic beach huts into nothing more than splintered, brightly coloured driftwood. Already, enterprising Brighton artists are collecting this bounty, recrafting it into a series of high-end storm-related art-pieces to sell to unsuspecting tourists at extortionate prices.

Street signs still lie fallen, but the collapsed trees, vegetation and rubbish has mostly been cleared away. Brightonians are not the type of folk to let the century's biggest storm put them off their stride. They came out in their droves to help with the clear-up. Some saying it was no worse than the aftermath of the summer Pride Parade, while quietly admitting this was on a totally different scale altogether. Politicians arrived to walk awkwardly around in suits, creating ample opportunity for protesters to jeer and throw ethically-grown organic fruit and vegetables at them, while reporters and journalists infested every street corner, marvelling at the fantastic mix of cultures, genders, cross-dressers, lesbians, gays, transgender people and everyone in between who mostly told them to 'fuck off back to London'.

Most importantly, the pubs stayed open. Thirsty punters invited inside to drink a variety of storm-themed cocktails, beers and lagers while engaging in post-tempest chit-chat.

The Cathedral Bar is no different. And Donnie Coogan, keen

no doubt to show 'business as usual' after recent events, has put on a special 'Comedy Wrath Of the Gods' storm celebration night, featuring headliner, Shirley Sands' final performance.

It's a whole week since I was here last, and a lot has happened in between.

Too much.

I enter the loud, sweaty bar, and head to the back room, my injured leg still hurting. It reminds me of what I've been through. That I am a survivor. And, with what I'm about to do, survival is at the front of my mind.

Pari Chabra's eyes widen as she sees me approaching. Everyone has heard what happened to Billy Belter and Jozee. I should imagine it's the biggest news that's ever hit the Brighton comedy scene. I guess tongues have been wagging on overtime, although there must've been tough competition from Sunday night's tempest. Tonight, Pari wears a more restrained sari, purple with a paisley pattern in gold.

"Oh Adam," Pari says in exaggerated tones, her thick makeup cracking around her ruby-painted lips. "I'm so pleased you found Jozee alive. Especially after what that pig, Belter, was about to do. What a terrible, terrible thing."

"Thanks," I reply, my voice purposely cold.

"Poor, poor Jozee. When will she be leaving hospital?"

"Soon," I say.

"Is everything okay, Adam?" Pari asks, one hand absently playing with her thick, grey dreadlocks. "You seem a little distant."

I've bigger fish to fry tonight, but that doesn't mean I'm going to leave this stone unturned. I take out my phone and show her the screen.

"Do you recognise this?" I ask.

Her eyesight isn't that good, and the screen is small, but the garish colour scheme is easily recognisable.

"The Cackle Comedy Forum?" she ventures.

"Yes. That's it."

"I only ever use my laptop for the internet. These modern phones are not made for old eyes," she says with a shrug of her shoulders. "Is it something important?"

"You're a regular visitor to the forums, aren't you? In fact, you could say you're on there all the time."

Her eyes narrow. "I'm sorry Adam, I don't understand. Cackle is one of the ways I like to relax. Catching up with other comics. Swapping jokes and stories. I can't be like all you youngsters, galivanting off to the pub every night."

"Did you perhaps hear about a guy called David Gentry? He was on the Cackle Comedy Forum making up stories about Jozee Jackson. He sure had it in for her."

"No. Never. But he sounds like a very nasty customer. I hope you reported him to the forum admin."

"Oh, I did more than that. I went to see the company that runs Cackle and spoke to the administrator personally. I told him about the police investigation into Jozee's disappearance, and more particularly, how a known stalker had used their forum to target her. He was, as you might imagine, very upset and worried that Cackle could come under fire should this information ever get out to the press."

"Well done you, Adam. People on there are out of control. Some of the things I read are quite, quite disgusting."

"Yes, we had a lovely chat. Rather than calling attention to the part he and Cackle had played in the disappearance of a female comedian, I was instead keen to insist that something be done to fix this problem. Forums should be a safe place for all, don't you agree?"

"Yes, very much so."

"He was so keen in fact, that he gave me access to certain user accounts and IP Addresses."

"He did, did he?"

"Oh yes. A dreadful breaking of privacy laws, but we deemed that it was absolutely necessary under such exceptional circumstances. It made for quite an interesting discovery—the majority of the vile, disgusting posts on the forum were coming from a single person with multiple accounts. A user whose IP Address matched various forum pseudonyms. Do you know who that user was?"

Pari goes a little pale behind her thick makeup and says nothing.

"Nearly all those nasty posts came from your computer. Indeed, the first accusation that Jozee was stealing gags came from you, Pari, not David Gentry. Also, there was a certain video of Jozee and her boyfriend arguing the night before he tried to kill himself. You posted that. And I've made it my business to make sure that everyone knows. An admin post has just gone up, shall I read it to you?"

I don't wait for a reply.

> *Cackle and its comedy forum takes user safety very importantly.*
>
> *New rules are now in place to prevent users using pseudonyms.*
>
> *You will only be able to post using your full name. As a result, all future posts will now bear the name of the account associated with your IP Address.*
>
> *You will be asked to enter your full name the next time you login.*

Pari's face is now almost white. She takes a drink from a gin-filled glass, swallowing loudly, her mouth remaining open afterwards, a thin line of gin dribbling from her lips.

"Yes, Pari. You won't be able to ply your vile accusations in anonymity any more. I also got one final concession. Your account has been suspended, but all your previous replies and posts will now bear your name. Everyone on the Cackle Comedy Forum will now know who you are and what you've said."

I lean in close to her and smile.

"It's over Pari. By morning, everyone will know about you. I suggest you go back to your little one-person flat and never come out again. Goodbye."

I leave Pari to ponder my words. I lied about her posts being exposed, but her account has been suspended. My guess is that she won't go back to check and that I'll never see her again. It's more than she deserves for the heartache she's caused. I sigh. I thought exposing Pari like this would give me pleasure, but instead I feel intensely sorry for her. It's her own fault. It's time she got some payback.

No one sees me as I enter the back of the Comedy Gods club. It's jam-packed with people. Mostly comedians and regular fans. Shirley is doing her stuff in the pulpit. Donnie waits on the staircase wearing his familiar silver suit with a pink, rather effete shirt, ready to close the show. His eyes on his headliner.

I scan the room spotting Scott Wong, Nat Naylor and other familiar comedians. Jim Laker and his fiancée, Ruth, sit to one side, his arm protectively around her shoulders. I asked Shirley to make sure he turned up. Tonight is Shirley's final performance and everybody who is anybody has come out to see her, including the local press, although I'm sure they will be writing a different story in tomorrow's papers. *And that's just how we planned it…*

85

SHIRLEY SANDS finishes her last joke and the crowd roars in appreciation.

When the laughs have calmed down, she takes a reflective step forward and waits for absolute quiet.

"Tonight, is my last night. I've mostly enjoyed entertaining you sad pathetic losers, but sometimes you have to move on and do other things. Sometimes you just have to round things off. That's what tonight is all about. Doing what's right, no matter how painful it might be."

More cheers and applause.

"Now it's my time to fuck off, but before I go, let me just say to Donnie…" She waits until everybody is hanging off her next words. *"Donnie, you're gonna get what's coming to you. Goodnight!"*

Donnie emerges at the top of the staircase opening his arms to give Shirley a hug. She blanks him to even more laughs, pushing past him to trot down the staircase in her high-heeled boots.

"Many thanks to Shirley Sands!" Donnie says over the mic. *"And that's it, folks, until next Thursday when on the bill we will have…"*

I push through the crowd, and make my way to the stage, my heart thumping.

This is it. What we planned for.

A few other faces turn to me, their eyes widening in recognition. Everyone has heard about Billy Belter and Jozee. People try to speak to me, but I ignore them and jump onto the spiral staircase, jogging up to the stage, ignoring the pain lancing through my damaged leg.

The crowd goes quiet. Donnie is puzzled until he sees where they are all looking. He grins towards me, his hand reflexively covering the mic.

"Don't you dare!" he hisses.

I ignore his words and put on my biggest smile, waving to the audience.

"Feck off, Adam!" Donnie warns me.

I stride over to him and give him a hug, before grabbing at the mic. Donnie struggles with me for a few seconds, the audience laughing, thinking this is some sort of play-fight. Donnie tries to make light of what is happening, but I don't give up and Donnie is forced to let go.

"Thanks Donnie," I say, stepping away from him, seriously worried he will push me over the balcony. But he moves to one side, a pained smile on his face.

"I just have a few words to say from Jozee," I begin. *"But first, let me thank you all for your complete and utter support."*

This gets a big laugh as I'm guessing everyone was convinced of my guilt after I was arrested.

"But enough about me. Jozee wants me to tell you that she's coming home from hospital soon and is expected to make a full recovery."

This news is met with cheers. Donnie steps forward and tries to take the mic off me, but I won't let him. He gives me a *I'm going to kill you* look and the crowd roar with laughter again.

"While I'm here, I want to mention another comic. You may or may not have heard of him, a guy going by the name of Tom Blunt..."

I look down into the audience to find Shirley Sands. She stands at the side of the room. We both know what I'm about to do. We decided that it must be done. She nods, lowering her eyes. I take a deep breath.

"Tom Blunt was the driver in a nasty hit and run a couple of years back. Does anyone remember?"

Donnie comes aggressively towards me and I'm forced to step away.

"But Tom wasn't alone. Donnie Coogan and Jim Laker were in the car as well, isn't that right Donnie?"

The club goes deathly silent.

"You little shit!" Donnie spits, his words clearly heard by everyone.

"Yeah, I found this out when I was looking for Jozee. That and a lot more. Did you know Donnie here was a member of the IRA? A real nasty piece of work. Implicated in multiple Irish abductions and killings. A fixer and drug runner. And if you don't believe me, why not ask his right-hand man, Jim Laker. It's well known he likes to trade a line of coke for

a quick leg-over."

I can't see Laker under the lights, but a commotion in the general area of where he's sitting tells me his fiancée isn't very happy with this news.

The audience is confused. Unsure if this is some part of the show. But I don't care. The truth will come out about Donnie very soon indeed.

"Let me be absolutely clear," I continue. *"This is no joke, gag or a comedy routine. I'm deadly serious. Donnie's real name is Sean Donald Coogan. He's not who he seems. But don't take my word for it, go talk to the police. They told me all about him. The guy is a nasty shit, isn't that right Sean?"*

Donnie lifts his fists against me.

"I've got a helluva a lot more tell you about him, and if you want to hear what that is, meet me afterwards down the Wagon and Horses, I'll be more than happy to fill you in with all the—"

Donnie steps forward and punches me in the kidneys. I go down like a sack of potatoes, the wind knocked out of me. He grabs the mic and tries to talk to the crowd. But he's drowned out by the barrage of boos and shouts.

I pull myself up to shaking feet and make a slow way down the staircase while Donnie tries to make light of my words, but it's too late for him.

Shirley meets me, and, with a few other people helping, I'm dragged out of the club and into the fresh air, pleased to see that Pari Chabra has disappeared.

86

I SIT outside the Wagon and Horses opposite Shirley Sands on one of the many wooden benches where Jozee sat with Billy Belter only three weeks ago. We have the table to ourselves. Despite my call for everyone to come and talk to me about Donnie, the comedians that have arrived, keep their distance. I understand why. They are a fickle lot, and Donnie is one of the top Brighton promoters. They are playing a game of 'wait and see' before taking sides. I don't blame them. I'm not interested whether they believe me or not. I had to speak out against Donnie. There was no other way.

Shirley, real name Charlotte Blunt, disappears to buy me a pint and I'm left on my own for a few minutes. Unlike me, Shirley is popular tonight. Others go up to her for a chat, to which she rebuffs them with a heartfelt 'fuck off'.

People love to be insulted by her. Only Shirley can do this I realise. And although everyone thinks she's being funny, I know otherwise. She's incandescent with anger at Donnie and terrifically upset that the truth about Tom has come out. No one knows that she's Tom's sister. That secret belongs to me, Stevo, the police and Jozee.

Shirley returns a short while later and sits opposite me. She's very probably one of the most strikingly beautiful women I've ever met. Even under the heavy make-up of Shirley Sands, her beauty shines through. And those legs. I've been so besotted with Jozee that I never really noticed.

"I'm glad we did it," she says, taking a gulp from a large vodka and coke, followed by a deep drag on a cigarette. "None of this would've happened if not for Donnie and Laker. Tom wouldn't have taken any coke, he wouldn't have hit those girls, and he'd be here tonight."

My rational side wants to tell her that this is a simplistic view, but one of the lessons I've learned in life is that upset people don't want anything more than simple support.

"He'd be proud of what you did," I say. "And of your act, you're one very funny comedian."

"Thanks, Adam. You know when I first met you, I thought you were a real twat."

"Yeah, I get that a lot," I reply, wincing.

"But now I can see Jozee is a lucky girl."

"She's going to leave me. To give up comedy and move to London."

"She is? Why? And after everything you've done."

"She blames herself for all of this. For Billy, Clive and Tom, even though she had nothing to do with what happened to him."

Shirley takes an angry swig of her vodka and coke. "No. But we know who is guilty of that, don't we?"

"Yeah, we do."

Nat Naylor emerges from inside the pub, holding a pint that's almost as big as she is, spots us and comes to sit down. I share a look with Shirley. She knows about Jim Laker and his predilection for coke and POV phone porn. Shirley wasn't impressed. I give her an unspoken warning, 'don't make a scene'. She nods back in return.

"So sad you're hanging up the mic," Nat says in her breezy, little girl voice. She turns to me. "And I want to thank you for… for talking to me the way you did the other day at the beach. I needed a good telling off. I've been foolish. Making an effing tit of myself. I'd like to blame it all on Laker, but you know what? It's me. I'm just a fucked-up mess."

"It's not like you to use the f-word," I reply.

"My boyfriend left me yonks ago. Messed me up. I pretended otherwise because… because I didn't want to accept it. I've been terrible on stage for months. I can't believe he's gone and not coming back." Tears form in her baby-doll eyes. "I'm using the f-bomb because *I am fucked up*. One big fucking mess."

"Join the club," I say, raising my glass.

We all drink.

"Forget men," Shirley says in her classic angry stage voice, slamming her vodka onto the table. "Or keep them as pets and feed them corn. You don't need no boyfriend to define you or make you happy."

Nat nods in agreement, but her eyes tell another story. I guess she does need a man. I know I'm nothing without Jozee. I suppose how we feel inside isn't always to do with gender, but just how we're programmed.

Out the corner of my eye, I see a big guy in a leather jacket approaching our table. I turn towards him, knowing who it is already.

Jim Laker and he's angry.

Ruth walks behind him, her arms crossed defensively, her makeup streaked by tears, her face a mask of controlled thunder.

Laker grabs me by the shoulder and pulls me off the bench. I fall to the floor, struggling to find my feet.

"Get up and face me, you lying bastard!" Laker shouts, so that everyone can hear him. "You'd better apologise for what you said! That's slander! You hear me? Slander!"

I stand up, aware of what a big guy Laker is.

He grabs my shirt with his left hand and pulls back his right fist threateningly. I ignore it, instead looking into the tiny black pupils of his angry, glittering eyes.

"Tell Ruth I had nothing to do with that hit and run, otherwise there's gonna be one helluva lot of hitting and no bloody running, you get me?"

"You were in the car with Donnie and Tom," I say, unafraid of Laker or his fist. "You can hit me as many times as you like. It won't change the facts."

Laker's fist tightens even more, his knuckles turning white. "I'm warning you!"

"Leave him alone!" The voice comes from Nat Naylor. Gone is her girlie tone and everyone turns towards her. "Leave him the fuck alone!"

And suddenly, she's between me and Laker, punching and hitting him with her tiny fists.

Laker pushes her away. "Don't get involved in this," he says. "This is between me and him."

"No!" Nat shouts. "It's not! This is between you and me, me and your fiancée and every other girl you've been fucking on that phone of yours."

"What?" says Ruth, her face trembling. "What are you saying?"

Nat turns to her. "I'm sorry, but you need to know. Your husband-to-be is a full-time creep. Getting silly girls into bed on the promise of a few free drugs. It's pathetic but that's what he does. Like Adam said on stage."

"But you told me that was a lie," Ruth says, turning on Laker.

Laker lets go of me, his fist dropping to his side. "It is. It all is. Can't you see they're all in this together? They're lying."

"Lies, is it?" Nat says, winding up for another tirade.

I say nothing, allowing Nat to carry on. We all need to deal with our demons and Nat was giving hers both barrels of the shotgun.

"If I'm lying," Nat shouts, "Laker won't mind showing you his little video collection on that fancy phone of his, will he?"

"She's talking nonsense," Laker spits in reply.

"Then show us," Nat says, putting her hands on her hips.

"I'm doing nothing of the kind."

"Is that why you're always so secretive about the damn thing?" Ruth asks. "I've always wondered why you're so paranoid about me touching or looking at it."

"Well now you know," Nat says. "Although I wouldn't let him film me, at least I'm not that stupid."

"What do you mean? You slept with this little tart," she screams at Laker. "You slept with *her?*"

"It's all lies," Laker says. He pushes Nat out of the way and stalks off, followed by Ruth screaming at his back.

"Well, that was intense," says Nat, aware of everyone staring at her. "It's true," she shouts. "I'm a fraud. I don't have a boyfriend. The pig left me, okay? Now who wants to buy me a drink? I effing need one after all of that."

Nat disappears into the pub with a few eager guys and girls.

I sit back down opposite Shirley.

"Well done to Nat," she says. "I was about to stab my fingernails into Laker's eyes before she exploded. Although I think she's going to regret what just happened tomorrow when she wakes up. Admitting to sleeping with a creep for drugs is gonna be hard to live down."

"I disagree. Getting the truth out there, no matter how painful, is always for the best. I didn't notice before, like I don't notice most things, but Nat has been suffering. Vulnerable. And that twat Laker took advantage of her. I think everyone will understand what happened."

Scott Wong appears and sits down next to me. "It's all happening tonight, isn't it?" he says jovially.

"It sure is," I reply.

"That true about Donnie?" he asks.

Both me and Shirley nod.

"I always thought there was something shifty about him. I suppose when this gets out, the Comedy Gods will be no more. Shame. That's a cool gig."

"Someone else will take it over," Shirley says.

"But it won't be the same."

Shirley lights a cigarette and offers one to Wong who accepts with a 'I shouldn't be doing this but why not' shake of his head.

"You're funny," Wong says, after Shirley lights him. "One of the best comics I've seen. My agent is looking for a female comedian to boost the ranks. Are you one-hundred percent sure you wanna quit comedy?"

I'm shocked. This is a great offer.

Shirley doesn't even blink. "I'm done, finished. Didn't you see the gig? It's over."

"I'd rethink if I was you."

"If you want to get into my knickers, you'll have to try harder than that."

Wong digests her words for a few moments, taking a thoughtful drag on his cigarette. "Think it over. With my recommendation, I'm sure I can get you aboard with Blowback." He stands up to go. "Don't give up the comedy." He walks away, lifting his hand to his ear. "Call me."

"You can't turn down the chance to join Blowback," I say when Wong is out of earshot. "You'd be made for life. It's what Tom wanted, it's what we all want. You'd be a fool not to take it up."

Shirley frowns at the mention of her brother, but it turns into a slow smile. "Yeah. Tom would've leapt at a chance like this. But there's still Donnie. I ain't doing anything until he's fucked good and proper, either behind bars or dead."

We stare at each other for a few moments.

It's a big ask.

87

SHIRLEY CHATS to me like I'm an old friend. It's the most I've ever talked to her. She tells me all about her big brother, Tom, who she idolised. I see glimpses of Charlotte, a warm, sweet, kind-hearted girl, and yet here and there I spot her other side. The side that's capable of creating a new persona, of becoming a successful stand-up, of dramatically changing her appearance all in the pursuit of revenge. She is, I realise, a very complicated but fascinating individual. An individual I'm privileged to know.

Time passes slowly. I unashamedly allow myself to drink a little bit too much. Shirley regulates her intake, and even though my conversation becomes slurred and difficult to follow, she stays with me until kicking out time. Until we are the only two people left sitting outside in the balmy night.

And that's when I make a move on her. Lunging in for a kiss. She returns it for the barest of seconds, her lips fleshy and urgent against mine, before pushing me away and slapping me resoundingly in the face.

"Creep!" she shouts and, grabbing her handbag, Shirley Sands disappears into the night.

I get a sympathetic shrug from one of the girls clearing the tables and decide it's time for me to go home. I'm woozy. Boozed up and feeling more than a little light-headed. I head towards the taxi rank, but instead of joining the queue, I lean unsteadily against the wall, wondering if I'm going to throw up. I give the queue of taxis a shake of my head and walk home.

I make my way up to Queens Road, past Churchill Square and down Dyke Street towards Hove, where I become aware of a car following behind me. I turn to see a large pick-up with blacked out windows. I've seen it before, I remember... leaving the mansion house where I was held prisoner.

As this information attempts to turn itself into some form of action, like running or… um… something else I can't think off, one of the doors is flung open, a thick arm darts out and grabs me, pulling me inside.

Harsh words in a threatening foreign accent. An accent I've heard before. I'm punched heavily in the stomach, a foul-smelling rag is pushed into my mouth, a hood put over my head and I'm thrust down behind one of the seats, someone sitting on me.

The pick-up drives away.

"Now, you little feck," says a voice I recognise, "you're gonna get what's coming to you!"

THE DRIVE is long, and I begin to sober up, adrenaline and fear pushing away the fog of booze, although I keep retching, fearing that I'm going to chuck up while gagged and choke on my own vomit.

The sound of passing cars diminishes and I guess we've left Brighton behind. I've been kidnapped by those guys who came for me before… to kill me. And Donnie Coogan is with them.

What have I gotten myself into?

Rough hands search through my clothing. I have nothing on me, only my wallet and some loose change that they take off me. I don't have a phone. It was lost in the flood in Blenheim Towers underground car park and I haven't yet got a replacement. I do however, wear a watch that Stevo gave me earlier today. An old-fashioned electronic model from a bygone age. You press a button and the time pops up in red, digital numbers that would've made any number of 70s schoolchildren wet themselves with delight. The world has moved on significantly since then.

Finally, after what seems like an age, the engine slows down and stops. I'm hauled out of the pick-up and taken down a series of stairs to enter a cold room. A basement is my guess. Not that I want to think about that too much. It's a relief to be back on my feet again, if it wasn't for what is probably waiting for me.

I'm sat down. My wrists and ankles roughly manacled, and the hood is pulled free. I'm blinded by bright lights which I seem to be at the centre of. After a few moments, my eyes adjust. I'm sitting, manacled to a chair in a room that is indeed a basement. It's similar but not the same as the mansion house. Cameras point at me on stands, while another hand-held camera lies unattended on the floor near to me.

The cameras I saw in the mansion before.

I'm surrounded by professional-looking stage lights and a white backdrop. I also spot a bank of monitors opposite me, in front of which is a seedy-looking man in jeans, t-shirt and professional looking headphones eating a cheese roll, his fingers dancing over a couple of keyboards. There's an accompanying hum of machinery. To my right is a man in stained leather overalls standing in front of a bench of tools. I see power-saws, screwdrivers, drills, knives and hammers. It's then that I notice his overalls are stained with old blood. And, as if in sympathy to this information, my own blood runs suddenly cold.

I spit out the gag and start screaming for help.

The men laugh at me. I look at them properly for the first time. They are big guys. Bald-headed, muscular, and covered in tattoos. Their black clothing stretched over powerful muscles like a second skin.

Donnie is with them. He's still wearing the grey suit and pink shirt from the Comedy Gods, patches of sweat leaking through. His face is passive, but his eyes are gleaming.

"You fecked up, laddie."

"What are you gonna do to me?" I ask, although I can guess the answer. This is no porn operation. It's far more sinister.

"You know what they say in comedy, Adam? 'Dying is easy'. And it is, I've seen it hundreds of times. A simple cut to the throat or the thigh. A bullet to the head… and off they pop. All done and dusted. But dying won't be easy for you, Adam. Especially after what you pulled tonight."

"What do you mean?" My voice is a shaky flutter, breathlessly spoken over the frantic thudding of my heart.

"We're going to kill you. But you guessed that, didn't you, laddie? We're going to cut bits off you, burn you, pull out your teeth and stab you in the eyes. We're gonna crush your bollocks and stuff your cock down your throat, pull off your fingernails and stick a hot poker up your arsehole… and that will be just for starters." Donnie turns to one of the guys. "How long before the transmission goes live?"

"Five or so minutes," the guy answers in a heavy accent. "Waiting on the satellite."

"Five minutes!" I shout. "You're starting in five bloody minutes?" I try to ignore what Donnie just told me. The unimaginable horror of what they're planning to do, but it's impossible.

"That's right, Adam. And I can't wait for this particular little show to start."

"So it wasn't porn you were filming but…. *but this?*" I say, swallowing hard, trying not to think about the guy in the leather apron and all his tools.

"No. Of course not. When you found our little operation in the basement of the house in the back end of Sussex, you didn't realise it was a far more sinister setup. Call it a torture chamber. A torture chamber with a paying audience. Once I realised what you had stumbled onto, there was no way I could let you go after that."

"So that's why you arranged for these guys to come and get me that night?"

"It wasn't personal then. Just business. As I told you. Although that changed when you pulled tonight's little stunt. You're going to get the full five-star treatment, and this time I'm going to be watching."

"You torture people and film it?" I say, aware of the time running out. The five minutes will be up soon and then…

"Not just torture. I told you, Adam, I'm a businessman. It's also a convenient way to get rid of problematic or useless stock and to scare the other stock into obedience. And to make a tasty little earner by streaming their demise to the eastern bloc. You'd be surprised how much those creeps pay to watch this messed up shit."

"What do you mean by *stock?*"

"Human stock of course. A never-ending line of illegals desperate to take any chance to get into this country. And when they're here? A nice little resource to be exploited in any way we want. You know what I mean?"

"You're a human trafficker?"

"That's exactly what I am. I was always wheeling and dealing back in the good old days in Ireland. I made a lot of contacts. Trade routes at first, then arms, then drugs and now people. People are messier to deal with. It's surprising how they don't take to slavery and forced prostitution, even with all the smack we give them. But when they know the alternative…" He glances at the tools laid out on what I'm guessing is a torture table and smiles. "What else are they going to do?"

"You're sick!"

"I'm afraid you're quite wrong there, laddie. I don't normally involve myself with this side of the business. Not my cup of tea at all. But after your performance tonight, I had to come down and take a looksee."

"So you're gonna torture me and stream it live to a bunch of perverts?"

"Paying perverts." Donnie nods. "But yes, that's pretty much it."

"And that satellite dish I saw in the mansion garden, that was also part of your set up?"

"You ought to become a detective, Adam. Although you'll soon find out that we on this side of the law have the most fun and the most money.

"Thirty seconds."

"Almost showtime," Donnie says, finding a chair and pulling it up to sit behind the cameras. "Strip him!"

My clothes are cut off me by a rough-looking guy with one of those military knives—all gleaming curves and wickedly serrated edges. A blade is a blade in my world. You can kill someone with a fruit knife if you have the inclination. No, this knife has another purpose. It is to instil terror and fear. As I look at the eight-inch, horrific shank, I realise that it's doing its job pretty much as intended.

While I'm being 'prepared', the guy in the apron puts on a terrifying, smiling pig-mask and runs his fingers lovingly over his set of macabre tools.. One of the other guys picks up the handheld and goes over to him. I watch the feed on the monitors, transfixed.

Oh fuck!

"Live in five, four, three…"

The handheld starts with a closeup of the guy in the apron, his smiling pig-mask filling the screen. It pulls back to reveal him standing above his bench. He selects a large rough-looking metal file, throws it up in the air and expertly catches it. The feed changes to myself sitting naked in the chair. The torturer comes into shot and stands next to me.

"No! Don't!" I shriek. What the hell have I gotten myself into?

Before I realise what's happening, he expertly scrapes the metal file over my left hand, stripping the nail from my forefinger.

I throw myself back in the chair, screaming in agony as the nail rips free. In the same moment, the room is filled with a terrific bang. I hear shouting and the slap of boots, followed by a plume of smoke that turns everything black. There are more bangs and shouts until everything goes silent apart from the stinging of my destroyed fingernail.

"He's over here!" A voice shouts. "And hurt. Call a medic!"

I'm dazed and a little confused until I hear a familiar voice by my ear.

"You did it, mate! We caught the twat-bastard red-handed."

89

THE SMOKE finally clears, and I can see what's happening. The room is full of men in military style uniforms carrying machine guns. They stand over the guys who abducted me, the technician, the torturer and Donnie Coogan, all lying face down, their hands tied with plastic strips like Billy used on Jozee. Stevo stands at my side, almost beside himself with concern. His face bearing stitches and bruises from his recent injuries.

"They bloody hurt you. But you're okay, though? Yeah?"

I nod, still a little dazed.

"I told you there was a bloody risk to this. That you might end up hurt or worse."

One of the military-garbed guys comes over and attends to my finger. Covering it with antiseptic cream and wrapping it in a bandage. He gives me the once over and nods. "That finger is gonna hurt like hell, but you'll be okay."

"Someone get him out of this bloody chair," Stevo says, his voice booming off the walls. "And put some clothes on him. I don't want to look at his dick no more."

90

HALF AN hour later, I'm sitting outside under a bright, starry night. Drinking coffee with a still-concerned Stevo and watching the operation dial down.

Stevo told me about his job a few times, but I never really listened. The reason? Stevo was being deliberately vague. Turns out he works as a code breaker. One of the top few guys and girls who work on deprogramming enemy software, making sense of encrypted messages and generally being an all-round Bletchley Park-esque superhero. And, as it happens, an invaluable asset to Her Majesty's Government. He not only works for a covert branch of the Foreign Office but is also occasionally sequestered by MI5.

My idiot mate, Stevo!

I was shocked when he explained it all to me, his job and how he was going to use it to track down Donnie. To get him put in jail. Until I came up with a better plan that is.

It turns out human trafficking in the south of England was a big problem. A problem no one was solving any time soon. As evidenced by those bodies found washed up on Sussex beaches. Or what was left of them. It wasn't a leap of imagination for us both to realise what was going on down in Donnie's basements. MI5 had been after the kingpin behind this human trafficking for a long time but had gotten nowhere. They knew about the live streaming of torture, but as Donnie's crew were using a tight-beam from unknown and changing locations to an eastern bloc satellite, there was no way of tracking them.

Hence tonight's little performance.

With what I knew about Donnie and the expertise Stevo could call upon, we decided to set Donnie up. To get all the main players and bastards in one place, with me as bait.

I had to sign up as a temporary operative—civilians cannot be allowed to do what I did. A more common occurrence than we are led to believe.

Tonight had been one big set up to lure Donnie out. My lunge at Shirley was just dressing. A way for me to end up alone, drunk and vulnerable. Donnie and his crew had to be convinced I was alone and pliable… and easy to capture. Which I was. I also needed the booze to calm my nerves.

"What now?" I ask Stevo.

"Now? Well, don't tell anyone, but I've got my eye on this 1970s S-Type Jag. She's a beaut'. Needs a bit of love and attention, but I think she's gonna be mine very soon, very soon indeed."

91
FRIDAY MORNING

I'M DRIVEN back to my flat where I get changed and wait for the day to start, hitting the paracetamol as the pain in my injured finger starts to chafe at me. It and my leg are both good pains. Pains that remind me who I am and what I've done. A missing fingernail is nothing compared to what could've happened to me or Jozee.

Stevo gave me a brand-new iPhone to replace the one I smashed and lost, which I accepted graciously. In return, I removed the watch and tried to return it to him.

"Keep it," he said.

"But I'm guessing it's an expensive piece of kit."

"Yeah, about that," he said.

"What about it?"

"Yeah, well. It's just a watch. They thought you'd feel safer thinking it was a tracker or sumfin. Soz, mate."

"Huh? But you told me—"

"Naw, that was just bollux. We knew where you were at all times. You were in no danger."

"But—"

"But what? You did it Adam. You bloody did it."

I was too tired to be angry. "I'm keeping it then," I said. "A keepsake."

"Sure, it's an antique, innit. Or as close to an antique as can be."

I phone Charlotte Blunt—aka Shirley Sands—and she answers before it rings.

"Adam, how did it go?"

"Donnie is in custody. His operation is shut down. It's being dismantled, and hundreds of people being freed as we speak. Watch the news for an announcement."

Charlotte squeals at the other end of the phone. "And you, are you okay?"

"I snagged a nail, but all is fine. I'm now off to pick up Jozee, she's being discharged from hospital today."

"Is she still hellbent on leaving Brighton?"

"Yeah, she is."

"But she can't leave you, not after what you did tonight. No way."

"I'm not telling her anything about it."

"What? Why not?"

"I'll tell her another time, later. I want her to stay because of me. Not because I caught Donnie."

"Why not?"

"It's got nothing to do with Jozee. That was between you, me and him."

"If you don't tell her, I will."

"No, you won't," I reply.

"No, I suppose I won't. Although I'm sure she'd like to hear about our kiss."

"I thought you weren't going to stop."

"Let's say you caught me off-guard."

We both laugh.

"Have you thought more about Wong's offer?"

Charlotte pauses. "A little bit. I'll have to go ask Shirley, see what she says."

"You do that. But be careful, she's got a tongue on her that can cut glass."

We laugh again.

"I've got to go," I say. "See you soon."

"Good luck, Adam. I owe you."

It's another sunny Friday morning. I leave my flat and walk through Hove and into Brighton, getting a little sweaty as I stride up the hill to the Royal Sussex Hospital. My leg is hurting, but not as bad as it once was. The exercise is good for it, I was told, but that seems to be the default medical advice for everything these days.

I arrive at Jozee's ward and find that she's gone. I'm annoyed and a little let down. A nurse tells me she was discharged a short while ago. The Royal Sussex County Hospital is a confusing maze, but I manage to navigate myself outside and jog around the buildings until I spot Jozee sitting in a wheelchair.

"So, you found me, huh?" she says.

"I've had plenty of practice, or don't you remember?"

"You can't make me change my mind, Adam. I've phoned Angela. I'm going straight to the train station and she's going to meet me at Victoria."

"No," I say and we're both surprised by the power of this simple word. "Not after what I've gone through to get you back. There's no way I'm returning to that empty flat again without you. Do you hear me, Jozee? No bloody way. And don't you ever think you are ever going to leave me again, because I'm not going to let that happen. Okay?"

I'm expecting Jozee to fight back, to grit her teeth and stick out her jaw, to rail against me, but instead, she sags back into her chair and sighs, the air escaping from her lips in a long, single exhale.

"Okay?" I repeat, softly.

She nods.

"Promise me."

"Oh Adam, I do love you."

"Promise me!"

"I promise."

"Thank the comedy gods for that!" I reply and we both start to giggle. Jozee is back and that's the way it is going to be forever.

NOW

THAT WAS three months ago and me and Jozee are going strong. We moved out of the flat into a new place with a garden and a dog. Neither of us wanted to stay there any more. And besides, it was my place before Jozee moved in and she was never comfortable living there. Especially with poor Clive on her case all the time. We were the only people at his funeral, apart from DC Marley and DCI Evans. I guess all Clive wanted to do in the end was to help. I judged him harshly, too harshly.

I tried to return to work but handed in my notice after a day or two. There was no way I could go back to that office and the Gannet, not after what I'd been through. I need a bigger challenge than sodding web databases. I was sad to leave Ollie on his own, but we went out for goodbye drinks and repaired our friendship. After he learned everything that happened, he was more than forgiving.

Shirley Sands made a triumphant return to comedy. Scott Wong was true to his word and she was signed up to the prestigious Blowback agency a few weeks later. It's still a shock to see her on TV, even if it is on some stupid baking program after-show, or similar. But she deserves it.

Nat Naylor overcame her slump, becoming funny again almost overnight. It was good to see the change in her, watching her smash it again and again. And despite everything that happened, we have become firm friends.

Jim Laker was arrested for perverting the course of justice and is presently out on bail awaiting his court case. His engagement and his comedy career are both over. I don't think about him any more.

And as for Jozee Jackson?

Wonderful Jozee Jackson?

She is moving onward and upwards. She also signed to an agency. Not Blowback, but one of the others, gigging around the country and making a fine living from it.

As for me, Adam Hanson? I took over the Comedy Gods night as the new promoter and compere. Not as slick or as funny as Donnie, but I'm getting there.

Donnie told me dying was easy. He was right. But one thing is for sure…

Staying alive is an entirely different matter.

Reviews

If you loved reading *DYING IS EASY* as much as I did writing it, can I ask you to please leave a review. This is not just for me and other readers, but for a whole host of other boring marketing reasons that I won't go into right now.

Suffice it so say, if you leave me a review on any of the e-book stores, or Goodreads or anywhere else, I'll be *well-chuffed*, and it will certainly increase the likelihood of further novels in this and other series.

Thanks in advance!

For information on further releases, please join my newsletter:

http://mostlywriting.com/join

Or you can pop over to my Mostly Readers Facebook Group. It's a friendly fun place to hang out.

And, of course, there is also my Twitter account @MostlyWriting – with over 100K followers!

Please read on for full links details.

About *DYING IS EASY*

Like Adam Hanson, I too was an aspiring Brighton stand-up comic, so this world is very well known by me. And like me, Adam is also on the Autistic Spectrum, something that came as a shock as I was diagnosed only a few years ago. I'm still coming to terms with it. I didn't know I had the condition when I started my stand-up 'career', but I shared the same motives as Adam. Crippling anxiety was and still is a chronic problem in my life, and doing stand-up was a great way to focus my terror on something legitimately terrifying. And believe me, stand-up is exactly that.

This is my first contemporary mystery. I really hope you like it. If you do, can I ask you to please give it a star rating and, if you have the time, to write a review? It really makes a difference, and we authors always value a good honest critique.

I will retweet links to reviews to my Twitter followers, and post on Facebook and elsewhere - and possibly include them as quotes in publicity releases.

Over to you…

Many thanks in advance!

Kev

Acknowledgements

Thanks for the red-pen, scribbling and 'telling me off in no uncertain terms' talents of my lovely editors:

Suzanne Buist
Blossom Young
Kevin Starns

Also by K.J.Heritage

Crime & Mystery
Dying Is Easy
The Peculiar Case of the Missing Mondrian

Science Fiction
Shattered Helix *(Vatic #1)*
Shattered Web *(Vatic #2)*
Blue Into The Rip
Quick-Kill & The Galactic Secret Service
The Lady In The Glass - 12 Tales Of Death & Dying

Sci-Fi Compilations
Once Upon A Time In Gravity City
Chronicle Worlds: Legacy Fleet
From The Indie Side

Fantasy
The Scowl

Non-Fiction
All About Editing: 55 Easy edits to improve your writing skills forever
3000 Writing & Plot Prompts A-C: Supercharge Your Creativity & Improve Your Writing Forever!

Online stores
Find all ebooks, paperbacks, hardbacks & audiobooks
by *K.J.Heritage* at the following stores:

Amazon & Audible
Apple
KOBO
Barnes & Noble/Nook
Google
Smashwords & more

Get to know me!

Join K.J.Heritage's *Mostly Readers Club!*
Get an inside track on all future releases, access to early reading
copies (ARCs), sneak previews, and more.
http://mostlywriting.com/join

Twitter:
Over 100,000 followers and growing
@MostlyWriting

Instagram
Photos of my wonderful Shollie rescue #RescueJack, piccies of my
best mugs of tea, and various and shameless images of all my books.
Oh and maybe yours truly on a good hair day!
https://www.instagram.com/k.j.heritage

TikTok
General silliness and book stuff. Search for #kjhtok
https://www.tiktok.com/@k.j.heritage

BookBub:
Not only can you check out the latest cool book deals, but you can
also get an alert when I publish my next book
https://www.bookbub.com/authors/k-j-heritage

Goodreads:
Friend me here:
https://www.goodreads.com/kjheritage

K.J.Heritage Facebook Group: *Mostly Readers*
Fun chat and posts about reading… *mostly.*
https://www.facebook.com/groups/mostlyreaders

K.J.Heritage Facebook page: *Mostly Writing*
Follow/like and keep in touch with even more writery stuff!
https://www.facebook.com/mostlywriting/

Website:
Both links go to the same site. Take your pick!
http://www.mostlywriting.com/
http://kjheritage.co.uk/

Email:
Want to get in touch? Well here's your chance
contact@mostlywriting.com

About *K.J.Heritage*

**"K.J.Heritage's uncanny sense of pacing and
story puts him at the forefront of today's
speculative fiction writers."
Samuel Peralta, Amazon bestselling author
and creator of The Future Chronicles**

When K.J.Heritage isn't penning third-person descriptions about himself, he's an international bestselling author writing the books he likes to read. From military/action science fiction and adventure to contemporary mysteries, crime thrillers, comedy, and paranormal fantasy. He should really stick to one genre, but he's not that kind of writer... or reader.

His first short story, 'ESCAPING THE CRADLE' was runner-up in the 2005 Clarke-Bradbury International Science Fiction Competition. His other short stories have appeared in several anthologies with such self-publishing sci-fi luminaries as Hugh Howey, Samuel Peralta, and Michael Bunker.

K.J.Heritage's short story, CHURCHILL'S ROCK, part of the 'Chronicle Worlds: Legacy Fleet' anthology, will be aboard the Astrobotic's Peregrine Lunar Lander set for launch on the United Launch Alliance's Vulcan Centaur rocket platform bound for the moon in 2022.

K.J.Heritage has worked all the requisite 'writer jobs' such as driver's mate, factory gateman, barman, labourer, telesales operative, sales assistant, warehouseman, IT contractor, Student Union President, university IT helpdesk guy, British Rail signal software designer, Premiership football website designer, gigging musician, company director, graphic designer, stand-up comedian, sound engineer, improv artist, magazine editor and web journo... Although he doesn't like to talk about it. *Mostly... Maybe a little bit.*

He was born in the UK in one of the more interesting previous centuries. Originally from Derbyshire, he now lives in the seaside town of Brighton. He is a tea drinker, avid Twitterer, and neurodiverse (ASD) human being.